The Detour

I0544707

The legend of the book of Fatima

An Edward Fleming Novel

By

I.M.Hussaini

I.M.Hussaini

ISBN: 978-0-9839023-2-4

DEDICATION

For her, a woman like no other.

In the darkest night, where there is nothing but despair and anxiety, I close my eyes, and I can feel the warmth of her watching eye.

Hussaini seamlessly blends compelling characters, thought-provoking situations, an impeccable discourse on Islamic history and a unique style and language to deliver an unparalleled historical thriller that will have readers anticipating his next novel, *Echos of Fatima.*

- Kirkus reviews

Fast-paced thriller, good job of integrating the historical part within the plot... And good humor too...

-Malone Editorial

Clever and engaging plot, and terrifically interesting historical data that even has worldwide implications...

-Rainbow Editorial

A controversial subject... the historical research and theory is very interesting and plausible.

-Department of External Studies,
The Iraqi Museum.

Other books by I.M.Hussaini:

Once Upon A Time In Baghdad

The Tributum: Echoes of Fatima. Edward Fleming 2nd novel.

PROLOGUE

James Archer lifted the unconscious bodyguard and seated him on the couch. This was the fourth and last of his target's security personnel.

Archer walked past the mahogany-wood bar at the entrance. Fighting an urge to try the beverage collection, he carefully put the stool back in position. It had been knocked over when he took out the guards. Two beer cans sat on the living room table, next to an ashtray filled with cigarette butts; someone didn't take his job seriously enough. But again, in a hotel like this in the middle of Dubai, why should they? The lush golden brown carpet made him suddenly aware of how dirty his shoes were. The dark night outside reflected only his image on the enormous glass window that faced the sea. He imagined himself sitting on one of the big luxurious couches watching the sunset, the sea extending endlessly, the roaring waves crashing against the elegant building that stood in the middle of the water. His weathered face stared back at him, bringing him to reality. In the dimmed light of the living room, the scar under his left eye was more prominent than ever. He looked stupid in the black suit he had snatched from the hotel security room.

Breaking into the Burj Al-Arab hotel had proved trickier than he thought. With the hotel built entirely on the water, security was tight and only people with an invitation or confirmed appointment were allowed on the small bridge road which crossed to the hotel. A nightmare of security cameras, security personnel, and security access control, whoever designed it had made sure people like Archer would have a hard time getting in.

He took the stairs to the right. The first floor had one desk with a laptop and a multifunction printer-scanner with phone. A complete office setup, in case the guest felt bored, or maybe guilty for having too much fun, and decided to do some work. But again, looking at the lush carpet and the ornate walls, the fine mahogany wood of the desk and the stair railing, it wasn't likely that anyone who could afford this six-thou-a-night room would actually care to do any work. There were two rooms on the floor; one of them was his target's. He chose the one to the right, following his instinct and, well, the fact that it was the master bedroom and the only one with the door slightly opened.

He reached for the doorknob and pushed it. The room, dark and quiet, was as big as the living room. The old millionaire should be asleep at this hour. Archer stopped before stepping inside. A familiar spasm. Something wasn't right. Call it a hunch or a decade of experience working as an undercover agent. His target was awake. He pointed his flashlight at the king-sized bed. Empty.

"I see you got my invitation, Mr. Archer." A voice, raspy and tired, came from the other side of the room.

His flashlight scanned toward the source of the sound, another desk with another computer. A skinny man sat behind the desk. The old man moved his pale face away from the light beam.

Archer was about to ask the usual, "How do you know my name?" but a man as rich as Kareem would find the resources. Besides, the message this man had sent suggested that he knew much more than Archer's name.

A faint blue light reflecting from the computer screen on the old man's thin face gave him a creepy look. His sunken dark eyes peered at Archer as if looking into his soul. If he had one, that was.

"How do you know about her?" Archer asked. Although he didn't mention her name, something clutched his heart and squeezed. After all this time, it still hurt like hell.

The old man shook his head, his blue-lit face as if from a class-B horror movie, his bushy white mustache and white eyebrows illuminated. "We can spend the night chatting about how a bored rich man could get any information he wanted once he hired the right people. But I am afraid that will be beside the point."

"Which is?"

"I can help you to avenge your wife."

The invisible hand squeezed his heart more. He was still standing at the door. It felt awkward and uncomfortable. Two love seats were next to him. He wished he could collapse on one of them, but instead walked to the desk where the man sat. A hammer smacked his chest.

Kareem gestured to a chair in front of the desk and Archer took it.

"For the sake of, umm… quality control," Kareem asked, "did the guards give you any trouble?"

Archer shook his head. "Not really."

Kareem nodded, with a hint of disappointment leaning back in the chair. "I see."

"To be fair to them, they didn't make many mistakes."

The old man nodded again. Their eyes locked for a moment. Archer searched for any signs of fear in the man's face, a nervous look or an edgy tone. Nothing. When he got the message the millionaire had left for him this morning, mentioning Archer's deceased wife and a better way to avenge her, Archer thought paying him a visit at night in Burj would not be expected. Apparently he was wrong.

"I already avenged her," he said.

"You killed some people that you believed to be behind the … attack."

Again, Archer didn't opt for the obvious how-do-you-know. "So?"

Kareem took a cigar from the ornate wooden cigar box that was big enough to carry the Queen's jewels but contained only three cigars. Rich people and their peculiarities. As if using some less-expensive box was too tacky, too human for his taste.

Kareem lit the cigar with a lighter that looked like a gadget from a James Bond movie, then took a long breath in and then out, watching the cloud of smoke ascending to the ceiling. No smoke rings appeared but they should have.

"I lost a dear one myself," Kareem said. His voice wasn't bored anymore. "Forty years ago. You may think it's a long time even for a big loss. Anyway, that's what I thought at the beginning... that time would ease the pain."

He paused, letting go another breath of smoke. The smoke that was beginning to fill the room gave the entire scene a surreal feeling. "I was wrong, Mr. Archer. Damn wrong. Pain is only worse after all those years. Not only the pain of loss, but guilt as well. You see, there is a reason why many religions granted the right of revenge to those who suffered injustice; it's a human need. A primitive one."

Archer was about to repeat what he said before. That he killed the people who planned the attack. Those who actually committed the attack were dead anyway. Leaving no one else to exact revenge from. But he decided to wait.

"You know why, Mr. Archer?"

Archer didn't answer. Kareem didn't wait either. "It's not because revenge brings peace to the soul, or a closure, or any of that crap. It is simply because revenge is what stops people from hurting you more."

"What do you want from me?"

He hadn't broken into here to listen to Doctor Phil.

If Kareem was offended, he hid it well. "As I said in my message, I want to give you the right revenge. Oh, and by the way, I know about your... What's the word... work, as The Shadow."

Archer swallowed. Only three people in the world knew that. "The right revenge?"

4

"Precisely." Elongated skinny fingers tapped on the cigar. "An opportunity to cut the evil from its roots, Mr. Archer. If someone slapped me on the face, I wouldn't feel comfortable until I cut off the man's hand, both hands if I could, to make sure he wouldn't do it again. If my son died in a school shooting, I wouldn't feel he was at peace until a law incriminating selling fire arms to the public was legislated."

Kareem stopped, leaning toward him, his brown eyes glittering with something akin to madness. "And if a group of extremists killed people I cared for, I wouldn't feel peace until I brought the entire religion to the ground."

"The entire religion?" Archer frowned. Another thing about rich people: because they had some more zeros in their bank account than others, they thought anything stupid they said should be treated like ancient wisdom.

Kareem rotated his laptop computer until it faced Archer. Archer squinted into the bright light. Three Internet Explorer windows were open. The one at the front showed a blank web page with a black message box in the middle. A one-line message had a counter under it.

Archer read the message; he was familiar with it. The counter showed:

1 Day: 21 hours: 50 minutes left.

Below the counter was an hourglass with most of the sand moved to the bottom part. He didn't need to check the computer clock to know that zero hour was the day after tomorrow's midnight.

"This is just a virus," Archer said.

Kareem brought up the second browser window. It was of a Saudi newspaper. The same message and the counter were displayed on two locations on the page where the web ads were normally placed. The third page was some real-estate site with the counter being displayed in the middle of the screen where a photo of the property should be.

"Okay, a widely-spread virus."

"Maybe." Kareem nodded slowly. "I have asked a programmer who works for one of my companies to give me a program to ... what's the word ... *track* the virus spread. See for yourself."

Kareem clicked on an icon on the computer's desktop. A program launched. A message popped up saying:

Number of infected websites: 23,453.

Below the message were two buttons, the standard "OK" and another one that read "Details." Kareem clicked on the Details. Another window popped up, showing a long list of websites. Infected websites, Archer assumed.

To his surprise, the list had some well-known websites. News sites, sports sites, and even some .gov ones.

"This is not just a virus, Mr. Archer."

"So you are trying to say that the message displayed is for real?"

Kareem nodded.

"But what kind of secret could bring down a nation of one billion followers?" Then he thought of a more important question. "I understand you are a Muslim yourself."

Kareem took another puff from his cigar. "I don't think this is the right question."

"No?"

"You should ask: what kind of religion can be brought down by a secret?"

Archer waited. Kareem turned off the laptop and switched on the nearby table lamp. "The answer is: not mine," he said in a theatrical way.

Archer thought about it for a second, then shrugged. There was no reason for him to trust this man.

"As for your question," Kareem said, "you will figure out the secret for yourself. As a matter of fact, this is why you are here. I am hiring you to finish the investigation."

"Finish?"

Kareem pushed a manila envelope toward him. "I hired someone to start it. They've done some good work. But they don't have your... what is the word... *edge*. That's why I need you to finish the investigation."

"And find out about this virus?"

"I don't give a rat's ass about this virus." Kareem scowled. "But the book it's talking about is quite true and it does exist. I want you to make sure that it is revealed. After you find it, of course. You will find everything you need in this envelope."

For the first time — maybe in his life — Archer felt perplexed.

"Interesting tattoo," Kareem squinted at the tattoo on Archer's right arm. "Do you know what it means?"

"A palm with five fingers, the hand of revenge."

"There is more to it," Kareem said. "Anyway, allow me to offer something that will cover your expenses."

The old millionaire opened the drawer, took out his checkbook, and wrote. He pushed it across the table. Archer counted the zeros twice, the six of them, then took it and put it in his pocket.

"Very well, then," Kareem said, standing.

Archer did the same. Kareem offered his hand. Archer shook the cold, skinny hand, unable to miss seeing the big silver ring with a blood-red stone.

———————

One thousand mile away from Dubai, in a small town in Saudi Arabia, sat a man wearing an identical blood-red ring on his right hand. His gaze wandered around the small room examining his collection of souvenirs and old weapons one by one. Strange how things looked different when one knew he was seeing them for the last time. His gaze lingered on the crystal ball of that fruit. He had never had the chance to tell the story of how a strange fruit could prove everything. He had never had the chance to do a lot of things he should have done.

This room had once been his sanctuary. Not anymore. They were watching him. He knew that.

It was over.

Abdul Zahra couldn't allow it. His death shouldn't prevent him from carrying out his mission. It was his responsibility, his legacy ... his honor.

He had to do something.

And the answer was right in front of him, he just didn't have the nerve to carry on. Time. Time was slipping away. He took the army knife from his desk. Without another thought he put the cold tip of the metal to his chest.

Then he pushed.

PART ONE

"She grows up to be either someone's slave or a whore. She dies, and the family's honor remains intact."
With these words, Arabs used to bury their girls before they reached puberty. Islam came in and stopped this habit. As for the mind-set ... well, that's another story.

-1-

<Dulles International Airport– Washington DC>
<Time left until Zero hour is 1Day:17H:10min>
<Number of infected websites: 34,952>

"This is your suite, sir!" The flight attendant — a blond wearing a red cap with a matching scarf dangling from one side and pinned to her shoulder in what looked like an Arabic style — announced with the enthusiasm of a game-show host.

Edward tried to force a smile, but ended up with a grimace. "Suite? Um... nice... I guess," he said, examining the *Star-Trek*-like first-class cabin.

With unruffled zeal, she demonstrated how the chair could turn into a bed, how to use the wardrobe behind him, how to close the cabin for total privacy. Despite how hard Edward tried to focus on what she was saying, all his mental aptitude — what was left of it anyway — was focused on the small device he held. So he kept nodding, hoping this would make her move on and finally allow him to sit.

"See, very easy." The flight attendant beamed as she pressed on the edge of the small desk in front of his chair and a mini-shelf filled with a variety of beverages rose up from the desk with a hiss, steam seeping out as it did. Yep, *Star-Trek*.

He collapsed. Even with his six-foot-three, one-eighty body, the seat couldn't be more comfortable for a fourteen-hour flight. The air hostess then showed him how to control the entertainment system — they didn't call it TV — then the phone. Finally she told him, with an ear-to-ear smile, that her name was Sasha and she would be his air hostess. Just in case he had mistaken her for his lawyer or financial consultant.

"Thank you," Edward said, his fingers pressing hard on his iPhone.

Ring. For God's sake, just ring.

His cell ignored the prayers, which was a shame for a phone that could do almost everything. One day he would complain to Apple about that.

He tried to call Kimberly, his colleague, again. He listened to the slow beeps, then the operator's voice came, almost mocking him, apologizing that the phone was switched off. Edward hung up without leaving a message. The half-dozen he left already should be enough.

Would life be better without the cell phones and emails and texting and tweeting? Back in the days you used to try someone's office or home number; if he were out you just left a message and waited. You didn't have to wonder why his cell was off, why he didn't text back. Or even better, back in the times when people used pigeons to communicate. Life must have been something back then.

He let his mind dwell a little in that fantasy world. He needed a break, something else to think about, something other than Kimberly's last call two... three hours ago. Jesus, it felt as if it happened days ago. How things had changed from the normal and slow-pace of what was supposed to be a special day in his career — in their career actually, both of them — to the madness that was going on.

Early that evening, when FBI agent Summers had nabbed him right after his presentation in the annual projects-review seminar the Library of Congress held, Edward knew that something was wrong. He finally convinced Summers to wait until he finished his twenty-minute presentation about the new historical documents verification method Edward and his colleagues had developed. They called it HILDA, short for Historical Information Lie Detector Analysis: a system that could not only help determine the age of a given document, but also verify the information within the manuscript. Advanced handwriting, comparison, and analysis techniques were applied to extract certain information. Yeah, okay, it was a long twenty minutes for agent Summers. And probably that was why he hammered Edward with questions afterward. Questions about his case that the FBI and the CIA had long since closed.

But it wasn't Summers' relentless and repeated questioning that turned Edward's day upside down. Not even Summers' insinuation that Edward was suspected for possible connections to overseas operations and armed groups in the Middle East. It was the call that came right after the agent had allowed him to use his phone. The very phone he was now squeezing, as if that would make it receive another call.

Other first-class passengers arrived. A forty-ish woman in a gray business suit and short red hair sat in front of him. Then his friend came, swaggering as if enjoying a day on the beach. He wore one of his custom-made black Gucci suits, and a silk burgundy shirt that had an extra-button undone. His arm circled around the waist of a beautiful Korean flight attendant, who really didn't have any waist. She giggled as if he told her a joke.

With an undulating body and batting eye-lashes, the air hostess took his friend through the tour of the suite. The no-waist flight attendant finally said, "Oh my God, I can't believe I am talking to Vampire Vane face-to-face! It's like a dream coming true."

Although Vane — his real name was Vensel Vaserely — hadn't been on TV for more than four years now, his role in the two-season successful TV show as the teenage, extra-hot vampire gave him a lifetime of fame. The handsome young man with delicate, porcelain-like features and wavy golden hair parted by gods played the role of a deadly Vampire.

"Anything else?" she asked Vane after he whispered something in her ear. Her tone double entendre.

"Just your soul, Yoki," Vane hissed. It was his line from the TV show.

Edward had watched several episodes after he and Vane became best friends. A series of worn-out clichés, and not even good ones. The sexy vampire lured ladies to remote and empty places and killed them, or sucked their blood, whatever they call that crap. But not before boring the viewer with the same lines every time. Finally, the merciless vampire met the innocent, pure and naïve (polite terms for extra-dumb) Margarita, the daughter of a Van-Helsing-like vampire hunter and fell in love with her. Another cliché. But thousands of teenage girls would stone Edward to death if he as much as criticized the beloved hotty vampire.

When Yoki was gone, Vane turned to him, his face showed nothing except his usual haughty expression and flat eyes as if engraved on a marble statue. "Any word from your old Jed buddy?"

Jed was Edward's boss back in the days when he used to work with the FBI himself. Ten years ago, in 2000, Edward had ended his three-year career with the bureau and used his experience to work as a freelance document examiner. A decision he was still unable to remember the reason for. One of many things Edward couldn't recollect about his life before the accident.

"No," Edward said. "He wasn't even aware the FBI was re-opening my case."

Vane nodded.

"I don't like the timing of it," Edward said. "Why now, after four years, are they re-investigating that accident? And then Kim called and…" He couldn't finish. The word felt as if a dreadful disease.

"Nothing from Kim, *Je suppose?*" Vane crackled his fingers.

"No." Edward sighed, hearing the exasperation in his tone. It might sound sexist, but he always felt somehow responsible, maybe even protective when it came to the welfare of his female colleague and the only other person in the world — besides Vane — Edward could call a friend. A real one.

The plane was taxiing now. Vane rested his head on the chair and stared at the TV screen in front of him. Edward did likewise.

Then his phone finally rang.

-2-

"Hello," Edward said, his heart about to burst from his chest.

"Hello, Edward."

It wasn't Kimberly. The hoarse and cigarette-raspy voice of Doctor Fayazi was unmistakable.

Doctor Fayazi. The Jordanian historian whom Edward blamed for everything that had happened. In addition to blaming himself, of course.

Kimberly, the photographic specialist of the agency, worked with Doctor Fayazi as part of a project the Library of Congress outsourced to their small agency.

"I'm afraid I have some bad news," Fayazi said.

Edward's stomach rolled. He wanted to tell the doctor that since the day they met him a week ago, nothing but bad news had come their way.

Kimberly was, as always, too enthusiastic about the photo collection the old historian had, covering some civil unrest in 1925 Saudi Arabia. Because she needed to see the photos herself, and despite Edward's concerns, Kimberly traveled to Jordan to meet the old man. Edward was supposed to go with her, but last-minute changes forced him to stay. One of the many what-ifs that Edward kept thinking of, knowing well they would haunt him for the rest of his life.

"I am unable to reach Majida, too," Fayazi said.

Majida was Fayazi's student who went with Kimberly to Saudi. Because Majida lived in Saudi, it made her the perfect choice to accompany Kimberly. But why did Kimberly decide to go to Saudi in the first place? Their scope of work was to examine the photos in Jordan and go back. When Kimberly called him three hours ago, she spoke fast and didn't make a lot of sense. She told him she was in Saudi, in a town near Madeena called Hayett. Why? Edward didn't quite understand. But she was excited that she was about to meet someone who could help her on her own research.

Her own research.

If he had just paid attention to what she was telling him for the past month. If he had just asked a follow-up question about the manuscript that she was working on. The signs were all there. He should have suspected that Kimberly's insistence to meet the Arab historian was not only because of those Saudi civil-unrest photos. Another what-if.

When Edward told Kimberly that she shouldn't travel alone to Saudi, she comforted him that she wasn't alone. Majida was with her. And now, they were both...

"She is missing, too." Fayazi sighed.

"Kidnapped," Edward corrected. For the first time he spoke the word. Now that he did, Edward felt a mixture of rage and anguish that left him paralyzed as in one of those dreams where one wanted to run from danger but was unable to move.

"We..." Fayazi stammered. "We shouldn't rush... to conclusions —"

"The hell we shouldn't!" Edward shouted. People around him turned with curious looks. "They are kidnapped and probably in danger, and we both know why."

Edward paused, his voice and hands — his entire body — shook when he remembered the way Kimberly had ended her phone call. That terrifying shriek, then the sound of her cell phone hitting the floor. When he'd managed to call her fifteen minutes later — that was, when the FBI finally let him go — a man answered the phone, saying only two words. Two words that hit him as if a cement block had crushed his chest. "She's gone." Just like that. The man hung up, offering no explanation and leaving Edward with that cement block, unable to breathe, alone in the street where agent Summers had left him.

Sasha, the flight attendant, tapped him gently on the shoulder and signaled that he should switch off the phone as they were about to take off.

"Edward," Fayazi said. "You don't know what you're talking about. There are things —"

"My friend is kidnapped," Edward fired back. "This is all I know."

Shouting 'kidnapped' in a plane that was about to take off, into a cell phone that was supposed to be off, wasn't really a good idea. He lowered his voice and added, "They told us what they want. Let's give it to them. We have to, Doctor."

"I don't *have* it," Fayazi said, his voice on edge. "I swear to God I don't. I wish I did. You have no idea how many people are willing to kill to get that—"

Sasha and another flight attendant came and asked him to switch off the cell. They pointed at the iPhone as if it were radioactive. The other lady mentioned something about calling someone if he didn't comply. NATO, maybe.

"I am on the plane going to Saudi," Edward said. "I need to hang up. Please, Doctor —."

"Don't go..." Fayazi shouted as Edward was hanging up. "You have no idea what you are up against. They will—"

The call ended. Edward put the iPhone on the small desk in front of him. Sasha and her friend didn't look very happy, but they smiled anyway.

"I don't trust that guy," Vane said.

"Who? Doctor Fayazi?"

"No, Abraham Lincoln."

Another thing about Vane: a wiseass.

"I asked Abbie to do a background check on him," Edward said. "The Library of Congress already cleared him, but after... well, the second call, I thought that she might be able to find something about him."

Abbie was their secretary-slash-programmer-slash-everything-else in the office. Vane had taken care of all the financial and administrative work through his company that owned the building in Washington. Edward and Kimberly did the actual document-verification job.

"You got anything?" Vane asked.

"There's some interesting stuff about him," Edward said, watching Yoki who stood in the middle of the isle while a video on the screen demonstrated the safety procedure. "He studied in Saudi, in the early '60s. His degree was some long name in Islamic Salafism."

"As in Wahhabism? I thought that was where all the friendly terrorists came from?" Vane asked, examining the collection of beverages in the minibar. "Vodka and Cognac?"

"Yeah, but here is the thing: Fayazi then went and studied Islamic history in Egypt. He changed his field to history and got the Ph.D. there."

"Yoki," Vane called out. Yoki came right away. "I didn't quite grasp the part of blowing the life-jacket. Care for *une démonstration?*"

Yoki giggled and went to her seat not far from them.

Edward watched from his window as the plane took off. The lights from the airport quickly became an unrecognizable blur.

"Do you think they have red wine here?" Vane asked, checking another bottle. "I remember Kimberly mentioned Fayazi was lecturing in King-something university. Alcohol-free Beer? Why the hell would someone want that?"

"King Hussain University in Jordan," Edward said. "Fayazi had published four books in Arabic, English, and French and guess what were they about?"

"*Please.*" Vane did something between a bored yawn and a sigh, another trademark of his that he saved only for Edward. "Assume I have made several guesses and they were all wrong and now you have my undivided attention." Meanwhile, Vane opened one of those alcohol-free beers and poured the contents into his mouth in one gulp. "Preposterous!" He almost spat it. "*Absurde.*"

So much for undivided attention. Edward went on anyway. "See this," he said, showing Vane a picture in his iPhone; it was the report about Fayazi that Abbie managed to compile within the last hour.

"*Une protestation?*" Vane squinted at the image, feigning to be shocked. "*Pourquoi?*"

Edward almost asked for a translator. What idiot convinced Vane that Vampires don't speak English?

"This was in Egypt ten years ago after Fayazi published his book about Saladin, titled *Saladin, A Liberationist Or A Butcher.*"

"Balls," Vane said, opening another bottle. "Fayazi has balls."

"Fayazi accused Saladin of lobbying against the Fatimies State that ruled Egypt during the crusade wars. Not only that but of conducting a massacre slaughtering more than 300 of the royal Fatimi family, including women and children."

"And those Fatimies were the good guys?" Vane asked.

"It sounds like they were better than the corrupted Abbasid State centered in Baghdad. This was why Saladin wiped out the Fatimies, he was working for the Abbasid."

Vane smiled and waved to someone, probably a flight attendant, but he motioned Edward to go on.

"A senior member in Al-Ulmaa community in Saudi Arabia denounced Fayazi as an infidel. He was forced to apologize for some parts of his third book about the transition of authority in Islam. In short, all of his books and theories seemed a little..."

"Off tangent." Vane said.

"To put it mildly." And maybe that was why the guys at the library trusted him.

The Fasten Seat Belt sign turned off. According to the information system, the flight would take thirteen hours to reach Dubai and then one more hour for transit to Saudi. Vane remained perfectly still. The screen in front of him showed a feed that read: Front Camera. The front camera showed, as expected, nothing but a black sky. Edward was not sure which was dumber, putting a camera in front of the plane for passengers to see or his friend looking at it while it showed nothing but darkness. It reminded him of an old joke about a man who liked calmness so he listened to a blank cassette.

Vane lifted the phone and dialed. He waited a second then swiped in his credit card. He said, "Fire him." Then he hung up.

"You fired the pilot?" Edward asked. Earlier in the day, Vane and Edward were supposed to travel in Vane's private jet. When Vane called his pilot, he told him that the plane wasn't ready.

"Yes." Vane stared at the black screen in front of him.

"Why?"

"His duty was to have the plane ready when I need it. He failed."

"Vane, this man might have a family to support. It was a mistake. Give him a warning, punish him."

"This is the least punishment I could think of." Vane shrugged.

"For Christ's sake, Vane."

"My family has a certain reputation. It is my duty to maintain it."

"A reputation of being ruthless, merciless capitalists?"

Vane tapped on his chin, then said, "Yeah, pretty much."

Vane and his family owned V&V, one of America's — if not the world's — biggest hunting equipment manufacturers. The company designed, manufactured and sold hunting gear ranging from rifles to binoculars to camouflage clothes; in short, everything to do with hunting, or as their smart advertisement said: "The hunt, the hunter, and the hunted and everything in between." Vane himself was a hunter, like his father and his grandfather and great-grandfather. The TV producers liked him, unknown face, old aristocratic money, and worked as a hunter, which was probably the closest profession to a vampire, if you excluded lawyers and politicians. Then there was his European blood and the semi-albino skin. It was as if young Dracula himself were applying for the job. The viewers worshiped him, especially girls. He was rated America's sexiest man alive for two years during 2004 and 2005, but of course Edward was not there to know any of that.

They fell into an uncomfortable silence. At least it was for Edward. Vane seemed to enjoy watching the black sky. Yoki asked if they would like something to drink. Edward shook his head. Vane whispered something in her ear. She giggled, nodded, and hurried back.

"My family runs a special kind of business. Selling hunting gear is just the front, the tip of the iceberg, if you will. Not to sound dramatic, but our real business is slightly more competitive in which such a reputation will not only ensure our clients' trust, but also make any competitors think twice before stepping in our way." Vane's face remained calm; he rarely showed any emotion. "I am not talking about piling more money in the bank account, this is the survivor's nitty-gritty, you don't show fear, you don't show mercy, you don't show weakness. Once you do, your opponents will eat you alive."

Edward arched an eyebrow. Vane had never discussed his family business before. "Don't tell me your uncle works for the mob." Vane's uncle, a man Edward hoped he wouldn't have to see ever again, was the only family member Edward had met. He was Chairman of the Board of V&V Corporation; Vane was the CEO of one subsidiary company. Vane's parents were alive but that was the only thing Edward knew about them.

Vane smiled. "You know me well enough to know I wouldn't accept being part of anything illegal."

That he did. "Okay, promise me you will help him find another job, indirectly."

Vane yawned. "If that will help you sleep better."

Yoki brought Vane a glass of wine. He took a sip, smiled at her. She leaned forward and whispered something in his ear. Vane took another sip then rose and followed her.

"I'll be back," he said, putting a steel hand on Edward's shoulder, then stopped and shook his head in disgust. "I can't believe I just said that line."

"Why? It fits with the reputation of ruthless, merciless, umm … terminator."

But Vane was gone. He and Yoki disappeared behind the curtains of the separator between first class and business class.

Edward might be old school, but he always looked at sex as part of the package. A relationship, even short ones, should be based on some mutual understanding or likeness. Even if it was not verbally said, sleeping with a woman meant a commitment. At least for him. Probably that's why he was dumped more frequently than America got itself into an overseas muddle.

Alone in his... um, suite, Edward took out the yellow folder he'd found earlier on Kimberly's desk. The same folder in which she had kept photocopies of everything she gathered in her research. The same folder he and Abbie had scanned an hour ago and uploaded to that FTP site they were given.

Edward examined the first page. He had seen other research Kimberly had prepared. Her early ones were about Mother Teresa, Madam Cory, and Queen Elizabeth. Now, her collection reached thirty. Women from different religions and nationalities throughout different times. Her essays ranged from a single page to fifty and were always filled with photos of some sort.

Kimberly loved taking photos. There was a time before she met Edward and Vane when Kimberly had sold her photos for hundreds and sometimes thousands of dollars, but like Edward, she had abandoned her career and joined their small agency.

The first page of each essay was always the same, and it was normally the only thing Edward read. Not because he didn't take his colleague's hobby — if that what it was — seriously, but because on the first page, Kimberly always wrote one line that paraphrased the research from her point of view.

He read the line. And he had the same feeling as when he read it in the office for the first time a few hours ago, right after the second call. A robotic voice called and gave his instructions if they wanted Kimberly back alive. He read the words and remembered what the robotic voice told him.

"Your friend and Fayazi took a very sacred book that doesn't belong to them. It is our right. If we don't get it back, your friend will pay."

Edward had tried to reason with the man — assuming he was a man — to tell him that there was no way Kimberly would take anything that didn't belong to her and even if she did, he would make sure to return it. But the voice cut him off immediately. "You have to send us everything she worked on, all the documents. So does Professor Fayazi."

"Send you?" Edward said. "Sure, but how?"

"Check your email."

And the voice hung up.

Via email, the kidnappers gave him an FTP site — which was a file-uploading site according to Abbie, their computer wizard — to be used to upload all scanned images of the documents they had. Then the kidnappers added a potpourri of mob clichés threatening to send Kimberly back in pieces if they didn't comply.

Somehow, reading that email wasn't as shocking as seeing Kimberly's own handwriting confirming what the voice said and what Fayazi told him when he contacted him immediately after he received the email. That it was too dangerous and he had no idea what he was up against. It might even explain the sudden interest of the FBI.

Edward read Kimberly's words and closed his eyes. The words, still echoing in his brain:

"Fatima, the daughter of Mohammed. There is a reason why, whenever her name was mentioned, crowns started falling and the cruelty of men got exposed. Find her book and history is not the only thing that will be changed."

-3-

Fatima's book. If that book was indeed valuable, how could Kimberly put her hands on it? The obvious answer would be through her work in the Library of Congress. The library acquired an enormous number of manuscripts and letters from Iraq and Afghanistan, mostly donated by the Pentagon. This was how Edward and Kimberly's agency got subcontracted to help with the document examination and verification. It made sense, except Edward knew it was impossible. Because he was the only one in their small agency who could read Arabic, all documents had to go through him first to filter the valuable ones and to see if they deserved verification with the HILDA system. He would definitely remember seeing such a history-altering book if they had it. So the question remained: how did Kimberly get that book?. From Fayazi? Why would he give it to her? Maybe to examine it? But how did Fayazi get such a book? Was it possible that during her trip she stumbled upon it?

Sasha and another blond flight attendant asked him about his choice for the meal. The food cart she brought was something that could solve world hunger. Edward couldn't recognize half of the contents.

"What is this?" He pointed to something wrapped with green leaves.

"It's a grape leaf stuffed with rice and spices, a Lebanese appetizer," Sasha said with a plastered smile.

"And this?" He pointed to a plate with what looked like yogurt but yellow and dressed with pomegranate seeds.

The smile fainted. *"Baba Ganooje,* an appetizer from egg plant mixed with yogurt."

"And this?"

"This is just steak, *sir."*

"And this?"

The smile was gone. "Just small hot dogs with spice."

"Do you have lobsters?" Edward asked, giving her his sweetest smile. Not the full wattage one. He didn't want her to disrobe.

She shook her head, her lips tight.

"Shrimps then?"

Some people lose their appetite when nervous, others start eating anything. Edward had a funny habit of craving seafood when anxious.

"This is our new seafood dish." She almost threw it at him. Maybe she didn't like seafood.

He asked what was the old seafood dish. She glared and asked for his choice of beverage.

Nope, definitely not into seafood.

The flight attendant pushed her trolley away. Edward started reading through the file. The first ten pages or so were the Arabic and English versions of the discourse Fatima gave in the great mosque a few days after her father's death. Edward reviewed his own comments on the document. He had personally verified this document and it was authenticated. The first part was pretty much like Mohammed's sermons, praising God and thanking him for his blessings. The second part was slightly different, the tone was bitter and maybe even offensive. There were parts where Fatima had paused and wept before she talked again. He couldn't understand why Kimberly had been so interested in this speech, nor if it had anything to do with what happened to her. He flipped through the pages, around fifty pages of printout from Internet websites. All about Fatima. He skimmed through the articles. Again, nothing stood out. Edward hoped that he would find a reference about a book of some kind or anything that would shed light on the document the kidnappers wanted. His heart skipped a beat when he reached the last page. Another empty page, except for a few lines in Kimberly's handwriting. The first line was:

"Check with Dr Fayazi about the farm. Is this the same as in his photo? Is it real? Can we go there?"

Which farm did Kimberly want to go to? Was this why she went to Saudi? She told him she was about to meet someone. Hmm. Probably it'd be better to read those pages Kimberly had included after the speech. There must be a reference to the farm Kimberly wanted to go to, or to the book they were looking for.

Edward rubbed his face and eyes. He put the folder on the table and leaned back. Vane sat in his suite as if he just materialized. "When did you come back?"

Vane's face showed nothing, but Edward knew that inside he was smiling. Nothing made Vane more happy than sneaking up on people.

Another flight attendant passed. Vane waved and gave her a full-wattage smile. Okay, maybe sneaking up on people was the second thing that made him most happy.

"I know you like to act like a vampire," Edward said. "But, for God's sake, I am already on edge today."

Vane shrugged, the annoying smile still there. "Just for the record, I don't do this because I became attached to the role, or any other psychological crap people are saying about me."

"No?"

Vane shook his golden curls. "I was raised as a hunter, I live like one and think like one."

"Uh huh."

"All the Vaserely family were raised this way. Hunting is more than a tradition in our family," Vane said, holding up the glass of wine and examining his reflection — read, *admiring* his reflection — "Being a hunter is the proof that man is on top of the food chain. It is the ultimate test of our superiority, blah blah blah."

"Blah blah blah? I thought this was your family's credo?"

Vane waved it off. "It's just the bull of rationalization my uncle starts every family gathering with."

"And what do you think?"

Vane shrugged. "It's simpler. Being a hunter, a real one, will give you an edge on everyone else."

The lady in a gray business suit who sat in front of Edward turned back, flashing a shy smile. "I am sorry to interrupt." She looked at Vane. "You are Vampire Vane, right?"

Vane said yes. She asked for an autograph for her daughter, as she was a big fan.

"But of course — it's the least I can do for a fan," Vane said, then wrote her one on the back of a charitable-donation envelope.

"My daughter will be so happy about that," the woman said, putting the envelop in her purse. "She was a big fan of the show. I mean, she still is... it's a shame it was stopped."

Vane offered a non-committal nod.

"I remember I read that you were chosen to be the president of...what was it?"

She read, not her daughter. Who was the fan here?

"Yes," she recalled, "the American Hunters Association."

Count on the tabloids.

"Yes," Vane said. "It's the family business."

But it wasn't his family business or Vane's hunting skills that made the American Hunters Association offer him that position. On the TV show, Vampire Vane promised his love, Mary, that he would not kill humans anymore, another cliché, so the vegetarian vampire started feeding on bears and lions and deer. To keep up with his diet, Vampire Vane went on hunting. And it became a part of every episode to see the sexy vampire wearing his camouflage clothes and his blue cap, and wielding his rifle. Why a super-strong and super-fast predator like a vampire needed a rifle to catch a deer, or why for example he didn't just buy his groceries from the supermarket, such questions were irrelevant. Apparently, the viewers liked the *sacrifice* the vampire did, and more to the point, the Hunters' Association saw a golden opportunity to use this to enhance its image. Vane liked it as well: between the Association and V&V corporation, which shared the same building with their agency, Vane had instant access to the best hunters in the United States, which took V&V business to new levels.

Done with his commitment to his fans, Vane shifted in his chair-slash-suite and turned so that he completely faced Edward. "Have you found what the kidnappers want?"

"I am almost sure it's about the book of Fatima," Edward said.

"And this Fatima is..."

"The daughter of Mohammed."

"As in... Mohammed the prophet?" Vane arched an eyebrow. Major mannerism for him.

Edward nodded. "Kimberly was so busy lately researching Fatima. You know how she gets obsessed when it comes to famous women."

"Fatima Bint Mohammed," Vane said as if trying the name. Then he shook his head. "Never heard of her."

"According to Wikipedia," Edward shuffled some papers in Kimberly's file and started reading to Vane: "Fatima was Mohammad's daughter from his first wife Khadeeja. Many people believed that Fatima was Mohammed's only surviving offspring. He had other sons and daughters who died when he was alive. To date, all Mohammed's offspring are descendants of Fatima."

Vane frowned. He sniffed, looking at Edward's still-covered plate. "Is that what I think it is," Vane said, pointing at Edward's meal as if it was something the dog left behind.

"What about it?"

"Shrimp with barbecue sauce." Vane shook his head. "There must be regulations against this."

"Where are the politicians when you need them."

"Tragic when you think about it. Anyway," Vane said, unwrapping the knife and fork. "So Mohammed had offspring?"

"Yep." Edward referred to Kimberly's papers. "It says here that Mohammed adored Fatima, always repeated that she was a part of him, that he who hurts her hurts him. He cherished her children and carried them around wherever he went."

"Duh," Vane said. "She was his daughter; of course whoever hurts her hurts him. Why do people like to state the obvious?"

"Maybe," Edward said, trying to remember what one of the historians had once told him about Arabs and how they treated their daughters. "But in the society of 600 AD Arabia, men used to bury their daughters alive because women were nothing but shame to their families. So, no, I think it was really unorthodox for a man to do that with his daughter or her children." Edward looked at the paper and read more: "Mohammed was often seen with one of his grandsons on his neck or even carrying him on his back."

Yoki came holding a plate for Vane. Vane adored special orders and special dishes and special treatment. Steam seeped out as Vane removed the lid. The barbecue smell wafted. Edward couldn't see what was on the plate but he would bet his lunch money that it was raw steak.

The plane went over a bumpy air pocket or whatever they call it. Through the window he saw nothing but darkness.

"Mohammed had also chosen his cousin Ali-Bin-Abi-Taleb as a husband for Fatima after rejecting many rich men who proposed to her. Fatima and Ali both lived in a small house next to Mohammed's in Madeena, the city to which Mohammed and his followers migrated. Mohammed always referred to Fatima, her husband and their sons as the household of Mohammed, promising heaven to those who revered them."

"I see, so Mohammed had pushed the envelope a little further here," Vane said as he finished cutting the supposedly-raw steak into small pieces and started picking them up with his fork. "What do you make of that?"

Edward opened his mouth but didn't know what to say. He wasn't really sure what to make of all that so he just shrugged. "Well, I have no intention of writing Fatima's biography. Let's focus on finding clues about that book."

Vane nodded while chewing. "Go on, please."

Edward shuffled more papers, looking at Kimberly's own notes. There was something about the handwriting of a person. Edward wasn't big on psychic revelations, but seeing the words she scribbled, the way the letters always leaned to the right, the neat curves she ended the G and Y with, it sent a pang to his chest as if he could see his friend writing those notes, asking questions, and cross-referencing between articles about Fatima's life and her famous speech.

"There is nothing much I can see," Edward finally said, trying as hard as possible to make his voice normal and to focus on the matter at hand. "Lots of long stories about their difficult life in poverty. Even after her father conquered the entire Arabic peninsula, Fatima and Ali's life was marked by poverty. Lots of stories about them donating their food to the poor. Fatima was practically giving away everything she had, sharing it with others. She died too young. A month after her father. Apparently because of her grieving. No one knew when exactly she died."

"Interesting."

"It gets weirder," Edward said. "Only five men attended her funeral. And it looks like her grave is missing. Kim wrote at least three notes about her wish to find Fatima's grave."

Vane counted with his fingers. "Died young, right after her father, practically no funeral, missing tomb, and no one knew when exactly." He reached five. "Why do I have the feeling that something doesn't add up with what you just said about how Mohammed loved her."

Edward wanted to repeat the comment that he wasn't interested in Fatima's life. He tried to shrug but couldn't pull it off. Kimberly's notes filled this page, as if demanding attention. Edward skimmed them, searching for any reference to Fatima's book. There wasn't any.

Most of the cross-references with the speech were about a section that described the dispute between Ali and the rest of the Muslims about who should succeed Mohammed after his death.

"There is an interesting piece here," Edward said, mostly to himself as he turned the page. The plane hit another series of air pockets. This one lasted longer. "It's more of a prophecy really. Mohammed told the people that Fatima would stand at judgment day before God and ask him to take all her followers to heaven. Mohammed kept repeating that those who pleased Fatima were pleasing God, those who aggravated her were to expect God's wrath."

Sasha came pushing a trolley and asked them if they would like some coffee or a cold drink. Edward asked for lemon-flavored green tea. She checked but what they had was regular green tea. She poured him a cup anyway.

"Okay," Vane said. "So Fatima was important, at least for Mohammed. Is that what we found so far?"

Edward nodded. "There is one more article, but I think it's a mistake from Kimberly's side."

"*Comment cela?*"

"There is a story about Fatima's church in Portugal where a holy woman that called herself Fatima materialized to three poor children and told them about future events."

"I know the story," Vane said, taking a sip of the red wine. "A touching one, but wasn't that holy lady Saint Mary?"

"Yep," Edward said. Despite the name similarities, the lady was not Fatima the daughter of Mohammed. "There were books written by one of the former popes about this Fatima and the prophecies she told."

"Most probably Kimberly was in such a hurry that she just included this article without paying attention to the fact that it had nothing to do with the subject," Vane suggested.

Edward concluded the same, but then he saw Kimberly's notes on that story, linking it with another story in the previous article about a similar appearance of Fatima, centuries after her death, to a group of Indian Muslims. Then to an Iraqi lady in one of Sadam's prisons. Interesting, but he wasn't in the mood to read old wives' tales, and his eyes became sore from all the reading in the low light.

The cabin lights were dimmed and tiny dots of light filled the ceiling giving it a twilight mood, so peaceful and beautiful that Edward wanted nothing but to stare at it and sleep.

"You probably should get some rest," Vane said, as if he read his mind. "However, I wanted to give you *this* before, and I think now is the best time." He handed Edward a wristwatch.

Baffled by the sudden change of subject and, well... the personal gift — which wasn't Vane's style, to say the least — Edward took the watch. It was metallic, heavy and slightly bulky. The time digits were also big and filled the rounded screen.

"Press on those, together." Vane pointed to two of many buttons on the side.

Edward did. The time digits were replaced by a whole new set of symbols and menus.

"It's a GPS tracker," Vane said. "The wrist band is an antenna that provides communication with satellite dishes. There is also a cell-phone chip that can connect to almost any cell-phone provider."

"Okay..."

"With this," Vane pointed at a similar watch he wore, "I can see your location all the time, and you can see mine on the map in the screen. The watch is able to provide a one-way audio signal. Once you press on that button, the small microphone in the watch will send the audio to a server in Europe, which will dial my number and let me listen to what's going on around you. Both our phone lines are encrypted and being routed through several servers via a set of secure and untraceable connections."

"So..." Edward said, having trouble digesting all the information at once. "I can use my cell phone while I am in Saudi without being tracked?"

Vane gave him a flat eye. "What part of secure and untraceable do you have difficulty understanding?"

The silver watch showed the world map on the background with red and green dots somewhere above the Atlantic. Edward deduced that the dots were his and Vane's location but he didn't brag about his conclusion. On the back of the watch was the V&V symbol of the Vaserely Corporation logo.

"This was manufactured by my uncle's company," Vane said. "And it's better not to ask about their business."

Edward tried the green tea and it took all his restraint not to spit it out. It was so disgusting that it could be dubbed inhuman even in Guantanamo Bay. Maybe he should consider ceasing to drink green tea. He wasn't sure where he picked up this habit.

One of many things that he couldn't explain about himself after he woke up from his coma with no memories of the two years before his accident — like his ability to understand Arabic, which was of far more a concern than the habit of drinking tea.

"Thank you," Edward said, putting on the watch. "Is there something I should know?"

"My God." Vane puffed. "Friends can give each other gifts."

Edward just stared at him.

"All right, all right." Vane raised his hand in a mock surrender. "My contacts brought me some *décocertant* news about Summers. Nothing to worry about."

"Vane."

Vane rolled his eyes and sighed. "Okay, Summers is actually with the CIA, not the FBI."

That explained why Jed didn't know him. "That's it?"

"Pretty much." Vane smiled. "He was heading the covert ops division for ten years."

Edward blinked. He tried to ask a follow-up but didn't find his voice.

"My source believes that it was the first time in three years Summers got personally involved in an interrogation."

"I feel privileged."

"I think whoever sent him wanted to scare us," Vane said. "It won't work."

Edward swallowed. "It might, a little."

Vane still had the icy smile.

"Is there more?"

"Not, really." Vane rubbed his hands with the wet tissue and pushed the dish aside. "You might find it intriguing that for the last five years, Summers was based in Saudi Arabia."

-4-

<Ryadh City– Saudi Arabia>
<Time left until Zero hour is 1Day:16hrs:05min>
<Number of infected websites: 49,664>

Archer looked at the unconscious old man tied to the bed. Then he glanced at his wristwatch. Eight in the morning, Saudi Arabia time. That meant he had spent more than one hour in this villa in Ryadh. Very risky, given the fact that the man, even after his retirement, had enough connections and influence to raise a small war.

Time was running out. Not that he had plenty to start with. What Kareem showed him on the computer meant that he had until tomorrow midnight before it happened.

Ever since he watched that message, he kept asking himself the same question.

Was it for real?

But Kareem had put it right. His job was not to question whether it was real or not. His job was to make it happen in the way it should. In the way that would eliminate once and for all the cancer. The cancer that took his wife and the daughter she carried.

His fist tightened when her image flashed in his mind. Her eyes. Even in his memories, her eyes were looking through his soul. As if she knew what he had done. Of all the lives he had taken, of the promises he broke in his long journey through the valley of death. To avenge her.

Maybe there was a place dead people went after death. Otherwise how could she know? Perhaps he had lost his head and started imagining things. Which was a very likely scenario. He wasn't the sanest person on the planet anyway.

The old man tied to the bed, spread-eagled, made a noise. He was in pain. His wrists and ankles had turned blue. Another person, a normal one, might have something against doing this to an old man. Not him.

According to the files Kareem gave him, this man, Jassem, was one of the key players in a big campaign launched against Saudi people in the Eastern area. A campaign during which hundreds of people were arrested under martial law, some of them sentenced to public mortification. It normally meant twenty lashes, but in their case, based on Jassem's suggestion, their hair was fully shaven as a way of humiliation.

But Archer wasn't after that. His interest was focused on one particular arrest, a month after the public mortification.

Archer walked to the minibar and got a can of beer. He jumped over the motionless body of the bodyguard lying on the red carpet. He liked the color, which was the same as the curtains and the bed sheets. Not because red was his favorite color or anything, but, given what he planned to do in this room today, red would make things easier for him.

The fancy cordless phone on the bedside table rang. Time to get back to work. He took the perfume stick he had been using to bring the old man into consciousness whenever he lost him.

Jassem opened his eyes. "Who are you?" he yelled. "Where are my guards? Where is everyone? Where is my wife?"

"1965."

"What?"

"Answer me, where were you working in 1965?"

Jassem grimaced. "I can't remember."

Archer pressed on the man's ankle, right on the pressure point.

Jassem moaned. "In the special guards."

"In the Arabian month of Muharam that year, you arrested a man and tortured him."

Jassem closed his eyes. "We arrested too many people, I am not sure."

Archer pressed harder. The old man screamed. The screaming went on for another half an hour. When Archer finally put him down he had all the answers he came for.

-5-

The new seafood meal on Edward's table started getting cold, so he opened the aluminum cover. No steam. But, and despite what Vane said, the smoky smell of barbecue was encouraging.

Vane was gone, perhaps chasing another flight attendant. Sometimes Edward suspected that Vane acted like this just to keep his reputation as a ladies' man. Only a few who dealt with Vane as a member of the Vaserely family saw past the playful, handsome skinny male model. Others who were taken in by the soft appearance made a big mistake, often a lethal one.

Edward plugged the headset into the chair and searched for something to watch on the nine-inch display of his ICE system, standing for Information, Communication, and Entertainment.

The food wasn't so bad. The vegetables outnumbered the shrimps by a ten-to-one ratio and the orphan fried ring of calamari got so soaked up with the barbecue sauce that Edward felt pity for it. He debated asking Sasha for something else, but wasn't sure he wanted to be the first Emirates passenger to be thrown out of the plane.

If he could only watch one of the blockbuster movies the plane had. *Angel and Demons* with Tom Hanks was on the list. Wasn't it released in May? Which meant the airline guys got it only two months after it was in theaters. Not bad. Edward almost went for it. Vane would not be so happy about that. Vane – through his contacts – got it recently on DVD so that they could watch it together at Edward's place, which was more of a private cinema with the seventy-inch plasma screen and the seven-speaker surround-sound system. A humble gift from his humble rich friend.

Despite being close friends for four years now, Edward and Vane had very little in common. Watching Tom Hanks movies was one of those little things. Okay, maybe the right word here was not watching. Try memorizing. They would sit for hours during the first weekend the DVD was out. Starting with the trailer, then the movie, then the special behind-the-scene clips —

Vane always bought the collectors' limited-edition version —
then the interviews. The next week, they would watch the movie
twice more. Sometimes Kimberly would join them. For Edward
and Vane, there was no bad movie when it came to Tom Hanks.
That was how the two first came to know each other in the
hospital. When Edward first awakened from his coma, his
brother brought him a collection of DVDs to kill time as his
body was too weak to walk. Vane, recovering from his alleged
car accident that ended his career as a movie star, heard the
sounds when he was taking his daily walk. He knocked on
Edward's door and that was the start.

Finally, Edward decided to wait on the movie. He had more
on his mind anyway. He tried the Information section on the
screen. Google's web page appeared. That could be useful. He
didn't want to think how the Internet connection worked on the
airplane. Using the touch screen wasn't as smooth as he expected
but he managed to type the words "the book of Fatima" in the
Google search box and clicked on the search button.

After a while, ten results appeared.

Musehaf Fatima, the proof of Shia's diversion from Islam,
one link suggested. Another had a similar title. The third said that
this book was a record of the epiphany Fatima had and
contained prophecies about the future. The fourth link said
something like: what other proof do you need to believe Shia's
infidelity than them having another Quran?

Another Quran? Was the Book of Fatima another Quran?
Other than the one Muslims read? If he wasn't mistaken,
Musehaf was another word for Quran in Arabic.

Edward swallowed. Fayazi's words warning him that this
matter was worth killing for resonated in his mind. He clicked on
the first link. After a minute the screen turned black. A message
appeared in both Arabic and English:

"Musehaf Fatima will be revealed. The nation of lies calling
themselves Muslims will be exposed."

Underneath was a counter showing one day and less than
twelve hours left.

A cold shiver went all over him. He tried the other two links. The same thing. The sites were apparently hacked. But what did this message mean? And the counter? It wasn't just a threat. Someone was actually setting a precise time for things to happen. Why? If someone wanted to reveal the truth about a subject, why set a time for it? But above all, he didn't like the language, that tone, the anger, the threats.

Edward went back to the search page. The fifth link had the title: 'Musehaf Fatima,' another false accusation. The link pointed to a site named ShiaSearch.org.

The page took more time to load. When it finally did, he read through, but it wasn't much. Basically, the site claimed that there was no such thing as Musehaf Fatima. "There is only one Quran for all Muslims," the web site repeated over and over.

Tell that to the people who kidnapped Kimberly.

A discussion forum talked about why there was only one Quran. Edward was tempted to read through the discussion, but the page went black. When it loaded again, a cold sweat peppered his forehead.

The same message with the counter.

He switched off the browser and went back to the main screen. The big colored I.C.E. letters greeted him. Enough reading. Edward pressed on the E letter for entertainment. He start navigating through the movie list, fighting the temptation to watch the Tom Hanks one.

Like a bad horror film, his TV screen started to change to black. The message with the counter materialized. He tried switching channels, pressing the back button. Nothing worked. He turned off the screen and switched it on again. The message remained.

The counter below the message kept its silent countdown.

Oh, God.

What if it was all connected?

What if this was not only the zero hour for the Musehaf but also for Kimberly? It kind of fit with the forty-eight-hour-notice they were given. Edward pressed buttons on the touch screen feverishly.

"Sir, can I help you?" a flight attendant asked. This one looked Arabic.

"I am ... I think there is a problem with my screen."

The women looked at the monitor. Her forehead furrowed, her face twitched in something between disgust and confusion. "What is *this*?"

"I don't know, I was just browsing the Internet."

She gave him a flat look, as if he just told her that the dog ate his homework. She tried pressing different buttons on the touch screen. Nothing worked.

"Please leave it as it is," the flight attendant said, going to attend another passenger.

Ten minutes later, at least three more passengers had the same problem on their screens. The black-framed message with the countdown was now everywhere.

What did you get yourself into, Kimberly?

-6-

Edward had trouble sleeping. He tried different positions, he tried to bribe the sleep fairy with an additional pillow, then an additional blanket. His mind wouldn't let go. Despite all the rationalization about how much he needed to sleep, about how he would need to be at full speed when in Saudi Arabia, anxiety gnawed at him. He couldn't help it. Dark thoughts hovered above his mind like vultures above a lost traveler. Waiting for him to fall, to feed on him.

Edward couldn't stop imagining Kimberly. Her scream replayed over and over in his ears. Was she being tortured? Interrogated in a dark room for information she had no idea about? Was she swearing to them that she knew nothing about any document?

— Or did she?

The idea sounded bizarre. One only a sleepless mind could conjure. And yet it sounded — in the same way all bizarre ideas sounded when one was sleepless — very possible.

Okay, Kimberly would never hide anything from him. Maybe from Vane, but not him. On the other hand, she had been away for several days now. Kimberly might have found something when she was with Fayazi, or during the brief time she was in Saudi Arabia.

What about before her travel?

Kimberly was consumed by this research, which was probably the main reason she insisted on going even after Edward couldn't go with her.

Okay, so Kimberly might have found out something about whatever document those people were after. So what? Whatever she had discovered wasn't going to help him find her unless he knew what it was.

Numbness started as sleep crawled all over his body. Edward welcomed it, letting his mind drift into that bliss of losing senses in his surroundings. Normally that was when another anxiety took over. During the day, he managed not to think of his accident — more precisely, what he didn't *remember* of his accident and the years before. Sleep became his time to catch up with his fears, with the crazy dreams about another life he might have lived. Faces of people he didn't know haunted him.

But tonight was slightly different. Edward felt the presence of another... ghost. But this one was of an angelic nature. A comfort took over his mind. An overwhelming confidence assured him that everything would be fine.

Tonight he slept with his thoughts hovering on a new name. A name that kept echoing in his mind, probably due to the time he spent reading about her today.

Fatima.

\<Saudi Arabia>
\<Time left until Zero hour is 1Day:1hrs:15min>
\<Number of infected websites: 82,106>

"What the hell happened here?" Captain Adnan demanded, entering the crime scene.

The two policemen closer to the door jolted like students caught by the principal in the teachers' area. As head of the police department in Madeena, Adnan had that effect on all uniforms. His short and chubby figure, with his bulldog-like face and thick mustache, was a nightmare for every policeman.

He counted six uniforms in the small shack. All stood staring at the body with yellow tape in their hands, not sure what to do with it.

Adnan wasn't an angry man; he didn't even shout when he talked. As a matter of fact, Adnan often greeted people with his wide smile, and shook hands with them. He did that even with low-ranking employees and janitors and office runners. For a Saudi local, greeting an Afghani was the equivalent of a politician shaking hands with people at the mall in a non-election year.

Adnan's gaze wandered around the interior of the small house. Amazing. From the outside, this house, like all others in this small town, was nothing but four walls of clay. But the inside was totally different. The clay was cleaner, maybe even painted or something. The big green carpet had mud stains left from the footsteps that crowded in the relatively small room. Talk about crime-scene contamination. Bookshelves hung on two of the walls. A large cupboard with some souvenirs was placed next to the door. A fancy crystal bowl that didn't belong in the place was filled with some... stones?

Everyone stared at the big wooden desk. On the chair behind the desk, a man slumped forward in the middle of a big pool of blood.

"What the hell happened here?" Adnan repeated.

A tall officer with a mustache was the first to answer. "We got a call that a man died here, sir."

"Who called in?" Adnan asked in his low, almost whispering voice, putting his palm under his left cheek and resting it on the other hand, as if listening to a boring lecture on nano-physics on a Sunday afternoon.

The two policemen exchanged glances. The other officer, a younger and shorter version of his colleague, said finally, "We don't know, sir."

"Why?" His tone was slower, lower, and had that menacing edge now.

"It looks like an anonymous call; we cannot even get the caller ID."

For those who were not lucky enough to visit Saudi Arabia, the word anonymous had the same effect as saying "tax free." Everyone wanted it and no one could get it.

Communication systems were thrown away and replaced because they supported anonymous accounts. Business cases were rejected if this word appeared even on an irrelevant reference. To use a "public" pay phone, you had to use your personal smart card. To use "free" wireless, you had to log in with your phone number, which was in turn linked to your passport. All phone calls, messages, and Internet access was recorded, monitored, and traced. Bottom line, everyone had to be stark naked in front of the all-seeing eyes of the law-enforcement authorities. One could not so much as fart without all information being logged and analyzed.

Talk about restriction of information flow in China.

But Adnan couldn't complain. It just made his job so much easier. Until now.

Adnan's eyes bulged. "*Anonymous?*"

"We are still investigating this, sir."

"I thought you are investigating the murder here?"

They looked at each other again. The taller guy said, "We are, sir."

The shorter said, "It is ... just ... this looked more dangerous."

Adnan nodded. Shorty was right. A murder was a breach of security in one small place. And let's face it, this part of the kingdom was the kind of place where everything happened. Where only one family out of ten owned a house, and having two meals a day was considered a luxury. That was why they assigned him to this city in the first place. An anonymous call, however, meant a breach in the entire system.

But that wasn't what worried Adnan. He wouldn't come to this place in this muddy town at night to investigate a murder. What worried him was the call he got from his superior that his team was interfering with another team. A complaint was already made and he had to go there to sort it out.

What other team?

If the head of the police department didn't know about it then it wasn't there. Unless … He paused, not sure he would like the answer.

"Was there anyone outside?" he asked.

"No sir, just our guys. The area was empty."

Adnan examined the dead man. Due to the way the man was leaning on the table with his face down, it was impossible to see where the blood was coming from.

"Adjust him," Adnan commanded. "I want to see what the hell happened to him."

Three uniforms hurried to carry out the order, surrounding the dead man, preparing to lift him.

Before they could, a voice came from the back. "Don't touch anything."

Everyone, including Adnan, turned. A man wearing a khaki uniform, red beret, and black sunglasses — although it was 9 in the evening — stepped in. Sunglasses strolled slowly, with a raised chin and inflated chest. He might even have flexed his arms. All signs of an asshole.

The uniform suggested the special forces, but Adnan knew better. Even the army had to report any activity in the area to the head of the police.

"I want all of you out of here … *Now!*" Sunglasses yelled.

Like the sea giving way to Moses, all the policemen in the room gave way between Adnan and Sunglasses. His men waited for him to say something.

"And you are?" Adnan asked calmly.

"Agent Fahad." Sunglasses huffed.

"Are you taking charge of the case now?" Adnan asked in his calm, whispery tone.

"Yes," Sunglasses answered as if he were asked, are you the greatest man in this room? Too enthusiastic, too eager to challenge, and too happy with his special-forces badge.

"Fine then." Adnan gestured to his men to follow him. He stopped midway and turned to Sunglasses as if just remembering something. "By the way, I hope you brought enough manpower to handle those." He gestured at the opened door. People gathered at the narrow road in front of the house.

Sunglasses cursed, then shouted, "Close the door and keep everyone out!"

No one moved.

"I thought you didn't want us to get involved."

Sunglasses sighed. "Okay, you are here to close the case and after that I want everyone out. You hear me? Just to close it, no investigation."

They glared at each other for a moment. Neither broke eye contact.

Adnan finally said, "We will close the case."

"Good, because I will personally make sure to kick your old ass out of here."

Sad. This was all that Adnan could feel. Not angry, not intimidated, just sad. He wasn't big on melodrama but after twenty-five years of service, getting a threat from someone who was twenty years younger was … sad.

"You two." Adnan turned back to his men, who were relieved to see their boss on top of things. At least temporarily. "Bring the man up. I want to see how he was killed."

Two police uniforms approached the dead man, grabbing him by the shoulders and pulling him to sit upright. Everyone in the room gasped once they saw the man's chest.

"What in the name of God is this?" Sunglasses said, stepping back.

"Deep shit," Adnan said, mostly to himself.

Dubai International Airport was huge. The lack of personal touch was further emphasized by the spacious halls and large steel structure, reminding Edward of sci-fi movies of a post-apocalypse future where surviving humans lived in those extra-clean, ultra-protected compounds.

They had landed in the new Terminal 3, which was dedicated for Emirates Airlines flights. Edward would take the connecting flight to Madeena. The visa to Saudi that Doctor Fayazi had sent him a week ago became useful now. And yet, Edward couldn't help wondering if Fayazi had planned for this from the beginning. A week ago, in his first phone call with the Jordanian historian, Edward casually asked if one could visit the locations shown in the photos, where demolition of historical landmarks had triggered civil unrest. Fayazi said that he would look into it. Two days later, Edward and Kimberly's visas were faxed. Fayazi then told them that he had misinterpreted Edward's question as a request to facilitate the visit.

But Kimberly then used her visa to go to Saudi, as Edward was doing now. Was this the plan from day one? To lure them to Saudi, and then what? Arrange for them to get kidnapped to extort some cooperation Fayazi was already getting from them?

"So what are you going to do?" he asked Vane who just finished a phone call.

"Arrangements were made," Vane said squinting at the information board. "I will take the flight to Bahrain."

"Then? I mean how will you get the visa?"

In the past few hours, Edward learned that getting a visa to Saudi for a non-Muslim American proved harder than he thought.

"Do you really want to know how I am going to get into a third-world Arab country without a visa?"

Edward shrugged. "As long as you don't get yourself in trouble, do what you want. But remember, I already have someone to save."

"Don't worry, O'noble one." Vane semi bowed. "You worry not about saving *mon derriére.*"

"So where shall we meet?"

"We'll be in touch." Vane pointed at Edward's watch.

It took Edward some time to remember that his watch was now a high-tech gizmo. "One more thing, Vane."

Vane frowned. "Is this the part where you tell me to be careful?"

"I..."

"One minute." Vane held up his hand then started playing an air violin. "Now go on, I got the sound track for you."

"Very funny. I actually wanted to tell you: don't rely on your super-fame powers, no one knows about Vampire Vane in the Arabian desert."

"Is that so?"

A group of teenagers passed them. All blondes, all talking loudly at the same time and all carrying back bags. European tourists.

"I guess this time you have to watch me scoring hot chicks while you stand and watch." Edward pointed at his forearm and wiggled. "It's gonna be muscular handsome versus skinny handsome."

Vane made a face. "Scoring hot chicks?"

Edward shrugged. "Been a tough day."

The public announcer called for the Bahrain flight passengers to start boarding at Gate 3. Vane headed that way.

Edward watched his friend walk onto the red carpet of first class and into the gate. Edward flashed back to when he had last seen Kimberly, disappearing inside another gate in another airport. Fayazi's words brushed the inside of his chest like a bat trapped in a house.

"There are dangerous people who would kill to get this thing."

Should he ask Vane to stay while he searched for Kimberly alone? At least not risk another life? But what chance did he have without Vane? What about taking Fayazi's advice and leaving it to the authorities? Abbie had contacted the state department and the police more than fourteen hours ago. All she got was that we-have-to-wait-for-forty-eight-hours crap.

Finally, Edward walked toward the Madeena flight, hoping that this moment wouldn't join the long list of what-ifs that tormented him.

-9-

<Madeena Airport– Saudi Arabia>
<Time left until Zero hour is 23hrs:50min>
<Number of infected websites: 123,950>

The queue at the immigration officer's desk in Madeena Airport was longer than Edward had anticipated, and much longer than he could wait. Edward tried to count the people in front of him but the heads seemed to blur after ten. He saw lots of passports. Afghanis, Pakistanis, Bengalis, and Indians. Not to sound racist, but they all looked the same. Some spat on the floor more often than others, some were picking their noses, and all of them were talking, loud and fast and at the same time. It still could be an intelligent conversation, Edward just couldn't understand how. He spotted white people as well, all males, all Europeans but they too looked somehow … off. Despite the confident looks and the straight backs they tried to maintain, Edward could sense the trepidation and anxiety behind the façades. He could almost hear them asking themselves if the inflated salaries they were offered were really worth this volunteer jail.

Mr. Psychic.

Maybe he'd better get one of those 900 lines for fortune tellers.

Above each of the four cubical desks was a sign in Arabic and English. The first one read "VIP," another was dedicated to Saudis, the third was GCC citizens, the fourth lane was left for

"Others." The first three lanes were empty, everyone stood in the "Others" lane. For a moment, he debated going to the GCC lane, hoping it meant something like Great and Cool Chaps. But then he read the Arabic label: Gulf Countries Citizens.

So much for the great and cool.

Enjoying being with the *Others*, Edward watched the immigration officers at the cubical desks at the end of each lane. Three of them wore the white sheets they call dishdash. The fourth wore a green uniform. Was he of a higher or lower rank than the others? The four officers were all bearded. One had a beard so long and thick that it looked like bad makeup for one of the extras in *Pirates of the Caribbean*. What made it even worse was the shaved mustache. No matter how open-minded he tried to be, seeing a man with this... um... facial style and not judging him for either an extremist or something worse was beyond Edward's human capabilities.

"Reason for the visit," the bearded man with the white tablecloth asked him, almost spitting the words.

"Tourism." Edward made an innocent smile. "As it says in the visa."

Edward thought a lot about the best answer to this question when he was on the plane.

He ended up with none.

"What kind of tourism?"

Edward's smile got wider. That was exactly what he was trying to figure out during the past hour. For what kind of tourism in a country where non-Muslims were barely allowed to breathe could he aim?

"I like skiing."

"So?"

Edward shrugged. "So I thought about doing that on the sand."

The officer frowned. Not that he was smiling before.

Edward kept the innocent smile. Five minutes more and Long Beard might adopt him. "You know, sand skiing." In case the officer did not get the point.

Long Beard nodded.

Edward kept the smile despite the pain in his facial muscles. But instead of letting him in, Long Beard picked up the phone and whispered something. He then waved for another security guard. A black man wearing a green uniform with a black hat strode up.

Once the uniform came, Long Beard handed him Edward's documents and murmured something. Edward waited for the part where the officer told him to wait or go or anything. Long Beard just waved for the next...um... customer.

The uniform gestured for Edward to follow him.

"Bye." He smiled once more to the nice long-beard officer. The man didn't respond.

Too busy with customer service. Yeah, that must be it.

The uniform escorted Edward to a nearby glass office where a big man sat behind a small black desk with a computer terminal and a phone. Big, was Edward's first impression; however, now that he could see him, rounded might be a better description. Everything on the man was rounded and blown up as if he wore one of those air-filled costumes. His small nose and small eyes were lost in his big rounded face. The black beard covered only a tiny bit of his multi-flapped chin. He wore the standard-issue white dishdash with a white head cover wrapped around his head. The desk teetered on his knees — it was like when an adult tried to sit at his son's desk in elementary school. The image was more like a polar bear being jammed into a matchbox.

Two chairs sat in front of the desk. Edward waited for the fat man to tell him to sit. He didn't. Polar Bear asked him the same question Long Beard had asked. So Edward gave exactly the same answers.

For some reason Edward couldn't quite grasp, he wasn't comfortable telling them that Fayazi had provided him with the visa. For one, he wasn't sure if he mentioned Fayazi that he would get any response. Second, based on what he read, the old historian wasn't very popular in Saudi.

"How do you write your name?" Polar Bear asked, frowning at the computer.

Edward spelled out his name.

Polar Bear shook his head. "You sure you never spelled it with a double D, for example."

"No, this is the only way I spell my name."

The man nodded and typed something on his computer terminal.

"Is there a problem with my name?"

Polar Bear frowned more. His small eyes were only two slits now. A little more frowning and the man could touch his eyebrows with his lips. "Your eye-scan print," Polar Bear said.

Edward waited for elaboration but that was it. "What eye-scan?"

Polar Bear sighed. "When you get in this airport, you see that big machine with little peep-hole, no?"

"Oh, yes." Edward remembered going into a machine for the eye-scan when he first entered the airport. "You mean the—"

"Well yeah, that's the one." Polar bear scowled, typing on his keyboard one letter at a time using only his index finger. "Stupid system," he finally said to the computer, then lifted his face and addressed Edward. "It look like you came here before with a different name. It could be a small change in the letters; I don't know. But the system detected it, you understand?"

Edward shook his head, the smile plastered on his face. "There must be a mistake. I never came to Saudi."

Polar Bear arched an eyebrow. "You *sure*?" Edward did not like the tone. "It says year 2001. As I said, the system is not responding so I don't have other details but I can see…"

All voices faded away. All that Edward could hear was a seashell noise on his ear. The year 2001. Was it possible? Had he came to Saudi before his accident and totally forgotten about it?

As with friendly Long Beard, Big Polar Bear made a phone call. The red handset was so small next to Polar Bear's chubby face that the phone looked like a toy phone used by a grown-up. Edward heard words like "Ameeri visa," which meant a visa issued by a prince. It looked like his visa wasn't a normal one. Something of a VIP guest. Polar Bear mentioned the issue of the eye-scan and the non-responding system many times to whoever was on the other end.

Finally Polar Bear nodded to the speaker and hung up. "I am sorry, Mr. Fleming," Polar Bear said, "I must ask you to permit a full search."

Before Edward could respond, Polar Bear waved, with a hand that could have been mistaken for an airplane wing, to the uniform outside the room. The man hurried in.

"Take Mr. Fleming here for full search. You understand full search." Then he turned to Edward. "Please go to the search. Meanwhile I will see what I can do."

"I don't understand, why the search?"

Polar Bear puffed up. A gust of wind blew on Edward's face. Hurricane Katrina with a garlic smell. "Listen, Mr. Fleming, I went to United State last summer, right, to Disneyland with my wife and three daughters. Do you know what your government did to me in the airport?" He pushed the chair and the desk and stood up, or tried to.

The image reminded Edward of the *Titanic* movie: the ship just about to launch.

After a minute, Polar Bear was standing in front of Edward. "Do you know how thorough they have searched me?" he said, gesturing to the layer of flaps where normally the hip was. "Do you want me to go to details?"

"No," Edward said, terrorized. "I understand."

"They took me to a close room and their hands were all over me, two men, you know?" He gestured to his upper thigh. "They frisked me as if someone tipped them I might be smuggling a diamond or something. There was this guy who—"

"Please," Edward pleaded, "I get the picture, believe me." He wished he didn't, though.

Edward wanted to argue that this wasn't the case before 9/11, and it was terrorists' attacks that forced the American government to do such searches. But arguing might encourage Polar Bear to give further visual details.

They went to an empty room with nothing but one table. Because Edward had only his *Barry Smith* shoulder bag, the search took no more than ten minutes. They asked him to take off his shoes and they searched them. They searched all his papers, reading them one by one. Edward was a bit concerned when they came to the yellow file with photocopies of Kimberly's notes. Fortunately, they examined it quickly and put it back in the bag.

After the search was finished, Polar Bear gave him his passport and visa, both stamped.

Ten minutes later he was out of the airport and into the hot, sticky night air. The street was empty of any other buildings. Desert extended endlessly, no lights, no sign of life except from the few people exiting the airport and walking to the lined-up cars not far from him. Taxis, presumably.

What now? His best chance would be to follow Kimberly's lead. Which meant going to the town from where she called him.

Edward got into the first taxi and told the driver that he wanted to go to the town of Al-Hayett.

The Indian driver turned back to him. "What?"

"Al-Hayett," Edward repeated.

"What?"

Sure about the town's name, he repeated it.

The driver repeated his "What?" then he added, "Sir, I never heard about this place before."

Edward pointed at a small screen attached to the dashboard. "This is a GPS, right? Can you check it?"

The driver slammed the steering wheel. "This no GPS. Why everyone think this GPS. This taxi company-system. Okay? Company system."

Some people got attached to their gadgets.

"I am telling you, there is no *Hayett*," the cab driver said.

Kimberly had mentioned that it was near Madeena. "Okay, take me to Madeena."

"We *are* in Madeena."

"Yes, I know, but I want to go downtown, to the city itself."

The driver shook his head. "You cannot get there, sir."

"Why not?"

More impatience, everyone in this place was impatient. "Sir, Madeena is a holy city. Foreigners are not allowed in there."

"You mean non-Muslims are not allowed."

The driver tilted his head left and right.

Edward took it as a yes. "So drop me at the border of the city."

The driver murmured something in Hindi, then shrugged and pressed on the gas.

-10-

During the trip from the airport to Al-Madeena, Edward had called Abbie and asked her for some help with the directions. The town wasn't on Google Maps or Mapquest or any gps/map site in the world. Still she finally managed to get it. He didn't know how and wasn't sure he cared to.

The GPS coordinates, when he entered them in his Google maps application on his iPhone, were in the middle of nowhere. It probably meant nothing. Middle East maps were all in the middle of nowhere as they were not updated frequently.

They had driven less than a hundred miles from the Madeena Airport. Noshad, the cab driver, kept mumbling about the futility of going there and that he was sure no city with the name of Al-Hayatt existed.

Edward thought of what he learned at the airport. Saudi Arabia? Was it possible? The answer kept flashing in his mind: his memory loss after the accident in 2001. When he awoke from the coma, four years later, Edward couldn't remember a thing from the year and a half before his injury. He couldn't explain to the FBI why he was found, beaten, bound, and gagged, in the trunk of a crashed car, several blocks away from the World Trade Center. Police records showed that the same car left the parking area of the Trade Center one hour before the attack.

Despite the three months of investigation, the authorities found nothing on him. He left the States for London in 2000 and had flown back only one day before the attack. While in London, after checking into the Ritz for two days, Edward Fleming hadn't used a credit card or checked into any other hotel. It was as if he had crawled under a rock for one year and came back to the States just before 9/11.

So how come no one found out about this trip? Why did he go there in the first place? Hold the phone, Polar Bear told him something about his name being changed. Maybe he, somehow, got himself another passport with another name and traveled to Saudi with that passport. That could explain why he vanished after arriving in London.

"Take the next right turn on the highway, please," he told the driver, looking at the map on his iPhone. His phone was getting the data connection from a local service provider through roaming service. Which meant he would be paying a premium rate. Maybe one day he would care.

They went into a small town called Hayl. Noshad tried to convince Edward that this was the town he was looking for. No, Edward was sure the name was Al-Hayett.

Without streetlights, the three-lane road was pitch black. The road itself was in a fairly good condition, except for the artificial bumps preceded by a sign that read: "Careful. Camel Crossing Area." Camels were nowhere to be seen. A pity.

The trip could have been more painful, Edward just couldn't imagine how. During the past hour, Noshad entertained him with his special collection of Indian songs. The lyrics were in English. For the first two minutes, Edward enjoyed the Eastern theme, whatever that meant, but soon, when the singer repeated the words, "Oh, baby, baby," for the hundredth time and then screamed, "Don't leave!" Edward felt a steel hammer pounding on his skull.

"He is Sundra Rajan." The taxi driver smiled, probably noticed him trying to concentrate on the song. "Modern music."

Modern torturing.

"He is on a tour in England now. Very successful."

Thank God England was not on their route today.

Edward tried to *get* the music. But every time he ended up by wondering if this Sundra Rajan's girlfriend left him before or after the song.

Probably after.

When the tape was over, Noshad gave Edward a white-tooth smile, asking him something Edward didn't hear well but he surmised it was whether he liked the song. Edward settled for "Yeah," sparing himself the extra communication. Noshad then re-wound the tape and started it from the beginning. Sundra Rajan's voice sang loudly, teasing him: "Oh baby, baby."

Edward eventually found himself singing "Oh baby, baby" with the tape.

The road significantly changed after they took the intersection for the Hayl town. Fifty miles of the worst highway Edward could imagine. It was bumpy, and rough and uneven to the point of nausea. No fences, no lane marks. Herds of camels — finally Edward got to see camels — crossed the road twice. Both times they came from areas not marked for camel crossing. The second time, the cab driver almost hit one big animal, which reacted by turning toward the car's headlights, totally uninterested, while it chewed, and continued walking as slowly as possible as if on purpose.

They took another turn in a town called Khalifa and after thirty kilometers — Edward had given up on miles as all the road signs and the dashboard meter were in kilometers — they finally came across a small traffic circle that had a big sign on its left turn. Made of bricks, the sign had the shape of a big cup or something like that. The writing, which was in Arabic, said the name "Al-Hayett" in big letters.

At last.

Edward checked his watch. Almost 1 in the morning. They took a right from the roundabout that led to a narrow and uneven road. Ten minutes later, they reached the destination.

Edward and the driver both gasped. Noshad whispered some prayers. It was as if they entered a time warp, where time had long since stopped at one sad moment that it couldn't pass. Calling it a ghost town would be as much an understatement as describing a civil war as a power-sharing dispute. There were no buildings, no clear roads. Instead, lots of what looked like mud houses scattered everywhere. The small dark silhouettes were forty square feet, maximum. There were no fences, no doors, no windows; just two small openings at the top of the wall with no glass. With no light from the inside, the openings looked like two peering eyes in a giant black skull. And if that wasn't creepy enough, the palm trees, and there were a lot of them, were just empty trunks. No fins, no leaves, no dates, nothing. Long spikes into the skies. So surreal. As if happiness and hope and life itself were sucked away from this place, leaving only a dead shell empty except for sorrow.

"What is this town?" Noshad whispered. "It's so much scary."

"Yes. So much scary." Were they in the right place?

He asked the driver to keep on the main road. Noshad obeyed. Now they could see different levels of the land. The skull-like houses peered at them from the level above and the one beneath. The empty palm trees guarded the houses like old sentries. On the other side of the road, separated by a low land full of mud houses, the palm trees were normal with fins and looked somehow less scary. He told the driver to try to cross to the other side. Noshad carefully guided the car through a small cliff into the low land passing between the dark clay structures. Edward avoided looking into the windows, not that he was scared or anything. Just to give whoever lived there some privacy.

Edward Fleming's travel tip number ten: don't look at dark windows in a creepy city.

Noshad found a road that took him again to the higher ground. The houses on this side were more scattered, the empty windows were still trying to swallow everything into their dark void, but now they could maintain some distance, they looked less intimidating.

"You thinking anyone living here?" Noshad asked, his accent more pronounced now.

"I can't see any sign of anyone."

As if on cue, the sign came. And with it all doubts were gone. They were absolutely on the right track.

In front of a relatively big mud shack, the only one that was lit from the inside, were four police vehicles and what looked like a small demonstration. People, mostly men in dishdash, gathered around the house. Police uniforms stood between them and the house, trying to keep them away.

"I think this is my stop," Edward said, handing the driver two one hundred dollar bills. "And keep the change."

-11-

<Al Hayett town– Saudi Arabia>
<Time left until Zero hour is 22hrs:45min>
<Number of infected websites: 148,122>

Edward walked across the street toward the lit house. Civilian vehicles were parked a block away. Aside from the lights coming from the police cars and the faint moonlight, the place was pitch black.

"*Emshou Min Huna!* (Move away) "*Yallah, Yalla,*" a police officer who came out of the small house yelled at the crowd.

The gathered men looked at each other and then at the officer. The flashing red and blue lights from the top of the police vehicles reflected on their faces and clothes. No one moved. The officer kept shouting. Several uniforms swung long black sticks at the crowd. That worked a little, sending the sea of dishdashes several yards back. Several women stood at the back, as if hiding. They all wore long black baggy dresses that covered them from head to toe, so that not even a face was visible.

So much for scoring hot chicks.

Edward's first guess was to go directly to one of the officers and tell him about Kimberly. Whatever happened here, it was clearly big, given the number of cars gathered. It had to do with Kimberly. She was in this city, she was kidnapped, and then the police came here. Did the kidnappers assault someone else while kidnapping her? Maybe Fayazi's student? Was Kimberly still here? With every thought, his heart did a two-step jump. He considered asking the police, but the uniforms guarding the door, the angry and threatening moves they cast away the crowds with, the solemn faces, were not very encouraging. Not to mention what he knew about non-Muslims being in the holy land of Madeena. No, he didn't want to start with this option.

Ah, Kimberly's phone. He dialed. The call went through. Again, the quickening in his pulse. The heavy weight on his chest increased with every ring. No one picked up. He tried again. This time, the phone was switched off.

The hair on the back of Edward's neck stood. His spider-senses tingled. Someone was watching him. He turned left and right. A group of men stood not far from him. He walked toward them and their attention immediately shifted to the tall white man. Not surprising that they looked at him, but somehow Edward felt whatever set off that tingling feeling was more intense than their curious gazes.

Maybe Edward had missed the part where Peter Parker explained how his spider-senses worked.

The men were all Pakistanis, from the look of their clothes. The knee-length wide shirt, which looked exactly like a dishdash cut from the knee down, the matching pants, and the head cover, which looked like a yamaka but was white and slightly bigger than its Jewish counterpart.

"Hey guys." Edward waved to the men with a smile.

Mr. Smooth.

They stared.

Should he start with one of his ice-breaking lines or give them a stock tip?

"Nice weather, very cool, yeah?" he said.

It was hot, sticky and smelled dusty. Yet he flashed them his full-wattage smile. If they were ladies, they would be on their knees by now. The men looked at each other. One of them, a guy wearing a light blue matching set with a face like Denzel Washington's if Denzel grew a beard, barked something Edward didn't quite understand. He should have tried the stock tip.

"*Matha Hadath Huna?*" (What happened here?) Edward asked.

They all spoke at the same time. A murder, he managed to understand. Something in his chest built up. It felt like a cement block.

"Who got killed?"

They frowned.

He repeated in Arabic, "*Mann Hua Al Maktool?*"

Again they all spoke at the same time. He debated lecturing them about manners of speech. Later. Edward understood that an old man got killed. An old man, not an American lady. Good.

He thanked them. Again they stared.

Edward smiled. "When someone says thank you--"

A blue car pulled up. From the driver's window a man signaled for him to approach. Okay, he could play Robinson Crusoe another time. Edward walked to the car. The driver, a white man with a marine-buzz-cut and a scar under his left eye, sat alone.

"Edward Fleming," the man said, it wasn't a question. Still, Edward nodded. "Get in the car, please."

"Umm, I don't ride with strangers. Unless you offer me a candy."

Buzz-cut closed his eyes and opened them slowly. "Please, get in the car, Mr. Fleming." Edward was about to crack another joke but buzz-cut added, "It's about Kimberly."

Edward swallowed. What option did he have? He moved to the passenger seat of the Honda Civic. The seats were disgustingly dirty. Edward actually debated wiping them with a wet tissue before sliding in.

Buzz-cut sped through the narrow roads into the darkness.

"Where is Kimberly?" Edward asked.

Buzz-cut's gaze remained on the road. A tattoo of a palm, with all fingers up except for the thumb and pinky slightly twisted outward, was on the man's right wrist. The car CD player played "Moonlight Sonata" by Beethoven, which was — under the circumstances of driving back into the ghost town — creepy to say the least.

"You don't happen to have Sundra Rajan's latest concert, do you?" Edward asked.

"Who?"

"Never mind, how do you know my name? Did Kimberly tell you? Have you seen her?"

Buzz-cut veered onto a side road. No houses, lots of rocks and palm trees. They were inside a farm of some sort.

"Who are you? Hey, at least you can tell me your name. I can call you scar-face but I don't think you will like it."

Buzz-cut gazed at him, smiled, then pulled the car to a stop. Edward looked through the window. They were in the middle of open farmland. In other words, isolated. Not good.

"Step out of the car, please," Buzz-cut said calmly.

Edward hated when goons acted politely. "You know you haven't given me any candies. Now when my dad asks me why I got into a car with a stranger—"

"Please step outside the car, Mr. Fleming."

Edward never believed what people normally said about the eyes being the window to the soul or any of that rubbish. He never believed in anything in the realm of souls, ghosts and spirits, but if he ever did, these eyes had a soul as empty and dark as the small windows in the mud houses back there.

Edward stepped out of the car. He might try to attack or run away, but what was the point? This man knew something about Kimberly and Edward needed to know what it was.

Buzz-cut, too, stepped out. He left the engine running and walked to face Edward. There were no crickets, no sound of leaves moved by the wind, no dogs barking. Total silence except for the engine's sound and Edward's drum-like heart beats.

"What do you know about Kimberly?" Edward asked the man who was less than a foot away.

A sharp pain shot into his body. The man had punched him in the kidney. Edward didn't even see it coming. Buzz-cut slid to the side and kicked Edward's leg. It landed behind the kneecap, sending him to the ground. Another kick crushed his kidney. Edward saw stars. His face was inches from the sand, he inhaled some of it.

"You shouldn't have come here, you idiot," the man said in the same calm voice, as if reading a newspaper. Edward's only chance was to roll away, gain some distance, and maybe then rise and fight back. Another kick on his side made everything go black. He heard himself making a noise like "Arghhh."

"That was your liver, by the way," Buzz-cut said.

A click of metal. The safety trigger of a gun being released. A sound Edward's ear couldn't mistake. Then as if to confirm it, the cold metal pressed on the back of his neck. The man's whisper made him shiver more than the cold object. "We gave you a chance to pull away, Mr. Fleming, you are forcing me to do this." He punched him in the kidney again. The punches were so accurate and economical, no effort wasted, and always on target. Pain paralyzed Edward. The man flipped him with his foot. Edward lay on his back, the gun barrel pointed at his face. He stared at the black hole of the gun and spoke, spitting blood. "Where is Kimberly?"

Something in Buzz-cut's face gave away... pity maybe, a confusion about what to do next. For a split second he looked up as if to get inspiration about whether to fire the gun. Edward rolled away from the line of fire. It was futile and useless but would save him from the first bullet. He kept rolling. Tires screeched. Another engine roared nearby, not the Honda. Buzz-cut jumped to the other side of the road. The engine sound got louder. A white car passed, almost hitting Buzz-cut.

Guns fired. Edward kept rolling away. Rocks cut through his shoulders and ribs. He ignored them. When he was away enough to stand up, he did.

Dizzy because of the rolling and the beating, he ran behind the white car for cover. The blue Honda sped forward. A cloud of dust arose. The red tail lights of the speeding vehicle disappeared in the darkness.

The white Mercedes driver's door opened. A young man stepped outside, his face lost color. "Are you okay?"

Edward nodded.

"Please get in the car," the young man said, "I think you need medical care."

Another car and another no-option situation. Edward stepped in, then turned to the young man. "Your car was parked in front of the house where ..."

The young man nodded. He had black hair, dark skin, and a thin-trimmed beard, his nose straight with an arched 'T' at the point where it met the forehead, giving the young man a muscular look that probably made him look older. "My name is Zain, I work as a driver for ..." He stopped as if searching for the word. "The victim."

-12-

"You don't look like someone from around here, mister…"

"Fleming, Edward Fleming."

Zain brought him some Kleenex tissues from the car and helped wipe dirt and blood from his face and clothes. Edward sank into the leather seat of the Mercedes. Now that the adrenalin had worn off, the pain was back. His side, the kidney probably, felt like a knife had been stabbed in it and left there.

Edward shook his head. "No, I am not from around here." Mere talking was painful. He lost Buzz-cut, the first —and maybe only— lead to Kimberly's whereabouts.

"American?"

Edward nodded. "You said you knew the victim."

Zain nodded.

Okay, he needed to be subtle about this. This man might know something about Kimberly, or at least he could shed some light on what was going on. "Was it a robbery?"

Zain shook his head. He had sad black eyes. Somehow they reminded him of Vane's. The sadness, the hurt, as if he were looking at someone who had just insulted him for no reason. "He was assassinated."

Yet again the cement wall in his stomach. A cement wall in his stomach, a knife in his kidney, dust and blood all over him. Edward sure knew how to enjoy himself.

"Was he alone?"

Zain tilted his head like a dog hearing a new sound. "Alone?"

"I mean, was he the only one who got killed?"

"Yeah…" Then, "I guess."

Relief.

"Do you see a lot of tourists here?" Edward asked. Subtlety, he reminded himself. Zain did the head tilt again. "Tourist, as in a person who is traveling to a place for pleasure," Edward explained.

Zain frowned.

"Americans?" Edward finally said.

So much for the subtlety.

Zain shook his head. "No," he said slowly. But there was something there. The "No" was not definitive. As if he knew something and was afraid to talk about it. Or maybe Edward was just projecting too much. After flying for fourteen hours and then two hours of Hindi-English songs, then ending it with a massage session by doctor By-the-Way-This-Was-Your-Liver, one never knew what to think.

"I thought because there were many cops, there could be some tourists involved," Edward said. "I heard that you have few of them here."

Zain shook his dark head again. "The victim was the owner of a construction company that runs this place... among other things."

"*Runs* this place." Edward almost sneered. "I can't imagine someone is taking care of this place."

The young man frowned.

Edward immediately tried to take it back. "I mean it's just—"

"It's a historical place."

That explained a lot. The old clay-like houses, the ghost town, it wasn't a real town. A historical one.

"And the man who was killed tonight was the one taking care of this town and the farm," Zain added.

Hmm. If Kimberly came here because it was a historical place, it would make sense for her to meet the man in charge. Kimberly went to meet the old man, asking him for some information, probably after Fayazi referred him. Some bad guys knew about that meeting and they attacked the house, killed the man, and kidnapped Kimberly and now they wanted all the information Kimberly and Fayazi had. It fit. Still, there were holes in this scenario. Like why those people waited all this time to attack the man, and why they killed him and spared Kimberly. If they were after manuscripts, then it was the old man who should have them, not Kimberly. And why didn't Fayazi get those documents from the man by another means, rather than sending Kimberly?

Edward took a Tylenol from his shoulder bag.

"Wait, let me get you some water," Zain said. He brought a water bottle from the car trunk and handed it to Edward.

Edward swallowed the pill. "I don't understand how this can be a historical town and you don't have tourists coming here."

"It's complicated," Zain said. "Not many people know about this."

"Is there some landmark or point of interest? You know, some place in this town with significant historical importance."

If this town were a historical site, then there should be some points of interest that Kimberly might go to.

"Not really, no." Zain shook his head.

"What was his name, your employer."

"Abdul Zahra." Zain said, "He is... was... a great man. Everyone here loves him, as you can see."

"Did you witness the crime? Do you know how they killed him."

Something passed over Zain's face. "Why do you ask?"

Better go for the truth. "I have a friend who I believe came here earlier today."

"Here? In this town? Why?"

"We are sort of experts. We investigate historical documents, photographs and the like."

Zain nodded slowly then turned on the car radio, searched for channels, then turned it off. Edward felt suddenly sick, the white leather of the seats was so clean and polished. So he stepped out, Zain followed him. His lungs welcomed the fresh air.

"So do you think there are historical documents here?" Zain asked as they leaned against the car.

"Maybe, I don't know." Edward had no other option but to give some information, hoping this would encourage Zain to talk. "She called and told me that she came here to see someone."

"And you think this someone is … Mr. Abdul Zahra?"

"All the other houses are empty in this town."

Zain nodded. "Fadak, the name is Fadak."

"I thought it was Al-Hayett."

Zain smiled. "Al-Hayett is just the name they made up to cover the original name."

"They? Who are they?"

Zain shrugged. "The government, the Arabs, the rest of the Muslims... Everyone."

"Why did they want to cover the original name?"

"It's a doomed land," Zain said then shook his head, holding up his hand as if to try again. "Do you know when something is supposed to be all good and all blessed and it was handled in the wrong way. Not just a wrong way but the most diabolic and evil way, that it changed it something... I am not sure what is the right word."

The beam of light from the car headlights shone on the elongated palm trees rising high in the dark clear sky until they blurred out before the tips of the trees could be seen, making the trunks look like stalactites dangling from the sky.

Edward said, "Cursed..."

"It goes back to fourteen centuries ago, back to the days of the Prophet," Zain explained, leaning on the car, hugging himself with both hands as if feeling cold. "It used to be a big farm full of palms when it belonged to Fatima —"

"The prophet's daughter."

Zain's mouth became a perfect 'O,' his eyebrows half moons. "So you know what happened."

"Well, I just—"

"You are Christian, right?"

"I was raised Catholic."

Zain said, "If Jesus left a son, well forget about a son, if he left a piece of clothes or a cane, wouldn't you treat it with respect and keep it in the most secure museums?"

"Sure, I guess."

"And yet, you know what they have done." Zain separated his hands, gesturing to the trees or the farm. "No wonder those palm trees and town ended up like this."

"What have they done exactly?"

"Have you seen that movie when a man goes back in time and changes something small, something really negligible in history and when he travels back to the present he finds everything has changed? Have you seen this movie?"

Edward wanted to say that if it wasn't Tom Hanks then probably he wouldn't remember it. "I know the type."

"Right, and then the hero understood that the tiny change he made led to all those big changes after some hundreds of years."

"Uh-huh."

"So you asked me about what happened to this land. Well, imagine a big event, not a tiny change, but a big one happened fourteen centuries ago. Even if some details are vague and the truth was covered up, we know that the ramifications will be enormous today. What is the phrase people always use... yes... alter the history. That is what happened."

Edward wanted to tell Zain that he was babbling and nothing he said made any sense.

Zain's face lit up. "Hey, wait... it's better to show you." The young man rushed to one of the palm trees, then to another, searching the ground. Soon, he was back with something in his hand. "See this." He gave it to Edward.

It looked like a peach, except it was brown as if burned and was as hard as a stone.

"See it with the car light," Zain said, beckoning Edward to step in the lights.

Edward did. He could see it better. It looked more like a big date but was charcoaled as if someone had left it for hours in a griller, except that the hard surface was smooth and even shiny. He shook it, and felt something rattling inside as if the real fruit were underneath that hard shell.

"All the dates from this farm are like this. There aren't many either. You hardly find one unless you search hard."

Edward looked up at the dark sky, the silence, the still trees. "Spooky," he said, examining the fruit.

"Cursed," Zain corrected, then made a move of checking his watch. "I need to go, man, I have to go on an errand. If you want, I can drop you somewhere."

"I... don't know..." Edward scratched his head, looking at the road down where the blue Honda Accord disappeared. Small, yellow, dried shrubs were on both sides right under the tree trunks. He doubted that this path led to anywhere; the only reason Buzz-cut brought him here was to kill him. Which brought up an interesting question: what was Zain doing here? Did he follow him from the house? Why? And what sort of errand did a driver whose employer just died need to carry out in the middle of the night in such a town? Whatever it was, this guy might still be able to help him. It couldn't be just a coincidence that the keeper of the place was killed on the same night Kimberly was kidnapped.

A bright light came toward them. A car engine roared. They both turned at the sound. A black hummer H2 parked next to the Mercedes. Chrome wheels, chrome front bumper, and several other additions Edward couldn't identify. The vehicle looked more like an accessory shop than a car. The headlights beamed through the rising dust. Another too-surreal scene. Edward half expected two men to come out of the car with a black suitcase, no, a silver suitcase, and engage in a drug deal of some sort.

You can take the boy out of the TV, but you cannot take the TV out of the boy.

The driver's window rolled down. A bald elderly man with a friendly smile peered out. An old driver? If this was a mob drug deal, it was a limited-budget gang. Understandable, given the current economy.

"*Salam Alykum,*" the driver said.

Zain greeted him back.

"Do you know where I can find Abdul Zahra's house?"

They looked at each other. Zain's gaze fixed on the front bumper of the car. A small black sign with white letters read "V.I.P.".

For a moment no one said anything. The back window rolled down, and a jasmine smell filled the air. A lady in her late twenties with tanned skin and black hair that reminded Edward of poems about moons and seas and nights at sandy beaches looked at him.

Did gangs in Saudi need references for joining?

"We have been trying to find this house for the past half hour," the lady said in a British accent, her gaze fixed on Edward making him feel light headed. "Could you help us, please?" She didn't bat her eyelashes but she might as well have. The way she said please was enough to make a movie R-rated.

"Sure," Edward said when he finally found his voice.

Zain gave him a reproachful look, slightly shaking his head. He stepped back and waved apologetically. "Sorry, I need to go. See you *later*."

Okay, later.

"Take me with you," Edward said to Miss Gorgeous. "Um...I meant, I can show you the way."

Ever the gentleman.

"Sweet," she said, "hop in."

Seconds later Edward was in the back seat of the black hummer, sitting next to the first person his eyes were happy to look at since he landed.

"Drive ahead and take the first turn to the right," Edward told the driver.

"Thank you so much for your help," she said, looking at him with her wide... green eyes? Black hair, tanned skin, and green eyes and a face like Charlie's Angels, all three of them. Okay, maybe the Tylenol was taking effect.

"My name is Edward Fleming," he said, extending his hand. "I am a history detective."

Modesty.

Something crossed her face as if surprised by what he did. "Safiya." She then laughed and shook his hand as if it was some kind of a game. "Princess Safiya."

-13-

Edward glanced again at his beautiful companion. Her balanced and delicate features with the Arabian... um... flavor stirred up a warm feeling, something he couldn't place. She had an electrifying beauty with prominent and yet feminine features. Even her skin wasn't a Caucasian-white that was tanned, more of a natural color that long hours at the beach — or in tanning booths — had little to do with. Her white Egyptian-cotton shirt and dark blue jeans spoke of simplicity and good taste. Although sitting, she was petite and looked as though she spent regular time at the gym. Her face seemed familiar. Edward had seen it somewhere, he just couldn't place it.

Nothing new: He rarely met someone without having the unease of seeing him somewhere he couldn't remember. One of the blessings of his memory loss.

On the car radio, or probably the CD player, Michael Jackson was so happy being *"Bad."* Edward suddenly missed Sundra Rajan.

"So what brought a history detective to *this* forsaken town?" Safiya asked.

Edward shrugged. "An autograph. Where I come from we don't see many princesses."

She laughed, a charming laugh. Edward's laugh stopped midway. The pain in his lower back reminded him of the situation. "I am here to find a friend of mine. I think she was kidnapped."

Safiya stopped laughing and squinted at him as if he just told a joke without the punch line. When Edward said nothing, she gasped. "Oh my God. You are serious."

Edward nodded. He wasn't sure why, but sensed he could trust Safiya. Call him naïve, or weak against green eyes and blue-black hair, or simply a man who needed to speak what was on his mind to someone. He told her everything.

"And are you going to give them the documents they want?" she asked when he finished.

"Do I have another choice?"

Safiya looked down, then at her driver, then through the tinted-glass window. Her gaze didn't meet his. When it finally did, she bit her lips and nodded slowly.

They were back in front of the house. All the police cars were there as well. An ambulance was parked right next to the door.

"But I still don't get it," Safiya said. "What is this Musehaf of Fatima?"

"I'm not sure it's the document they wanted but—"

"It has to be." It was Abdullah, the driver. "It is the secret Quran of Shia. They claimed that it had more knowledge and teaching than this Quran." He sneered. Edward and Safiya looked at him. "What? you don't believe me? Check out the Internet or the email or the Facebook. You keep saying that Internet has everything one need, all the information in the world. Check it."

"Oh, come on, Uncle Abdullah." Safiya rolled her eyes.

Uncle? Edward arched an eyebrow. Safiya waved her hands dismissively. "If you know my uncle, you would know that this is not a compliment." She and Abdullah chuckled. "No, I am kidding. But Uncle Abdullah here is the closest person in the world to me."

Edward said after a minute, "You know what, it might not be a bad idea."

"I beg your pardon."

"Checking the Internet. Do you have an Internet connection here?"

Safiya handed him a red Sony laptop. He winced as he adjusted in his seat. Ouch. All his body ached. She smiled, tapping on his knee. "So are you going to show me some history-detective secrets?" Safiya shifted closer to him in order to see the screen. Her hair smelled like wildflowers after the rain. Her neck, smooth and tanned and too… fragile; it made the word swan-neck sound like an understatement.

"Have you heard about Fadak?" Edward asked her, remembering what Zain had told him about the land.

Safiya shook her head. "Never heard the name. You, Uncle?"

The old man looked back at them through the rear-view mirror. "What?" Abdullah said. "Because I heard about the Musehaf, means I am an i-pedia."

"It's Wikipedia, Uncle. I keep telling you that."

"Right, Wikipedia. So what was that thing you plug to you ears when your mood is cranky?"

"That's the i-pod." Safiya rolled her eyes, the way teens did when their parents were not hip enough to know those basic facts of life.

"See, I knew there was an i-something there," Abdullah said, satisfied. "So, what is this Fadak anyway? I hope it will not turn out to be another i-Fadak."

Edward smiled. "No, according to what I heard, it's the old name of this place."

"Fadak," Safiya said, as if trying the word. "Odd."

"That's why I need to see what I can find about it online." Edward typed the word Fadak in the Google search engine browser that was already opened.

"Wow, Googling for the word. That must have taken you, what? — ten years of experience as a history detective?"

"I never thought I would say this to a princess, but Your Highness is a royal pain in the neck."

Safiya laughed and socked him on the shoulder. Again the *deja vu*. He ignored it and focused on the search results. The first one was from Wikipedia, then another link from a website that promised references from all Muslim sects about Fadak. There were some videos as well, YouTube. Edward tried the Wikipedia link. The page came with an error. He tried refreshing the page. No use.

"Maybe it's the local proxy server," Safiya suggested. "Many sites are forbidden here."

Edward went back to the search page. At the bottom, a link offered Fadak's real boundaries. Edward clicked on that link. The page took some time to load. It came back with a story about one of the famous Muslim kings, Haroon Al-Rashid, offering one of the descendants of Fatima to return Fadak land to him as the heir of Fatima. The man, the story called him Emam, told the king he would only accept the land with its real boundaries. The king asked what those boundaries were. The Emam explained that it was from the Atlantic ocean to China, which covered all the Islamic empire at that time. End of story.

"What is that?" Safiya said, her black brows furrowed.

"Better to check Wikipedia," Edward said. "Do you have any proxy bypass software on your computer?"

A knocking on the glass window startled them. A police uniform yelled something in Arabic. Edward recognized the word *"Emshi,"*(move). Abdullah pointed for the policeman to check the VIP sign. The uniform held up both his hands in apology and retreated.

Abdullah looked in the mirror at Safiya, as if waiting for orders.

"Edward, the police might be able to help," Safiya said. "I can go with you, if you like."

"I would appreciate that."

Safiya said something in Arabic to Abdullah who opened his window and talked to the policeman.

From a bag in the back seat, Safiya pulled out a black piece of cloth. She put it on, then another black piece on her head and face. Within seconds the sexy lady with the jeans had transformed into a black ninja with only her eyes visible. She smiled at him, or at least it looked like that. Hard to tell from the eyes only. "What? Even a princess has to respect the rules."

They went out. Two policemen escorted them through the crowd and ushered them inside the small house. Edward pressed the buttons on his watch. Vane needed to hear this. Once Edward and Safiya were in, the policemen closed the door nervously, as if something might get inside.

A gasp. Edward knew he was entering a crime scene, ergo there would be a body. But Lord, what was this? In the center of the room, a man sat at a big chair behind a wooden desk smeared with blood. The victim leaned backward as if looking at the celling. His opened shirt revealed a naked chest. Dark-crimson blood covered the man's skinny abdomen, coloring the gray body hairs in that dark repulsive color. But that wasn't it. The old man's eyes were still open, his mouth frozen in mid-scream. His face was contorted in a horrible way leaving no doubt that the man's last moments on earth were agonizing.

They say the worst kind of fear is the one that you cannot rationalize. The one that you cannot escape by analyzing the matter. Edward examined the dead man's face. A cold shiver crept up his spine. His knees buckled. Kimberly's scream resonating in his ears. Had she faced the same destiny?

Edward risked another glance at the man's face.

Another chill.

A short man wearing a police uniform addressed him in a low voice. "Who are you?"

Stars crowded on the man's shoulders — more than the other uniforms in the room. He must be running the show here.

"My name is Edward Fleming." Better to skip the history-detective part.

The officer was about to fire another question but Safiya cut him off. "He is with me, officer."

A young policeman approached the officer, whispering in his ears.

"Really?" the officer said in Arabic, his mouth a perfect 'O', his gaze shifted to Safiya. "Your Highness, it's a pleasure to meet you." His tone conveyed anything but pleasure.

"Officer," Safiya said in a semi-commanding tone.

"Captain Adnan, head of Madeena police department, Your Highness."

On a nearby shelf, a blue ceramic artifact stood. Edward recognized the shape immediately. The same open palm tattooed on Buzz-cut's right arm.

"An American lady disappeared today," Safiya said in English, gesturing at Edward. "And this man is here because she called him from this town."

"An American." Adnan arched an eyebrow. "How interesting."

Edward didn't like the way he said it.

"Mr. Fleming," Adnan scrutinized him, as if sizing him up for a fight. "I need to ask you several questions, but before I do let me show you this."

Adnan pointed at the dead man behind him, beckoning for Edward to step forward. Edward tried to avoid the contorted face.

"Do you have any idea who this man is?"

"I heard people outside calling him Abdul Zahra."

Adnan nodded as if Edward gave the right answer. "He is a big-time contractor, very respected one. You see all the people outside, no? This is just the beginning. By morning we will see hundreds gathering here."

"They must love him," Edward said.

"*Love* him? Who are you? Cupid?" Adnan scowled. "Okay, they might, but that is beside the point. You see, all those people outside and many more were living on the charity funded by Abdul Zahra. Now he is dead, they will blame the government. If we don't find his killer before morning, well, we are in deep shit." He raised his eyebrows. "You get it?"

"Got it, deep shit," Edward said. But something felt amiss. "Why will they blame the government?"

Adnan sighed, shaking his head. He looked to his left where a man sat on a chair in the other corner of the room. He wore a Khaki uniform, different from the green one the other policemen wore, and sunglass. Sunglasses at midnight. Get real.

Sunglasses gave Adnan an it's-your-call shrug. Adnan turned back to Edward. "I am sorry, it's just that the name is so obvious that I forget you cannot understand it."

Edward was about to say which name then it hit him. Abdul meant 'the servant of' in Arabic. Al-Zahraa was, as he read today, another name for Fatima.

"The servant of Fatima," Edward said in a low voice.

Adnan stuck out his thick lips and gave him an impressed nod. "So you understand Arabic."

"A little, but I don't understand what this has to do with anything."

Adnan frowned like a teacher disappointed by his pupil. "The man is—" He looked over his shoulder to his staff. "What the hell we call them now?"

"Iranians? Sir."

"Infidels? Sir."

"No, you morons." Adnan waved in disgust. "Ah, yes, minority, fucking minority. This is what we have to call them now. Anyway, this man was a pain in the ass, for the last two decades with all that human-rights bullshit. We have enough trouble on our plate because of—" He waved it off.

Edward had a fair guess what the officer was about to say. The message on the Internet.

Through his peripheral vision, he saw Safiya's shoulders had slumped. Whatever confidence she had entered the room with was gone now. Matters of national security trumped a princess's influence.

Getting used to a dead body in the room, Edward stepped closer to the desk where the victim was. Something was strange regarding the wounds on his chest.

"What are these?" Edward asked.

"We are still *working* on it," Adnan snapped.

Edward stepped closer until Adnan shot him a glare that said "that's it."

"Jesus." Edward murmured. The cuts on Abdul Zahra's chest were in the form of some symbols. Four Arabic letters surrounded by a rectangular shape. Something uncomfortably familiar, as if from a dream he just recalled. He couldn't place where or when he had seen such symbols.

"What is the name of your friend, Mr. Fleming?" Adnan's voice brought him back to reality.

"Kimberly Green," Edward said after a beat.

"Description, please?"

"White, brown hair, five-seven, and one-twenty--"

"What? What is that?" Adnan scowled. "Speak English, will you, no mumble jumble."

Edward blinked. What did he say wrong?

"Captain," Safiya sighed, "this is the American system, they don't use metric." Then she smiled at Edward. "One-twenty, boy, I wish I could change my diet regime to whatever your friend was into."

"Change the regime!" Adnan's eyebrows shot up to his hair.

"Must be that American system, sir," a uniform whispered conspiratorially.

In the background, Edward imagined someone hailing "Long live the King."

"What is going on here?" Adnan demanded. "Your Highness, please, this American is crossing the line. We are not here to discuss politics, please, Your Highness."

It took Safiya two minutes to explain. Then another ten explaining to Adnan how to convert from feet to meters. The beauty of traveling. You get to meet people who never heard of yard or pound.

"It's okay now." Adnan nodded, gesturing for his uniforms who were whispering to each other. Edward kept hearing the words "Regime" and "Change" and "American" in a too-conspiratorial way. They all calmed down. The Papal approval for the feet and pounds was issued.

"So tell me, Mr. Fleming," Adnan said, "why your friend was here?"

"She called me and said she was in Saudi Arabia in a town called Al-Hayett, and she was about to meet someone here." Edward had thought about this question and decided that too much information would sidetrack things. Better keep it simple, a missing person.

"But you don't know for sure she was in this house?"

"No, not really."

"I see." Adnan exhaled, his heavy gaze never left Edward. "So tell me, Mr. Fleming, what is exactly your relationship with your friend."

"She is a colleague... at work... we work together."

"And what is your work exactly?"

Patience, he told himself. "We work as freelance researchers." Awkward, but it would spare the confusion of saying history detectives.

Still, Adnan made a face. "Researching what?"

Edward shrugged. "Subjects of academic nature."

Mr. Elusive had arrived in Saudi.

"Like?" Adnan asked.

Mr. Elusive met Mr. Stubborn.

"History, social studies, that kind of stuff."

Adnan nodded, looking back at Sunglasses on the chair. "I am sorry, Mr. Fleming, but help me understand this." Adnan rubbed his shaved beard hard, as if desperately willing the hair to grow. "Your colleague, who is a researcher working on subjects of *academic* nature," he made quotation marks with his fingers, "had just decided to travel thousands of miles to a small town in Saudi Arabia to meet someone, then she disappeared, is that what are trying to tell me?"

Mr. Stubborn kicks Mr. Elusive's behind.

"Pretty much, yes."

"Did I miss anything?" Adnan's tone got lower, calmer, yet Edward felt the words crawl up the back of his neck. He shook his head. Adnan's gaze was more intense now. "Had your office done any work with Abdul Zahra directly or indirectly?"

"Not that I am aware of." Not that I am aware of. Too much *Boston Legal*. "We normally work for the American government."

Something crossed Adnan's face but he didn't speak a word.

Edward knew he'd better stop talking and yet he added, "Sometimes we contact universities in different parts of the world. But we've never had the chance to work with anyone in Saudi Arabia."

"Mr. Fleming, may I ask you one question?" Adnan said, as if catching up with him about old times. "How did you and your friend come to Saudi Arabia?"

"By plane."

Mr. Elusive never gave up.

"How did you get the visa?" Adnan's eyes narrowed, his voice was more of a grunt.

"We received them by email." Edward put on his best sweet-boy smile. If Adnan was a little older and a female, he wouldn't be able to resist pinching Edward's cheeks.

Adnan gave him a cut-the-crap look.

So much for the sweet-boy smile.

The problem was, once he mentioned Fayazi, his research and Fatima, things would go in a different direction.

"Captain Adnan," Safiya said, "can we skip this part and focus on finding the missing lady?"

"Your Highness." Sunglasses stood up and strolled to Safiya. "We need to have a little chat, if that is okay with you."

Edward felt each word slithering on the floor toward him and Safiya. Safiya nodded silently then turned to Edward. Her big green eyes looked directly into his. This time it didn't remind him of shimmering stars on water, but rather, the eyes of someone who was or would be in trouble.

"Mr. Fleming," Adnan opened the house door, "would you please wait outside."

"Sure."

Edward stepped outside. The uniforms in the room waved at him with mocking smiles. He didn't wave back; that would show them.

Once the door closed behind him, whether because of the loud way it slammed, or the lack of confidence in Safiya's tone, or Adnan's suspicious look, that feeling was there.

They were in trouble.

-14-

Abdullah, the driver, chatted outside Abdul Zahra's house with two uniforms. Policemen secured the outside perimeter, forming half a circle in front of the ancient house, occasionally waving with their sticks at the gathering crowd and pushing them back.

Far from city lights, this sky was the clearest and probably the most amazing he had ever seen. Hundreds of stars —real ones not choppers or satellites— shimmered in the black sky. As if he could see deeper into space, his mind traveled through the light years, the stars getting closer and closer. With such majesty, he felt as if someone were watching him. That he was part of something far bigger than anything he knew.

Corny, yes, but after what he'd been through, cut him some slack.

When he was seven years old, young Edward asked his father why he had that mysterious sensation, the awe whenever he looked up at the sky. His father smiled and explained that the physical act of tilting the head up caused less blood to go to the brain, and hence the dizziness that some people might associate with spirituality.

While growing up, Edward heard, learned, and eventually came up with hundreds of similar explanations for different spiritual experiences. Everything could be traced back to physics and a simple scientific explanation. And no, he wouldn't blame his parents for his materialistic beliefs. As a matter of fact, his mom and dad had raised him the best they could; most parents did, or tried to. They constantly took him and his brothers to church on Sundays. In the old days, his father used to say a prayer before they ate. But those memories where in black and white, faint and muted, and no matter how hard he tried to hold onto them, they were slipping away, fading, like the more recent memories did after the accident, leaving him in total darkness.

Edward took a deep breath. Those were not helpful thoughts, but he understood why his mind wanted to go there. Replaying Kimberly's scream over and over was hard enough before things started to get complicated. Now, he was not even sure he could do anything for her, or even for himself for that matter.

His phone vibrated. He picked it up.

"It's me, Dr. Fayazi." The voice was much clearer than the previous time.

"Oh, hello, Doctor, I didn't recognize the number."

"Edward, where are you?"

"Saudi Arabia."

Silence. Fayazi then said with a deep exhale, "You shouldn't have gone there."

"And you shouldn't have allowed Kimberly to come here."

"Edward, *please*." Fayazi's voice was weary and tired. "It's not the time for this. You have no idea what you are getting involved in."

"I know it's about Fatima and her book."

"You know nothing, you are just risking your own life for nothing."

"I know about Fadak." Fayazi's silence confirmed his suspicions. Everything was connected, somehow. "I know that Kimberly came to Fadak to meet Abdul Zahra."

"They killed him, Edward, and they will do the same to everyone who steps in their way."

"Who are *they*, Doctor?" And how did he know about the murder?

"Please go home, son."

Son?

"I won't leave this town until I find her, I just can't."

"Okay, okay." Fayazi sighed. "Let's meet. I am in Saudi as well. I can help, but we cannot do this on the phone."

In the background, people started shouting, demanding to get inside the house and see Abdul Zahra.

"I still need about an hour. The police want to talk to me and I think they know something."

"Don't trust them, Edward."

"It's not like I have a choice here. This is my only lead to where Kim is."

"Wrong." Fayazi's voice became calm.

"What do you mean?"

"I know one man in Saudi who will know about anyone who is involved in this matter. You can still make it within one hour to his house if you hit the road now."

Another police car pulled up. Four green uniforms stepped out, yelling at the gathered crowd, then with the help of other uniforms started beating those who were close. People ran away.

Two women got caught in the middle. Policemen circled them. Wooden sticks rose up and down; women cried for help. Edward instinctively walked toward them. A uniform pushed him. The cell phone dropped, his sour body protested.

"Edward, you there?"

"Yes," Edward said, walking away from the commotion.

"They don't trust you or your friend," Fayazi said.

"Right."

"They will arrest you, I am sure of that. And when they do, that will be it, you can no longer help anyone."

Something in the old doctor's tone made him pause. He looked back at the house surrounded by policemen, and remembered the way everyone glared at him when he arrived.

"*Edward*," Fayazi pleaded, "if you insist on staying here and searching for your friend, then you have to listen very carefully to what I say."

Edward remained silent.

"Go to Nakheela, it's a small town within an hour's drive. Ask for Sheikh Essa and tell him that you are a friend of mine. He will help you. I am sorry but this the only thing I can help you with now. You have to trust me on this."

He hung up.

Fayazi asked for trust. Just as he probably asked Kimberly to trust him when he sent her to Saudi. But what was his other option? The police who were stuck with the high-profile murder case? Or Princess Safiya? As much as he felt comfortable with her, she was a stranger. A stranger looking for Abdul Zahra's house at midnight.

Zain's Mercedes was back, parked next to the black Hummer of Princess Safiya. Zain and two other elderly men wearing Arabic dishdash were talking with an officer. Talking might not be the word, given their body language. A heated discussion, if not more.

Edward stepped toward Zain and his companions. One of the elderly men with Zain, who had a thick white beard and held a cane, was telling the officer something about a decent burial. He hit the ground with his cane for emphasize. The officer mentioned something about an ongoing investigation. White-beard pointed the cane at the officer's face, repeating the same words about burial.

Was this the errand Zain had to do? To bring some elderly people to talk to the police about taking the body? Edward remembered what Adnan said about how people loved Abdul Zahra. Maybe Zain realized that if he demanded the body no one would listen to him, so he summoned some people with influence to help. The question was, why would Zain or his friends be so eager to bury the body now? Was it some religious thing not to autopsy? Or was there something more to it?

Zain spotted him and waved. Edward waved back. The young man left the two men talking with the officer and walked to Edward. "Does your friend have brown ponytail hair?" Zain asked.

"Yes." Edward's heart skipped a beat. He wanted to add, "Have you found her?" but he let it hang in the air.

Zain bit on his lower lip then said in something close to a whisper, "Someone saw her today morning, forced into a black GMC outside of Abdul Zahra's house."

"Where did they take her? Did anyone manage to get a plate number or anything?"

Zain shoved his index finger to his lips. "Not now." He pointed with his chin to the policemen.

People gathered again, this time keeping more distance from the uniforms. The house door opened. Safiya emerged. A humming noise came from the gathered crowd. A man shouted, demanding something. A policeman shouted back. Another struck a blow with his stick, hitting a nearby Pakistani.

Safiya looked left and right. She saw Edward and walked toward him, shoulders slumped. Even through the face cover, he could tell that she was frowning. Covered in black clothes with only her eyes visible, the way she walked, she could be more miserable but he couldn't imagine how.

"They want to talk to you," she said, her gaze fixed at the crowd.

"Okay."

"You don't understand," Safiya said. Then she stepped aside, giving her shoulder to Zain and facing Edward. "They have witnesses that your friend was at the old man's house."

So Kimberly went to meet Abdul Zahra. Safiya looked at him for a brief second then broke contact as a policeman knocked down a young man in the crowd. People ran away again.

"There is more," Safiya said. "They have evidence that Kimberly was in the house when Abdul Zahra was alive. She is their primary suspect."

"*What?*" His voice was harsher than he intended. Fayazi's words echoed in his head. The old man knew somehow. "I am sorry but that's... that's beyond ridiculous."

Safiya nodded, staring at the ground.

"Why would Kim want to kill him? And look at the way the poor man was killed, I mean... Jesus, no way in hell would she do that."

"Their theory is," Safiya held up her soft and delicate hand, "Abdul Zahra attacked her. It was in self-defense and she fought back with the knife."

Zain grumbled something.

"Right." Edward sneered. "What self-defense leaves cuts like Arabic letters on the chest of the offender?"

Safiya still avoided looking at him. "Listen, Edward, I don't know Kimberly, but what I know for sure is that this case, the entire situation today, is bigger than you and maybe even me. And those guys inside will be more than happy to nail an American ass to get the heat off them."

Did she just say an American ass? So much for the Royal prestige.

"I want to help you, honestly, I just don't know how," she added.

Edward took a long breath. He saw her point. A lot of people were offering to help him, and all of them were telling him that whatever was going on here was big. His body still ached from the beating. The murder of the old man, the police, that strange virus, and Kimberly's kidnapping, it all pointed to the same fact: these people were serious. The problem was, he couldn't just quit. So what should he do? Going back to the police didn't seem very attractive. They would arrest him, or at least deport him back to the United States. Contacting the embassy was risky given Agent Summers' involvement with his past in covert missions and his insinuation about Edward's engagement with armed groups in the Middle East. And how exactly did Summers and the CIA fit into what was going on? Strange enough, everything Agent Summers inquired about was happening.

A coincidence? Right.

What about Zain and what he just told him about seeing Kimberly? That should be his priority. And the Wizard of Oz Fayazi told him about, Sheikh Essa? Fayazi was holding back something, no question about it. How to make him talk?

He excused himself from Safiya and Zain and walked a few steps, just enough to get out of hearing distance. Edward dialed the first name on his favorite list, shame that the iPhone didn't have speed dial.

One more thing to complain to Apple about.

Vane picked up on the first ring. As usual he said nothing. Annoying and creepy.

"It's me, Edward."

"Yes, I can see the caller ID."

Vane, always with the pleasantries.

"Can you see my location?"

" *Oui.*"

"Vane, I need you."

"Nine hours," Vane said.

"Nine hours to be here?"

"No, nine hours to Rama, it's a nice movie. Or perhaps, nine hours for the light to travel from Orion constellation to earth or—"

"Okay, okay, I got it." Why did everyone enjoy being a wiseass? "Sheesh, you could've just said, yes. But why nine."

"I am working on a lead."

"A lead?" This fast?

Vane sighed. "A Saudi ex-arms dealer named Saud. The man was kidnapped by Al-Qaeda in Baghdad three years ago with his brother. Since then he has become a nut job."

"An arms-dealer and a nut-job." Edward chuckled. "God, I feel comfortable."

"He won't lie to me. Is there anything else I can do for you, O'great one."

"As a matter of fact, yes." Edward told Vane about his plan.

Vane listened until he finished, then finally said, "Very risky,"

"So?"

"*J'aime ça.*"

"I knew you would. See you in nine hours."

"Nine hours it is, Kimosaby."

They hung up.

"Princess Safiya," Edward said, headed back to where she was with Zain. "Can I ask you a favor?"

-15-

Adnan watched the civil-defense personnel put Abdul Zahra's body in the gurney to send him to the station. The process took less than ten minutes. During which he couldn't stop looking at the victim's face.

Adnan had seen, during his thirty years of service, a lot of dead bodies. But there was something in the man's face that made his policeman's antennas vibrate. Something beyond that agony and pain Abdul Zahra had clearly gone through.

"I need the American locked up and secure now," Fahad said, just finishing a phone call. "By all means, no loose ends."

Adnan did not comment. Fahad had told him that he was on a covert mission he could not disclose to the local police. Not uncommon. But there was no way for Adnan to make sure that Fahad's actions would not backfire on him. He had seen it before. Now, under the pressure, approvals would be granted generously. But once the dust settled, only the local police had to deal with the aftermath. If the long-term political agenda required a scapegoat, none other than the local police would take the heat.

But not him. Adnan wouldn't have survived so long in such a critical position if he didn't know how to protect himself. And man, he was good at it. He might not have made it to the top of his career, but it wasn't his fault that only people with the proper connections made it there.

The two civil-defense men carried the gurney heading for the door. Three policemen surrounded them to make sure no one interfered. Before the first uniform reached the door, it swung open. A policeman rushed in. He was the one assigned to get Edward. "Sir," the man said out of breath, "the American escaped."

"What!" both he and Fahad shouted in unison. "How did that happen."

"He was talking to her Highness so I waited till they finished... I was only a few steps away... giving them some space... respecting her privacy and all..."

"Where did he go?" Adnan asked calmly, no point in scaring him.

"He took the Mercedes car that was parked in front of the house, you know, the one that belongs to the victim. The American snatched the keys from the driver and sprinted to the car. No one could stop him... it all happened too fast."

Americans... they watched too many action movies. Adnan smiled. "Have you alerted other units?"

"Yes, Sir." The policeman looked more relaxed now, seeing Adnan smiling. "Two cars went after him, and the two control points outside the farm were alerted too. We know where he was heading and we will close in on him."

Adnan nodded. Nowhere to run. All the town's entrance and exit points were guarded by police. Standard procedure when civil unrest was expected. Police forces were already on alert for the last three days because of some strange threat on the Internet. Now with a murder of a high-profile human-rights activist, the tension couldn't be worse. Before he came here,

Adnan made sure that a force of twelve patrol cars were distributed around the city in addition to the town police.

Catching this idiot could not be easier.

"What about her Highness?" Adnan asked.

Fahad examined one of the books on the shelf, his fingers flipped the pages too fast, his gaze on the empty space beyond the book.

"She is safe," the policeman replied. "She called for her driver to pick her up and I think I heard her saying she is going to leave this town."

Better. Although Agent Fahad had pointed out to her, in the most polite way possible, that any interference was not welcomed, Adnan would feel much more comfortable without a Royal Family member protecting a suspect.

Adnan turned back to a large man. "Lieutenant Sami."

"Sir."

"I want you on this chase."

"Yes, Sir."

The Lieutenant took his radio and turned the channel selector knob a few times until he was on the right one. "All road patrol, all road patrol, this is Lieutenant Sami from the Madeena police department."

Sami then gave the description of the white Mercedes the American ran in. Adnan listened to the radio feed. Several patrols were in the chase now. Fahad looked at Sami's radio like someone waiting for important stock-market information from his broker.

His legs ached from standing. Adnan was no longer at the age that allowed for long hours on his feet anymore. Long gone were the days where he stood guard for an important post, as in his early assignments on the force. He refrained from dwelling on the philosophical irony of what life gives and takes; important things demanded his attention now. Things such as the fact that the only chair in the room was occupied by the friendly Agent Fahad. Adnan yelled at a policeman, ordering him to bring a chair to the house.

The officer sprinted out.

The radio in Sami's hand crackled to life once more. Everyone in the room leaned toward the small black thing.

"We surrounded the car, Sir. Over."

Then another voice. "The driver stopped with no resistance, car engine is still running. Over."

"Arrest him. Over," Sami said.

"Proceeding to the car, Sir. Over."

After a minute that lasted forever, the radio crackled. "We have him, Sir. Over."

"Great, bring him in," Sami said.

"Sir, one issue. Suspect does not match description."

Sami looked at Adnan, both confused

"What do you mean? Over."

The house door opened. The young policeman brought a folding chair, opened it, and put it next to Adnan.

The radio crackled. "Sir, the description we got for the suspect is: an American, tall and fit, brown curly hair, in his thirties. But this man is a local. Fifties or sixties. And definitely not fit. Over."

Adnan fell to the chair.

"He said his name is Abdullah, and he works for the Princess. Over."

-16-

<Saudi Arabia>
<Time left until Zero hour is 20hrs:45min>
<Number of infected websites: 171,100>

Edward looked through the tinted side windows of the black Hummer. The few lights from the town's gate had disappeared in the darkness. They were safe now.

"Do you call this *fun*?" Safiya grimaced. She sat next to him on the back seat. "We hardly broke any rules."

"Next time I'll make sure we exchange some fire," Edward said.

Safiya's pink cellphone rang. She snapped it open. "Uncle Abdullah." Her hands clutched into fists. Safiya listened for a while then she let go a long exhale. "I knew you could manage it." Then she said to Edward and Zain, who was behind the wheel. "He is fine. They let him go. Not that they could hurt him anyway."

"What did he tell them?"

"As we agreed, that you saw his car parked on the road and you took the car from him while he was, you know... taking a leak."

As if on cue, the pain in his kidney erupted. He too, needed to discharge and was sure that he would be pissing blood today. So far they hadn't passed anything even remotely resembling a public toilet. And... Well, Edward didn't really cherish the idea of using the Arabian desert. So he would wait till they got to Essa's place. The important thing was they were all safe, at least for now. His plan was simple. They faked the act of him snapping the keys and running away in Zain's Mercedes. Then Edward drove the car to the first turn where they agreed that Abdullah would be waiting with the Hummer. They switched cars and Abdullah drove fast in the Mercedes while Edward got back in the Hummer to pick up Zain and the princess. The only thing he didn't like was endangering an innocent man like Abdullah. But Safiya had assured him that they couldn't touch someone who worked for a princess.

"You sure you know the way to that town, Zain?" Edward asked.

"Right to Sheikh Essa's house."

"Lucky us," Edward said, trying to hide his concern. He was lucky today. Too lucky, as a matter of fact. First to meet Abdul Zahra's driver, a man who not only knew Abdul Zahra very well but also the roads to every small town in this desert. Second, and maybe most importantly, Safiya. Having a princess with you is like having a free get-out-of-prison card. It was all too convenient. He might accept getting lucky to find Zain, but the friendly way the young man acted and offered to help him although he knew nothing about him was... well, suspicious at least.

Edward wasn't paranoid. Not in normal circumstances. Even if he ignored Zain's too friendly behavior, and accepted that it was merely good luck. Fine. But what about Safiya? Could he really believe that he was so lucky that he met her by coincidence on a farm in the middle of the desert, and she decided to help him in his quest? If he were that lucky, he would have won the lottery a long time ago.

No. There was something going on here. One of his companions, if not both of them, was not telling him everything. The question was how to get to the truth without losing them. So far, both of them, especially Safiya, were of great help.

He had to be subtle and delicate.

"So." Safiya slammed his knee. The move was gentle and too casual as if they had known each other for a long time. "Is this your first time to Saudi?"

For the second time, Edward wasn't sure why he opted for the truth. "I am not sure."

"That's funny." She laughed, it wasn't the musical laugh he heard the first time he saw her. Nervous and maybe forced. "How come you are not sure."

"I had an accident in September 2001." Edward fought to make his voice neutral and low. "I went into a coma for four years and when I woke up... I..."

"Oh, my God."

"It wasn't as bad as it might sound." He tried to smile. "It's just the last year or so before the accident that I have no account for." No need to mention the slipping away of older memories.

She murmured, almost to herself, "2000 to 2001."

"At first, it was maddening. I found that I quit my job with the FBI and started working as a document analyst. Something I have little experience with. Then, there was that part of understanding Arabic and other stuff I couldn't place."

"Must be terrible." Safiya's gaze stayed fixed on the window. It was pitch black outside, but she kept staring.

"I've gotten used to most of it now." He shrugged. "Seeing people you think you know from somewhere. Fragments of memories. Flash of images. Sometimes I am not even sure what I see is myself—" He paused. Why did he want to tell her? What if she thought he was crazy?

"Have you tried hypnosis?" Her tone was of sympathy. As warm as the look in her ardent eyes.

He shook his head. "Doctors said I am blocking. That... you know... something bad had—"

The car veered right. She leaned against him. An electric shock went through him as his arm touched hers. She shifted back, her hand tucking wisps of the blue-dark hair behind her ear.

Zain apologized. They both told him that it was okay. Safiya took out her cell and fiddled with it as if checking her messages. Maybe she was. Edward made a move of checking his watch: 3:00 AM. He pressed on the two buttons in the watch as Vane had showed him, then from the miniature menu he chose the location map. The red dot, presumably Vane's location, was in the eastern part of Saudi. Edward was in the west.

"So Safiya," Edward said, breaking the uncomfortable silence. "Do you live in a palace, I mean like ..um... a princess."

She smiled, revealing a set of pearly-white teeth. "Sort of." She tapped on her red lips. "It's a big, very big villa with a big garden, gardens actually. So you might call it a palace as well."

"Is it nearby?"

"In Ryadh."

Edward had no idea how far Ryadh was, knowing only it was the capitol.

"So do you come here often, to this town?"

She arched an eyebrow, opened her mouth, closed it, then said in a measured voice, "You want to know why I came here, right?" No smile now.

Edward shrugged. "I was just wondering—"

"Fine."

Subtlety wasn't his forte.

"I was just looking for an adventure, something to break the boring routine." He remind silent. Better to leave her to fill in the silence. "I know how that might sound. The spoiled, reckless girl who had everything but she want to break the rules just to fill her empty life. But the truth is different. Yes, I am a member of one of the wealthiest royal families in the world. Yes, I have many things, I can buy anything. But, and I know how this will sound, I don't have the most important thing everyone else has. And there is no point talking about it because everyone is judgmental when comes to the rich."

"That being…"

"Forget about it." She waved her hand in dismissal. "You won't understand anyway."

"Who's being judgmental here?" Edward gave her his charming smile. When it came to women, Edward had a Jedi-like charm. He didn't use it on Safiya though, instead he wowed her with an eyebrow wiggle.

Safiya frowned. "Just forget about it, okay."

"Okay." He shrugged. Maybe he should've used the charm. "But if it will help you, I know a rich-people support group."

Safiya squinted.

Edward went on, "You know, you go there and sit with other wealthy people who need condolence for their inability to spend all their money."

"Very funny." Safiya stuck out her tongue. "I know how to spend all my money. The perfect way."

"By using it in the fireplace?"

She shook her head. "Nah, that won't work, it's too hot here."

"Good point, so what? You threw it from a plane?"

Safiya rubbed her chin. "Hmm, I will consider that, but no, it's simpler."

She smiled, she had a beautiful smile, attractive and daring and the kind that seduces a man to jump off a cliff.

"One word," she said playfully, "racing cars."

Edward frowned. "Racing cars?"

"Yep."

"Those were two words."

She poked him in the shoulder. "Don't be a smart-ass with me."

Now that she was relaxed, Edward decided to hit again. "When we first met, back at the farm, you were looking for Abdul Zahra's house."

Safiya nodded. "I will tell you later," she said in a low voice, pointing with her chin to their silent driver.

Fair enough. She didn't have a reason to trust Zain.

The young man looked at him in the rear-view mirror as if he heard his thoughts. "I know you are wondering why am I helping you," Zain said, glancing at the dark road ahead and then at them. "Mr. Abdul Zahra was like a father to me. Someone had killed him and I need to know who."

Edward didn't know what to say.

Zain kept talking anyway. "The police theory is rubbish. Not only Abdul Zahra won't attack her but also what you said about the symbols on his chest. Not to mention that he was sitting on the chair behind his office. If he was attacking her, he wouldn't be sitting."

Valid point. "So whom do you think killed him?"

"The same people who kidnapped your friend and put her in the car."

"About that," Edward said. "When I asked you about the car, you couldn't talk because we were near the police."

Zain nodded. He slowed, turning right to take an exit off the highway onto a narrow road. The only lights those of their headlamps. Small bushes covered both sides of the road.

"It was a black GMC," Zain said, looking into the rear mirror.

Edward said, "Yes, you said that before—" but Zain was looking at Safiya.

"That doesn't mean anything," Safiya said. This was the first time she talked to Zain.

"Am I missing something here?" Edward said.

Zain nodded to Safiya.

The Saudi princess finally said, "Black GMC is commonly used by the religion police." She sighed then immediately followed up, "But that doesn't means it's exclusive or anything.

Many other people drive this car. It's a nice car and—" She probably realized how defensive she sounded.

Edward had an idea about the notorious Saudi religious police. One of his friends once told him how they used to raid restaurants searching for liquor, checking if couples were married or having an affair. Basically, their job was to make sure everyone followed the Sharia rules, which was equivalent to… well… marshal law. No drinking of alcohol even in your house, no woman could go out without the full ninja-dress. No walking or working or even sleeping during prayer times, among other things, which you wouldn't know were forbidden until you got a lash by the religious police with their long sticks and then someone might explain what you had done wrong.

Safiya raised her chin high and added, "However, given the circumstances today, I wouldn't be surprised if I saw the religious police get involved."

Edward had enough of cryptic talking for one night. But he didn't want to interrupt Zain.

"What else?" he asked the young driver.

"Nothing much. They were at least three men. It was early at morning, around 6."

The exact time she called him and he heard that scream. So she was taken right after that.

"Who saw this? I need to speak with them."

"Why?" Zain snapped. "I told you everything they told me."

"Maybe they missed something; little details can sometimes make a lot of difference."

The car hit a bump. Edward jumped, his ribs and shoulder ached. Man, he needed some rest.

"I am not sure they will talk to you," Zain said. "They are just simple villagers, no one want to get into trouble."

Edward wanted to protest but saved it for later. They were driving to another city, following another lead. Zain remained silent, gaze fixed on the road. The young driver had narrow shoulders and was probably five-six. In the rear-view mirror, Edward saw the young Saudi's furrowed brow, his expression set on gloomy. Their eyes met for a brief moment. Zain reminded him of Vane. The two men had the same wall around them, the fence with barbed wires and a do-not-cross sign. A sea of emotions hid behind that fence. Emotions so complicated they made having that wall look like a good idea.

Priorities. He need to focus on finding Kim. And so far, he'd gotten only more riddles.

"Do you know what that symbol means?" Edward asked, making a stop sign with his palm.

"The *Hamsa*," Zain said. "Not really sure about its meaning."

"Hamsa is five in Arabic, right?" Edward asked.

"Yes," Safiya said. "I have seen this symbol before, but with an eye in the palm, the evil eye." She tapped on her ruby-red lips then said, "There was a story but I forgot the details."

"Edward." Zain adjusted the rear-view mirror to look at him. "Why you are really here?".

Edward frowned. "I told you why."

"You want to find your friend, I know. But is there any other reason?"

Zain stared at him. Safiya did likewise.

Edward could guess what Zain referred to. "What other reason?"

Zain shrugged. "I don't know, maybe you are here to finish what she came to do here. And before you ask, no, I don't know what she came to do here, I never met her, as I told you. But you see, there has to be something that brought her to this particular place."

Edward closed his eyes. When he spoke his voice was calmer than he expected. "You know what, Zain, all that you said makes perfect sense except that I don't know what she was doing here."

Zain nodded, focusing back at the road.

Safiya turned to Edward and whispered, "There is something going on you need to know."

PART TWO

To ensure segregation between men and women, all stores and restaurants in Saudi have two doors. The main one, big and shiny, and a smaller, service-entrance type. It goes without saying which one is the women's door.

"So what is it you want to tell me, Princess?" Edward asked. Princess Safiya gnawed at her lower lip, her eyes narrowed, looking at Zain.

Zain half smiled —half being very optimistic percentage here. The corner of his mouth quivered up as if it took a lot of effort to pull it off. "I don't mean to be rude, your Highness, but I live here so I doubt whatever you will say is new information."

"*Anta Ala Hak,*" (you are right,) Safiya said. She shifted in her seat to face Edward, her right leg under her left, pulling her knee closer to her chest. Edward tried to do the same but ended up strangled by his seat belt.

"It all started a week ago," Safiya said with enthusiasm. "It wasn't so big as to be noticed the first three days but on its fourth day, people started noticing it to the point of public concern."

"You are talking about that...um... thing on the Internet, right?"

She nodded and turned on her laptop. "You have no idea how embarrassing this message is. Not only because of what it says, but the fact that it exists flags a serious threat to the *national security*." Safiya made quote marks with her fingers.

"The best local experts were hired, other measurements were taken but it kept getting worse. More websites are infected now. You see, it started with only Islamic websites, you know, there are a lot of those hosted locally in the Kingdom. But now this message and that bloody counter is almost everywhere."

"I don't get it," Edward said, "what's the big deal about it? It's just a virus, right? Why do you make it sound like—"

"National security?" Zain sneered.

She typed something while speaking. "Here in the Kingdom, Internet access is strictly controlled. Authorities keep detailed records of who, when, and what."

Safiya turned the screen in Edward's direction. The black screen showed the same message he saw on the plane:

0 Days, 20 Hours, 20 minutes for Zero hour.

"Yeah, I have seen it," Edward said. "So, the authorities believe that it's a local job because it started with local sites?"

Something flickered in her eyes. Admiration?

He should've warned her that his deduction skills were seductive.

"Exactly, otherwise they wouldn't think that someone was able to penetrate the security system."

Zain sneered. "Freedom of speech, Saudi style."

"There are rules and *regulations*," Safiya snapped. "People have to respect those, otherwise—" She shook her head and murmured something that sounded like a curse. "I am sorry. I didn't mean to sound like I am defending this policy. God knows I don't like it a bit."

Zain whistled. His dark eyebrows rose.

"Anyhow, back to our subject," Safiya said, forcing the smile back. "I got this software that can show you how many sites are affected by this virus."

Safiya clicked on one of the icons and another window popped up. It said:

Number Of Web Sites Infected : 205,701 sites.

Underneath the message was an option of more details. Safiya clicked it. After one minute the screen came back with a long list of websites.

Safiya pointed at the screen and said, "Only yesterday the number was forty thousand."

"Those are *all* infected sites?" Edward asked.

"Yes."

"Impossible," Edward said. "It says even the *Washington Post* website is hacked. No way in hell a local hacker in Saudi can do that."

Safiya opened her web browser and wrote the URL of the newspaper. The website loaded with the familiar *Washington Post* website, no sign of the message or the countdown.

"I don't understand," Safiya said. "I checked it for other websites and this program was accurate."

Zain said, "Make sure you have entered the entire web address. Some newspapers have different versions, local, international. What does the program list says?"

Both Edward and Safiya's jaws dropped.

"What?" the young man said. "Not that I work as a driver means I don't know how use the Internet."

Edward scanned the list reported by the program. The entry said http://Washingtonpost.com/local.html. He typed the new web address and pressed the enter key. The page loaded again. When it came back, it was almost the same page, except one thing. On the top of the screen, where the web ads were normally displayed, a black rectangular box showed the message and the countdown.

"Holy cow!" Edward said. "How did they get here?"

"Not only that," Safiya raised her finger, pointing at the laptop, "see this."

She ran the software again. The window came up with this message:

Number Of Websites Infected : 206,580 sites.

"Jesus," Edward exclaimed, trying to do the math. Eight hundred and seventy-nine sites were infected within... how long? Three minutes?"

"Click on the details." Safiya gave an I-told-you-so smile.

He did. The same report came back. Edward scrolled down to the last, there were now two entries for the *Washington Post*. The local one they saw before and another one, showing the international version of the newspaper.

"Try it," Safiya said.

Edward did, but he already knew the result. The message and the counter were there on the right column of the page.

Edward rubbed his face. "I don't understand... they were what? Monitoring our browsing and when we went there they hacked this website?"

Zain laughed. "Spooky.. imagine that, viruses with artificial intelligence. Soon they will decided that human race should be terminated."

"It's not funny, Zain," Edward said. "Whoever did this might possess the means to carry out their threat. There is a good chance that this group is after hurting people... who knows, maybe some computer-generated terrorists' attacks."

"Or maybe they want to use human as batteries." Zain laughed teasingly.

"Not funny." It was Safiya this time.

Safiya said she was after an adventure, but what did this have to do with this town and the virus? Could it be that Abdul Zahra was responsible for this? Edward didn't recall a computer in the house. That didn't mean anything; the man was rich and maybe hired someone to do it.

Edward remembered something. "Zain, do you know what Musehaf Fatima is?" Zain had told him about this land story, Fadak. Maybe the young man could relate another story about Musehaf, some local heritage of some kind.

"There are some theories about it," Zain said. "But why you don't ask the expert?" He gestured at a house in front of them in a theatrical way.

They were in another town. This one with normal houses. Small and old but not ancient like those in Fadak.

"We reached to Sheikh Essa's house," Zain announced.

-18-

The three of them stood in front of the old house of Sheikh Essa. Edward, so occupied with the discussion, hadn't paid attention to the other houses in the neighborhood. They all looked as old as this one. "Old" was a very polite word to describe the state of decay. It wasn't the peeling paint or the fungus-like spots on the walls or the rusted doors or the crooked windows or the missing bricks in the fence. The roof had caved in as if the main pillar had fallen, leaving the house in a post-Godzilla-attack status. The street —muddy, unpaved, uneven—

was silent but given the fact that it was almost 4 in the morning, that was expected.

Zain knocked gently on the once-white front door; Edward felt that the door would fall apart.

"What is this town?" Edward wondered mostly to himself.

Safiya, now in her black ninja disguise, remained silent.

Zain smiled, "Just another dump where less-fortunate people lives. And oh, it just happened that those less-fortunate are on a different sect than that the government embrace."

Edward glanced at Safiya. She didn't bother responding. Maybe she thought it was better not to defend. Or maybe she, too, had sensed this aura of sadness and anger surrounding Zain.

Zain knocked on the door again. Harder this time. There was no echoing of the sound through the silent night, not even the uncomfortable feeling that normally accompanies disturbing the silence.

"It's almost 4 in the morning," Edward said. "Don't you think we might be disturbing—"

Zain waved his hand. "It's pre-dawn hour. The old man must be praying now. Besides, we are here asking for help. Helping others is a crucial part of Islam."

Before Edward could comment, a voice, an irritated voice that didn't convey any enthusiasm about helping others, came from the front yard: "*Man Hunak*?" (Who is it?)

"We want to see Sheik Essa!" Zain shouted back.

"Do you know what time is it?" the man shouted back in an Arabic accent Edward could barely comprehend.

Edward gave Zain an I-told-you look.

"We need help, and it's urgent."

"Come back at morning."

"Um… Maybe he isn't rehearsed in the part about 'helping others is a crucial part of Islam'," Edward teased Zain.

Safiya let out a low snicker.

Zain made a face and turned toward the sound. "I am not leaving here until I talk to someone."

A door creaked opened. Footsteps thudded in the front yard, which despite the darkness looked nothing more than a short walkway with one tree in what some might loosely be referred to as a garden.

A man's face, correction, a very *angry* man's face, grimaced at them over the rusted door. Through the faint light of the moon and what reached from the far streetlight, Edward could see him. Old, cranky, angry... give him a candle and a hat and he'd be Mr. Scrooge from *A Christmas Carol*.

Okay, he didn't hear the part about helping others. Fine. Hopefully, at least, Mr. Scrooge here wasn't in favor of beheading.

The man grunted something about them not having respect for time. Surprisingly, Zain was even more angry than Scrooge. The young man fired back something about respect for urgency.

Scrooge blinked, slightly taken aback. "The Sheikh is over seventy years old. You people are killing him by keep knocking on his door whenever you have as silly stuff as gazes."

Zain was about to respond, his face red. Edward stepped forward and said, "*Nahnu Huna An Tareek Dr. Fayazi*"

Either Fayazi's name or the sight of an American speaking Arabic got Scrooge's attention.

"*Dakeeka*," (one minute.) Scrooge said and went inside.

Zain pointed with his thumb to where Scrooge stood a minute ago. "You might think I am rude but this man is just acting on his own."

Edward winced. "It *is* late, Zain."

"It's not the first time we go to the Sheikh on a bad time, and he is always welcoming. You see, he understands that there are emergencies and he always tell his man-in-service or assistant or whoever this guy is not to cast people away."

Edward shrugged. Zain might be right, but at the end of the day he was just a stranger.

"Why does a cleric need an assistant?" Safiya asked.

Zain smirked. "Do you have an idea who is this man? He might be of minority but he is the highest cleric of his sect in Saudi Arabia. The man report directly to the Ayatollah in Najaf in Iraq."

Safiya just stared at him, she might have nodded. But not very convincingly.

"What?" Zain said. "You don't believe me? Do you know how much charity this man receive annually?"

"Oh, let me guess?" Safiya put her finger on the piece of black cloth that covered her mouth. "Given the fancy house and the rich neighborhood, I wouldn't expect anything less than a hundred dollar, in good seasons."

"Ha, it's millions!" Zain yelled.

Safiya laughed and turned her back on Zain. Zain looked at Edward for support. Edward raised his hands in a mock surrender. He wasn't part of these children's fight.

"People who work on this amount of money," Safiya said, "even if it's charity, they don't live in such places or such neighborhood, how can someone trust them with his money?"

"You know, its a good point," Zain said, his brown face turning red. "You see, this is what Islam teaches the leader to do, to live as poor as their poorest subject. This is what the prophet and Imam Ali did. They were real leaders. I am sorry if your perception is clouded by other type of leaderships who lives in palaces."

Zain made at least three quotation-mark gestures with his hands. Edward stopped counting.

"Let me ask you a question, *Zain*," Safiya said. Edward would bet his lunch money that under her face cover she was angry red. "Would you dare to say what you just said if it wasn't me. If it was one of my cousins, for example. Or just because I am more ... liberal... you find it so convenient to keep criticizing my family."

Zain shrugged.

"Or is it because I am a *woman*." Her eyes glistened with something. Strange how the eyes of a woman covered from top to toe became so expressive.

Zain's head lowered. He opened his mouth as if about to apologize but Scrooge's voice interrupted.

"*Tafadaloo*." (Come in.)

They did. The interior was slightly better than the outer facade. The walls could use some painting. The furniture was no more than four mattresses laid on the floor next to the walls with big pillows for back rests. But there was something besides simplicity in the room, warmness, coziness maybe. A small wooden cabinet had two drawers, one of them missing the handle, which was replaced with a metal wire.

Very handy.

A rusty air conditioner hummed a tad too loud as if trying its best to compensate in the hot weather.

"The Sheikh will see you in one minute," Scrooge raised his index finger in case Edward did not understand.

"Sure, one minute. Thanks."

The old assistant grinned as if to say "see! I can speak your language too."

Sheikh Essa trudged inside. Every step defied his seventy-plus years that hunched his back. The sunken hazel eyes, despite being almost covered by his bushy gray eyebrows, brought thoughts of afterlife and spirits and pursuing a goal beyond man's reach. Edward stood up instinctively. Zain and Safiya did likewise. The old man patted his three-inch gray beard and smiled at them. He looked at each one of them straight in the eye, concerned and welcoming, and as corny as it might sound, fatherly. Something about Essa made Edward unable to look at him nor to shift his gaze away. As if an aura of respect and wisdom surrounded the tiny old man.

"*Ahlan, Ahlan,*" the Sheikh greeted them with a smile, extending his hand to Edward. Careful not to break Essa's delicate warm hand, Edward shook it. A whiff of a sweet perfume hit Edward's nose. Sheikh Essa smelled as if he had just taken a bath in perfume.

"*Tafadaloo,*" Essa said, pointing at the mattresses.

They all sat. The man was like his room, simple to the point of modesty. It gave a friendly feeling.

Essa tucked away his flimsy black robe that covered his Obi-Wan-like white costume and sat on the mattress. Edward's heart skipped a beat as he noticed the painting on the wall.

A scene of blue sky and sun beaming on the sandy land. The sun was replaced by an open hand. The same symbol Edward saw tattooed on Buzz-cut's arm and sculptured in the ceramic artifact in Abdul Zahra's house.

-19-

The old Sheikh was anything but sleepy or tired. He sat on the mattress next to the wooden cabinet while the three of them sat on another mattress and had to turn their heads left to talk to him. Edward was the last one in the row and thus he had to tilt his head and body at an uncomfortable angle.

Sheikh Essa exchanged some pleasantries with Zain in Arabic, Edward understood the bigger part of it thanks to the slow and deliberate way the Sheikh spoke.

"Edward Fleming," the Sheikh said, after Zain finished his introduction as if trying the name. "I hear you and Dr. Fayazi friends," the old man said in broken English.

"*Tabadelna Rasael,*" (We exchanged mails) Edward said shifting to Arabic. Perhaps his Arabic sounded as funny as the Sheikh's English, but at least he could understand the Sheikh better if they all spoke Arabic. "We also talked on phone but I never met him."

Essa patted his beard. Then spoke in his slow and easy-to-understand Arabic. "Dr. Fayazi is a very respectful man. A man who would sacrifice for truth. A rare coin he is. Very objective and honest."

Okay, so the Sheikh was a fan of the old doctor. He wouldn't expect Fayazi to send him to someone who didn't like him anyway.

"*Nureed Musa'ada,*" (We came here asking for help.) Zain said, gesturing to Edward to get to the subject.

Maybe because he was tired after the long flight, or because Safiya was with them and he had told her everything, or maybe something about the old man inspired trust. Whatever, Edward told the Sheikh everything that happened to him since Kim's call. How he talked to two people, one who told him she was gone

104

then, later, the robotic voice who demanded the scan copies to be uploaded. To his credit, Sheikh Essa was a class-A listener. He never interrupted except with a nod or an encouraging smile. He also showed the interest and compassion of a man who was used to listening to people for long hours. Edward wasn't sure if Muslims had something equivalent to confession but whatever it was, Essa seemed more than good at it.

Mr. Scrooge came in with glasses of water and smaller ones for tea. Edward accepted both. He swallowed another Tylenol. The tea was too concentrated and too sweet, it might as well be sugar with some tea. But the small amount he managed to sip — mostly because of his embarrassment — gave a good surge of sugar and caffeine to his brain.

Essa remained silent after Edward finished his story. The Sheikh rubbed his chin, his thin fingers disappearing inside the thick beard. When the silence became a tad awkward, Essa spoke in a slow and calm Arabic. "Islam, like other religions, had set humans' well-being as its ultimate goal. Islam tries to make a balance between mind and body, life and after-life happiness. It is no surprise that all main religions emphasize the value of love. Love is the way for humans to reach their perfection, their true potential and true happiness."

Edward flashed back to the sight of the two towers of the World Trade Center, to the images he watched on TV and newspapers of the innocent people who died there. About all the people whose lives were ruined because of those attacks. Like him. He wanted to ask the Sheikh where was this love he talked about. But then he flashed to another memory. The sound of Kimberly's cry. Weakness took over the rage. He kept his mouth shut.

"Unfortunately, many Muslims do not realize this." Essa sighed. "While we are not trying to force our understanding of Islam on others, we are also trying to correct the dangerous path that some might take. I have seen cases where Muslims were so driven by their enthusiasm to the point that they caused damage to others. This is not only an improper act, but it also contradicts what the religion is trying to teach us of loving each other."

The Sheikh stopped, as if he remembered something. "I am sorry, I didn't mean to sell you Islam or anything like it, but it was an important introduction to what I am about to say."

Okay, the sales pitch was over.

"Because of my position, I am aware of more than one group who is trying to make a difference. I listen to them. I try to keep the bridges open between us. After all, we wouldn't be better than them if we sat back and made a judgment on others."

Another pause. Sheikh Essa rubbed his chin. "What you told me clearly indicates three things." He raised three fingers in the air like a referee in a boxing match.

"One, this group is interested in the Musehaf of Fatima. Two, they have a good knowledge of computers and technology." Essa lowered two fingers leaving one in the air. The old man wasn't bad for a game-show host. "Three, they are willing to hurt people to achieve their goals."

He held the last finger as if this point was very important, looking at the three of them in turn, with a smile of someone who just made a discovery.

"I could simply say that no group that I know —or more precisely— a group that talks to me, matches this profile. But you will not take my word for it, would you?"

Essa looked him in the eye. He was embarrassed by the sudden bluntness but this wasn't the time for maneuvering. "I guess I was hoping for more insight."

Essa nodded. "Allow me to explain what Musehaf Fatima really is and then you... I hope... will understand who might be willing to hurt people to get it."

The air conditioner roared puffing dust. Essa continued, "Quran, as you might know, is very special not only because it's a holy book, it is so because Quran, unlike other holy books, was perfectly preserved across centuries. There is one version of Quran and Muslims can show evidences that this printed Quran today is the same that was written on leather parchments fourteen hundred years ago in the era of Mohammed, God's peace upon him and his offspring."

Edward actually knew a lot about this part, a lot of the document-verification method he studied used the Quran as an example. The Quran was indeed a bullet-proof document when it came to accuracy to the letter, across all the manuscripts.

"You see, Mr. Fleming, what made the Quran a great book is not only its content. Yes, I wouldn't be exaggerating if I said Quran is a remarkable book that talked in a miraculous language about faith, morals, rules, economy, war and peace, and other subjects in a way that inspired each generation in a different way, and they were able to dig more meaning out of this great book. But again, it is not about the content only. Muslims accepted Quran as a reference because there is only one version. All Muslims agree that this book, with every single Surah, every single phrase, every single word, is from God."

The old sheikh reached for the glass of water on the floor in front of him and took a sip. Edward did the same. "Now you can all imagine the catastrophic ramifications if another version of this book were found, or even believed to exist."

"It will lose its credibility," Zain said.

"Entirely," Essa said. "The Quran itself declares more than once that its content were preserved and protected by God himself. If another version is found, the entire contents would be questionable. No one can say for sure that this phrase —we call it Ayah— is part of the Quran or not. It is as if you have a contract of one hundred paragraphs, and you know that one of those was changed but you don't know which one. At the end of the day, you cannot use this contract in a court of law."

Edward said, "Because any paragraph, any clause could be the one that was changed."

"Indeed."

"So?"

"So, saying that there is something such as the Quran of Fatima is as if questioning the entire Islamic religion, as this Quran is the basic pillar for the all the Sharia laws."

Edward remembered the message in the Internet, the threat of bringing down the nation of lies.

"It is an accusation some people are trying to throw at us, saying that we are not Muslims, we are infidels because we believe that there is another version of Quran." Sheikh Essa's face clouded the same way it did when he first mentioned the Musehaf. "You have to understand this, no Muslim believes there is another version of the Quran. It's only one book from one God."

"So as far as... umm, you're concerned, Musehaf Fatima does not exist?" Edward asked, feeling somehow disappointed that the long discussion led to nothing new.

Essa shook his head. "Actually, there is no doubt that Musehaf Fatima exists and will be found and published one day."

"I am lost," Edward said, unable to shift his gaze from the imposing painting of the hand. What was this symbol?

Sheikh Essa took a long breath, as if the old man was about to dive into the water. "That is why I was reluctant to discuss this matter. People might misunderstand or deliberately pretend to not understand."

"Uh huh."

"The evidences that back up the fact that something called Musehaf Fatima does exist are too many to be ignored."

Scrooge came in, telling the Sheik that some people wanted to talk to him about an important matter. Essa asked him to apologize and that he already had guests and they could come in an hour.

"I'm sorry to interrupt," Edward said, before the Sheik continued. "But what does this hand stand for." He pointed at the painting.

Essa turned and examined the drawings as if seeing it for the first time. "The hand of Fatima." He finally said.

The hand of Fatima? "Is it some kind of a group?"

Essa shook his head.

Scrooge said, "It's the protection against the evil eye. We received it as a gift two weeks ago. And I thought it would be good to hide the hole in the wall."

"To hide a hole in the wall?" Edward didn't bother to hide the skeptic tone.

Essa said, "Some believe that Fatima and her family, the five including her two sons, husband, and her father, are a protection from the evil eye. Others, however, believe that the symbol is for something different."

"And that thing is?" Safiya said.

Essa took a deep breath and let it out. "Some believe that the five represent the five degrees of relatives, the circle who are entitled to carry on a certain right when it comes to Fatima."

Edward swallowed, somehow, he knew where this was going. "And this right is..."

Essa nodded. "Avenge her."

-20-

"Avenge Fatima?" Safiya asked. "Why?"

Essa took another long breath. "It's a long story and you are not here for that. To keep it short, there is more to Fatima's death than the history books tell us."

Edward said, "So is there a group of people who —"

"No," Essa snapped. "Not a group, never in this way." He closed his eyes and when he opened them, he spoke in a low voice, choosing simple Arabic words as if to make sure Edward would understand. "What we know is that there is something called Musehaf Fatima. And that this Musehaf has a tremendous knowledge that when revealed will change the world. What we don't know is what this Musehaf really is."

"But why do they call it Musehaf Fatima?" Safiya asked.

The Sheikh then opened the drawer and took a thick, old book out of it, the brown leather peeled pages had long since turned into that brownish color of old paper. He held the book in both hands with extra care then raised it to his face, put it on his lips, and kissed it. "This is a Quran," Essa said. "It is also my Quran because my wife had given it to me as a gift. And when I say it's my Quran, it does not mean that I have another version, God forbid no."

"So Musehaf Fatima," Safiya said, "could be Fatima's own Quran, but I can't see how this could be so... I don't know... dangerous."

"There are some theories, but you need to understand the way the Quran was written first," the sheik said, putting the book back on the table.

"The history, and even the Quran for that matter, tells us that Quran was recited to Mohammed by Allah, through the angel Gabriel, in what we call the epiphany. However, the Quran was not recited at one time, rather the process took two decades. The Quran was recited on different occasions, different events. There are some Surrahs recited to Mohammed at times of peace, others at wartime, and others came answering questions some unbelievers challenged the prophet with. All in all, the Quran came in pieces. The history also tells us that as soon as the prophet got a new part of the Quran, he called one of what was later called the epiphany writers to write the new Surrah or group of Ayah."

Edward asked, "The Surrah is a collection of Ayah, right? Ayah is one phrase."

They all nodded.

"The official account is that the Quran remained as a collection of manuscripts and parchments even after the prophet died. It wasn't until the rule of Omar, the second ruler after Abu Baker, that the Quran was collected in one big book and hence the name Musehaf came."

Sheikh Essa took another sip of water. "According to this, the Quran was only collected five or six years after the prophet's death. Not a long period, but also long enough to ask why the prophet did not do it himself. After all, Quran was his biggest miracle. It is also a valid question to ask how come Fatima and her husband Ali, the two closest persons to the prophet and the only two he allowed to live in a house attached to the mosque with him, how come those two did not have a copy of the Quran? We all know that Ali was one of the first epiphany writers. The answer to this is simple: Fatima and Ali *did* have a full copy of the Quran. As a matter of fact, we knew that Ali, after burying the prophet, took an oath on himself not to go out until he finished putting all the manuscripts he had into one Musehaf."

"I am sorry but I think this is not accurate," Safiya said. "You are saying that among all his companions, Mohammed had chosen Fatima, an eighteen-year-old girl and Ali, how old was he? Twenty, thirty—"

"Thirty-five," Esaa said.

"Yeah, whatever, my point is why Mohammed didn't pick one of the elder men around him, one of the tribal leaders, for such an important task?"

"And when was age or sex the guideline to choose the fitted one?" Essa smiled. "Jesus died at thirty-three, Moses was forty when God called him. And Virgin Mary was thirteen when Angel Gabriel came to her."

"So what happened to that Musehaf?" Edward asked. They were sidetracked and he wanted to focus on his quest.

"There are records that Ali, after three days, went out of his home and talked to the people, that he did what he promised his cousin Mohammed to do. And he offered them the Musehaf, the first collected Quran. But they refused it."

"Why?" Safiya asked.

Zain sneered, shaking his head, his gaze fixed on the ground.

"It was part of the unfortunate events that happened right after the prophet died." Essa sighed. "There are many other and more depressing 'Whys'. But this is hardly the point. Most likely Fatima's Musehaf was *this* Musehaf. That Emam Ali, peace be upon him, had given this Quran to Fatima to keep it with her."

Edward massaged his forehead with his thumb and middle finger. God, he needed to sleep. "But, if this is true, and this Quran Ali had collected is the same one other Muslims have now, then why would revealing that Quran change the world?"

"Good point." Essa nodded. "The answer is, Musehaf Fatima had, besides the normal Quran, a lot of footnotes, explanations and remarks made by Ali and Fatima. Those were the questions and answers Ali and Fatima asked the prophet immediately after

the particular Ayah or group of Ayahs was recited to Mohammed
—"

"Excuse me," Edward said. His iPhone chirped. Vane.
Edward answered it.

"I need your translation *compétences*." Vane's calm and bored
voice came.

"O..k..a..y." Edward stood up and moved to the corner.

Essa told him that he could go to the corridor if he needed
privacy. Edward thanked him and went back to the corridor they
came from. Once he closed the door behind him, he was
plunged into darkness.

"Go on," Edward whispered.

A man's voice came screaming, pleading, "*Arjook!*"

"He's saying please. Jesus, Vane, what are you doing to him?"

More screaming: the man was swearing he didn't know.
Edward translated it to Vane.

"Tell him I know they are working for Othman," Vane said.
Edward translated.

"*La Aaref.*" (I don't know) the man cried. Two muffled thuds
came, then a crackling sound. More screaming. Then in barely
fathomable Arabic, "The warehouse! The control is there."

Edward relayed this to Vane. Vane hung up.

God. Edward collapsed against the wall. His mind took him to
places he didn't want to go, questions he couldn't answer, didn't
want to.

Kimberly. Focus.

Edward went back to the room. Everyone stared at him as if
it were written on his forehead that he helped torturing a man
for information. Edward apologized to the sheikh and asked him
to continue.

Essa did. "If you think about it, what Ali and Fatima
supposedly did, by writing the explanation of each Ayah the
moment it came, is what any good student would do: ask
questions and take notes on what the grand master said. All big
teachers, prophets, and great leaders across history did that;
Mohammed wasn't the first to choose people close to him to be
his students, to write and document his teaching. And what

better than his only daughter and his cousin, whom he himself had raised and took under his wing since he was a newborn."

"So Musehaf Fatima is the Quran plus notes and comments made by the prophet?" Edward asked. "I still don't see how this will change the world."

Essa smiled. "Maybe because you are new to Quran. Otherwise you would have known that the biggest challenge Muslim clerics have with Quran is when it comes to unclear or somehow vague phrases. The Quran is a great source of spiritual inspiration and was actually more of a constitution for Muslims because of the extensive way the Quran explained the important Sharia laws. Quran still amazes scientists by pointing to theories in different fields of life, theories that were in Quran but people didn't pay attention to it because of the way it was mentioned — either too casual or too vague."

Edward hardly refrained from rolling his eyes. He didn't like when people started their sales pitches. Clerics were the worst.

Essa cleared his throat and said, "My point is: if Musehaf Fatima really had her notes it would be a breakthrough in many fields of life. It would put an end to long discussions about if Quran meant this or that."

Edward didn't know what to say. Safiya tilted her head. Hard to read someone's expression when her face was covered, yet, Edward had more than a hunch that she had difficulty accepting part or all of what Sheikh Essa said.

A knock came on the outside door. The room had no windows so it wasn't possible to know who was there.

"More visitors?" Zain smiled to the Sheikh.

Sheikh Essa glanced at the circular wall clock: 4:30 AM.

"You said there are other theories." Edward tried to get back to the subject.

The old man nodded. "You see, Edward, we are trying to avoid confusing people. There are a lot of... what do you call them... people with a hidden agenda, who keep accusing us of breaking Muslim unity. We don't want to give a chance to those who accuse us. Consider this, we are officially declining anything related to the Musehaf and yet there is all that noise about us having another version of Quran. What if we actually said that there *is* something called Musehaf Fatima? They wouldn't give us a chance to explain what theories we have. We would be branded as unbelievers. Take any book about Islam that is printed in Saudi Arabia and see what they say about us. Anyone who disagrees with them is an unbeliever, and that is us, what else? Anyone who doesn't believe that we are unbelievers is also an unbeliever, *Kafer*. People are killed by the hundreds in Iraq and Pakistan just because they were branded as infidels by some narrow-minded cleric. We say Musehaf Fatima, and we have open season on us; for God sake, it is open season on us now." Sheik Essa sighed.

The door opened and Scrooge came in. He stepped forward to the Sheikh, whispering something in his ear. The Sheik smiled and nodded.

"I still don't understand," Edward said. "You said whoever did this cannot be from your people. I cannot see why. You said yourself that this Musehaf had valuable knowledge, so maybe there's someone... um... maybe someone from your people, desperate to lay their hands on this knowledge."

Essa glanced at Zain, who whispered something Edward couldn't hear.

The Sheik nodded. "There are two reasons why I am saying this." He again lifted his fingers in the air.

The Sheikh loved counting, no doubt about that.

"First, as I said before, public knowledge about the Musehaf is that either it doesn't exist or it's proof of Shia's infidelity, *KUFUR*. So if someone was looking for this, it would not be someone who belongs to us."

"They might know about this explanation you just told us about," Edward said. "So for them it would still be a great discovery."

Sheik Essa smiled. "Here comes the second reason."

The door opened and another old man, slightly taller than the Sheik, with white hair and glasses and broad shoulders, walked in with a cane. "*Salam Alycum,*" the man greeted them, walking toward Sheikh Essa.

"*Salam*, Dr. Fayazi." Essa hugged the man. The two embraced a tad too long. They exchanged something about a long time having passed since their last meeting. Zain stared at Fayazi with his mouth open. He shook Fayazi's hand firmly with both his hands. Edward half expected Zain to yell out, "Hi, I'm your biggest fan!"

Safiya did not stand.

Then Fayazi came to him. Edward stood. He was unsure of what to say. So was Fayazi.

"I...am ... sorry. For what happened to Kim," Fayazi finally said.

"Let's work on getting her back," Edward said. No point blaming now.

"That's why I came here," Fayazi said, extending his hand. They shook.

PART THREE

Eight of ten expatriate women in Saudi are subjected to different levels of sexual harassment.

Thirty percent of those who are working at Saudi houses are subjected to either beatings, starvation, or rape.

Only a handful of cases make their way to court.

-21-
<Al Nakhawla town – Saudi Arabia>
<Time left until Zero hour is 19hrs:30min>
<Number of infected websites: 220,880>

Sheikh Essa resumed the discussion after they all sat again. Fayazi sat on the other side of the room, facing Edward.

"The second reason," Essa said, "that I don't believe the one who did this is one of us, is that only the elite know about this story and they will not try to get this Musehaf — not to mention hurting someone to get it."

"Why not?" Edward asked.

"Because they will know that it is not meant for them to have it."

"Why not?" He felt like a curious child.

"Because the other part of the story — if it was true of course — says that after Muslims rejected Emam Ali's Musehaf and he gave it to Fatima, the book remained with her until her death. Then it was with her sons, they passed it from one to another. And it would be with them until the last one of her offspring — that is Emam Mahdi — will come and reveal it to the public."

Both Fayazi and Zain nodded in some kind of salute when Essa mentioned the name Emam Mahdi. This name, and the gesture they did, gave Edward a disorienting sense of *de-ja-vu*. This time hard enough it actually hurt.

"The Mahdi," Edward tried to breathe, "isn't that the one who will fight all unbelievers and conquer the world?"

Where did he hear that before?

Essa said, "The prophecy is that he is the one who will finally bring justice and peace to all the world."

"Uh huh, by killing everyone else."

Essa shook his head, took a long breath. "The prophecy says some wars will happen but that doesn't mean the Emam will start them."

Fayazi cleared his throat. Essa nodded for him to continue.

"Interestingly enough..." Fayazi began. He had a theatrical edge in his tone, his Arabic accent was different from that of Essa. Yet Edward had no trouble understanding it. "All the battles the Mahdi will fight, according to the prophecy, are only with other Muslims. And here in this region."

Edward arched an eyebrow.

Fayazi went on, "On the other hand, when it comes to the Western world, the prophecy mentions that he will *talk* to them. It's a peaceful dialogue with people who will give him the chance to talk and listen to him. Sadly, it looks like it's not the situation with Arabs..."

Edward didn't know what to say. Did he even care about what a one-thousand-year-old prophecy said? But that nostalgic feeling of remembering the same discussion got stronger, painful, as if related to a sad memory.

"Anyway," Edward said, trying to clear his head and at the same time not be rude, "so what you are saying is that whoever did this is not someone you know."

"I am afraid not." Essa sighed and shook his head.

"So is that it? We don't have a clue who kidnapped her or why?" To hell with not being rude. Somewhere his friend might be facing death and he was sitting here listening to lectures on Islamic history.

"Actually, we have a clue," Fayazi said.

Everyone looked at the old doctor. His thick and bushy white hair, his rosy face and the wide, almost-zealous grin, he didn't strike Edward as a very sane man, rather, a man who spent too much time in the sun.

Fayazi cleared his throat again. "For the past ten years, I have dedicated my work to one thing only. Only recently did I have some real evidence that could help me find it."

"The Musehaf of Fatima," Safiya said as if she just found her voice again.

"*Naam...*" (Yes) Fayazi squinted at her, then turned back to Edward. "The last piece of the puzzle was given to me by Kimberly. I never saw anyone like her. Kimberly did one great job on her own, gathering a lot of information about Fatima. Her enthusiasm about supporting women's causes is akin to a religious zeal."

Edward half smiled, remembering Kimberly and her fascination with feminism.

"Anyway, I showed Kimberly what I had found so far and how, if we found this Musehaf, we could change the world. And how what she had given me helped me in my research." He paused, looking at Edward again.

Edward took the chance to ask, "Are you saying that Kim had something that relates to the Musehaf of Fatima?"

"Yes, but she didn't realize how that was related. It's a document that you have in your office. I was so happy with my discovery that I shared it with her. I wasn't about to keep it for myself anyway."

"Kimberly was supposed to get some photos verified," Edward said. "How did this turn into a treasure hunt?"

"The photos were about the events of 1925, when the Saudi government demolished historical places and the shrines of Fatima's sons. It's a long story, and to my surprise, Kimberly insisted on helping me. I explained the dangers and the risks. She did not listen. One of my students lives in Saudi, Majida, so I thought it would be safe for her to take Kimberly. Now, in hindsight, I realize that was a mistake. Anyway, she left and Majida called me from the airport after she picked up Kimberly. But they haven't called me since."

Edward frowned. "What was she trying to do here? She mentioned something about meeting a man, was he Abdul Zahra?"

Fayazi nodded. "Yes. I had some doubts before but I am almost certain now that Abdul Zahra is connected to everything."

Everyone waited for Fayazi to elaborate. The old professor took his time. Some people thrived on attention and the spotlight. Edward didn't know the man but he seemed quite comfortable with all gazes upon him.

"It is true," Fayazi finally said. "And that's why I believe that whatever happened to Abdul Zahra and to Kim is connected with the Book of Fatima. Someone is digging for it and they will not stop until they find the book even if it means killing everyone in their path."

Scrooge came to serve tea again, including Fayazi this time. "Thank you, Hameed," the professor said courteously.

Edward said, "No thanks." Hameed put it in front of him and left.

"I don't understand. It's just that nothing makes sense here," Safiya protested. "People being killed. Others kidnapped. And strange threats on the Internet talking about bringing everything down in on-me-and-on-my-enemies sort of thing. And all that because of a *book*."

Fayazi frowned, the lines on his forehead and under his cheeks more prominent, as if someone pinched them. "Do you realize that this book changed the course of history, and maybe not just Islamic history but that of all humanity? The secrets in this book have enough power that its influence left clear marks."

Safiya sneered. "*Secrets?* You make it sound like some bloody magic spell. With all due respect to Quran, a version with some notes won't cause the catastrophic damage you are talking about."

Fayazi chuckled. "Sheikh Essa told you that Musehaf Fatima is Quran?"

Safiya shrugged, looking at the Sheikh, "What else could it be? It's a Musehaf. Musehaf mean Quran."

"It has been widely used to refer to the Quran." Fayazi made a yes-no gesture with his hand. "The word was originally derived from *Saheefa,* which means document. The word Musehaf means collection of documents." Dr. Fayazi turned to the sheikh.

Essa shook his head. "Please don't go there, Professor."

"Why? They deserve to know, the world deserves to know for the sake of Allah."

Sheikh Essa shook his head, his lips tight.

Now Edward protested, speaking in English, knowing they all could understand. "I don't mean to be rude or anything but we are wasting valuable time here. What is going on?"

Fayazi, maybe out of respect to the sheikh, did not speak. Essa finally spoke in his slow and easy-to-understand Arabic. "You remember when I told you that there are other theories about the Musehaf of Fatima?"

Edward nodded.

"Well, they are weak and based on speculations. Except a new theory the professor came up with."

"What theory?" Zain said, rubbing his eyes as if he had just woken up.

Essa raised his hands in mock surrender. "The man is here, ask him."

Zain, Safiya, and Edward turned back to Fayazi. Fayazi cleared his throat. This time it turned into continuous coughing. When the coughing ceased, the doctor apologized and began in a voice that had the emotion of someone telling the story of meeting his true love. His English, too, had that theatrical tone, as if rehearsing for *King Lear.*

"The general belief was that Fatima's Musehaf is a Quran because of the word Musehaf, used mostly to refer to the holy Quran. However, the word's actual meaning is a collection of documents. There is no evidence to indicate that Fatima's book is the holy Quran, other than some propositions."

Edward started feeling numbness in his legs from the uncomfortable sitting position. He moved them; it got worse.

"I found very few references about the nature of those documents but they confirmed two main facts. The first is, whatever the contents of Fatima's Musehaf were, they had nothing to do with the Quran. As I said before, the word Musehaf here is used to refer to documents Fatima kept with her after her father's death."

Edward wanted to ask but Fayazi signaled for him to wait.

"The other fact that became clear to me is that the information in these documents is very sensitive — to the point that, across history, it played a crucial role in shaping the struggle for power in the region."

Safiya said, "The way you talk about it, it sounds like other people had put their hands on the Musehaf of Fatima."

"Of course they did," Fayazi said. "Do you think that it was locked up in a safe and no one touched it?" Fayazi chuckled. The chuckle turned into serious coughing. "If you examined the history of the Islamic empire, you would notice a strange trend. It's a good indicator not only that the Musehaf was there, but also of how powerful it was. Our history, like any other history, was written by kings and for kings. But you can see the holes if you just look carefully. You can see the great power of the secrets this Musehaf holds."

Edward stood. The numbness became unbearable. The others had no difficulty with the way they were sitting. Maybe they were used to it. "I'm sorry but I need to rest my legs."

Essa gave him a suit-yourself smile. Safiya snickered.

"Doctor Fayazi," Edward said, "can we please skip the cryptic talk? For the past hour, I have heard nothing but theories and lectures. You said that you had a good clue about what happened to Kim and I want to hear about it now."

Zain bit his lower lip and shook his head. Edward didn't care. The truth was, on another occasion, one that did not include his friend being kidnapped, he would love to listen to all of those theories. Partly because it was what he did for a living now. And partly because of his natural interest in stories about mysteries from the past. But not now.

"I am coming to that, Edward," Fayazi said. "But the background is important. Besides..." Fayazi's sunken brown eyes lit up with vigorous zeal. "This is the interesting part."

Edward took a long breath and said with surrender, sitting back on the mattress, "Okay, please go on." He accidentally tipped over his glass of tea. It spilled on the floor. Essa told him it wasn't a problem, wiping it up with two tissues.

"That should take care of it," Essa said, panting. "Doctor, please, continue."

"Our story begins somewhere in the second half of the Seventh Century, right after Prophet Mohammed died. The tragic events after the prophet's death made Fatima practically boycott almost everyone in Madeena —which was the Muslim capitol at the prophet's time. In her will, she asked to hide her tomb's location so that those who hurt her wouldn't come and try to make amends, which should give you an example of how discontented she was. The Musehaf of Fatima was born in those days. And that's why it probably got mixed with the Quran that Ali had collected. But I am almost sure it was not the same thing. Yes, maybe they were kept together at a later stage but the sources I was able to find in both Shia and Sunnie books suggested that the Musehaf had begun its journey not with Fatima but with someone else. I couldn't put a finger on a particular name. As a matter of fact I found an old letter from the Eleventh Century referring to different companions of the prophet as previous owners of the Musehaf or parts of the Musehaf."

"Which means..." Edward said. "It's not the Quran Ali had written and collected."

"Precisely. Anyway, in her last days, I believe the Musehaf was given to Fatima, peace be upon her, or she might be just another owner, it's really hard to be sure. Right after her death, a month or two after her father's death, the Musehaf was kept by a very... how to pick the word... interesting person. His name was Mohammed Bin Abu Baker. His father, Abu Baker, was the first ruler after the prophet. Abu Baker died after four years. At that time, Emam Ali was a widow after Fatima's death. So Ali married Abu Baker's widow, a good woman called Esmaa. Mohammed Bin Abu Baker was raised by Emam Ali during his youth and was very loyal to him."

"So why is he interesting?" Safiya asked.

"You must be aware of how Muslims were divided between following Abu Baker or Emam Ali as a successor to Mohammed after the prophet's death. Anyway, Mohammed Bin Abu Baker was on the good side of his family, although he made it clear that he was on Emam Ali's side. And I believe that he was the first one who owned the complete version of this Musehaf. I am not sure how, but it looks like he got it a few months before his execution."

"Mohammed bin Abu Baker was *executed?*" Safiya asked.

"Yes, executed by Muawya when he captured Egypt," Fayazi replied.

"Who is Muawya?" Edward asked.

"The man who ruled Muslims after Emam Ali. The fifth ruler," Fayazi said. "Muawya was the most ferocious enemy of Emam Ali, just as his father was the most ferocious enemy of Mohammed. Anyway, during the war between Emam Ali and Muawya, Ali made Mohammed Bin Abu Baker the ruler of Egypt. And when Egypt fell, Bin Abu Baker was tortured, Muawya ordered him to be dressed in a mule skin and burned alive."

"How come Muawya would do such a thing to the son of Abu Baker?" Safiya asked. "Maybe he hates Emam Ali, but why would he do that to Abu Baker's son?"

Zain sneered. "Do you think a scumbag like Muawya, who killed thousands of Muslims to be a king, cared about Abu Baker's son."

"As a matter of fact, it's a good point," Fayazi said. "I would understand the killing, but the brutality of the execution tells me that there was something more to it."

"Revenge?" Safiya asked.

Fayazi shook his head and smiled. Despite his seventy years, Fayazi wore a ten-year-old-boy's crooked smile.

Edward ventured, "The Musehaf?"

"Aha, that's my theory." Fayazi jumped, pointing at Edward with a wide grin. "My guess: Muawya got a whiff that Mohammed Bin Abu Baker had it. Anyway, Muawya did not get it, and the Musehaf disappeared, but it was still with those I call The Followers."

"The *Followers?*" Edward tried to remember if he had heard the name before. It sounded like the title of a bad horror movie.

"A group of elite Muslims who believed that Ali, Fatima and their sons were the natural extension to Mohammed. That they were — and pay extra attention to this one — the living Quran. That Mohammed's miracle was not only bringing the Quran, which is the guideline to perfection, but also creating and raising the living examples of such a product: Fatima and Ali. A perfect man and woman."

Back to the sales pitch.

"So the Musehaf stayed with those... um... followers?" Edward asked.

"That is what it looks like," Fayazi said. "Muawya and the kings who followed him — all from his clan, as they declared it was monarchy — tortured and killed a lot of those followers. Men and women who were the true believers of Mohammed, anyway. The Musehaf appeared with another famous name seven decades after that." Fayazi stopped to give dramatic effect to what he was about to say. "Jabir Bin Hayyan."

"The alchemist." Edward knew the name. He had seen one of his books, as well.

"Another mark for Edward," Fayazi announced. "Yes, the famous alchemist and astronomer. The man considered to be the father of the chemistry; his books were breakthroughs far ahead of anyone in his time. His work with chemistry was close to magic. But the interesting thing about Jaber was that he had only one teacher."

Fayazi looked at Edward as if expecting an answer. Edward shrugged. Just because he recognized the name didn't mean that he was his biographer.

"Emam Sadeq," Zain said.

Fayazi did the same thing of jumping and pointing at Zain.

Did the old man do this in his class?

"Exactly, Jabir had only one teacher, Emam Sadeq, the grandson of the grandson of Fatima. Emam Sadeq is the sixth Emam of the twelve Emams who shall lead the Muslims, according to prophecy. The first one is Emam Ali and the last one is Emam Mahdi."

Zain and Essa did that salute thing again. Edward made a mental note to ask about it later.

Fayazi took his glass of tea and drank it in one gulp. "It looks like Jabir got this valuable Musehaf to do one important task. The preservation."

Edward had seen this done before. "To prevent the paper from aging through time, it has to be kept in special conditions. At the Library of Congress, they keep old manuscripts in vacuum storage. But in the Eighth Century, this technology wasn't known. So maybe Jabir came up with an alternative."

"Exactly." Fayazi clapped. "I personally have no doubt that the master of chemistry came up with something perfect. After that there were other references to the Musehaf. By the way, I found that during this era it was called by different names. Maybe to hide it or maybe for other reasons. The peculiar thing about that book is it kept disappearing and popping up again all of a sudden with some famous followers, like Ibn Seena and Farabi, the philosophers, and Al-Yakoobi, the geographer, and Al-Masoudi, the historian. Often associated with serious genocide against those opposing the king or demanding reform. For example, during the massacre that ended the Fatimian kingdom in Egypt in 1171. Then in the Safawi era, the strong Persian empire, then during the Mongolian campaign. Then the Ottoman empire. During each of these periods, the followers of Mohammed and his offspring — the followers of Fatima — were in grave danger. Often a massacre was about to be carried out against them or one had just started. Then all of a sudden, a famous cleric or philosopher or scientist talked to the ruler, and the killing stopped —"

Edward's phone rang. Again Vane.

"I need to go outside," he said, apologizing, and already regretting interrupting the discussion at this point.

The old Sheik pointed at the same corridor door.

"One second, Vane," he said, walking to the corridor then to the front yard. Once out, Edward filled his lungs with the refreshing breeze. Crickets' chirps made the quiet night even more pronounced.

"I found out something from the fellows I... *talked* to," Vane said.

"I'm listening,"

"I heard the name Abdul Zahra Al-Makki when you were talking to the police."

"Yes, he is the house owner who was murdered," Edward said. "The police were very edgy about it."

"Oh, I wouldn't blame them."

"Why?"

"It says here that Abdul Zahra was a human rights activist," Vane said. Then, "*très* active."

"One minute, is the paper written in English?"

"No," Vane said, too bored. "I bought one of those learn Arabic in two-hours books."

"Really?" Edward teased.

"Good Lord, of course not. It's in English." Then he chuckled. "Ah, you got me."

The man, or men, Vane *talked to* were Arabs. No question about it. So why did they have documents about Abdul Zahra written in English?

"Okay, what else did you find?" Edward asked.

"The man was arrested in 1965 with twenty people, most of them sentenced to life."

"And he got out?"

"Nope, that's why I saved it for last."

A shiver crept over Edward's spine. From a distance a car engine roared.

"In 1965 after a long and tough interrogation," Vane said, "Abdul Zahra Al-Makki was executed."

-23-

Edward stayed for another five minutes in the front yard, hoping that the fresh air could bring him answers. He couldn't hear the crickets anymore. Maybe because Vane's words still hammered in his skull. Abdul Zahra was executed in 1965? How was this possible? And who was this man with knife cuts on his chest? Was he an imposter and killed because of that? Who killed him? And why the strange symbol on his chest? And most importantly, how did Kimberly fit into all of this?

He went back to the living room. Answers: he needed answers. And he hoped he would find some in the history lecture Fayazi offered.

"So, Doctor," Safiya said, "are you suggesting that those men you mentioned had something to threaten the rulers with?"

"What else?" Fayazi speared his hands. "The Persian Safawi king actually converted and took a pledge to take care of all the shrines of Fatima's sons that other kings had destroyed."

"Converted?" Edward asked, trying to keep up with the discussion.

"Yes," Fayazi said, "Muslims had different sects, despite what some might say. Different sects had different views of Fatima and her sons."

Great. So an entire sect of god-knows-what might all be looking for their lost book. Back to square one.

They fell silent. Safiya broke it. "And you think secrets in that Musehaf were used to force something on the kings of different Muslim empires?"

Fayazi nodded. "There are signs that those men had this book. Using it to save thousands of people is justifiable. However, our interesting part of the story starts in the year 1898."

Edward winced. "I thought you said *this* was the interesting part."

"Let's say it's the *really* interesting part." Fayazi grinned. "In that year, Grand Ayatollah Seerazi had written a letter to one of his students, telling him that he believed it was his duty to return the trusted secret to its original home. Ayatollah Seerazi gave some reasons for his decision, which are not part of our discussion, but it's enough for any scrutinizing eye to conclude that this trusted secret was nothing other than the legendary Musehaf of Fatima."

Fayazi stood and paced the room. Good to know that someone else had trouble sitting on these mattresses.

"Ayatollah Seerazi died a week later. And, interestingly enough, his student traveled to Saudi right after the burial ceremonies of his teacher in Najaf were over. I was able to trace his visit and it looks like he spent less than a week in Saudi."

"A short visit," Safiya said.

Edward found it more than strange. "How long did the trip take back in those days from Najaf to Saudi?"

Fayazi's face lit up. "Three weeks was the average time required for travel. You know, they used camels for travel in those days. In today's analogy, given that air flights take only two hours from Iraq to Saudi, our friend stayed for one hour and then went back home."

"And what did he do in Saudi?" Zain asked.

"That's the thing," Fayazi said, raising his index finger. "He met some people, merchants, but this is not the important part. What we need to focus on is that he hid the Musehaf in Saudi Arabia."

"Where?" Edward and Zain asked in unison.

"I don't know for sure," Fayazi said. "But I know this. It has something to do with the land of Fadak. Maybe he hid it there, maybe just left a clue in Fadak for the whereabouts of the Musehaf."

"That's why Kimberly went to meet Abdul Zahra," Edward said. "This was your only clue."

Fayazi nodded.

"But why not you, Doctor? Why send her?"

"As you might have guessed," Fayazi said, looking at the floor, "I am not very welcome in Saudi. Kimberly insisted and she said maybe Abdul Zahra would be more comfortable talking to an American researcher rather than me."

Should he ask Fayazi about what Vane had told him on the phone? Zain and Fayazi both believed that the victim was Abdul Zahra, so they were either lying or something was missing.

Safiya asked, "What is Fadak?"

Fayazi said, "Fadak is the land that the prophet Mohammed gave to Fatima. And then Abu Baker, the first king, confiscated it after the prophet's death."

Safiya frowned. "No way, why would Abu Baker do such a thing to the prophet's daughter."

Fayazi shrugged. "What I am saying is agreed-upon historical fact. Abu Baker claimed that this land should be used to fund the coming wars, the *Jihad*, he wanted to carry out. So he sent a letter to one of his men to kick out the guardian of the farm appointed by Fatima. When Fatima protested, he asked her to bring witnesses. She did. Abu Baker refused the witnesses, so she went to the mosque where all the Muslims gathered and she gave her famous speech, not only about her rights to Fadak, but about her political and religious views if you wish. Anyway, the land was not given to her but imagine all of this happening just days after the prophet's death. The effect was devastating to Fatima."

Edward needed some time to digest the information. "So, what document did Kim give you?" he finally asked.

"The letter from Ayatollah Seerazi to his student. She had called your office and someone had sent her a scanned copy of the letter."

"And because Abdul Zahra was the one looking after Fadak, you suspected he knew something?"

"Yes."

"Just like that?"

"What do you mean?" Fayazi asked.

"It just doesn't sound logical; he doesn't know her."

Fayazi opened his mouth, closed it, then rubbed his face with his hand. "I don't know, Edward, you might be right. I guess your friend had some sort of plan to get the man to talk. I admit I was too enthusiastic to stop her."

Edward was about to retort but Safiya held his hand. She shook her head. "Let's focus on finding her, remember?"

Edward took a deep breath. "So, Doctor, you think Kim's disappearance has to do with the Musehaf, but this is hardly new information. I don't see how this is going to help us."

"I think whoever did that to Abdul Zahra did not find the Musehaf," Fayazi said. "Otherwise he wouldn't ask you to give him your documents."

"So?"

"So he is still looking, and that will give us a clue where is he going to go."

"I don't see how. We don't know the location of the Musehaf," Edward said, trying to remember anything he had overlooked in the story that pointed to where the Musehaf might be.

Fayazi smiled. "We might, thanks to the letter Kimberly gave me. On the other hand, if Abdul Zahra knew something, we might find some clues, maybe in his house — I don't know."

Fayazi's plan wasn't bad. At least it *was* a plan. A door to knock. And maybe, if he could knock hard enough, something might come up. The problem was, Abdul Zahra might not be the man they thought he was. Unless the man somehow resurrected from the grave after being executed. Edward debated telling them about Abdul Zahra, but wasn't sure now was the best time. Better to play along and see what would come up.

"I can help," Safiya said. "I have good contacts in the police department and I might be able to find out if they have anything about Abdul Zahra's last moves."

Edward said, "I don't want to put you in danger."

She shook her head. "I want to do this."

What could he say to stop her? "Thank you."

"I will stay with you as well, Edward," Zain said. "I know the area and I was very close to Abdul Zahra. I have access to his house. I am also dying to lay my hands on the bastards who killed him."

Fayazi smiled. "And don't expect me to leave you alone just because I am old and will slow you down. This is my life dream."

"No," Edward replied, "Dr. Fayazi, I know you mean well, but I want to focus on finding Kim, and you... let's just say I understand you have other priorities."

"I see." Fayazi nodded. "And I understand what you are saying but there is something important you are missing."

Edward folded his arms, standing face to face in front of the doctor. He had two or three inches on Fayazi.

Fayazi continued, "Finding Kimberly and finding the Musehaf of Fatima is the same thing. I just explained that the only clue we have now is we know that the kidnappers are after the Musehaf. Maybe if we find the Musehaf, we find Kim — and Majida, don't forget that she is missing too."

Edward didn't like this. Too much of a treasure-hunt-movie cliché. Besides, he felt there were hidden agendas. Paranoid as it might sound, his mind kept telling him to be on guard until he knew these people better. For now, he had no choice but to accept their help. "Just promise me you will not endanger Kim," He finally said in surrender.

"You have my word." Fayazi raised his right palm as if making an oath.

Edward tried for an enthusiastic tone. "So what is our next step?"

The historian checked his watch. "I think the dawn prayer is due now, Sheikh."

Essa nodded.

Fayazi turned to Edward. "I need to pray, and after that we will go. I have one place in mind."

Maybe Fayazi saw the reluctance in Edward's face so he added, "Don't worry, it will take only ten minutes."

Essa opened the door. Addressing Zain and Fayazi, "We can pray in the next room." Then he turned to Safiya. "And you, my daughter, if you like I can show you the women's prayer room."

Safiya shook her head with embarrassment, murmuring something in Arabic.

"Um… Sheikh Essa."

"Yes, Edward."

"I need to use the bathroom." Edward smiled sheepishly. "And it's been a while since the last meal I had, so I was wondering…"

The old man chuckled. "But of course. I wouldn't accept to let you leave at this time without having something."

-24-

The bathroom experience was challenging... to spare the details. At least he didn't urinate blood after the beating. Still, he couldn't stop wondering how different people around the world had different ways to... um... answer nature's call.

Edward spent a longer time at the sink, not only to wash his hands but to rinse his head under the water. Ah, the cold refreshing water. When he got back to the visitors' room, he found only Safiya there. She had taken off the face cover, still had on the black head cover. The black color went well with her skin, making her beautiful face even more attractive.

Three dishes and some bread were placed on a plastic plate in front of her. The plate had a sunflower print with faded colors. One of the dishes was yogurt, the other had olive oil and pepper-like green and yellow seeds. The third one was walnuts and cheese.

"I like Sheikh Essa," Safiya said, once he was seated next to her. "I think he is cute."

"Cute?"

She took a piece of bread, cut it into two halves, and gave him one. She put some of the olive oil with the yellow-green things on her half.

"I mean, he did not comment or try to lecture me when I did not go to pray," she said, taking a bite of her bread. "And he doesn't know who I am."

Edward started with the cheese and walnuts. The taste wasn't great but his stomach welcomed the food. "Praying is a very personal choice."

"It's against the law here if you don't pray."

"That's stupid."

"Yeah, I know," she said while chewing. "That's why I did not defend the religious police when Zain accused them back when we were in the car. Those guys are driving everyone crazy."

Edward leaned back so he could have a better view of her face. "Since we are alone now, I am still curious about why you came to Fadak in the first place."

She stopped eating. Her almond-shaped green eyes stared at the floor where there was a small stain from the tea he had spilled. Was it sadness that he was seeing? Why? "I was following the virus."

He tilted his head, still trying to look her in the eye. "That crazy message on the Internet with the counter?"

She nodded, her eyes moist. "I had asked one of my contacts in the secret police about it and he just told me today, I mean yesterday, that the secret police had one suspect with the name Abdul Zahra, who was in an old farm in Al-Hayett town."

Interesting. "Do you think he is behind that message?"

She shrugged. "I didn't see any computers in his shack."

Probably the computers were somewhere else. But Safiya had a point, if he were behind such a thing, wouldn't it be logical to have a computer with him to follow the progress of his cyber attack?

"So you just decided to come to the town, to ... what? Interview him?"

She turned and looked at him. God, she was beautiful. Her green eyes glistened with tears, begging him to understand. What was he missing?

"I was bored." She shrugged, turning the other way and wiping her face.

"Safiya?"

A faint sniffle.

"Are you okay?" he asked, feeling a familiar pang in his chest. He had seen this before. Safiya crying. Where? No, *When*?

She wiped a tear from her face. "Sorry, silly me. It's just I didn't know that I would come across you... and Kimberly."

The embarrassment of her family because she was helping a wanted man must be hard on her.

"You should eat," Safiya said, her red lips quivered in a sad smile. Her eyes reddened of crying. Something about the way she looked at him made his mouth dry.

"What is this?" Edward asked, pointing at the pepper-like powder and trying his best to make his voice cheerful.

"*Zaatar*, smashed mint leafs with sesame. Very delicious and healthy on breakfast. Here, try it." Safiya cut a small piece of bread and put a mix of olive oil and the *Zaatar* and gave it to him.

He accepted it, feeling a quasi-electric shock when his fingers touched hers.

"How does it feel?" she asked, staring at the colorful plate. "Being unable to remember anything. Does seeing people or places trigger memories back?"

"Sometimes. Sometimes it's just an odd sense of deja vu."

She nodded, then said in the calmest way, "I wish I could forget who I am."

Neither spoke. He took another bite of cheese, bread, Zaatar and whatever else was mixed with it.

Finally he continued, "Sometimes I wake up at night not knowing who I am and where I am. My brother sent me a photo taken in our old house in Egypt, when Father used to work there for two years. He wrote saying: "This is the yard where you and I learned to ride bikes." The thing is, I couldn't remember any of it. My childhood memories? I mean come on, how can you forget something like that? What makes it worse is when I remember... stuff."

Edward shook his head, he wasn't sure he wanted to, or even could, go there.

"Unpleasant memories are hard to forget," she said bitterly.

"No, that isn't what I meant." He shook his head. "I have those... What do you call them? Not memories, I am not even sure they happened. Images flashing in my mind. I imagine doing things I know I would never do. Everything is like a damn half-remembered dream."

He stopped. Edward had never said this to anyone except Kimberly and Vane. It felt weird and comforting at the same time.

"Look at me," he said. "Complaining about memory loss when my best friend is kidnapped."

She held his hand. The electricity shot into his nerves again. "I will help you, Edward. It's a promise."

Her smile reminded him of an old song by George Michael. Something about smiling like Jesus to a child. Yeah, corny, but Edward blamed the too-much Tylenol for this.

"Thank you," he said.

The door opened and Sheikh Essa came in with Dr. Fayazi and Zain. Hameed followed with another plate, with the same three dishes.

"So where we are going now?" Edward said when they all got settled.

"As I said before," Fayazi answered, "there is a hint in the letter of Ayatollah Seerazi about where the trusted object should be placed. It's not very clear, and I am not sure how your knowledge of Arabic is, but the language can be very vague if you want it to be."

"So what is the lead?"

Fayzi took a folded piece of paper from his pants pocket. He unfolded it and started reading. "I am trying to translate what I understood. It says here in the end of the letter: 'I had a premonition that the time to return the trust will be due soon. What belongs to his honorable position, is no longer to be held here. To return it to its home is the proper thing to do. To make it close to the downtrodden and the betrayed scion.'"

"The betrayed scion?" Edward frowned.

"It is a common description of Fatima, God's peace be upon her," Fayazi explained. "Given what she went through."

Edward did not fully grasp what that meant, but he had heard enough history lessons today. "So where does this lead us?"

Fayazi made a fairly big wrap of bread with olive oil and *Zaatar*. He took the first bite. "It sounded like it should be kept in a place related to Fatima."

"Fadak?" Zain said.

"Probably," Fayazi said, still chewing. "To be honest, it doesn't strike me as the first place related to Fatima. And Fadak is a large place, so unless he left some clues or a map, we will not be able to find it."

Edward slammed his forehead with his hand. How had he forgotten this! "Abdul Zahra's wounds had Arabic letters."

"What?" Zain and Fayazi said in unison.

"Oh, yes! I've seen them too!" Safiya shouted.

Zain shook his head violently. "Letters? There was —"

"Do you remember what letters you have seen exactly?" Fayazi asked, his eyes bulging like in those cartoons when the greedy man has dollar signs rolling in his eyes.

Edward asked for a pen and paper. Essa gave it to him from his drawer. Edward drew the letters as he remembered them with Safiya's help. Then he enclosed them in a box exactly as it was on Abdul Zahra's chest.

He handed the paper to Fayazi. Zain moved next to him and they both studied the drawings.

"You sure this is all?" Fayazi frowned, turning the paper upside down, trying to get a better perspective.

Edward nodded.

Safiya said, "Yes, it was exactly like this."

They passed it to Sheikh Essa. His face slackened as if he aged ten years.

"Ya, Allah." Essa exhaled. Essa stood and walked outside.

A minute later he came back, flipping the pages of an old book. "It's a talisman, I have seen it before." He flipped more pages. Then he turned the book in their direction. "Here it is, a protection talisman."

"I don't understand," Edward said.

"It's like a written prayer," the sheikh explained in Arabic. "You write it in a certain way and hold it with you to give you what you want, protection mainly. Some people think that it really works." Essa shook his head. "Complete nonsense." His voice was calm but the revulsion was there. "Protection should be asked from God through prayer and good deeds. Talk to him by your heart. Allah will listen. I feel sorry for those who still believes in talismans and other voodoo-like stuff."

Zain said something in Arabic; from the sound of it he agreed with the sheikh. Safiya snapped a reply that Zain did not like. In a minute, Fayazi, Zain, and Safiya were deep into a discussion that Edward didn't care to follow.

Edward turned to Sheikh Essa, who was listening to the heated discussion without much interest. He got closer to the old man and asked, "Sheikh Essa, is there anything else about this talisman? Why would someone put it on a dead man? Is it kind of a ritual…"

Sheikh Essa shook his head. "Not someone put it."

The realization came to Edward in one shot, buried him like an avalanche. Maybe it was there from the beginning, or maybe he saw it in the old man's hazel eyes. "He cut his own chest!" Edward whispered.

Essa nodded. "You heard Professor Fayazi: if Abdul Zahra was the keeper of Fadak, he must have seen or known something about the Musehaf. My guess is this is the only thing he managed to do before he died to tell us where the book is."

The image of Abdul Zahra's twisted face flashed up. He tried to imagine the man with a knife in hand, cutting those letters onto his chest. He tried to imagine the pain. But why choose this way? Couldn't he write a note, for example?

"So where does this clue lead us?" Edward asked, still recoiling from the idea of what Abdul Zahra must have gone through.

Sheikh Essa pushed the book to Edward, his thin finger pointing at a line right under a sketch of the talisman symbol. It was in Arabic, and maybe a hundred years old when printed by the old mechanical machines. It took him longer than usual to read. The pounding grew louder in his chest.

The talisman of lady Khadeeja.

"Who is she?" Edward asked, pointing at the name.

"The prophet's first and dearest wife," Essa said with a trembling voice. "A great woman by all standards." He paused. When he spoke again his voice trembled with sadness. "And also Fatima's mother."

-25-

Fayazi and Safiya were still immersed in the discussion about the talisman. Zain stood in the corner, talking on his cell phone.

"You found something?" Zain asked, ending the phone call in a hurry.

Before Edward could answer him, the door opened and Hameed peered in, his face white. "The police... are here," he said, out of breath. "They are... in front of the house knocking... on our neighbor's door asking for an American."

Edward's heart skipped a beat. How did they know where he was?

"We must leave," Fayazi said.

An urgent pounding came on the outside door.

"No way to run," Hameed said. "They are all over the street."

Fayazi gave Essa a pleading look, his face pale.

"There is a way," Essa said in a calm Arabic tone. "Take our guests to the roof, Hameed."

"But they will know, their car is parked in front of the house. We have enough trouble with the authorities —"

The Sheikh glared at his man-in-service. "They... are... our... guests."

Hameed motioned for them to follow. They all did except Fayazi. He went to Essa and hugged him. Edward heard him saying something in Arabic about this being "the second time."

A minute later, they were jumping from Essa's rooftop to his neighbor's. Edward and Zain carried Fayazi while Safiya jumped. After few minutes they were running out of the neighbor's house to the back street.

Hameed did not come with them. Zain took the lead. He told them he had a friend who lived a block away. In five minutes they reached the designated house. And before the sun rose they were in a beat-up Honda Civic Zain had borrowed from his friend.

"Where are we going now?" Edward asked, fumbling for the seatbelt. The way Zain drove, he would need it.

There were no streets — just spaces between the scattered houses. Zain kept veering the car violently left and right to avoid crashing as the way narrowed suddenly, often blocked by other houses. "Don't worry, I am familiar with the area," Zain grinned. He almost crashed head-on with another car. Zain turned at the last minute into a small alley to avoid the crash.

"You will kill us all!" Safiya yelled from the back seat.

Zain just sneered.

"Where are we going, Zain?" Edward repeated.

"I just want to leave the town. Meanwhile, it will be really nice if one of you figure out where should we go next, before I reach the highway."

"If we stay alive…" Dr. Fayazi said, holding the handle in the car's roof with both hands. "I think we should head back to Fadak."

"It's the only lead we have," Safiya added.

"Not really," Edward said. "I think we have something else." Edward briefed them. "Sheikh Essa says that this Talisman is also known as *Herz Khadeeja*."

"Oh my God!" Fayazi gasped.

"*Herz* means a protection talisman," Zain explained. "As Sheikh Essa said: grannies' myths, no more, no less."

"Oh, dear Fatima," Fayazi murmured, his finger toying with his lower lip, his gaze fixed on the empty space in front of him. Then the doctor snapped his fingers. "It makes perfect sense, can't you see? Seerazi's letter said that the documents must return to their original place. I was always under the assumption that it had to do with Fatima, but it could also perfectly apply to her mother, Khadeeja."

"Why Khadeeja?" Safiya asked.

Fayazi rubbed his face. "Although Khadeeja died when Fatima was only eight years old, Fatima shared more than her DNA with her mother."

Zain made another sudden turn that threw Safiya practically into the old doctor's lap.

She said, "You will draw attention to us by this stupid driving."

Zain fired back something in Arabic.

Fayazi ignored them both and continued, "The two women had shared the same great goal and both of them had made sacrifices that did not stop until their deaths."

Could Fatima's Musehaf turn out to be something that was passed to her from her mother? He remembered Essa's words about Khadeeja being the first wife of Mohammed. Did that mean anything? Maybe Mohammed had given her something that he did not trust anyone else to hold?

Then the unsettling thought crossed his mind, again. How could Abdul Zahra have been executed in the '60s? Edward asked, "Zain, how well do you know Abdul Zahra?"

"Very well." Zain's gaze still on the road, but his grip tightened on the wheel. "And yet sometimes I felt I didn't know him at all."

"Why?"

Zain just shook his head.

They passed an area where houses were made of mud. They were small, maybe just one room. A single piece of old cloth performed the function of both door and fence. Clothes of different colors and sizes hung outside most of the houses.

"So, Doctor," Edward said, still forming the question. "Do you think Abdul Zahra wanted to tell us about Khadeeja because he suspected the Musehaf was there or it was a way to tell us who killed him? I mean, even if he knew the location of the Musehaf, leaving a clue this way doesn't make sense. Unless he expected us to come looking for the Musehaf. Which I can't see how."

"So maybe he wasn't pointing to the Musehaf," Safiya said. "Maybe he was pointing to his killer... Somehow."

"Or," Edward said, "he didn't put those marks on his chest —his killer did."

"Can I ask a stupid question?" Zain said, speeding over the bumpy road, his gaze fixed on the rear view mirror.

Edward turned. Car headlights followed them. The police?

"If Abdul Zahra did that cutting to himself," Zain said. "Then who killed him?"

Great, back to square one with more questions. But whatever the case, this clue had to be followed.

Edward asked, "So, is there any shrine for Khadeeja?"

"Shrine?" Fayazi snickered.

"Maybe he means a *palace*." Zain sneered. "Khadeeja's palace."

Why the sudden sarcastic attitude? For an important person such as the prophet's first wife, there should be some sort of shrine like that of the prophet himself in Madeena or other Muslims' shrines around the world.

"Oh, my friend," Zain said. "Some great minds here decided that the only thing this great woman deserves is a flat tomb in a neglected cemetery in Mecca."

"You can't get enough of criticism, can you?" Safiya muttered.

Two cars were following them now, closing in.

"I am afraid Zain is right, at least this time," Fayazi said, the way a father explains to his daughter why her brother was right. "You see, despite the fact that all Muslims agree that Khadeeja was the first to believe in Mohammed, along with his cousin Ali, the first to support him in spreading the religion, the only thing she got from this nation is a shameful tomb without her name on the stone."

Zain veered into a narrow passage between the houses, then into another one. He killed the engine and switched off the lights. Behind them, not too far from where they were hiding, two police cars passed.

"Were they following us?" Zain started the car again, watching the police taillights in the distance and turning in the opposite direction.

"Did you say it's in Mecca?" Edward asked, almost hearing the gears in his brain shifting to calculate the distance, transforming kilometers into miles, and KM per hour to MPH. "But that's another city, isn't it?"

"Yep." Zain wiggled his thick black eyebrows. He pressed on the gas, giving the car a shove forward. "And if we want to be there fast enough, you have to stop whining about my driving."

-26-

<Al Hayett town – Saudi Arabia>
<Time left until Zero hour is 18hrs:00min>
<Number of infected websites: 240,124>

Adnan stayed at the local police station in Al-Hayett. He considered going back to the police headquarters at Madeena, but his thirty-year policeman's instinct told him otherwise. During his professional life, Adnan had seen hundreds of cases. During the last nine years when he was heading the police force at Madeena, Adnan was personally involved in only a few investigations. Understandable; the higher the position, the less the work. The last case was a standard sexual assault.

Standard meant the offender was a local male, between thirty and fifty years old, and the victim was a female, often an expatriate. One of many cases police officers came across that never got published. The only reason he got involved was because the first one was a group of young Saudis, kidnapping a Palestinian college student and repeatedly raping her for five days before she managed to escape. The girl's father worked as a manager in a Saudi bank and was a friend of one of the bank owners. The investigation was short. Although the girl never saw the rapists as they kept blinders on her eyes, she was able to identify the villa and then the five young Saudis from their voices.

The case was closed after an agreement between the families of the young men and the girl's father, paying him to drop the charges. Adnan also remembered the real reason why the father agreed to drop the charges —threats of charging his daughter with prostitution and hence expelling the father and his family from Saudi.

But tonight's case was totally different. He had heard a lot about cases that changed the careers of the officers in charge. Adnan had seen incompetent men climb high up the ladder due to a single case they handled well. Read, they pleased the right people. He also knew some good men who lost their careers because of a single mistake. If he could consider one thing to be his real training, it would be the words of his former boss.

"If you want to survive in this job you have to know the key to success," the former head of police of Madeena told young Lieutenant Adnan, fifteen years ago.

"Keep the streets safe, Sir?" the naive Adnan replied.

"To please the right people."

That was the wisdom of an old police officer. An advice his boss did not follow himself six years later when he refused to drop the case of a female child who was found brutally murdered. After two weeks of investigation the murderer was found, but never was brought to justice. His boss was fired the next day and Adnan was assigned as the new chief of police.

The murderer was one of the right people, who obviously was not pleased by the result of the investigation.

Adnan walked silently into the old police station building, both hands behind his back, flanked by his assistant Sami and the officer in charge of the local police. From their edgy attitudes, both men probably assumed he was conducting one of his routine checks on police stations.

He wasn't. Adnan tried to solve a puzzle. Who were the right people to please in this situation? He had a murdered activist, whatever that meant, who happened to be a pain in the neck for the past two decades because of his roots in the society. The murder couldn't happen at a worse time. Recent reports predicted the probability of civil unrest because of some Internet message that had been circulated for the past two weeks.

Normally, investigation helped ease the tension when the case turned out to be some old revenge. Instead, Adnan had a high-ranking intelligence officer watching over his shoulder, first telling him to drop the investigation, then trying to push him to accuse two Americans. And just to make things messier, one of those Americans had a princess from the royal family on his side, trying to help him find the other American, who was the main suspect.

What a circus. No matter what he decided to do, he was screwed. Adnan sighed, looking at the detention area. Five people were there. He could hear in the background the voice of the officer in charge, giving him quick information on everyone's charges. Adnan couldn't be less interested.

The walkie-talkie his assistant held crackled. Sami held it closer to his ear and talked. Adnan pretended not to listen.

When he finished, Sami cleared his throat and relayed the news reluctantly. "Sir, the American escaped again."

Adnan nodded. "And Her Highness?"

"They found her car parked in front of the house but no sign of her either."

"Why is she doing this?" Adnan murmured, mostly to himself.

"One of my men heard something, Sir,"

Adnan motioned to Sami to walk with him. When they were alone in the corridor, Adnan told him to speak.

"The princess was talking to her driver," Sami said in a low, conspiratorial voice. "The driver asked her why she didn't tell him who she was."

"By *him*, you mean the American?"

"I think so, Sir. Then her highness told the driver that if he can't remember her, she would win his heart — again."

"Win his heart again?" Adnan frowned. "What the hell is this? The Princess and the Frog?"

"Sir." Sami scratched his head. "I think this American guy somehow forgot about her, and she will help him remember her. It's a different plot than... er... you know, The Princess and the Frog."

Adnan squinted at the tall officer. Sami shrunk. "And who the fuck are you? Walt Disney?"

"Sorry, Sir,"

"Then stop fooling around and go get me that frog... shit... American... get me that American."

Damn you, Walt Disney.

Sami did the military salute and was about to turn around but stopped. "Sir, there is one more thing."

"What?"

"Our medical examiner took a quick look at Abdul Zahra's body after we brought him here." Sami paused.

Fahad's instructions were clear that the body should be buried immediately even without the consent of Abdul Zahra's family.

Adnan motioned to his assistant to continue.

"He is almost sure that the death was not caused by the knife wounds. He will need some time with the body to give the exact cause of death."

He left it hanging but the question was obvious: Should they proceed with the investigations or just follow Fahad's instructions?

"How long does he need to do the autopsy?"

"Maybe three hours if we push him," Sami replied, looking at his watch.

Adnan nodded again. "Where is Fahad now?"

"He is taking a nap at my office, Sir. He told me to awake him an hour from now, 7 exactly."

Adnan allowed a faint smile. "The man is tired, he was awake all night. It would be rude to wake him. Is that clear?"

"Yes, Sir."

"I will need an office here," Adnan commanded, clapping his hands the way one does when sitting in a Shisha café, ready to order. "We have lot of work to do."

-27-

<Somewhere between Mecca and Madeena– Saudi Arabia>
<Time left until Zero hour is 17hrs:30min>
<Number of infected websites: 245,154>

"We're wasting our time," Edward said after a long silence. He wasn't sure if Fayazi and Safiya were still awake. "I doubt that they will take Kim to Mecca."

"It's the only thing we can do right now," Zain said in English.

"Actually there is one more thing," Fayazi murmured, his eyes still closed.

When he didn't elaborate, Edward asked, "What is that?"

"Majida had a fiancé, a young teacher in the University of Technology. I guess he works in the labs or something. Anyway, he lives in Mecca."

"So why we don't call him right now and ask him if he heard from Majida?"

Fayazi grinned. "Let's say he is not crazy about me. Besides, it is still too early for a phone call."

As if to emphasize, Fayazi pointed at the window. Over a sea of endless orange sand, the sun started to rise. Its red light reflected on a sheet of flimsy clouds that looked like pink cotton candy in the dark blue sky. Edward had seen a lot of sunrises, and this wasn't the most spectacular one. Yet something about the colors of the sand and the sky, the glistening mirage in the horizon, the retreating darkness giving way to the light, made him smile. Not a smile of joy or happiness, rather — and as corny as it might sound— one of hope.

"So we just pop in at his place?" Edward asked.

"He lives in a condo very close to here. The next exit would be good, as a matter of fact."

"Thanks for letting me know," Zain moved the car into the right lane.

It was 6:00 AM when he got the second call yesterday. Half of the forty-eight hours had elapsed. They had uploaded all the documents to the FTP site as instructed. Would the kidnappers be true to their word? Edward didn't count on that, so he and Abbie had prepared a plan. A long shot but it could work. He took out his cell phone and called her.

"You realize that there is a nine-hour time difference," Abbie said, picking up the phone after the first ring.

"You aren't asleep."

"I could be."

"With Kim kidnapped, and me and Vane here looking for her? I doubt it."

"Okay, what do you want?"

"Any luck with the website?"

The agreement was that Abbie would try hacking into the FTP site the kidnapper gave them. Then she'd monitor all the incoming connections to see where the kidnapper would connect to download the documents.

"No. Security measures are good there."

He nodded silently. She had explained to him that hacking a website was not as easy as movies kept showing. Only in certain cases when security measures were light, or there was a software bug, could a website be hacked and only after proper planning.

"Even if I was able to hack the website, chances are they'd use VPN connections so I couldn't trace them."

"I know." He didn't know what the VPN was but it sounded like something untraceable. Maybe a VIP-like connection. "I just hoped we could do something to track them."

"Who said we didn't?" She giggled.

"Sheesh, Abbie, don't play games with me."

"Relax, big boy, I had a better idea and I think they took the bait already."

"So, did we find anything on them?"

"Not y..e..t," Abbie said. "But don't worry, there's a good chance we will."

He could do nothing about it now. Edward thanked her and they hung up.

"Any good news?" Safiya asked him mid-yawn. She was just waking.

"Not really, we have given them what they wanted and we're still waiting." The anxiety in his voice surprised him. He had little hope about this. But still, it was a thin strand of hope that was snapped.

"I don't understand one thing," Zain said, adjusting the rear-view mirror to see Safiya. "If those people in the black GMC were from the religious police, why you cannot check with one of your contacts to verify this."

For the first time, Zain addressed Safiya without the sarcastic tone.

"I am trying to do that," Safiya said. She too sounded normal. "But, and I know how this will sound, being a princess doesn't mean that I can do miracles. A woman is a second-class citizen here. Edward, you saw how this guy from the special forces talked to me."

Edward nodded. True. And he had sensed how defeated she felt when she talked to the man.

"If anything," Safiya said, looking the other way, facing the window, "I am the most helpless of you all. At least there is no bunch of jerks waiting for your slightest mistake."

-28-

Minutes later they were driving in a desert area filled with buildings under construction. Only a handful of these buildings were ready to be inhabited.

White buses were parked all along the street. Edward watched in curiosity as hundreds of men in blue jumpsuits queued in endless lines starting from the buses and ending up in some sort of a security checkpoint in front of each building.

Although most of the activity was on the right side of the two-lane street, Zain had to reduce speed considerably, while driving to the address scribbled on the small paper Fayazi had handed over to him.

Two workers crossed the street in front of the car. Zain slammed on the brakes, barely missing them. Everyone in the car jolted forward. Zain fumed. One of the men stared at them. The worker had dark brown skin, his blue suit was dirty, covered with small black stains around the hands and legs. A once-red towel was wrapped on top of the man's head, apparently for protection from the sun. The man's gaze met Edward's for a split second. His eyes were bloodshot; his expression was dull and disinterested. And for that split second Edward had the feeling

150

that the man did not really care if he got crushed under a vehicle or died of dehydration while working in that dreadful heat.

When the car finally moved, Zain let out a long breath, "I am sorry. But I... I don't feel well."

After a while, Zain pointed at a ten-story white building with red stripes. "I think it's this building."

He managed to find a place to park. They got out and started stretching.

"Is it okay if we all go up?" Edward asked.

Fayazi shrugged. "I am not dying to see this arrogant bastard. But I think I have to go with you."

Safiya and Zain exchanged looks as if they wondered whether they could stand being left alone together.

Then Fayazi waved his hand. "Oh, come on, the more of us the better the fun."

So they went.

An Indian security guard wearing a blue uniform with golden rings on both his thumbs, asked them with a heavy accent where they wanted to go. Zain answered gruffly that they were going to apartment 501. The man nodded left and right, and let them in with an apologetic smile.

They were in front of the elevator when his cell phone buzzed. Edward looked at the caller ID. Abbie. He pressed the answer button.

"I forget to tell you," she said, chewing on gum so loudly Edward felt it in his ears. "Regarding that thing you asked me to investigate."

He was in the lift now with the rest of them. Zain pressed on the button for the fifth floor. The door started closing.

"Which one?" he asked. There were lots of things he had asked Abbie to investigate recently.

"What? Ed, I can't hear you!" Abbie shouted.

"I am in the lift now, I will call you once I am out!" he yelled back as if talking loudly would solve the problem.

"Whatever." Abbie's voice became distorted. "I just wanted to tell you that the rumor on the Net is that someone is hiring —"

Her voice broke up again. The dotted LED panel indicated the second floor.

Edward sighed. "I can't hear you. I'll call you later."

He was about to press the end call button when Abbie's voice came in clear. "Someone is hiring zombies."

The call was disconnected. What the hell was that supposed to mean? Probably nothing. Despite being a computer genius and good at almost any task given to her, Abbie was sort of a lunatic when it came to her theories about conspiracies of the underworld. Her favorite one was that Vane was a real vampire. She also had other interesting theories, such as the U.S. government was run by aliens, and that Bin Laden was cloning his mujahedeen in the Afghanistan mountains... well, the last one probably explained the number of brainless suicidal bombers.

When the lift opened, they found themselves standing in front of apartment 501. Edward looked with hesitation at Safiya who turned to Zain, who passed the bucket to Fayazi.

"What?" Fayazi said. "One of you has to ring the bell. I am sorry but if you want to get anything useful out of this man, it's better that someone else do the talking."

"Shy?" Safiya teased.

Fayazi grimaced. "Shy of this ignorant extremist? No way."

The apartment door was slightly ajar. Edward rang the bell.

Zain took a step back, his Adam's apple bouncing up and down. "It's open!"

Safiya pushed the door open. The room looked like a bomb had exploded inside. Chairs were knocked down, the contents of the only cupboard thrown on the floor. Books and papers and notebooks, tens of them, were scattered on the floor.

"*Ya Allah!*" Fayazi exclaimed with horror-filled eyes.

No one moved.

Edward stepped on the pile of papers toward the bedroom on the right. His mind flashed back to his old days of training. He should take a gun and sweep the apartment, tip-toeing from one room to another, beckoning for his companions to follow him, and probably do a couple of rollovers Sean-Connery style. That always impressed the girls.

Edward opened the bedroom door. Safiya shrieked behind him. She covered her mouth and started weeping. Edward involuntarily took her in his arms and held her so she would not see.

In front of them, tied to a chair, half naked in the bedroom was a young man with blood and bruises covering his face and upper torso. His face contorted in the same agonized way Abdul Zahra's was. The upper right part of his head was missing. Dark red blood and a white substance were splattered on the nearby wall.

Edward's stomach rolled.

"We have to leave," Zain said. "Right now."

Ten minutes later, they were sitting in the car again driving toward Mecca.

No one spoke a word.

-29-

Safiya was still weeping in the back seat next to him. They changed seats so Fayazi sat in the front next to Zain, who silently drove away from the condominium area.

"We should have searched the apartment," Edward said. "We might have found something."

"You mean more brain matter on the floor!" Zain fired back. "For God's sake, Edward, someone had tortured and killed that guy in cold blood. What makes you think they will not come after us?"

Safiya jolted at the brain-matter remark. She had seen two dead bodies in one day. Too much for any normal person.

"Please pull over," Safiya said in a choking voice.

Zain parked in the emergency lane. The princess ran to nearby bushes, throwing off the head cover. Edward's heart plunged. He was the one who dragged them all into this. He, too, needed fresh air. Edward stepped out of the car and walked aimlessly. The old doctor joined him.

"What do you reckon happened there?" Fayazi asked, watching Safiya from distance.

"I am afraid there's only one explanation," Edward said. "It doesn't make sense but it's the only thing I have." A big truck passed on the highway. They waited for the noise to subside.

Fayazi rubbed his chin. "The kidnappers are thinking the same way we are."

"But this man has nothing to do with the Musehaf. I don't see why they killed him."

Fayazi plucked his lower lip. "Maybe someone else did. Maybe it has nothing to do with all of this."

No, it had to be connected.

"What if we were wrong from the beginning?" Edward took a deep breath, filling his lungs with the fresh air. "What if the whole thing was not about this legendary Musehaf. What if it was from day one about Majida, your student, or her fiancé."

Fayazi made a face. "Majida? I can't see how."

"What if her fiancé was working on research that upset someone."

Fayazi sneered. "Who, Omer? No way. You remember when I told you we don't like each other?"

Edward nodded.

Fayazi leaned closer, almost whispering, "It's not polite to talk bad about the dead, but this man was a narrow-minded Wahhabi. An extremist that will make Abu Ayob look like a liberal."

"Who is this Abu Ayob?"

Fayazi shrugged. "A leader of the Al-Qaeda in Iraq. The man is suspected of being responsible for more than three hundred beheadings personally."

"And Majida's fiancé was worse?"

"Maybe that is an exaggeration on my part." Fayazi raised his hands. "I once had a discussion with him in which he blamed me for criticizing an Ottoman Sultan who had mass murdered twelve hundred Shia civilians in one big massacre during the Nineteenth Century."

"So you don't think that he was up to something that got him killed?"

Fayazi chuckled, shaking his big head. "How to put it? Let's say he was floating with the current."

Safiya came back, her face yellow, her eyes swollen.

"Are you okay?" he asked her.

Edward Fleming, master of witty remarks.

She gave him a wry smile. "Better." Then, "I need to ask you something, Doctor Fayazi."

"Sure." Fayazi smiled dubiously.

Edward excused himself and went back to the car, despite Safiya's assurance that this was not a personal matter.

When he reached the Honda Civic, Zain was talking on the phone with his face turned the other way. He didn't notice Edward approaching.

"*La Astatee' Alan.*" (I cannot now) Zain said. "*Yajeb An Urakebahum.*"

Edward's jaw fell. If he was not mistaken, Zain was saying: "I have to watch them."

-30-

<Mecca borders– Saudi Arabia>
<Time left until Zero hour is 15hrs:00min>
<Number of infected websites: 335,450>

Edward remained silent for the rest of the trip to Mecca. He chose the seat right behind Zain to avoid looking at him. Otherwise his emotions would surely betray him and make Zain aware of what he had overheard.

It all made sense now. How the police managed to track them to Nakheela to Sheikh Essa's house. And why Majida's fiancé was killed. Zain must have been working against them from the beginning. He'd had a nagging feeling all day about Zain. Something about him was unsettling. A fine line existed between not being paranoid and being careless. Edward might have erred on the careless part.

They passed the checkpoint. Edward had heard a lot of warnings and stories about non-Muslims not being allowed in

Mecca and Medina, the two holy cities in Saudi. But as he had guessed, no one was checking.

Mecca was a strange city, looking as if built on a mountain. No, not a mountain... hills. A group of scattered, red-rocked hills that gave the entire city an eerie look. The buildings varied from one to fifty stories in an area that Zain had pointed to as *ALHARAM*. Which was where the holy Kaaba was located.

The morning sun burst from behind the reddish hills, unmercifully burning even at this early hour. Old and dusty cars drove in the semi-deserted streets. Zain explained that Mecca's economy was based on the Haj season. Around two million Muslims come to do the Haj every year. Aside from that event, which lasted for ten days, the economy depended upon Umra.

"It is similar to Haj but easier, faster, and it can be done any time in the year," Zain explained. "This is the off-season for Mecca."

"So why do Muslims do Haj, not Umra?" Edward asked, trying to sound normal. "I mean why do they all rush to do it in the peak season when they can do it any time of the year?"

Fayazi took this one. "Haj is a key part of Islam, a spiritual trip like no other. It is one of the five pillars Islam is based on. Salat, which is the daily prayer, is another pillar, for example."

Fayazi gave him a crash course on the other pillars and how each one participates in forming the character of the true Muslim. Edward couldn't pay attention. Should he focus on finding the Musehaf and Kimberly, or escape from whoever wanted him dead or the police? Or watch Zain? His mind kept flashing "Overload Warning" every now and then.

Fayazi finished, with a sarcastic remark that most Muslims were not making use of this wonderful teaching and had lost the real meaning behind the acts of worship.

Edward replied with a thoughtful, "Oh," happy that he did not miss any critical information.

Or so he thought.

At a highway overpass, Zain pointed to a deserted piece of land, saying it was the historical cemetery of Mecca.

Edward saw nothing but nodded anyway. The more he scrutinized what Zain was probably doing, the more contradictory it appeared. For example, Zain was probably the one who tipped the police about their whereabouts. But what about Zain's arguments with the police to get his boss's body? And his resentment against the authorities, not to mention that Zain was the one who helped him escape by giving Edward his car. Zain was also the one who led them to Essa's house, and who kept accusing the religion police of being behind everything. It could be an act, of course. Edward had seen people with acting skills that would make Tom Hanks retire. Still, it didn't add up.

He pondered his next move. Should he confront Zain? But if Zain were watching them for some group he worked for or the police, confronting him would just complicate things. He might be armed. Or he might signal them somehow. Too risky. Maybe he could use Zain to get information about the people he worked for.

They drove through an old industrial area. The highest building nearby was three stories. A small bakery that had once been white was now ash-gray. What caught his attention were two doors at the front of the shop. A big one with a big sign in Arabic saying, "Entrance," and a smaller one that looked pretty much like a service door, with a sign that read "For Women."

"A separate entrance for women?" Edward scowled, talking to himself.

"You have seen nothing." Safiya sneered.

Zain turned back with a wide grin. "Hey, sarcastic criticizing is *my* forte."

"Try to be faster next time." Safiya stuck out her tongue teasingly.

Fayazi chuckled. "You two have to fight even when you agree on something, don't you?"

Zain parked and killed the engine. They all got out. The highway overpass they just passed was now above them. To their left was a big traffic circle with palm trees in the middle. To the right was a long brick wall.

Zain pointed at the fence. "This is the cemetery where all the prophet's companions who died in Mecca were buried."

They walked alongside the fence for five minutes. The air felt as if someone had turned on a giant hair dryer. Finally they reached an area where the brick wall ended and was replaced by an iron fence. Through the bars, they could see inside the deserted graveyard.

The same empty area of sand Edward saw from the highway overpass stretched in front of them. Where were the graves and the gold-plated domes Muslims were famous for?

A gate of rusted metal formed the only entrance to the cemetery. In front of it stood a group of Pakistani pilgrims. Around twenty men and women all wearing white clothes, all sweating, all reading from small books they carried tightly as if a favorite stuffed animal. A man stood in the middle, reading out loud in what sounded like chanting.

"What are they doing?" Edward asked. He couldn't help noticing the dagger-like glares from two bearded men on the other side of the gate inside the cemetery. Clearly they were upset by whatever the Pakistanis were doing.

"They are performing the visit ceremonies," Fayazi replied, looking at the large sandy area behind the fence with subdued eyes.

Zain said, "Muslims, at least some of them, believe that the souls of people — and especially good people — do not die with the body and the dead can hear and see us." His eyes were moist. "That's why we pay respect to our great ancestors as if they were alive."

Safiya frowned. "That is not Islam. Dead are dead."

"Really?" Fayazi arched a bushy eyebrow. "So why do all the Muslims in their prayers address the prophet with a long phrase of Salam?"

Safiya frowned.

Fayazi added, "You might say it's nonsense, fine. But please do not say it's not Islam. Believing in life after death is key in Islam. And we keep the connection alive with the nation's leaders by those rituals."

"Stop! You infidels!" one of the two bearded men shouted at the Pakistani group. He wore a short white dishdash and his beard was messy, as if he had an electric shock. "You filthy pagans, whom are you talking to?"

The other guard talked in Arabic to the group. Edward heard the word *Mushrik* and *Kafer* several times.

"We need to get in," Fayazi finally said, looking at Safiya.

She nodded, biting her lower lip. Safiya took a long breath and strode to the gate. The princess exchanged words with the two men, then showed them her ID. Their expressions shifted from anger to revulsion to surprise and then to fear. Better.

Safiya turned and motioned for them to follow. The bearded guards opened the gate and stood aside. The four of them went inside, followed by envying looks from the Pakistani group.

-31-

Edward called Abbie. It was around midnight back in DC, but he needed her.

"Boss, thank God you called." She called him Boss. Something was wrong. "I've been trying to call you for the past half an hour with no luck."

"Yeah, about that." He wasn't sure how to start this. "Abbie, you mentioned something about zombies…"

"Y..e..s,"

"Well, we were just going to see this guy, Majida's fiancé, and his head—"

"Who's Majida?"

"It doesn't matter, you see, the thing is… Abbie, we found his brain splattered on the wall." He felt stupid.

"What do you mean?"

"Well… he looked like someone shot him in the head, but then I remembered what you said about someone hiring zombies and I thought—"

"What!" She let out a laugh. "You thought… because of his brain… and you call *me* silly." More laughing.

Edward rolled his eyes. "I'm glad I made you laugh, Abbie. Now, tell me what did you mean when you said someone was hiring zombies?"

Zain and Safiya signaled him to follow them inside the cemetery, he did.

"I can't imagine you thought I was talking about real zombies... That's really rich."

"Abbie."

"Okay, Scooby Doo, zombies are another word for bots." Abbie said.

"Ah, that explains everything. What are bots, Abbie?"

"Gee... you never watched *The Transformers*... The *autobots*?"

"Tattoo me ignorant."

"Sheesh, zombie is the best word to describe them. I'll talk in simple terms."

"The sacrifices you make..."

"Yeah, yeah... Anyway, first, forget about all the nonsense you see in movies about hacking into computers. That's just ridiculous, I mean, come on, a guy hacks into the traffic system while he is driving and turns all lights green. What a crap —"

"Abbie, please."

"Okay, okay, imagine you are a computer hacker, right? You hacked into someone's computer and now you have full control over the computer, right?"

"Right." He had a million questions about how to hack into someone's computer, but better not to interrupt.

"Now, you can command this bot, this zombie, this hacked computer, to launch attacks at other computers."

"Really?"

The two bearded men closed the rusty iron gate behind them. It made an awful screeching sound.

"Yeah, really, and after a while, you will have an army of zombies all controlled by you."

"I thought only Michael Jackson had an army of zombies."

"Yeah, very funny. Now professional hackers do this for money: they control hundreds of computers, personal computers like yours, and they hire them out."

Safiya signaled that they were waiting for him to come. He followed.

"*Hire* them? You mean if someone took control of my computer he can rent, um… its services to another person, who will ask my device to launch attacks at someone else."

"Pretty much, yes."

"That's sucks." He frowned. "So, when you said someone was hiring zombies you meant…"

"Thirteen thousands bots were hired last week. Someone is really up to something big."

"How big?"

Abbie took some time then answered, "With ten zombies, I can bring down a small newspaper website. Just to give you an example. But the scenarios are unlimited. It's just that the number is so scary. I never even knew there were thirteen thousands zombies around. It looks like a fucking cyber world war."

-32-

<Mecca – Saudi Arabia>
<Time left until Zero hour is 14hrs:00min>
<Number of infected websites: 406,013>

The narrow pavement took them through the sandy area in the cemetery. Edward turned left and right but all he could see was the high fence surrounding them. The place was quiet, but not that dreadful silence of a cemetery. Another kind of silence, another feeling. All sounds were muted. No birds, no wind, not even the noise from the street and the nearby highway. As if they were engulfed in a cocoon that wrapped this place in stillness. His heart clutched by a strange feeling of sadness. It sounded corny, but when he glanced at Safiya, he could almost swear the same gloomy feeling had crossed her heart.

The pavement cut the land into two halves, inclining to another sandy area on a small dune. Pieces of rocks were scattered everywhere in the sand. He first thought it was just garbage, especially with all the plastic bags here and there. But as he followed Zain and the rest of the group through the narrow aisle, he started noticing the pattern.

Dear Lord! Those scattered rocks *were* the tombstones. There were no markings of any kind. Nothing to indicate where the graves started and ended. Remains of demolished walls gave the impression that this once was a big structure, a shrine probably. Now it was stones and plastic bags and dirt. One rock per grave. One rock per person.

Zain took them across another small pavement, which went up on the mound. They all followed. Fayazi had difficulty walking so Zain helped him. They stopped before reaching the top of the dune. In front stretched another sandy area with twenty stones scattered around.

"Is that *it*?" Edward said, the disappointment echoed in his voice.

Zain nodded, his face more solemn than before if that were possible. Fayazi used his cane to bend and sit on the pavement. His mouth wide open as if frozen mid-gasp, his gaze fixed on the stones in front of them, he looked as if just took a heavy punch in the guts — maybe overwhelmed by the humiliation the place had gone through.

Fayazi and Zain motioned toward the area where Khadeeja's tomb was marked by a small gray rock.

The professor's chapped lips quivered. His brown eyes were moist and in a sad whisper he talked to the thin air above the grave.

Edward exchanged a puzzled look with Safiya. She shrugged.

"She was the wealthiest woman in Mecca," Fayazi said, wiping tears from his eyes, his voice barely audible. "A respectable business woman. Arabs never saw anyone like her." The doctor let out a long exhale, holding his cane with both hands now, his gaze following a sheet of paper the wind pushed in front of him. It looked like a magazine cover. "The merchants in Syria and Yemen who had conducted business with Khadeeja described her as a savvy and trustworthy businesswoman who managed to build a fortune that was more than the sum of all the merchants in Mecca."

"Wow, that rich?" Safiya said.

Fayazi nodded with a wry smile. "She asked Mohammed to lead one of her caravans to Syria, justifying that with Mohammad's reputation of an honest merchant. Her real reason was different though. Khadeeja had ordered one of her men to keep a close eye on Mohammed and report every single move he made. When the caravan was back, the man reported that he never encountered anyone as honest as Mohammed in his life. A few days later, Khadeeja asked Mohammed to marry her."

Edward frowned. "I thought the society was as conservative as nowadays."

"It was," Fayazi replied, extending his hand to Edward to help him stand up. Edward did. Fayazi went on, "What Khadeeja did was unprecedented. She justified it by saying Mohammed was an unprecedented man."

"Sure he was. He was the prophet, after all," Edward said.

Fayazi gave him a scolding look as if Edward admitted to drinking from the toilet. "That was ten years *before* he was chosen as a prophet."

"Oh."

"Mohammad had developed a habit of going to the nearby mountains for meditation. One night he returned earlier than normal, confused. He told Khadeeja that he had seen Gabriel, the Archangel, informing him that he was chosen as a prophet."

Fayazi stepped carefully around the area where the tomb lay, examining every inch with intense care. Was he looking for a clue, for the hiding place of the Musehaf? But where?

"That night, Khadeeja talked to her husband. From the first moment, he knew what burden he was given. The responsibility, the difficulty of his mission, the danger. Mohammad was a wise man and he could see how his people would react. Paganism was not only a religion, it was the way the economy of Mecca had established itself throughout the past ten centuries. People came to Mecca to worship the stone statues of gods that were brought to Kaaba earlier in history."

"And Khadeeja was the one who encouraged him," Safiya said, maybe just to say that she knew something.

"Encourage is an understatement for what Khadeeja did." Fayazi shook his head, lifting the small gray rock carefully and looking underneath it. Nothing there.

"Khadeeja was one of two persons Mohammed credited with the spread of Islam. His word was that Islam would not have been spread without the money of Khadeeja and the protection of Abi Talib, Ali's father and Mohammed's uncle."

Fayazi stood, the lines in his forehead more prominent. He scanned the wide area of sand, searching for something he didn't find. The old man cocked his head, raising his index finger. Then said in monotone as if talking to himself, "It's actually very interesting how those two ended up."

"What do you mean?" Zain asked.

"After eight years, Khadeeja had spent her last penny to survive the boycott forced by Mecca's leaders who wanted to put pressure on Mohammed and his clan that protected him. During the boycott, both Abi Taleb and Khadeeja died."

A long-bearded man with an ankle-length dishdash and red head cover came nearby, looking curiously at them. Safiya turned and waved dismissively. He walked away.

"Khadeeja's death shook Mohammed. His words describing her were full of sorrow, longing, and acknowledgement of her support. He called that year the year of sorrows. Soon after, he left Mecca with a broken heart, heading to Madeena where he established Islam's first city. You see, even now, the society in Saudi in general is very violent against women. Mohammed's love for Khadeeja was something they couldn't fathom. He didn't marry another when she was alive. He cherished her, respected her, and loved her in a way Arabs never fully understood."

Zain's cell rang. He picked it up and walked away. Edward watched him. He wished he had Vane's sensitive ears now. Vane could probably hear the man on the other end of the call.

"Abi Taleb's protective rule was replaced by his son, Ali. And Fatima did the encouragement that her mother used to do."

Edward tried to focus on Zain's expressions, at the same time keeping pace with the conversation.

"Abi Taleb was branded a pagan in today's Muslim culture." Fayazi gestured to the piece of land next to them. "Khadeeja... well... you can see how she is being treated. For God's sake, is that a tomb for the first woman in Islam?"

"This is not accurate," Safiya protested. "It is not personal against Khadeeja, it is just the Wahhabi ideology of demolishing all the tombs."

"Is that so?" Fayazi arched an eyebrow. "Would you please explain why Mohammed's shrine is as big as this entire cemetery?"

"That is different," Safiya murmured.

"Don't you think Mohammed would want his wife to be included in whatever that exception is?"

Safiya shrugged giving him a don't-ask-me look.

"But what did Fatima have to do with all of this?" Edward asked, finally remembering why they came here.

"Fatima had a unique connection to her mother," Fayazi explained. "History tells us about Khadeeja saying that from the instant she was pregnant with Fatima, she could hear her daughter talking to her. She said that she started seeing things differently, and experienced a series of supernatural revelations. When she was born, Fatima followed in her mother's footsteps of supporting Mohammed. As a child, Fatima would go with him when he was going to pray in *Kaaba*, in order to wipe off the dirt people threw at her father."

"That was in the early days of Mohammed's movement, right?" Edward asked, trying to imagine how the situation looked back then. Mohammed was not a popular man after he claimed that he was a messenger of God. And how must Fatima have felt, seeing her father being treated this way by his people? What did her parents tell her when she asked them why people threw dirt on her father? Did she realize that her parents were following a different religion? Did they ever tell her that her father was a messenger of God?

Unlikely, Edward concluded based on his readings about Fatima.

Fayazi nodded. "Fatima was as exceptional as a child as she was when she grew up. On several occasions, she used to talk to her father, lifting his spirits and reminding him of the greater cause. That it was his responsibility to stop the enslavement of people, to establish equality between men and women. That all prophets before him had gone through such ordeals."

So much for his readings.

"Fatima was described by her family as her father's mother, referring to the way she used to take care of Mohammed. What history has saved from conversations between the daughter and the father leaves no doubt about who tutored Fatima. Khadeeja took the matter of supporting Islam and Mohammed as her goal in life. And Khadeeja left her daughter with this heritage."

A strong wind blew sand in their direction. Fayazi paused, waiting for the wind to subside. When it did, he continued, "Fatima pushed the envelope even further, as you Americans say. Fatima participated in the wars with her father. She was the one whom Mohammed saw last when he left the house and greeted first when he got back. Fatima was brought up to carry the message of Islam, to help the poor, to feed the orphans, and this is what people often miss when they study her early life."

"There is nothing here..." Zain said, coming up from behind.

"How are you so sure?" Edward asked.

"Unless you want to dig in the ground, I don't see where a book could be hidden here."

That was exactly what Edward thought. A lot of sand. A lot of unmarked graves. The Musehaf could be hidden anywhere.

Fayazi put a hand on Edward's shoulder. "Even if the people here have disrespected this great woman by obscuring her grave and neglecting it, there is no way a man who had a drop of love for Mohammed in his heart would dare to dig a hole next to his wife's grave."

Zain and Safiya agreed. Edward had to give up.

As they prepared to leave, Fayazi and Zain faced the tomb and almost kneeled, in some kind of a salute. Safiya watched them, then did likewise.

They all headed back. Even then they had to follow Zain so as not to lose their way through the maze of pavement.

Hmmm. Edward asked Safiya, "How difficult was it getting us inside?"

Safiya broke a charming smile. "You mean what were your chances of getting in here without me?" She put her finger on her chin, pretending to think about it. "Slightly more difficult than impossible, and I am not bragging."

He believed her. Zain was a few steps ahead, talking with Fayazi. "I don't trust him," Edward whispered.

Safiya's pretty face clouded with concern. Edward quickly filled her in on what he overheard Zain saying on the phone. She nodded slowly. "But he—"

Edward knew what she was about to say. It didn't make sense. But he had another reason to suspect Zain now. So he waited until they were outside the cemetery gate, then pulled Zain by the shoulder. "It's over, Zain."

"What... hey, man, what's wrong with you?" Zain pushed Edward's hand away.

Edward tightened his grip on Zain's collar. "I know about you."

"What are you *talking* about?" Zain's eyes moved left and right. Cornered.

"I heard you talking to someone, saying that you want to watch our moves."

Zain shook his head.

Edward told them about his suspicions. Fayazi and Safiya said nothing. Another group of pilgrims went by, all looking at the angry tall American holding a young Arab in a driver's uniform. He didn't care.

"And one more thing," Edward added, "how come you know the way into the cemetery if no one is allowed inside, unless you aren't what you pretend to be."

Zain snorted. "This one is right. I was entrusted by Abdul Zahra to keep things he didn't share with anyone else."

"Oh, yeah," Edward sneered, "like what?"

"Like for example, the symbol Abdul Zahra left is a message to me."

"What are you talking about?" Edward's hands relaxed but he still held Zain.

The young man didn't seem to care. "Two years ago, Abdul Zahra gave me a piece of paper with the same symbol as the one engraved on his chest. He insisted that I always keep it with me. I never opened it because, and these are his words, talismans are never meant to be opened."

Edward let go of Zain. What did that mean?

"So?" Fayazi said, rubbing his chin, "the knife wounds on his chest were…"

Zain nodded, his eyes blank. "I think it was his way of telling me to open the talisman."

-33-

"And where is that talisman?" Fayazi asked Zain, his eyes glittering with hope.

"I asked a friend to bring it from my home," Zain said, then looked at Edward. "The phone conversation you overheard was with that friend."

Edward said, "But it still doesn't explain what you were saying on the phone."

"You misunderstood what I said. He wanted me to attend to other matters but I told him that I need to keep an eye on you, to make sure you don't get into trouble."

"Okay," Safiya said, glancing toward the short dishdash strolling by again. "There is nothing we can do here, let's leave this place."

When they were out, Zain made another call to his friend, giving him their location. They agreed to meet in a small gas station not far from the abandoned cemetery.

Minutes later, a white Corolla parked at the gas station. A young man, who was Zain's age and height, and yes, looked exactly like Zain except he wore casual jeans and a red baseball cap, stepped out of his car and headed toward theirs.

Zain met the young man midway. They shook hands and exchanged words, then the young man gave Zain something so small Edward couldn't see.

"You got it?" Fayazi asked once Zain was back at the car.

Zain opened his palm. He had a white paper folded into a small rectangle and wrapped with a black strand of wool. On the back, the same symbol of Arabic letters was drawn in neat handwriting.

"What are we waiting for?" Fayazi's eyes almost popped out. "Let's open it."

With a meticulous care akin to disarming a bomb, Zain unwrapped the paper then unfolded it. The four-by-six inch paper contained a few lines. All in Arabic except for some numbers in English.

Fayazi frowned, turning the paper as if searching for a hidden message.

"I don't understand," Safiya said. "It's just verses from the Quran."

"It has to be something." Zain shook his head. "The old man kept insisting that it was very important, keep it with me all the time."

"Maybe because it's a protection Herz," Fayazi said, leaning back on his seat, rubbing his face with both hands. "He wanted you to carry it."

"He never believed in that stuff," Zain said. "And yet, he kept insisting that I always carry it. I just thought it was one of his peculiarities. Now it all makes sense."

"What do the verses say?" Edward asked. "It could be some kind of clue, right?"

Mr. History Detective.

Fayazi cocked his head, then snapped the paper from Zain and started reading it. "Exalted is *He* who took His Servant by night from al-Masjid al-Haram to al-Masjid al-Aqsa, whose surroundings We have blessed, to show him of Our signs. Indeed, He is the Hearing, the Seeing. And *We* gave Moses the

Scripture and made it a guidance for the Children of Israel that you not take other than *Me* as Disposer of affairs."

"That is Surah of Sons of Israel," Safiya said.

"What does it mean?" Edward asked.

The car was getting very hot. Edward wiped off the sweat from his forehead. The AC was still on, turned all way up.

"Well, it talks about the night of *Mi'erage*," Fayazi explained. "A night when Gabriel came to Mohammed when he was at his house in Mecca, in the early days of his prophecy. He flew him to the holy land in Jerusalem, then took him to the heavens. It could refer to a literal trip or a spiritual perception."

"Anything to do with Fatima?" Edward asked.

Fayazi rubbed his chin. "Actually, the story said that Mohammed was fasting for forty days before this journey so Gabriel brought Mohammed fruit from heaven, he ate it and that night he... um... approached Khadeeja, and Fatima was conceived this very night —from the fruit of heaven."

Edward mulled it over. So where was the lead taking them? Hopefully not to heaven. "What about the next verse?"

Fayazi read on: "You who covered himself with garment. Arise and warn your people. And your lord glorify." The doctor stopped, then said, "It is one of the early verses sent to Mohammed, the story says that after Mohammed first met Gabriel and was informed that he would be the prophet of Islam, he went down from the mountain he was meditating on and back to his house."

Fayazi paused for a while.

Safiya said, "Yes, I know the story, he was so scared and confused he went into bed and covered himself with heavy bed sheets so he was sweating... something like that."

Fayazi arched an eyebrow at Safiya. He shook his head and sighed. "One day, my young lady, I will give you a lesson or two on how to read Islamic history. Anyway, receiving the epiphany was a burden beyond normal human capabilities. Even great prophets like Mohammed, Jesus, and Moses had it hard especially at the beginning. Probably I am not the right person to talk about this, but look at it this way; seeing and hearing the angels and the epiphany requires a new set of senses that still need development. So it was perfectly normal for Mohammed to feel exhausted after the first encounter."

"Okay, okay." Edward held up his hand. Focus on the target. "Anything with Fatima?"

Fayazi shook his head. "Probably the event that foreshadowed this Ayah gave a hint as to the support Khadeeja gave Mohammed even before he was chosen as the messenger of God. But nothing specific."

Why did those who wanted to leave a clue to something always make it so hard? Did they enjoy watching —from their graves or places in heaven or wherever they were— people running around like headless chickens trying to solve the little riddles they came up with? "What does the third one say?"

Fayazi read again: "And warn your close clan."

Zain snapped his fingers. "*Wakeat Al-Dar!*"

Fayazi nodded. "Yes, exactly."

"The incident of the house? What does that mean?" Edward asked, not sure if his translation was right.

"Soon after Mohammed was informed he would be the prophet," Fayazi explained, "God ordered him to start with his close family, so he invited around forty members of his clan, mainly his uncles and their sons, to a big dinner he prepared at his house in Mecca. There he told them about his responsibility of getting God's message to all the Arabs, and asked for an ally."

"An ally?" Safiya frowned.

"Yes," Fayazi said, "he told them he would need someone to help as an ally, friend, a brother, and a next-in-command if you will."

"And what did they say?" Edward asked.

"No one said anything. It wasn't like they didn't believe him, not all of them anyway. Mohammed was known for his honesty, as I told you before. But it looks like they knew what that really meant — to be on the wrong side of all the Arabs. The only one who volunteered to help was Ali Bin Abi Taleb. Mohammed repeated the question three times and each time Ali was the only one who answered him. The third time, Mohammed took Ali's hand and told him: you are my brother, you are my ally, and you are my successor."

"Is that *all?*" Edward said, unable to hide the disappointment in his tone. "*Nothing* else?"

Fayazi scrutinized the paper. "There is something here, I cannot read." He handed the paper to Zain, pointing at the edge.

"It says, '*Ebdaa Min Hunak*, start from there,'" Zain said, squinting at the paper.

"There where?" Safiya said.

Edward closed his eyes. That sadistic treasure-hunt game. There should be law against it. "There must be something in the three verses that explain the next move."

Safiya asked, "What about the numbers?"

"They are the verses numbers." Zain said. "Surrah number then the Ayah number."

"Well maybe we can use it as GPS coordinates," she said, opening her Sony laptop and keying in the numbers. She stopped after a while and took another look at the numbers.

"Too short for coordinates?" Zain said.

Safiya shrugged. "Unless he wants us to go to Hawaii."

At least not heaven.

"Okay, maybe they are just plain house addresses," she said. "I still don't know what format they are, and they don't look like a house address in Mecca or any town in Saudi."

House in Mecca?

"The house!" Edward almost jumped. "The house is the common thing in the three verses. Mohammed's house. All the stories happened in Mohammed's house in Mecca."

Fayazi's eyes widened. He grabbed Edward's shoulders with both hands. "Son, you are a blessing. You are a blessing."

"It was nothing." Edward gave an embarrassed smile.

Mr. Humble.

"I don't recall there is a house of the prophet in Mecca," Safiya said, looking at Zain.

Zain shook his head too, but started the car anyway.

"Yes, there is." Fayazi said, wiping tears from his eye. "Go to the old city, dear Zain. Go to the old city."

PART FOUR

The largest number of unemployed female graduates in the world is in Saudi.

Zain drove to the address Fayazi gave him. They were closer to the high-rise buildings now. Safiya explained to Edward that the black cubical structure was Kaaba, the holy place Muslim pilgrims headed to. The area around it, called Al-Haram, was now one of the most developed areas in Saudi Arabia. Mecca was the name of the entire city.

"Millions of dollars were spent on the area around Al-Haram," Safiya said, pointing to the high-rise buildings. "Five-star hotels, office buildings, and even spas for rich pilgrims were built, all facing the Kaaba so that hotel guests could enjoy the holy—"

"Oh, *please*." Zain snorted. "They have turned the city from a spiritual place to a business investment."

The cynic was back.

"And what's wrong with having a good sense of business?" Safiya snapped. "Develop the town and flourish the economy."

"Right, the economy." Zain sneered.

"Yeah, the economy. Do you have a problem with that?"

"And by the economy, you mean what pocket exactly?"

"Knock it off, Zain," Edward said.

"She started it!"

She started it. As if they were in first grade.

"I did not, I was just trying to give Edward an overview of the area."

"Yeah, sure," Zain said.

Edward rolled his eyes. He looked at Fayazi for support, but the old man was staring out the window, probably at nothing. So immersed in his own world, Fayazi wasn't bothered with the kindergarten in the front seat.

Edward looked out his own window. He wasn't sure what to make of the neighborhood. It was too tacky to be modern, and yet not old enough to qualify as ancient. There were shops, small cubical shops. The ones you see in the movies when they show the Arabic Market. Most of the walls were not even painted, left with the eerie gray color of the cement. Tables in front of each shop displayed colorful and shiny clothes. Shades extended from the roof to protect the shoppers and the goods from the sun. White sheets covering a good part of the pavement held piles of small objects that could be anything from souvenirs to toy guns... hopefully, not real guns. People followed their car with gazes that were both too eager and too curious. Children wearing dishdashes in different shades of gray ran after each other and the car, yelling something he couldn't comprehend.

The fancy multi-million-dollar high-rises were less than two miles away.

So much for developing the town.

"Here," Fayazi said, pointing at an old house painted in a white color that was way beyond peeling.

Beside the big green flag of Saudi fixed on the wall, a sign in Arabic and Urdu hung on the wooden door. It said "Public Library," but the look of the only small door and the dingy area behind it suggested anything but books. Public toilets would have been more appropriate.

"This is the *prophet's* house?" both Zain and Safiya said in unison.

"You should have seen it in my days," Fayazi said. "It used to be public toilets."

Wow, sometimes Edward scared himself.

"Oh, God." Zain put both hands on his head as if he had a migraine.

"No way," Safiya snapped.

Fayazi was the first out of the car. They followed. Zain helped the old man crossing the street.

A little girl approached. She wore a pale purple dress and a green headscarf that didn't cover much of her hair. Grimy was too polite a word to describe her. The girl glanced at them, set her target, and hurried toward Safiya. She just extended her hand to the masked princess without saying a word.

Safiya made an "Oh" and reached in to her Gucci purse and handed the child a bill.

The child yelled, "*Shukran, Shukran!*" too loud to be talking to Safiya alone. Before they could reach the house/library/toilet, five or six, maybe seven more children — it was really hard to tell — surrounded Safiya, all younger than the first little girl and much grungier.

Safiya yelled at them and took Edward's hands as if pulling herself from the swirling group around her.

A man in a short white dishdash and a long beard sat at a desk just inside the entrance of the house. He looked the same as the two nice guards at the cemetery. Did whatever entity responsible for assigning them have some discount deal on the those short dishdashes?

"*Wesh Tibon?*" (what do you want) he asked them with the same tourist-friendly attitude as the cemetery guys.

Zain told him that they wanted to get into the library.

"*Mafee Dukhool,* (no entrance) today is closed." He waved Zain off and stood. His dishdash was midway between his knee and ankle, revealing brown and hairy legs.

Must be a really good discount on those dishdashes.

"Why?" Zain said in Arabic. "Your books are on vacation?"

Safiya signaled to them to step back. They did. She spoke with the man the same way she did at the cemetery.

Edward wasn't sure why, but he stared at the man's legs a second longer. Huge mistake. Nausea kicked in. The black heels had cracks big enough to hide Sadam Hussain's WMD arsenal.

"I remember this place," Zain said, examining the facade. "I have been here before, a long time ago. When I was a kid..."

He too had that distant look on his face as had Fayazi.

-35-

"Definitely not the knife wounds, sir," his assistant, Sami, reported. "The medical examiner believes it's some kind of heart attack."

"A heart attack?" Adnan said. It didn't make sense.

"Yes, sir, the medical examiner asked for another three hours to confirm that. He started the autopsy and —"

"You know what really bothers me, Sami?"

"What, sir?"

"Abdul Zahra was not tied to the chair. Not only that, there weren't any signs on his wrists to indicate he was tied."

Sami bit his lower lip. "So, how did the attacker manage to make those cuts, sir?"

"Exactly my point," Adnan said, resting his legs on the desk. "The way that symbol was engraved on the old man's chest, so careful and so clear, tells me that Abdul Zahra did not fight, did not even move his body. So the only way to do that is when he was tied up."

"Or maybe postmortem, sir."

"Nah, that amount of blood cannot be postmortem, his heart was beating when he got those cuts." Adnan examined his brown shoes. They were dirty and old. The edges of his green uniform pants had turned yellow. He needed a new outfit. Or retirement. "Beside, you just said that the death might be a heart attack, so tell me how that fits in?"

Sami stared at him, probably assuming this was a rhetorical question. When he realized that his boss was waiting for the answer, Sami cleared his throat. "Maybe he was drugged when the killer cut those symbols on his chest, then when he was awake he had the heart attack."

Or maybe it wasn't a heart attack. Adnan had lived long enough to know that there were many ways to fake such a thing.

"Sir, do you really think that this American lady killed him? Because —"

"Officially, yes," a voice said from the door. Fahad.

Sami jumped, turned around, and greeted the officer. Fahad ignored him. He carried a laptop and looked confused where to put it. Adnan left his feet on the desk for another second then took them off. "And unofficially?"

"Unofficially, you have to find a man for us," Fahad said. He put the laptop on the desk and turned it toward Adnan. The computer was already on. "A man was seen entering the house after the American lady left," Fahad said. "He is our primary suspect."

Adnan squinted at the laptop. A video filled half of the screen. There was a date and time stamp on the upper-right corner. The picture was dark and greenish. A night-vision camera.

The video showed the old house where Abdul Zahra was found dead. The camera was mounted to cover the entrance and the street. The time stamp showed 6:00 a.m. A green shadow wearing some kind of uniform walked toward the house. He turned left and right, as if to make sure he was not being watched. Then entered the house.

"He stayed in the house for five minutes," Fahad said, fast forwarding the video.

Adnan watched the man in the uniform hurrying out. "Why are you showing me this?"

"I thought you liked home movies." Fahad shrugged. Then, "I need you to get this man, Captain."

"It's too fucking late! You should have shown me this a long time ago."

Fahad nodded and said in a quiet voice, "We didn't know."

The video stopped. Adnan hit the play button again. Who put that camera there? Was Abdul Zahra under surveillance? What else did the camera capture? He had taken Fahad's word earlier that Kimberly was the only one who got into the house. Now Fahad was showing him new evidence. Why?

"It's too late," Adnan repeated. "We won't be able to identify him in time."

Fahad's lips parted. "And if we did?"

"Last known location?"

Fahad's smile widened. "I can get you that."

"And an official letter of appreciation for local police's role?"

Fahad squinted at him. "Granted," he said, putting a paper on the desk in a theatrical way. "I want him for questioning before midnight." Fahad left the office.

Adnan glanced at the paper. There was a name and four lines of information and an address.

The name read: Zain Mustafa.

Occupation: driver.

-36-

<Mecca – Saudi Arabia>
<Time left until Zero hour is 13hrs:15min>
<Number of infected websites: 446,315>

Aside from four or five shelves that contained books with leather covers and two wooden tables in the middle of the room, there was nothing in the library. The walls had recently been painted white. The bright color reminded Edward of hospitals, especially with the two neon lights fixed to the ceiling.

"It's made of brick," Edward said. "It can't be from fourteen hundred years ago."

"Renovation." Zain chuckled, but there was no humor in it.

Safiya turned from one wall to the other, touching the one next to her so gently, as if she expected the spirits from the past to rise. "I don't understand," she finally said in a low voice. "How can this be our prophet's house and no one is paying any attention to it?"

"Attention?" Zain said, pointing at the walls. "They have torn down the old house. And turned it into this… this…" He shook his head and waved it off.

Fayazi found a small door and opened it. He stuck his head inside. "It's the bathroom," he said in a wistful voice. Fayazi stood for another moment, looking inside. Then he trudged back, shaking his head and murmuring.

"What are we looking for?" Safiya said, pulling out a chair and sitting next to the wooden table.

"Let's check out the books," Edward said. The idea sounded silly even to his ears.

He, Safiya and Zain did that for ten minutes. All the books were relatively new. Most of them were Quran.

"We are searching in the wrong place," Fayazi said. "If Abdul Zahra hid the Musehaf here, it must be in the walls or under the tiles. It cannot be left in plain sight."

"Abdul Zahra *hid* it?" Edward asked.

"It doesn't matter who did," Fayazi said. "But apparently Abdul Zahra hid it here."

"How can you be so sure, Doctor?" Edward asked, Vane's words resonating in his mind. The man was executed in 1965.

Fayazi waved it off. "It's his talisman, isn't it?"

"But you know something else," Edward said. "Even before you read the talisman he left to Zain, you sent Kim to meet him not because he is the owner of the land, but because you suspected that he had the Musehaf of Fatima."

Zain and Safiya stared wide-eyed at Fayazi.

"Okay, I owe you an explanation," Fayazi said, rubbing his face, the wrinkles in his forehead and under his eyes again more prominent. "You remember when I told you that the student of Ayatollah Seerazi came to Saudi for one week?"

They all nodded.

"Well, he met a merchant."

"So?" Edward asked, but knew where this was heading.

"This merchant was Ismail Al-Makki."

Zain let out a muffled, "Dear God."

Fayazi took off his glasses. His eyes were small and swollen. "Ismail ran a very successful trade between Iraq and Saudi. At that time, travel was only by camel. This Ismail had around ten caravans to transport pilgrims to and from Mecca. But once he had that meeting with the clerk from Iraq, Al-Makki quit his business and started buying land."

"Fadak," Zain murmured.

Fayazi nodded.

Edward said, "So, this Ismail Al-Makki bought the land back. Why?"

"Not only that," Fayazi said, "Makki changed the name of his only son to Abdul Zahra."

Silence.

Edward assumed that they were all doing the same math he ran in his head. But Fayazi spoke before anyone objected to the impossible timelines. "This Abdul Zahra was known later as Senior, as he had named his first-born son Abdul Zahra as well."

Ah! "So the man killed yesterday was…"

"Abdul Zahra Junior, that's right," Fayazi said. "Abdul Zahra Senior, had a very eventful life. Not as a businessman, although he somehow managed to make some good investments that tripled his family's fortune, but he was involved in lots of activities that made him not best friends with the authorities. Abdul Zahra junior followed in his father's footsteps. A successful businessman, a lot of charity work, and a pain in the neck for the authorities."

"So that's why they killed him." Edward dropped the bomb. "Abdul Zahra Senior was executed in 1965 after the interrogation."

Fayazi's lips trembled, his hand started shaking violently. "Yes, someone gave him to the religion police."

"And you think that Abdul Zahra has the Musehaf?" Edward asked.

"I had my doubts at the beginning." Fayazi nodded. "But now after he was murdered, and that talisman thing, I am almost sure. Lots of Saudi families, by the way, had the tradition of keeping certain items of historical value within the family, and they passed them down from the father to the elder son. So my guess is that Abdul Zahra Junior inherited this Musehaf from his father and he was the trustee, per se."

"Does he have any sons?" Safiya asked.

Fayazi shook his head. "I don't think so. He was once married but he divorced his wife when he was forty. I don't really know if he had any offspring."

"You should have *told* us this when we were in *Nakheela*, Doctor," Edward snapped.

Fayazi looked at his glasses, took a napkin, and started wiping them. "I was afraid you would refuse to come if you knew that it was about the Musehaf."

He was right. If Abdul Zahra were really the trustee of this ancient secret, his first worry would be to protect it and make sure that it wasn't lost. But why the elaborate scheme? Why not leave a bank account or a map? And why did he give the talisman to Zain?

"Don't worry, Edward," Fayazi said. "Whoever killed Abdul Zahra killed him to get the Musehaf, and Kimberly's kidnapping was related to the Musehaf as well. So —"

"Finding the Musehaf is our only chance." Edward sighed. He wasn't sure of that. There were still lots of holes. For example, why did the kidnappers tell him that Kimberly had something? Why did they kill Abdul Zahra if they knew he was the only one who knew the location of the Musehaf? Why not torture him to get the information?

Blackbeard sat at the other end of the room, holding what looked like a thick toothpick and pretending to be busy using it as a toothbrush to clean his teeth. The keyword here was, pretended. Blackbeard never took his gaze off of them.

Edward considered offering him a newspaper with a hole in the middle. But he didn't want to interrupt the tooth-cleaning process.

"You've got eggs in your beard," Edward said in Arabic to Blackbeard, who zeroed in on him.

Safiya signaled to the man to leave the room. He did. Nice to have a princess on your side.

Safiya shook her head. "I just don't get it, why this place to hide such an important thing? If that Musehaf does exist."

Fayazi put the glasses back on, his hand still shaking. "This is not the right question."

Everyone looked at him.

"The question is, how did Abdul Zahra manage to hide it here? This place is owned by the government. You have seen how the guard greeted us. He wouldn't let anyone in, much less let him hide something."

Zain snapped his fingers, hurried to the back of the room, and started searching for something on the floor.

"What?" Edward asked him.

Zain just kept looking in all the corners. They followed him. The floor tiles were made of something that looked like orange clay. Zain went to the door that led to the bathroom.

"Yes!" he shouted, stabbing the air with his fist. "It's here."

They ran to him. He leaned over a metal plate that looked like a small manhole cover. The plate, rusty and old, was fixed to the floor. They all gasped when they saw the markings on the plate.

"Oh my God," Safiya said, her hands on her cheeks.

On the metal plate were the same rectangular symbols that were on Abdul Zahra's chest and on Zain's talisman. Below the rectangle was a number:

3-165.

"Do you think what I'm thinking?" Fayazi said, looking at the number with a wide smile.

"It is a reference for Surah in Quran," Zain said, grabbing one of the Quran copies from the nearby shelf. He flipped the pages. "Number 3 must be Surah of Imran, father of Lady Mary." Zain glanced at Edward.

Edward refrained from rolling his eyes. Okay, he got it, they had a Surah, a chapter in Quran about Lady Mary. When would they understand that all of this meant nothing to him? Not when that terrible guilt gnawed at him.

"The second number must be this Ayah..." Zain flipped more pages, stopped at one, and started reading out loud: "Why when a disaster struck you, although you had struck with one twice as great, you said, 'From where is this?' Say, 'It is from yourselves.' Indeed, Allah is over all things competent."

Edward frowned. "Is this about the Virgin Mary?"

"No," Fayazi said, "it's the Battle of Uhud."

"But I thought the Surah name was—"

"Yeah," Fayazi said, "sometimes the Quran talks about different, albeit related, subjects in one Surah. This particular Surah is as long as five percent of the Quran."

"Wow." They would keep trying to impress him, so better to get over it. "Impressive, one complete Surah about the Virgin Mary."

"Two," Zain said. "This one and there is another one named after Lady Mary herself, not her father. Mariam. She is the only woman mentioned by name in Quran."

Then Fayazi gave him a crash course on how the Virgin Mary was one of the four most respected women in the Islamic culture. The righteous women. Khadeeja was another one and the mother of Prophet Moses was another.

"Please, Doctor." Edward winced. They were not about to get over it.

Why did Muslims always want to show that their religion respects other prophets mentioned in the Bible? To prove that their religion was as friendly as others? Was it because they knew how the extremists made Islam look? Or was it something else? Maybe deep inside they knew that tolerance and accepting different opinions were amiss in their cultures and their minds. So, when they saw their Quran repeatedly mentioning mercy and tolerance, they hurried to non-Muslims, trying to sell the idea.

Wow, that was deep. Maybe next Edward would conclude that Muslims were a bunch of hypocrites, taking from Quran only what suited them. Stay tuned.

Fayazi nodded. "Back to the subject. This Ayah is about the battle Muslims lost, Uhud. The second battle, in the third year after Mohammed's migration to Madeena and establishment of the first Islamic state."

Safiya said, "Ah. The one where they disobeyed his commands, wasn't it?"

"Yes, Princess, that particular one." Fayazi nodded.

Zain was trying to move the plate. It didn't budge. Edward tried to help, but the plate was fixed with cement to the floor. He knocked on it. The sound was muffled. No echo. Nothing was underneath.

"Nothing to do with Fatima, I assume," Edward said.

They all looked at Fayazi. The old historian gave a crooked smile. "Actually it does, big time."

Finally a glimpse of hope.

"And this time there is no question about it," Fayazi said. "This place was one of Fatima's favorites."

Edward rolled his eyes. "Oh, please don't tell me we have to go to another place."

"Even better." Fayazi grinned. "We have to go back to Madeena."

He slammed his head. "It's a three hour drive."

Safiya smiled playfully. "Not necessarily."

"Unless you have a plane—" Edward opened his eyes wide. "Do you?"

"Very close." The playful smile was wider. "Have you tried a Lamborghini before?"

-37-

<Mecca – Saudi Arabia>
<Time left until Zero hour is 12hrs:45min>
<Number of infected websites: 520,197>

Safiya had her Lamborghini, *one* of her Lamborghinis, stored in a warehouse just outside Mecca. She and Edward went to fetch the car while Zain and Fayazi waited in the Honda Civic. Two security guards greeted Safiya and opened the warehouse door for her. Neon lights turned on automatically one by one in something of a theatrical touch.

Welcome to the Bat Cave.

Edward gasped. The size of a football stadium, the warehouse was full of cars. Cars he didn't even recognize. All shiny and elegant, with shapes and lines that screamed 'way out of your payroll'.

"Wow," Edward said when he found his voice.

Safiya took off her black head cover. Letting her raven-black hair slide down over her shoulders, she strolled down the aisle, her hand gently patting the thin air above each car.

So that was how rich people took care of their automobiles.

She turned to face him, arms spread wide, the playful smile was back. "Say, what car you would like to try?"

Edward turned left, then right, then left again. Should he choose based on the color, shape or size? He recognized the B for Bentley and the Ferrari horse, so he waved a hello at them. Other cars were way too haughty for him to have rapport.

"Are those all yours?"

Safiya giggled. "No, this warehouse is shared with my brothers."

"Your brothers? How many do you have?"

"Eleven, twelve." Safiya shrugged. "All step-brothers."

"And sisters?"

"Maybe ten."

Maybe. Very strong family ties.

"But anyway, only me and two boys share this hobby. The rest are just assholes."

"Well, Princess, if you're looking for additional members of your family, I might be able to find some spare time."

She put a hand on her heart. "Very kind of you. Now let's pick a babe and hit the road."

-38-

They didn't go with the Lamborghini. Shame. To make room for four passengers, Safiya decided to take the Bentley. Or at least that was what Edward assumed the name was. The car wasn't like any Bentley Edward had seen before, on the *Wheels* magazine cover of course. A limited edition. Edward made a mental note that next time he chose his career, he would be a Saudi prince, or marry a royal.

The road around them didn't blur. Another disappointment. Safiya drove over 160 miles per hour but with nothing around but the endless desert, it was hard to notice the speed. Life could be unfair.

"How far to the site of Uhud?" he asked.

"*Normally* three hours and a half." Safiya grinned.

"Okay, so it's ten minutes with you."

She laughed. Her vibrant laughter tickled him. Edward could feel the happiness and the joy and the screw-the-world attitude in her tone.

"Is it somewhere downtown?" he asked Zain, just for distraction.

Zain shook his head. "Uhud is outside Madeena, in the direction toward Mecca."

"Here, look at it here." Safiya pointed at the car's GPS. Even the GPS looked fancy and futuristic with iPhone-like sleek design and touch screen. The location was a dot in the middle of nowhere.

Fayazi adjusted his wire-rimmed glasses, cleared his throat, and looked as if preparing for another history lecture. Why not. Edward could use some sleep now.

"After Mohammed and the Muslims migrated to Madeena and started the first Islamic state, Quraish, the Arab tribe of Mecca decided that it would be too risky for them to allow Mohammed to build his own city."

"So they declared war?"

"Yes, the first war was Badder," Fayazi said. "Despite that Quraish had more than triple the Muslim army, Mohammed achieved a victory. That was in the second year after the Migration to Madeena. Quraish's defeat was so bad they lost their grip on other Arab tribes in other cities. Their reputation as indestructible tribe was ended by the small army of Mohammed. So the next year, they gathered an even bigger army and marched to Madeena, where Muslims were not ready."

"And they defeated the Muslims," Edward concluded.

"Not in the beginning. You see, this entire Uhud battle was a lesson to Muslims to obey the prophet, which one might conclude from the Ayah Zain read in the library. At first, when Mohammed knew about the attack, his plan was to stay in Madeena and re-enforce the defenses. He told other Muslims that if they listened to him, he would lead them to another victory."

"And they didn't."

Fayazi nodded. "They insisted on taking the war outside the city. They forced Mohammed to take their opinion and they went out and met the Quraish army next to a hill called Uhud, hence the battle name."

Safiya added, "Is it the battle where the prophet ordered the archers to stay on top of the mountain and protect him? I remember that one from the movie."

"The same one," Fayazi said. "With the plan Mohammed made, the Muslim managed a victory in the very first hour of the battle. His cousin, Ali bin Abi Taleb, and his young uncle, Hamza, had a great role in the victory. Before the battle, they had that tradition of one-to-one challenge—"

"The best of the two armies fighting with each other," Edward said.

"Exactly." Fayzi pointed at him, maybe giving him extra marks. Then the old man's face clouded. "What is this?" He said, pointing at a big silver ring with a blood-red stone Zain was wearing.

"This?" Zain chuckled, a little tension in his voice. "It's just a ring."

Fayazi frowned, then shook his head and went on, "So, history tells us that the Quraish army chose a man no one from the Muslim army dared to challenge. They described him as a giant warrior who blocked the sun if he stood. Ali accepted the challenge, and he cut the big warrior into two halves in one stroke."

Fayazi made a move with his hand as if waving an imaginary sword. "Then the man's brother demanded revenge, another scary warrior. Ali killed that one too. Their brothers and cousins followed one after another, nine of them, each bigger and stronger than the one before, you see, that was why Quraish had the upper hand on other tribes —they had the best warriors, warriors no one dared to challenge."

"Until Mohammed and his Ali and Hamza came," Edward added.

Fayazi gave him a thumbs up.

"And the nine brothers?" Safiya asked.

Fayazi smirked. "Nine strikes, no more, no less. That's why they called Ali's strikes with many names. All meant one thing: fast death."

"Must've been a hell of a man." Edward laughed.

Fayazi said, taking another glance at Zain's big ring. "Actually, Ali was of average height and built. Everyone described Ali as a monk. A man who spent his nights praying to God, checking on poor people's houses, feeding them from the money he made farming his small land. Fighting was something he did to protect the religion. Hamza, on the other hand, was well known as one of Quraish's finest warriors before he converted to Islam. You see, it was the presence of Hamza, Ali and his father that prevented Quraish from killing Mohammed after the first day he declared the new religion. Muslims kept saying that God protected him, true, but how? God did not send angels as bodyguards. God protected Mohammed with believers, people, natural causes. This is the way the entire universe worked, natural causes to carry out God's will. God wanted a tree to come up, he created sun and prepared the rain. Rain is also a series of natural causes. But the believers look at those causes and see what's beyond them; they see wisdom, purpose, and the merciful hand of God."

Edward fought not to yawn.

His iPhone vibrated in his pocket. Edward picked it up. A blocked caller ID. "Hello?" he said tentatively, almost expecting another threat.

"Edward. It's me."

Edward's heart skipped a beat. "Kim! Is that you? Are you okay?"

She sniffled. "I'm fine."

He fought to keep the tears in. "Kim, where are you?"

More sniffling. "Please come and get me, Ed."

She started crying then gave him an address and asked him to be there in two hours.

"Why two hours? What's happened, Kim?"

"Just come... Alone and unarmed."

And she hung up.

"Was that Kimberly?" Safiya asked.

Zain and Fayazi leaning forward from the back seat to listen.

"Yes." He stared at the phone. Why didn't he feel comforted? He took a long breath and told them what she said.

"This address is in Madeena," Zain said. "I know the place. Actually it's five minutes from the site of Uhud."

"Why this place?" Fayazi frowned.

They all looked at each other. Fayazi rubbed his chin, Zain kept shaking his head, Safiya bit her lips. No one spoke.

Edward finally said it: "How did she know we were going there?"

-39-

<Somewhere between Mecca and Madeena – Saudi Arabia>
<Time left until Zero hour is 12hrs:15min>
<Number of infected websites: 571,349>

"It could be just a coincidence," Safiya said after some time. "Maybe Kimberly assumed you were going to Madeena."

"She wanted to meet us five minutes away from Uhud," Edward said. "Of all the places in Saudi."

"Maybe she is a psychic," Zain whispered, wiggling his fingers in front of his face.

"Relax, Edward." Safiya chuckled, nudging him in the shoulder. "You are just too happy — your mind doesn't know how to deal with it. Relax."

Maybe. Still, Edward's spider-senses tingled. Maybe he was paranoid or extra cautious today. Maybe Safiya was right and his spider-senses were wrong. Maybe he watched too much *Spiderman.*

"Do we still need to go to the Uhud site?" Edward asked.

Safiya checked the dashboard clock, then the GPS. "We need another hour to get to Madeena. If we stop for ten minutes in Uhud, we will still have plenty of time."

Zain said from the back seat, "There is a shortcut."

"No, this is the fastest route," Safiya said.

"And if I show you a faster one?"

"No way." She stuck out her tongue.

Zain leaned forward, his curly head between the two front seats now. "Tell me, Princess, can this car go in the sand?"

Safiya arched an eyebrow. "Where?"

190

Zain pointed to the right of the road. Safiya took a breath then veered and went onto the unpaved area.

"Careful!" Fayazi shouted.

Safiya maintained her speed. The road was bumpy and uneven, but the Bentley drove steadily, leaving a cloud of red dust behind it.

"This road was the original one between Mecca and Madeena," Zain said, too excited, his accent more pronounced. "The prophet used to take it when he went to Haj from Madeena."

"No! Not the pilgrims' route... Oh...my...God!" Fayazi said, sticking his head out the window like a child told that the circus was outside.

"The very same one," Zain said.

"Oh my God, so is it still there?"

"They are demolishing it, Doctor. I think someone told them that people knew about the place and tourists were starting to visit it."

Edward exchanged puzzled looks with Safiya. What were they talking about?

"God damn them," Fayazi finally said.

Safiya asked, "What are you talking about, Doctor?"

But the answer came to them. A construction site lay ahead. Bulldozers, pickup trucks, and other heavy machinery were scattered around. Red emergency cones and road barriers blocked their way.

"It's blocked," Safiya said, slowing.

Zain pointed at a small opening between the barriers, and guided Safiya through a narrow semi-paved road. "This is the road they are constructing. It serves no real value but as an excuse for them to demolish it."

"Demolish what?" Edward asked.

Zain pointed at a small dune that looked more like a two-headed rock where the remains of a tree trunk were buried. "This."

"Oh, dear God," Fayazi whispered. "The rock of Ghadeer."

Safiya asked, "What is Ghadeer?"

"On this rock, in this very same place, Mohammed had gathered around one hundred thousand pilgrims after finishing his last Haj. He foresaw his death after this Haj," Fayazi said, his body and voice shaking. "He climbed on this rock and called for all Muslims, telling them that if they were truly Muslims following him as a messenger of God, then they would follow Ali after his death."

"*Really*?" Safiya said, her head cocked.

"All Muslims agree on this event. Mohammed made sure those thousands acknowledged Ali as the man who would continue as the guardian to the message."

Edward examined the rock again and tried to imagine Mohammed holding Ali's hand in front of thousands of Muslims. The images didn't conjure up. "But it was not Mohammed's right to appoint someone after him."

"Indeed." Fayazi nodded. "It's God's decision. Every prophet, every messenger left a guardian to his religion. A man, appointed by God, who would make sure people always found the guidance they seek. It doesn't make sense for God to send a messenger, establish the faith, then a few years later, when the prophet dies, let his teaching be changed and let people lose track."

Edward wanted to argue about that, but a vibration in his pocket stopped him. His cell.

"Where are you heading?" Vane asked.

"A place called Uhud."

"Coordinates, please."

Edward gave him the coordinates.

"I'll be there," Vane said.

"Vane," he caught him before hanging up, "Kimberly called me." Edward briefed him on Kimberly's call.

"Did she actually say come alone and an unarmed?" Vane asked.

"I think it's a trap," Edward concluded. "Maybe she added that to warn us."

"*Je pense aussi.*"

"So?"

192

"Oh, we will be ready."

-40-

<Madeena – Saudi Arabia>
<Time left until Zero hour is 11hrs:00min>
<Number of infected websites: 641,329>

The site of the battle of Uhud was exactly as Fayazi and Zain described. In the middle of the desert. Which was true of almost everything in Saudi. In the distance, houses and buildings all hid behind the curtain of rising dust.

Uhud was hardly qualified as a hill, maybe six hundred feet in height, maximum. Another, smaller hill extended close to it. The other was darker, filled with rocks and holes, giving it an eery feeling. One day, on this very spot, a battle took place. Men were killed here. Fayazi pointed at the dark hill and said it was where the archers were positioned. A large cemetery extended beneath the second hill. The cemetery and the battle site enjoyed the same extra care the cemetery in Mecca did. Well, at least they were not turned into public toilets.

Whoever ran the heritage department in Saudi would not get a performance medal this year.

A high fence made of long steel bars surrounded the cemetery. A small concrete-gray single-room house stood in the middle of the graves, or rocks.

Three green signs guarded the cemetery entrance. In English, Arabic, and Urdu. What was it with the Urdu anyway? Edward read the English one, almost sure it would give a description of the battle. Nada. It talked about the danger of worshiping tombs and how one could lose his faith if his heart had any connection with the dead. The dead are dead, said the sign. Good intel. So at least now Edward could feel safe there were no zombies or vampires.

"The prophet told the archers to stay in their positions and not to come down if they saw the Muslim army win," Fayazi said, pointing at the small hill. "They did not listen to him, something you will keep noticing if you read Islamic history, which is pretty much like what happened with other prophets and their people."

Edward looked at the stones on the ground, the graves. Over a hundred. "So they did not listen and were defeated."

"The Quraish army was retreating when one of their generals, Khalid Bin Al-Waleed who commanded the cavalry, noticed that Muslims were vulnerable from the rear after the archers left their positions. Khalid and his riders turned around and attacked the Muslim army. A massacre, as you can see."

"Good that *Mohammed* didn't get killed," Edward said, not bothering to hide the sarcasm.

"He had a serious injury," Fayazi said, walking toward an empty area of the cemetery. Only one stone was there. "As a matter of fact, the Quraish spread the rumor that they killed Mohammed and all Muslims retreated to Madeena. The part of Quran we read back in Mecca referred to this incident. God reproached Muslims that Mohammed was only the prophet; if he was killed their faith in God should remain."

"But not all Muslims retreated," Safiya said. She had the head cover back on. "I remember I read somewhere that twelve people stayed with Mohammed. Fatima and another brave lady were among them."

"Actually only two stayed with him. Fatima was young, she couldn't hold the sword so she attended the wounded only. Others joined at a very later stage."

"Let me guess," Edward said, "Ali and Hamza."

Fayazi's mouth twitched in a sad smile. "Yeah, Hamza was killed during that battle, defending Mohammed. Ali stayed alone with his cousin. Historians say he killed around fifty men and got seventy wounds in his body. Fatima was the one who treated him when the battle was over. The funny thing is he had arrows in his legs and arms. They waited for the prayer time. Once he started praying, they took out the arrows. They say when Ali prayed to God, he would be in another world."

So Fatima had been in Uhud. Was that why this place was chosen? It still did not make a lot of sense. If someone wanted to hide such an important document, why hide it here in the middle of the desert?

The bankers in Zurich would not be particularly happy about that. But again, they rarely were.

Zain stood outside the fence, close to the lonely stone. Another sign there reminded people how bad praying next to a tomb was.

Hmm, so this stone marked a tomb.

Mr. History Detective.

Zain raised his hand, saluting the thin air above the stone. Something was off with this kid.

"It's Hamza's grave," Fayazi commented, looking at the deserted tomb.

"Why is it alone?" Edward asked.

"Hamza's body was dragged during the battle," Fayazi said, his eyes moist.

Edward shook his head. "I don't understand."

"Hamza, the prophet's uncle, was assassinated." Fayazi wiped his eyes. "You see, during the first battle, Badder, Hamza, and Ali killed a lot of people from Amoyeen, the big family in Mecca. A lady wanted to avenge her brother and father who got killed by Ali and Hamza, and hired assassins to kill them and bring their livers to her. Ali killed the assassins who were supposed to kill him. Hamza was caught off guard. The Amoyeen took advantage of Muslim defeat and of Mohammed and Ali barely surviving, so they dragged Hamza's body to this location where this woman cut open his chest and ate his liver."

"Oh, God." Safiya covered her mouth. "She was Hind, right?"

"Yes, Hind. The mother of the fifth Muslim king, Muawya." Fayazi shook his head.

"Wow, this guy must be really committed to Islam then." Edward laughed, but then immediately felt bad, seeing the tears in Fayazi's eyes.

A drama queen, this professor.

"Very committed," Fayazi said, still looking at the lonely stone. "You know that this king, Muawya, and his sons had ruled the Muslim empire for one hundred years. His son, Yazeed, the sixth Muslim king, killed Mohammed's grandson and what was left of Mohammed's family."

"Jesus, how come such people become rulers?" Edward asked. "I know Mohammed took control all over Saudi Arabia, so why didn't he just eliminate them? I mean, it was obvious that those Amoyeen guys were not big fans of his."

Safiya went to join Zain. She asked him what she should do to pay her respects to Hamza. Zain replied something Edward did not hear.

"Yes, they hated Mohammed and his new religion." Fayazi sighed. "And Mohammed knew it, but he chose to let them go. He warned Muslims not to put them in power, but, well…" Fayazi shrugged. "Arabs chose to ignore the messenger of God."

Fayazi pointed at the green sign next to Hamza's tomb. "You know, Fatima used to come to Hamza's tomb and pray every day after he died. Mohammed did not say this was wrong. On the contrary, he encouraged people to do the same."

A member of the long-beard club wearing the standard-issue short dishdash came out of the small gray house. With his baggy white dishdash and bushy black facial hair, he looked like something you would get if you crossed a pirate with a mad scientist. The man ran toward Zain, yelling and waving a small wooden stick. He opened the iron door in the fence and ran to where Safiya was standing. Short dishdash raised his stick-hand and aimed a blow at Safiya's arm. Zain stepped forward, taking the hit. Short dishdash hit Zain again, this time knocking him to the ground.

"*Kafer!*" the man shouted.

Safiya shouted back. Short dishdash whacked her on the face. She bit her lip, stifling a cry. Her eyes met Edward's. Nausea took over. Everything turned black. An image flashed. He was on a ship, no, a yacht in the middle of the sea. Safiya wore a white shirt over her swimming suit. A large man next to her wore a colorful Hawaiian shirt. The man slapped Safiya. She cried. She bit her lip, looking at him. Just like now. The next thing Edward knew, he was on top of Short dishdash, his fists smashing the man's nose.

Others came in. Edward kicked left and right. They pulled him away. Safiya managed to get her ID out, showing it to them. All he could hear was that sea-shell noise. His heart pounded like a hammer. The sudden flood of memories overwhelmed him.

He had known Safiya.

-41-

"He is saying that Hamza is rotten under the ground and there is no point of paying respect to rotten bones," Safiya told him when everyone calmed down.

The short dishdash clan went back inside the small house. Fayazi helped Zain to stand. Zain's arm and ear bled, but he told them he would be fine.

Safiya said, "We need to finish here as soon as possible."

Images flashed again in his mind. Safiya, him, another man in a yacht. Was he imagining?

But Safiya was right. He checked his watch. One in the afternoon. About time for Kimberly to appear. Zain showed him the location where Kimberly said she would be. The trap. A one-story building, relatively new. And a five minute walk. He couldn't read the sign but it was some government establishment.

"Edward," Fayazi said. "I know we are waiting for Kimberly here but we can still use the time to search for the Musehaf, meanwhile."

Edward shrugged. Fayazi trudged off alone, looking around the place.

"Edward," Safiya asked as she took a napkin from her purse and wiped the blood from Zain's ear. "Do you really believe that Abdul Zahra had that Musehaf of Fatima in the first place?"

Zain said, "He had it."

From a distance, Fayazi signaled them to come. When they were close, he shouted, "It's the same rectangular symbol, it has to be it!"

Edward shook his head. "It's a wild-goose chase."

Safiya added, "How are you so sure it's not just some marks left by the construction company?"

"No!" Fayazi yelled. "You don't understand. This has to be it, Abdul Zahra wouldn't leave it. Just like his father."

Zain stepped forward. "What do you mean?"

"You know exactly what I mean, *Zain*, if that's your real name." Fayazi stepped in front of Zain. The two men faced each other. Fayazi pointed at the red ring in Zain's hand. "It's your father's ring. Your grandfather used to wear a similar one as well. Abdulla Zahra Senior was killed the same way your father was, and I bet he left the same clues to him."

"No, no." Zain shook his head.

Abdul Zahra was Zain's father? "Hold on, why didn't you tell us you are Abdul Zahra's son!"

"It's beside the point."

Safiya said, "No it's not, Zain. We trusted you. And you should do the same with us."

"I shared with you the talisman that got us here so far, didn't I? What else you want?"

Through the haze, Edward saw Zain's point: hiding this detail was probably something personal. He remembered how Zain looked "off" the entire night. The strange way he talked, the sadness. It all made sense now. He had just seen his father killed in that horrible way.

"When my mother was pregnant, my father divorced her," Zain said, his voice a monotone. "He even arranged it in a way that I take another name, not his. But he kept visiting us, at the weekends. He took care of us, put me in a good school, everything. I had a grudge against him until one day I read your letter to him, Doctor."

Fayazi nodded. "My research led me to him, so I wrote, asking if he had the Musehaf. Your father never replied."

"I got this letter, he left it in a secure place but I used to search through his papers, I don't really know why, maybe I was looking for answers for all the strange things he was doing."

Two men with short dishdashs walked nearby, glaring at them. No one paid attention to them.

Safiya winked at Edward. "So he isn't a poor guy from the streets after all."

Edward tried to keep his face neutral. His mind was playing back every word Safiya had said to him. Did she remember him?

Zain smiled. "Guess not."

Edward stepped aside and signaled for her to join him. She did. "I need to ask you a question,"

Before she could answer, three four-by-four police cars sped to them. Sirens wailed and lights flashed.

Seven cops, all dressed in green, surrounded them. They did not pull their guns; no need to.

An officer approached. He reminded Edward of the Arab terrorist they always bust at the end of the movie: short, olive skinned, bearded, unsteady eyes. Probably it was easier this way, to stereotype people and contain the terrorist behavior with the same gene that gave this man his skin color. Or maybe Edward was just rambling in this pointless monologue to distract himself from the fact that everything went south in a blink.

The officer focused on Safiya, his face stern. "Your Highness," the officer said in a resolute tone. There was no apologetic smile, no embarrassed look. He pointed at Edward and Zain. "This will end... now."

-42-

Safiya looked at Edward, as if to ask what to do. Edward forced a smile and nodded. The officer said something about Edward and Zain coming with him to the police department downtown.

"She gave our location to the police," Zain whispered to him. "I *knew* it."

"Safiya?" Edward whispered back. "No way."

"She came for an adventure and now she wants out."

Edward couldn't tell Zain why he thought Safiya was with them, but deep inside, he knew he was right. Safiya wouldn't do anything to harm him. She was here because of *him*. The way she was arguing with the officer now, the fear, the desperation. Moving from reasoning to pleading. It wasn't a princess trying to protect her companion. Rather, a woman afraid to lose the man she... loved? Could that be? How could he forget such a thing? Oh, God.

Edward scanned the area. Vane should be here any moment now. But where could he hide? The hills? Those were protected by a fence. The roof of the building where Kimberly was supposed to meet them? Maybe. Vane would blend in a way no one could spot him, even if they looked directly at him. The policeman walked toward Edward. Edward held his watch, ready to press the connection button when his iPhone rang.

"Hello," he said.

"So, let's save Private Ryan." Vane's voice was bored, as if commenting on a game he saw hundreds of times. "Please hand over the phone to *l'officier courageux*."

Edward turned to the officer and extended the cell. "Um... it's for you, officer."

The young officer frowned, then looked at Safiya. She just stared at him. Maybe he expected one of Safiya's contacts to call him, one of her brothers maybe, or his boss's boss to call and tell him this was all a mistake and he should apologize to the Princess. Probably the young officer knew deep inside that his career was over even if he was following orders. There was no such thing as law-above-all in this place. Maybe he knew that later the Princess would avenge herself by firing him.

The officer took the phone. Edward could swear that the young man's hand was shaking. *"Meen Ma'ee?"* (Who is on the line?)

The officer frowned more. "What?" He listened, nodded, then turned to face the other side and squinted at the far buildings, then at the hills. His face lost its color. His shaking hand was more prominent. "What... are... you mean... what?" The officer looked down at his belly. A tiny red spot glowed below his belt. A laser light.

The officer listened some more, nodded, and then handed Edward the phone. *"Yalla!"* he called for his team, his voice choked. *"Erjaao Wara,"* (pull back).

It took the reluctant soldiers some time to comprehend the order. Finally they went to their cars and pulled back to the entrance of the site, some five hundred feet away. Only one large uniform with dark skin and the body of a bulldozer stayed with the officer.

"He is staying with me," the officer said on the cell. "What? Which house? Okay, I see it. I will go inside and wait for you. Remember... you cross me, my men will take you down." The officer cursed under his breath and took out his gun and tossed it away. Bulldozer did the same.

Gone were the confident postures and the arrogant grins, replaced now with weary looks and a shaking hand that gave Edward his cell back.

Edward put the iPhone back to his ear. Vane's voice came calm but urgent. "Leave... *now.*"

-43-

<Ryadh City – Saudi Arabia>
<Time left until Zero hour is 10hrs:50min>
<Number of infected websites: 695,550>

Archer stood inside the long corridor leading to the archives room in the Higher Community for Islamic Affairs building. Wooden doors were to his left and right. Metal plates carried writing in Arabic for different department names. The floor was covered with a yellow carpet that didn't quite go with the shiny green furniture and green wallpaper. A long window with one small opening, similar to what you might see at old banks extended in the wall, giving a partial view of the archiving department. A short, dark-skinned man sat behind the first desk after the window. Must be the place where documents were submitted for archiving. Behind him were a dozen cubical desks.

A man bent over his desktop computer; the blue page of Facebook filled the screen. Others chatted, gathering around one desk.

But this wasn't his target. The documents he was after should have been moved to the archiving storeroom at the end of the corridor. In the beginning, he couldn't understand what an institution like this had to do with a case from 1965, but what Jassem, the retired officer told him, started to make sense.

More and more on this mission, Archer was convinced that something big was going on. A cover-up, and not just any cover-up. One that had been going on for decades and maybe lot more. From his experience, such a cover-up meant fire behind the smoke. So maybe the old millionaire who hired him was not crazy after all. And maybe, just maybe, he would really have a chance to... no... too early to think about that. And yet, just the possibility that he could have another chance for revenge made him feel... alive.

Time to focus on the mission. Getting inside was a bit tricky but for someone who could perfect a disguise that got him into high-security buildings in North Korea and Iran, infiltrating a civilian building in Saudi hardly qualified as a challenge.

He looked at the wrist watch on his right hand. For some reason, religious police wore everything on the right. Except the ring, it had to be on the left. Whatever. Still five minutes before the midday prayer time. Archer had done enough missions in Saudi Arabia to know that at prayer time, no one was allowed to stay at his office. Everyone should go pray, except for non-Muslims, yet he doubted any non-Muslim would be hired to work in the Higher Community For Sharyaa Affairs.

Dishdashes passed him, leaving their offices, heading to the third-floor prayer room. One might think people would complain about forced prayer times. Well, they did, but not much. Most of them looked at it as a forced break. And let's face it, Saudis didn't strike him as workaholics. One peek at any workspace told you why five-minute paperwork took two days.

Prayer time. He could hear the Athan, the call for Salat, through the sound system. Employees, all males, all wearing the white tablecloths and the rosy head covers nodded to him with fear as they headed upstairs.

They should.

His choice of disguise was smart.

Once the corridor became empty, he strolled toward the archiving room, peeking at the offices. No one there. In front of the door now. The archive store. Shit. An electronic lock protected the metal door. This stupid tablecloth he wore didn't allow any room for his tools. Even if he had brought them, it would be very conspicuous to stand in front of a door in mid-day trying to hack a lock.

Fortunately, easier methods existed.

Footsteps approached from the other end of the corridor. A man with sleek black hair and a khaki uniform appeared. A security guard. They exchanged glances. Archer stepped toward him, waving his wooden stick in the air.

"*Salam Alycum,* Sir," the Indian security guard greeted him.

"*Enta Laysh Ma Ysali?*" (Why are you not praying?) Archer barked, already tuned into the role of the Islamic police inspector. The most feared authority figure in Saudi and the only man who could wander around during prayer time. A medieval inquisitor with the tools of the Twentieth Century and the mind-set of... well, a cave man.

Okay, maybe Archer had a grudge against men with long beards who shoved people to pray with wooden sticks.

Archer had studied the religious police of Saudi for enough time to know all the details about their methods, their privileges, what places they could access, and what information they could obtain. Forget about bureaucracy, forget about human rights, forget about inter-agency communications, whatever that was, these people had limitless power to get inside any place they wanted and do almost anything they wanted as long as the dear religion was protected. Protected from whom and against what, Archer couldn't understand. But when talking about places like this, human-rights-related debates seemed to be as relevant as talking about life in Mars.

Another benefit of studying the religious police was he could master his disguise. His long beard and the shade at the end of the eyes, the ID card he had stolen, along with the careful choice of the ankle-length dishdash, and most importantly the rude, scowling attitude made it impossible for anyone to recognize him.

"Me no Muslim, Sir," the security guard replied, his gaze fixed on the wooden stick.

Archer faked anger. His eyes bulged and he started swiping the thin stick in the air threatening to hit the man. "*Emshi, Emshi.*" (move, move.)

"I am no Muslim, Sir," the man pled, but two lashes on his thigh sent him running to the prayer room.

Talk about the power of faith.

Time to get in. He examined the electronic card reader. A small red LED light on a black plastic box. No keypad, no place to swipe a card, which meant only one thing, an RFID reader. He doubted that the real inspector from whom he had stolen identification and access card had access to this room. He tried his card anyway. The red light flashed then gave a long beep.

No go.

His second choice would be to get one of the employees to open it for him. It would be tricky to get someone out of the prayer room. After all, his job was to get people *in,* not out.

Archer checked the brand name on the card reader. TemaLine. He squinted at the ceiling and examined the fire-alarm speakers and the smoke detectors. The familiar red logo of Honeywell, which was the manufacturer of Temaline products as well. That meant both the card reader and the fire system were from the same company. Most likely part of one deal, and most likely integrated.

It wasn't the first time his thorough knowledge of various systems saved the day.

Archer took a lighter from his pocket and a piece of paper from one of the nearby desks. He lit the paper, letting the smoke go up to the smoke detector. Seconds later the fire alarm system crackled and gave a long beep. He glanced at the red LED light on the door. Still red. The fire alarm wasn't acknowledged yet. New systems had the feature of acknowledging the fire from a central computer, normally located in the security room or the facility control room. Still, all systems should allow for manual acknowledgement. That is, allow for normal people to report fire situations.

Archer looked for the familiar red fire box with the breakable glass. Bingo. It was ten feet away at the end of the corridor. He smashed the glass. The alarm got louder to the point of deafening. Water showered from the small sprinklers in the ceiling. The LED light turned green. A common practice during fire situations for all electronic doors to switch to an open state to facilitate evacuating personnel and valuable assets.

The downside was that he would not have much time before the security team arrived. Archer shrugged. Just more casualties.

He opened the door and slid inside.

-44-

<Madeena City – Saudi Arabia>
<Time left until Zero hour is 10hrs:30min>
<Number of infected websites: 789,778>

"Did you have a chance to look at the symbol, Doctor?" Zain asked after they were a safe distance from the police.

"Yes, the same plate with the same symbol," Fayazi said.

Edward looked back through the rear window. Where was Kim? Should he stay there and wait for her?

"What was the Ayah number?" Safiya asked.

"Two numbers, not one," Fayazi said, "42:23 and 76:9"

"We need a Quran," she said.

"I know the first one!" Zain yelled. "Say, O Muhammad, 'I do not ask you for this message any payment but only fellowship to kinship.' And whoever commits a good deed - We will increase for him good therein. Indeed, Allah is Forgiving and Appreciative."

"Fellowship to kinship?" Edward said, feeling that he had just awakened. His thoughts were with Vane and Kimberly. Vane would manage to get whatever information he wanted from the police. He would also manage to get out of there safe and sound. Still, the image of the two policemen getting inside that gray house where Vane supposedly would meet them kept gnawing at him. Guilt. "What kinship? It's about Fatima, right?"

"No," Safiya said. "I think it's asking the Muslim to be good with their relatives."

"A common misunderstanding." Fayazi shook his head. "Allah is telling Mohammed that when people ask you what to give in return for all your efforts of delivering the message, tell them the way to pay you is through fellowship to Mohammed's kinship."

"But how come?" Safiya protested, still looking at the road ahead. "The messenger of God should not ask anything for himself."

"He didn't," Fayazi said. "That's why there is another Ayah after this, saying: 'Whatever I asked you as a reward is actually for you.'"

Fayazi took a bottle of water from the small compartment in the back seat. He drank some, then said, "Don't you get it? Mohammed wanted to make sure that when he died, the nation would follow the track God pointed to them, that the people would have a guide, and that they would respect and follow that guide even if —"

"Even if that guide was a woman," Edward said. Strange as it might sound, pieces were coming together.

"And her sons," Fayazi said. "The same people Mohammed repeatedly said were his household. The family that he covered with his cloak and prayed to God to purify and be their guide so that they could guide the people, the students whom he personally supervised and made sure they were up to the task."

Okay, so it *was* about Fatima, but where did this lead them? And why should he care? Was this still their only lead to Kimberly? "What did the second Ayah say?" Edward asked.

Safiya reached into her pink purse and gave him the small Sony laptop. The car veered to the left as she did that.

"I got it," Edward said. "Focus on the road."

Her hands were shaking, and Edward doubted that it had anything to do with the laptop or even the Musehaf of Fatima.

Zain took the laptop from Edward, powered it up, and started Internet Explorer. "Get yourself Firefox, Princess, with all the security plug-ins, and don't browse the Internet while you are logged in with the Admin account."

"Huh?"

"Your computer is infected, Princess." Zain's fingers blurred on the small keyboard. The only person Edward had seen working on the computer this fast was Abbie.

Zain typed in a Quran website address. A web page loaded, then the same thing happened —another page started downloading and the message with the counter showed ten hours remaining. Zain opened a black window. His fingers danced even faster. He hummed a song, the typing sound of the keyboard followed the rhythm of the song.

And they said computer weenies didn't have good taste in music.

"Nice song," Edward said.

"It's not a song," Zain said, opening new windows.

Fayazi explained, "It's a sad poem, about attacking Fatima's house after the prophet's death."

So much for the taste in music.

Seconds later, Zain refreshed the browser screen. The message and the counter were gone and the Quran website was there with a search box in the middle.

Edward said, "Someone had a lot of spare time and decided to play around on the Web."

Without moving his gaze from the screen, Zain said, "I would take them seriously if I were you. Maybe they are not just bored computer hackers."

Zain typed the Surrah and Ayah numbers in the search box and waited.

The Ayah came in Arabic and English.

Fayazi closed his eyes and started reciting, before he looked at the screen: " 'And they give food for the love of Allah, the needy, the orphan and captive. We feed you only for the countenance of Allah. We wish not from you reward or gratitude.'"

"A bit late, Doctor, no marks for you this time," Edward chuckled.

"I know the Ayah." Fayazi smiled sheepishly. "It's the translation that always holds me."

"Don't tell me," Edward said. "Those giving the food were Fatima's family."

Fayazi smiled. "You don't need me anymore. But the story is very touching."

"Touching?" Edward frowned.

"Fatima gave up her food, and Ali's and her two sons', for three days in a row, first to a poor man, then to an orphan, then to a war prisoner from Quraish. For three days they had only water."

"But why give four shares for one man?" Edward asked. "Ali could donate his part and they share the rest together."

"First, this was always their way; Fatima's family never missed a chance to give and help. Second, and most importantly, their parts were just small pieces of bread. It wouldn't be enough."

Edward, ever the skeptic, shook his head. "But Fatima was the daughter of the prophet, the man who ruled the city."

"And the man who also said that the ruler should be as poor as the poorest man of his people."

"Mohammed said that?" Edward asked.

"He *lived* like that," Fayazi said. "This story is one among many other testimonies to the way Mohammed and his family lived."

"Doctor, listen to yourself." Safiya chuckled. "You sound like a campaign manager in the election year."

"Really?" Fayazi scoffed. "Doesn't it surprise you, Princess, how most Muslims know very little about Mohammed but they know everything about Jihad?"

She opened her mouth but said nothing.

Far behind them, a car followed, maintaining a considerable distance. Edward couldn't tell if it were a police vehicle, or if it even followed them, but that tiny dot in the deserted road made them all edgy.

"So where should we go?" Edward asked.

"To Fatima's house, in Madeena," Fayazi said. "Both Ayahs talked about what happened in that place. The problem is, like anything to do with Fatima and Ali, the house was demolished and it's now part of the big mosque."

"But the Baqee' is still there," Zain said.

Edward was about to ask what Baqee' was but Fayazi explained. "Baqee' is the cemetery next to the Mosque where Fatima's sons were buried. It has always been treated as the reminder of Fatima and her sons in Madeena."

"So should we go to the Baqee'?" Safiya said, typing into her GPS.

"For your GPS, put the address as Abu Thar street," Zain said. "It will put you directly in the street between the big mosque and the Baqee' cemetery."

"I didn't know the street name was Abu-Thar," Fayazi said, taking another gulp of water.

"Yeah, looks like a mistake." Zain smiled. "Or someone did not do his homework well and check on the man's background."

The car, still following them, turned out to be a black GMC. Safiya stepped on the gas pedal. The Bentley roared and the GMC turned into a small dot again before completely vanishing. They all cheered, except for Zain.

"I don't understand," Edward said, "who is Abu Thar?"

Fayazi said, "One of the prophet's few companions who stayed loyal to Fatima and the prophet's family after his death. The third king after Mohammed sensed a threat because Abu Thar kept reminding the people how Mohammed's rule was different from the new... well, *regime*, so he was expelled to Rabatha, a city close to Madeena."

"A desert with no people," Zain said. "He died alone. But he kept saying he never regretted supporting Fatima and the holy family. By the way, the Rabatha city has evolved since then,"

Zain messaged his neck where the bearded man had hit him. "People came and settled next to the grave of that brave man. And you cannot imagine the blessings at that place."

Another campaign for Abu Thar. It was election year, all right.

Once they reached the main road, Zain leaned forward and tapped on Safiya's shoulder. "Please drop me here."

She slowed down. "But—"

"That's it… I am afraid I cannot be with you guys. Someone is tipping the police about our whereabouts and there is just too much to lose, at least for me."

Fayazi grabbed Zain's arm. "But, son—"

Zain shook his head. "Sorry, Doctor." He gently pulled his arm away and stepped out.

-45-

<Madeena City – Saudi Arabia>
<Time left until Zero hour is 10hrs:10min>
<Number of infected websites: 860,700>

No one spoke a word for some time after Zane left. Edward wanted so badly to hold Safiya's hand and tell her that he trusted her. But they needed to be alone. He wasn't sure it was a good idea to discuss what he started remembering in front of Fayazi. Like the butterfly tattoo on her back. How could he know about that? And who was that man he remembered beating her? But above all, if he were right and he had met Safiya, it must have been during his alleged visit to Saudi. Talking to her might shed light on the year and a half of his life that he couldn't remember. And for some reason, he wasn't sure he was ready for that.

"I still don't get it, Doctor," Edward said, trying to change the mood. "What is so special about Fatima? Mohammed had some other children, even boys, right? Why all the focus on her?"

"First," Fayazi said, "it's not us who are focusing on Fatima. Mohammed never missed a chance to tell people how important

Fatima was. And that those who followed her and respected her would be the first to enter God's heaven. You have to understand the culture in the Arabic society back then, especially at Mecca. They treated women like objects; I don't say animals because animals were treated much better than women. Women were nothing but a shame to their families, and an object of sex to others. Most of the noblemen of Quraish, the clans who lived in Mecca, buried their newborns alive if female." Fayazi took a long breath, then said, "It was so common in their culture that Quran had several phrases reproaching them for doing this and reminding them that they would all be questioned about the innocent souls they have killed and that men and women were all the same in front of God."

Safiya spoke in a low voice. "You still see women treated as second-class citizens in many Arab countries. No right to vote, no right to work, hell, even no right to drive a fucking car." She exhaled, "Forgive my French."

Edward remembered the shop with the back entrance for ladies, the way Short-Dishdash in Uhud hit Safiya. "Do you think that might be the reason, Doctor? I mean Mohammed was trying to educate the people of his time to treat women better and he used Fatima as an example."

Fayazi shook his head. "Maybe. But, Fatima had another dimension in Islam. There are a lot of prayers told by the emams, the sons of Fatima and Ali, and some of them gave Fatima a unique status even in comparison to her father." Fayazi opened his pocket notebook to the first page. There were two printed lines in Arabic. The translation was something close to this:

"God, I ask you by Fatima, her father and her husband, her sons and the secret within her."

"You see," Fayazi's bushy eyebrows arched up, "it's all about Fatima. She is the center... the secret. If you ask me, Fatima was God's way to point to Muslims what they should do after the prophet's death. The failsafe for the big diversion to come."

They were inside the city now. The streets were cleaner, crowded with cars, all driven by males. Why were women not allowed to drive a car?

"There was no diversion after the prophet's death, Doctor." Safiya said. "It was the democracy of choosing the prophet's successor."

Fayazi sneered. "People can choose their kings, fine, but they cannot choose prophets or their successors. That's God's job."

They stopped at a traffic signal. A woman covered in black crossed the street guiding a child. Other drivers yelled at her, some honked, others threw comments about how attractive she was. Finally, one moved his car forward to block her path.

"This is the Saudi's way of flirting." Safiya sighed. "You, idiots! Can't you see the child?"

For Edward the child was one thing, these strange and barbaric customs were another, but the big question remained: with the woman covered from top to toe in black, with what were they flirting? Her sense of fashion?

"So what was Fatima's role in all of this?" Edward asked when the traffic moved again.

"Here is what made Fatima unique in my opinion." Fayazi raised his index finger. "Unlike everyone else, her expostulation on the way things went was not by words. Words could be, and often were, distorted and twisted. But Fatima expressed her position with actions, actions even Islam's twisted history could not misinterpret. And this is what makes anything from Fatima super-dangerous to the rulers — the kings, in the past and now."

"Like the Musehaf of Fatima," Edward said.

"Exactly." Fayazi gave him a thumbs up. "Look at how Fatima insisted that her grave be hidden. Till our day, the question remains why the grave of the prophet's daughter is not known. The answer is simple: because that was her will. Why? She condemned the changes to Islam, changing the religion to politics, replacing the prophet's successor chosen by God with a king they had chosen."

"There is no proof of all of this." Safiya shook her head.

"So why was her tomb hidden? Why was her house burned after the prophet's death? Why did she die so young? Why did she go to the mosque and give that historical speech of hers?" Fayazi started coughing, his face red. It took him a few seconds to calm down. "Do you know that most of this was documented in letters exchanged between the people participating in burning her house?"

"Just lies, all made up. History was twisted." Safiya shrugged.

"Yes, twisted for the sake of the kings. Look at the rulers who followed the Prophet, Safiya. They were all on the bad side of Fatima; she publicly condemned them. The only one who was really elected by *people,* not by *force,* was Ali. People forced him to accept the role after the rebellion killed the third king. But Ali was soon assassinated after the war with Muawya, the fifth king. Then all the kings who followed were Muawya's sons. They declared Islam as monarchy. That the Khalifa, which basically meant the man following the prophet, would be only from their family — the family who fought Mohammed and ate his uncle's liver! Each one of them had either killed or chased whoever survived of Fatima's offspring. The Amoyeen kings used to start the Friday prayers by cursing Fatima and Ali. How did *that* happen?"

Fayazi started coughing again. "History was written and twisted for the sake of those kings. Only God knew what happened back then, but what survived the alteration was more than enough to explain."

"Explain what?" Edward said.

Fayazi waved it off, making a growling, angry sound.

Edward wanted to ask about that, to ask about the message on the Internet and how it related to what happened to Fatima, about Abdul Zahra and his father and Zain and whether they were involved in something bigger. He did not ask. Partly because there were things he couldn't talk about. Things like the FBI and the man who almost killed him in Fadak. Another part was that Edward had a feeling that whatever was going on Saudi had something to do with his past. But the most important part was that he could see the four white minarets of the big mosque now.

They had reached the prophet's mosque. Almasjed Alnabawi.

-46-

If one word could describe the prophet's mosque in Madeena, it would be *enormous*. Safiya had been driving around the edifice for the past ten minutes and so far Edward could only see one side of the mosque. Five-star hotels surrounded the structure, leaving only the marble minarets visible from the main street.

"Why don't you use the road Zain mentioned?" Fayazi asked.

Safiya pointed with her chin to Edward.

"Can I get inside?" Edward asked. But he already knew the answer.

"Non-Muslims are not allowed inside," Safiya muttered. She was still upset by her discussion with Fayazi or because of what Zain had done. Or both.

Fayazi didn't comment. The old man stared from the window at the glass facades of the five-star hotels that crowded the street as if an idiot held the elevator door open shouting: "Come on, we can squeeze in one more hotel."

The crazy, enthusiastic professor who kept jumping around and throwing new theories at them was gone. An old man with a shaking hand, a wandering look, and long sighs took over. A man haunted by his own demons. Something Edward was familiar with. You are fine as long as you keep moving. As long as you don't think. The moment you stop, the moment you face your demons, your past will mercilessly get you.

Maybe Edward was not after the Musehaf, maybe he was not even after finding his friend. Yes, he wanted to help her. Yes, he wanted to satisfy his curiosity and find this secret Quran. But it was something more; he needed to run. He needed a distraction from his own past. For years he kept convincing himself that he wanted to discover the secret of what happened to him. It seemed that this was the normal thing to do. He wasn't sure anymore. His discussion with the FBI agent, added to what he knew now about his previous visit to Saudi, had awakened a fear that he wasn't the innocent victim everyone treated him as. The keyword here was *awakened*. Now when he thought about it, those fears were there, maybe in his subconscious, maybe in a dark corner of his mind locked behind whatever doors his defense mechanisms had created. Who knew?

Immersed in his thoughts, he didn't pay attention to where Safiya had parked. He followed them along a narrow paved road. A long fence lay ahead of them, behind it, a big green dome was surrounded by several large, shiny marble pillars, the minarets. Then next to it stretched a big structure with golden domes and smaller minarets.

"What is that?" Edward asked, pointing at the green dome.

"It's the original mosque of the prophet and his second house. He lived here in Madeena after leaving Mecca," Fayazi said. "It is where he was buried. The big building you see here was all added as an extension to the mosque in stages at different times since then."

Edward examined it. There was something about mosques, chapels, churches, and temples — he wasn't sure what it was. They were engulfed within an invisible cocoon where time stopped.

Probably the jet-lag and him needing a long sleep.

"What is that? The small rectangle on the dome," he asked.

Safiya cupped her eyes with her hands, looking where he had pointed. "I am not sure. It's like a small refrigerator."

"The cursed man." Fayazi chuckled without even looking up.

"What cursed man?" Safiya asked, wrapping the face cover on top of the head cover. Face cover, head cover, body cover — being a woman in Saudi must be a lot of fun.

"It's just a rumor everyone is talking about but no one can deny or prove." Fayazi shrugged.

They stood in front of a small house guarded by a long brick fence that extended all the way to the big mosque. Safiya knocked on the gray door of the house.

Fayazi continued, "They say that during the '20s when Saudis were demolishing all the shrines of the prophet's known companions and family members, including Khadeeja, his grandsons, and others, they tried to demolish the shrine of the prophet himself."

"Why?"

Safiya rolled her eyes, sighed, and said, knocking on the small door again, "It's part of the Wahhabi religion that all tombs must be demolished and must be flat with the ground."

"Thank you, Princess." Fayazi almost bowed. "The Wahhabi, the official sect of the Saudi rulers, was imposed on all Muslims, who had to watch the holy shrines in Saudi be demolished. No respect for history, no respect for other beliefs, and no respect for the dead..." Fayazi shook his head and took a long breath. "Anyway... the story is that they were reluctant about demolishing the prophet's mosque. On one hand, because the prophet was buried there, they looked at it as a tomb. On the other hand, it was the holy mosque all Muslims were attached to. So rumor had it that an extremist climbed on the green dome carrying a hammer to knock it down. Lighting struck. They said his body was so burned they couldn't get all of it out of the dome."

Safiya frowned. "So they covered it with this rectangular thing?"

Fayazi shrugged. "I am not saying I am buying this story, but it's the only explanation I heard."

Finally the door opened. A man wearing — surprise — a normal-length white dishdash and a red baseball cap with the Ferrari horse — greeted them with the same enthusiasm as someone opening the door to find a Jehovah's witness on the doorstep.

"What do you want?" the man asked, his gaze fixed on Edward.

Safiya said, "Your Facebook wall is empty, and no tweets for the last week. So we thought about paying you a visit."

Ferrari cap squinted at her then broke a smile. "Safiya! No way."

"Glad you still recognize my voice."

Ferrari cap put a hand on his chest, faking shock. "Oh, how can I forget our generous sponsor."

"Yeah, yeah, my phone record is filled with missed calls from you."

Ferrari winced. "I know, I should've called after that asshole divorced —"

"Yeah, whatever," Safiya snapped. "Keep giving us excuses while we stand in the sun."

He ushered them in. They sat in a small room that was meant to be an office but ended up as something between a studio apartment and a meeting room in which a meeting had dragged on for weeks. Besides the two desktop computers on the only desk in the room, a small plasma TV hung on the wall. A black leather couch was filled with files, books, and another white dishdash in a plastic bag as if it had just arrived from the laundry. A half-opened Pizza Hut box rested on the wooden table next to the couch with one family-sized Pepsi bottle and two empty plates. The only window in the room had a view of a large area of sand. Edward knew better now; the evenly laid rocks, the cement walkways in the sand. It was a cemetery.

"*Hal Hathi Janat Al-Baqee'*?" (Is this the Baqee' heaven?) Fayazi asked, looking out the window.

Ferrari cap nodded.

"Heaven?" Edward asked.

"Some people call it this way." Ferrari shrugged. His entire body undulated when he talked. "Lot of the prophet's companions buried here, several of his wives, and the rest of his family."

Safiya cleared a place on the couch and sat. "So, how is your GPS project, Rashid?"

Rashid brought two chairs from behind the desk and offered them to Fayazi and Edward. He sat next to Safiya on the couch. "Going on, we have all the graves from 1920 in the system now. Thanks to you, Safiya. Without your help we wouldn't get this approved."

Safiya poked him in the chest. "Stop the ass-kissing."

Fayazi cocked his head. "Do you mean you have all tombs marked with GPS locations and in the system?"

Rashid spoke with broken English and a vigorous zeal, "More than that. Give me a name and I can tell you if any of his relatives are in the cemetery. And the locations of their tombs."

"Great," Fayazi murmured, walking to the computer.

"Try for yourself, the search page is open." Rashid pointed at the screen.

Fayazi leaned over the desk and typed with one finger, each keystroke separated by a long breath and a lot of searching. If this were a movie, it would show clock arms moving fast, then calendar pages flipping one after another. Finally Fayazi frowned. "It's not working."

Rashid laughed. "It's working. We receive twenty requests per day from people who want to know where their dead ones are. What name you tried?"

"I put in the prophet Mohammed's name to see where his relatives are on your map. A lot of Mohammeds came up with the same last name but not the prophet. Those all died recently."

Rashid grinned. "I told you the records are only for 1920." He leaned on the table, grabbed a newspaper, and gave it to Safiya. "Here, see, they even wrote in Wattan newspaper about our project. See my name here."

Fayazi scowled. "So I can find a grave of some nobody who died forty years ago but you cannot mark the graves of the people who supported the prophet, the people who sacrificed their lives—"

Rashid held up his hand. "Easy on me, this foundation is for records, not historical data. We have in Saudi a complete department for historical sites."

Fayazi's face reddened. He took off his glasses with a shaking hand. "And they have managed to do a damn good job of wiping out all the names and grave markers, and demolishing all the shrines. Can someone tell me now where the prophet's grandsons were buried? How can I visit their graves and pay my respects?"

Rashid looked at Safiya. "What's going on?"

She forced a smile. "It's a long story. Listen, Rashid, I need to get to Baqee' cemetery, the old section, the one close to the big mosque. Can you help?"

Rashid shrugged. "Sure, it's all connected, we just walk from here."

They stood to leave when Edward's cell rang. Vane.

"Ed," Kimberly's voice came weak.

"Kim! My God, are you with Vane? Wh——"

"I am okay," she said. "Vane wants to speak with you."

Before Edward could say anything, Vane said, "I don't have time to explain, meet us in the Hilton Hotel. Al-Haram restaurant. It's right in front of the big mosque, five hundred yards from where you are now."

"On my way."

"And Edward," Vane said in his measured, calm tone. "Come alone, please."

-47-

The Hilton Hotel was a ten-story blue-glass facade that reflected the white marble minarets and the golden domes.

Edward took the stairs to the first floor. A well-dressed young man in a black suit greeted him with a wide smile and asked if he had a reservation. Edward told him he was supposed to meet a friend here. Keeping the wide smile, the young man told him he must have a reservation or a name.

After five minutes of discussion, Edward managed to get inside the restaurant. Four rows of tables covered with white cloths extended over fifty meters. All the windows had a view of the big courtyard inside the prophet's mosque. Edward let out a gasp. No, *enormous* was not the word to describe the big mosque. The way the sun reflected off the shiny alabaster floor that stretched endlessly, the line of small golden cupolas, the engraved Arabic calligraphy that covered the walls, the white clothes of the pilgrims... It felt like staring at a sea of lights. For a moment, Edward stood there admiring the spectacular view, immersed in unfamiliar thoughts about heaven and the afterlife.

How could he forget seeing such a thing? No, this *was* the first time he had visited this place.

The restaurant was almost empty. So much for "you need a reservation." At the last table, far from the door, sat a woman in all-black Islamic dress, similar to what Safiya wore when she wanted to go out. Unlike Safiya's, this woman's dress was baggy and at least two sizes too big. In front of her sat Vane, dressed in white cotton pants and a white long-sleeved shirt, his head covered with the white head cover local Saudis wore. His pale skin was sunburned, reminding Edward of Peter O'Toole from *Lawrence of Arabia.*

"Kimberly," Edward called, barely able to hear his own voice with the thud in his chest.

She turned, her freckly face swollen and tired, her eyes surrounded by black circles that spoke of a night of terror. Kimberly stifled a cry when their eyes met. She ran toward him and threw herself into his arms. "Oh my God." She sniffled, her shoulders heaving, her warm breath burning his shoulder. "Ed, you came for me."

"You are okay now." He patted her back. "It's over."

She pulled away slowly, looking at him with bloodshot eyes. "Not yet."

"What do you mean, not yet?"

Kimberly gestured to the table. "Let's sit and talk."

"There is no talking, Kim, we have to leave this place right now. Vane, talk to her."

"No use." Vane sipped from the glass of water in front of him. "But, we can always sedate her and put her on the plane."

Kimberly glared at him. Then she smiled, reaching for his hand. "I really appreciate what you did for me, Vane. But I need to finish this."

"Kimberly," Edward protested. "We just—"

Vane yawned. "Kids, you can both argue as long as you want, but Edward, I need your shoe. *dès maintenant, s'il vous plait.* Now, please."

"What?"

Vane opened his palm, feigning impatience. Edward took off his shoe and handed it over. Vane took out a knife and stabbed the shoe's heel, taking the cover out.

"What the h—"

"This," Vane held up a small, black object the size of a match box, "is how they were tracking you."

I.M.Hussaini

PART FIVE

Sixty percent of working women in Saudi get financially abused by their husbands. In many cases, the husband takes the money from his wife to buy a new home to marry another.

The good thing is, there aren't a lot of working women in Saudi.

-48-

Vane took Edward and Kimberly to another hotel, Dar-Al-Taqwa Intercontinental, which was around the corner. They sat in a similar restaurant to the one in the Hilton, with the same view of the mosque and its big courtyard, and with the same number of empty tables.

Off season.

They concluded that when Edward was in the airport, the police must have planted the tracking device.

"Back in Uhud," Edward said, "why did you ask the two policemen to go inside the house?"

"They weren't police," Vane said, beckoning for the groomed waiter, who was steps away.

"Special branch?" Edward asked.

Vane nodded. Then to the waiter: "One *Shish Tawook* for the lady, one *Kibbah Neeya* plate for me, and *Fatoosh* for my friend here."

"What is *Kibba neeya*?" Kimberly asked.

"Raw minced meat with spice and onion."

Edward frowned. "I thought vampires didn't like onion."

"Some are on a special diet."

The waiter, a young man with traces of acne on his cheeks and forehead, asked if they would like drinks. Vane asked for more mineral water. The waiter took the food menus and left.

"I still don't understand why you wanted to talk to the policemen," Edward said. "Did you suspect they knew where Kim was being held?"

"I knew that the warehouse Kim was held in was in that area," Vane said, moving his finger in a circle around the rim of the empty glass in front of him. "So I figured out that if those guys worked for the same people who kidnapped her, and they most likely did since they forced her to call you, then they should know where the place was. *Facile, non?*"

"Am I missing something?" Kimberly loosened her head cover and breathed as if it strangled her. "How did you know about the warehouse in the first place?"

Vane bared his teeth in a smile that sent chills all over Edward's spine. "Oh, people talk."

"And you can be persuasive." Edward heard himself saying.

"That I can."

The waiter came back with lunch. Edward's *Fatoosh* looked like a Cesar salad with lots of olive oil and crispy pieces of bread and a sour black sauce. Vane told him it was pomegranate sauce.

They ate in silence. Then Edward said, "Kim, you know it's better for you to leave this place."

Kimberly finished chewing on her *Shish Tawook,* which was small grilled cubes of chicken, swallowed, and said, "You know I'll say I can't."

"It's too dangerous. Whoever kidnapped you and whoever's watching me will not let us just walk away."

"That's exactly my point," Kimberly said. "We have to find the Musehaf."

Not again.

"I got involved in all of this," Kimberly said, staring at her dish. "For days I was reading Fatima's speech over and over and every time I found more proof of my theory."

Edward nodded, hoping she would skip this part. Kim talked a lot about her theory of the role of women in the political movements of the dark ages, and Edward wasn't in the mood for another historical lecture.

"Anyway, I discovered new things. I realized that Fatima was not just a woman playing a role in a political debate, or trying to get back her rights that the ruler had confiscated. Fatima established the principle that people could question their governments. She was talking about an ideology where the government is responsible to the people, men and women. And this was not just any woman; she was the one about whom their prophet was saying that God would be pleased if she was pleased."

"So, what happened?" Edward sneered.

"Exactly," Kimberly said, her penciled eyebrows in perfect half moons. "Figuring out what happened is more important than Fatima's movement itself. Because I think one can uncover a lot of things by opening this door."

Kimberly took another bite of her chicken, drank some water, then said, "Fatima and her movement might be history, but the way her people treated her is still the present. The cover-up is still happening. And the injustice against Fatima has evolved and has taken a dangerous shape now." She paused, her eyes glistening with something akin to a religious zeal. "Maybe if we revealed that, we would change the future."

"Probably." Edward tried to shrug but couldn't pull it off. Although dramatic, Kimberly was right. Her kidnapping, the message on the Internet, the number of people involved in this matter, made it clear that this wasn't about historical research. Something else made certain people so scared that they were ready to kill for it... Okay, maybe killing in this part of the world might not be a big deal, but using all these resources and money was something else.

"Tell me what happened with Fayazi," Edward asked. "Why did you decide to go to Fadak?"

"Fayazi just confirmed the doubts I had about what happened to Fatima. When I met him at the college in Jordan, he told me about his research and how he could prove that Islam took a dangerous route once the prophet died."

"Boring," Vane said, doing his best *Homer Simpson*.

"Maybe." Kimberly smiled. Her sweet smile that Edward had missed so much and was afraid he wouldn't see again. "But we are not here to evaluate the religion. All I'm trying to say is that something big happened and we need to understand what it is before assessing the ramifications."

Kimberly went on with her account, although adding nothing new to what Fayazi had told him. "Once Majida and I went inside the clay house in Fadak, we found Abdul Zahra..."

"Dead?" Edward said.

She nodded, looking down at the table. "It was horrible, I just can't forget his eyes." Kimberly wiped her own. "Then all I know is the room started spinning and everything turned black. When I opened my eyes again I was tied up in another place with men around me, asking me about Fatima's Musehaf."

"But why did they ask for the files to be uploaded? Why didn't they ask *you* to give them all the files. You have access to our server."

"Ed, what are you talking about?"

Edward told her about the calls he received from her phone.

"No way," Kim said, "my phone was lost in the house. They kept asking me for the phone all the time. Why would they do that if they had it?"

A family of four, parents and two girls, entered the restaurant and sat on the first table, far from them. The girls were fighting over what looked like a *Gameboy*. Mom and Dad kept hushing them.

"You mean the kidnappers didn't try to call me at all?"

She shook her head. "They were planning on killing me once they were sure I was no longer useful. I heard them talking about you as well."

So who called him? Who asked for the files to be uploaded to the FTP server and made all those threats about killing Kimberly otherwise?

"And you still want to go on with this search?" Edward asked her.

Kimberly nodded. "They are scared, Edward. I heard them saying that someone... an assassin of sorts, was killing people to extract information about the Musehaf of Fatima.

Edward looked at Vane. Vane wiggled his brown eyebrow. "*Un compétiteur.*"

"So it wasn't you?"

Vane put a hand on his chest, feigning insult. "*Moi?* Killing people for a book? Oh, my God."

"See," Edward told Kimberly rubbing his face. "Another reason why we should go back."

"By the way," Vane said, "the goon who beat the hell out of you in Fadak."

Edward's hand reflexively held his side. "What about him?"

"The tattoo you described and the scar..." Vane paused, cut a piece of bread put some of that *Kibbah Neyah* in it, then wrapped the bread and start eating. "He is bad news."

"How bad?"

"The kind that you want to keep the light turned on when you sleep."

"I already do."

"Get an extra one then." Vane smiled. He enjoyed this. In a sick way, Vane only became cheerful when there was a life threat.

"That bad?"

"A former CIA assassin, he lost his mind after his wife and daughter were killed in the bombing of the Hotel in Amman-Jordan in 2000 and started killing people, anyone who has links to the Qaeda or to extremists."

"Doesn't sound like a very bad guy to me," Kimberly said.

The corners of Vane's mouth curved up. "As I said, he lost his mind. Once he tortured an American businessman then killed him in front of his wife because he suspected that he was selling weapons to Hamas."

"Ah." Edward stabbed a slice of tomato with his fork but didn't feel like eating it.

"And that businessman was protected by a dozen of his body guards around the clock."

"He is dangerous," Edward said. "Even for you, Vane."

"Is that a challenge?" Vane's eyes glittered with... lunacy?

"Why is he after the Musehaf?" Kimberly asked, staring out the window as a flock of pigeons flew over the green dome.

Vane shrugged. "The rumor is that this Musehaf could end Islam and stop extremists for good. But that's just a rumor of course."

Again, the unlimited and fearsome power of the book of Fatima? But what could it be? A new Quran? Some buried teaching of Fatima or her father that condemned violence and terrorism? Fayazi had talked about the resistance Mohammed got from his people. How could his commands make any difference now when even in his time people found a way around them? The power of information could be huge when it touched on sensitive issues, but what could fourteen-hundred-year-old information do?

"Okay, we will go together," Edward said. "Let's go and get Dr. Fayazi and the others."

"About that." Vane batted his eye lashes. The same eye lashes thousands of teenage girls were willing to die for years ago when the show was on the silver screen. Maybe they still do. "Fayazi arranged for your VISAs."

"So?" Kimberly said.

Vane signaled for the waiter that they were ready to leave.

"Let's be careful," Vane said. The simplicity of his response combined with the glassy eyes and the stern face made Edward shiver. He often asked himself what it would be like if Vane weren't on his side, if Vane weren't his best friend. Then, Edward wasn't sure he wanted to know.

Edward let out a long breath. "I'll call Safiya and ask her to meet us alone."

Safiya picked up on the first ring. "I was about to call you, Edward," she said. The tenderness in her voice, the British accent, all were more prominent over the phone.

Good cellular networks could do that. It had nothing to do with her melodic voice, or the fact that each minute away from her felt like an eon.

"You okay?"

"It's Fayazi." She sniffled. "Zain came here, to the cemetery, and took him."

"What do you mean, *took* him?"

"Took him, for God sake, forced him to come with him... fucking kidnapped him."

<Madeena City – Saudi Arabia>
<Time left until Zero hour is 9hrs:15min>
<Number of infected websites: 973,760>

Edward led them to Rashid's office, where he had asked Safiya to wait.

Safiya opened the door even before they knocked. She threw herself on Edward and hugged him. "Oh my God, oh my God… It was—" She stepped back, noticing Kimberly and Vane. "I am sorry." She tucked away a wisp of raven black hair behind her ear. As she took another look at the dressed-in-black Kimberly, her eyes bulged. "My God, you are Kimberly, aren't you?" She gave her a hug.

What was with Safiya and hugging today?

"Let's go inside," Edward said.

For their convenience, Rashid had left the office.

Safiya's story was short. When they were in the Baqee' cemetery looking for the sign, Zain had appeared out of nowhere the moment Fayazi found the metal plate. Zain carried a knife and ordered the doctor to come with him.

A knife? So *West Side Story*.

"He said he didn't trust me and that I was the one who tipped the authorities about our whereabouts," Safiya said. Her mouth twitched as if stifling a cry. "After all I have done."

Despite how hard she wanted to look strong, the facade she put on, her moist eyes and quivering lips betrayed her. Safiya had tried to be part of something else, to belong to something other than the richest-royal-family-on-the-planet club. Or, maybe, just maybe, she wanted to be with him.

The sea-shell noise came back in his ears, the sound of the waves crashing on the big rock on the beach where they sat. Safiya —a younger version of her— looked at him, the emerald-green eyes filled with fear and gratitude. On the sand between them lay the man with the Hawaiian shirt. Motionless.

"I trust you, Safiya," he said, holding her hand, fighting to stay on his feet while the room spun. The words sounded corny even in his ears, but he would do anything to make her better.

"Do I *look* like I need a patronizing hero?" she snapped.

So much for making her feel better.

"—Hey," Safiya said, scrutinizing his face. "Are you okay?"

Vane pulled Kimberly aside and pretended to show her the cemetery out the window.

"It might sound silly," Edward forced a smile. "But I guess we've met before."

Safiya took a deep breath. Her cheeks reddened, her hands trembled. For a second, he thought she was going to slap him, but her breath grew shallow and her mouth quivered in a half smile. "Damn you!" Safiya threw herself at him and hugged him. "I... almost... gave up... that you would remember." She wept, her shoulders heaving.

Bewildered, Edward patted her on the back, her breath burning his neck. "I am sorry... Sofi."

This was her name. The name she had used to introduce herself to him. On that yacht.

"Oh, don't remind me." She pulled away, her eyes wet and her nose red from crying. "I was so stupid. If not for you, only God knows what that monster would've done."

"I killed him..." His own words made his knees buckle. Kimberly and Vane turned to look at him. Kimberly shocked. Vane as expressionless as ever.

"You didn't mean to," Safiya said. She tossed away Rashid's just-ironed dishdashes to make enough room on the couch. They both sat. "I was young and idiotic and he took advantage of that. I thought we could run away..." She waved it off, her cheeks flushed. "Oh, you know."

He didn't. Only fragments of memories. The man was beating her, she couldn't go back to her family after running away, or so she thought.

"But why was I there?"

She shrugged. "You were his friend. Sort of. I don't know. We were supposed to smuggle you into Saudi. He never told me anything..." Her voice choked with the agony of the memory. "You helped me. I don't know how you did it, but my uncle sent for me. And you... You never came back."

"I... I..." He bit on his lower lip. Edward could almost see the flood gate open. He shook his head, casting away the images, the guilt.

A knock on the door saved him. Vane opened it. Abdullah, Safiya's driver, stepped in.

"Oh, Abdullah." Safiya ran and hugged him.

Yep, hugging day.

"What happened, Safiya?" Abdullah asked, scanning Vane from head to toe.

"Nice to meet you too." Vane raised his palm, wiggling his fingers.

Safiya briefed Abdullah. The old man wiped the tears from her rosy cheeks with the back of his hand, something Edward wanted so badly to do himself.

"You will teach him the lesson of his life," Abdul said. "When you find that thing before him."

Safiya broke into a smile. She nodded at Edward. "He remembered."

"About time," Abdullah said, giving Edward the head-to-toe scan.

"So..." Edward rubbed the back of his skull, the overload message flashed again in his mind. "Umm, have you managed to see the plate, Safiya?"

"No." She shook her head. "Zain's timing couldn't have been worse. He jumped us right when Fayazi saw the plate. He was prepared this time with a tool to take it out. Hell, he was dressed as one of those construction workers, a helmet and jumpsuit so we couldn't recognize him approaching."

"What plate are you talking about?" Kimberly asked.

Edward told Kimberly about the way Abdul Zahra left the clues to what Fayazi believed was the Musehaf.

Kimberly asked, examining the computer screen that Fayazi had used earlier to access the cemetery database, "But why not put it in a bank? Why the elaborate scheme?"

"He is doing what his father did," Vane said.

Everyone stared at Vane, who stood, of course, expressionless.

Safiya finally asked, "How do *you* know about this?"

Vane put both hands in his white trouser pockets and strolled to the window overlooking the cemetery, his back to them. "More than forty years ago, the, um... bad guys... arrested Abdul Zahra Senior. He was a politically active man, which did not make him best friends with the authorities. He participated in lots of activities trying to lobby against the demolishing of historical sites in Saudi. Anyhow, Abdul Zahra Senior was arrested, tortured, and finally killed. His family, his two sons, were under surveillance for months, in hope that one of them would show up with the Musehaf, if Abdul Zahra really had possessed it. But they had no idea where it was. Twenty years later, Abdul Zahra Junior developed the same interest his father had. He suddenly got obsessed about all the historical sites in Mecca and Madeena."

Vane turned to face them. "My guess is that the father left some clues for his sons about where to find the secret he had hidden. Abdul Zahra Junior did not find it right away; it took him maybe ten years to connect the dots."

Where the hell did he get all of this? From the men he interrogated? "You said sons?" Edward asked. "Abdul Zahra had brothers?"

Vane held his head and tilted it to the left. His neck made a faint cracking noise. "Why not."

"Let's not get sidetracked," Kimberly said, holding up her hand. "I think the question is how to get to the next place without a clue?"

Edward thought the same thing the moment Safiya told him about Zain taking the plate. He couldn't blame Zain for doing that — not when they were trying to find something that his father left him. The grotesque image of Abdul Zahra in his chair, the horrific look of pain, and the blood, all rushed into Edward's mind. How desperate was the father to deliver this message to his son. To cut himself with a knife just to guarantee that his secret did not die with him, that whoever was watching him, whoever killed him, would not be able to stop him from fulfilling a promise he had made.

"I have an idea," Edward said. Everyone turned to him. Nice to be in the spotlight again. "I'll need a computer with an Internet connection and let's pray Abbie is not asleep now."

-50-

<Madeena City – Saudi Arabia>
<Time left until Zero hour is 8hrs:00min>
<Number of infected websites: 1,100,400>

Abbie wasn't asleep. She sent him a scanned copy of the old letter that Kimberly gave to Fayazi when she first met him. The same letter they sent to the mysterious caller. Before they hung up, he asked Abbie to run another search for him.

"Safiya." He beckoned for her to come and look at the monitor. "My Arabic might not be as good as yours. Could you help me with this?"

She leaned closer to the monitor. Her neck was practically on his lap. Heat radiated from her lavender-smelling skin. Safiya read through the letter. It took her a while before she pulled away. He felt light-headed and dizzy.

She said, "It's the same letter of Ayatollah Seerazi, that Fayazi read to us back in Sheikh Essa's house."

"Yes, I know," Edward said.

Safiya read: "I had a premonition that the time to return the trust will come soon. What belongs to his honorable position, is no longer to be held here. To return it to its home is the proper thing to do. To make it close to the downtrodden scion and the oppressed martyr. Where the hands of her enemies would not reach. Where the chosen one would eventually find it and reveal it to the world, so to establish justice again."

She pointed at the words while she spoke. He wasn't sure why the Ayatollah called Fatima the oppressed martyr, but for an Ayatollah, everyone was probably a martyr.

"So where does it lead us?" Kimberly took off the baggy black dress. Underneath she wore jeans and a green Lacoste T-shirt.

"Think about it," Edward said. "The student of Ayatollah, based on this letter, went to meet Ismael Al-Makki and his son, Abdul Zahra Senior, and gave them the Musehaf of Fatima to hide it. He must have told them where they should hide it, based on the instructions he had from the Ayatollah."

"The letter," Kimberly said. "Of course! It's a no- brainer."

Safiya read the scanned copy of the letter again. "Unless one of those words is a code of some sort, I don't see how this can lead us anywhere."

"What is this drawing here." Edward pointed at the bottom of the scanned page, to a drawing of a half circle and two long lines.

"His signature, I guess," Safiya said, squinting at the drawings. A lot of swirling lines were within the shape of the half circle.

"It's Arabic calligraphy art," Abdullah said. "Some sign this way."

"It's clear," Kimberly said. "The place has to be one of those historical sites, can't you see it? All the places you went to so far had one thing in common-- they were all historical ones, from the time of Fatima."

Edward pursed his lips. Something was missing. He couldn't quite put his finger on it, but it was there. Mecca and Madeena had lots of other places that went back to the first Islamic era. Why were only those chosen? They were related to Fatima? It made sense, especially considering the part of the letter about keeping the secret close to Fatima. How close? Edward wished they had Fayazi with them. The man must have taken a lot of time analyzing the meaning of this letter. There must be other references in history to such places, places where this chosen one would look for it.

Was Fayazi really working for the Saudis? But what about all the books he wrote criticizing the idols of the inherited Muslim culture? From what he read, Fayazi wasn't that popular. Hell, Saudis might even deny him coming to pilgrimage for the rest of his life. They had done worse. So, could that be it? Was it possible that Fayazi made a deal to help retrieve the book of Fatima in exchange for a pardon?

Edward shook his head. He might be unable to remember a lot of his past life, but being paranoid was definitely not one of his flaws.

He asked Safiya, "What is the closest historical landmark?"

"You mean besides the prophet's big mosque?"

"Is it possible it's hidden there?"

"You haven't seen the place." Abdullah chuckled. "It's a fortress of religion police; they are watching every inch and everyone."

The places they visited so far were almost deserted. Searching for marks left by Abdul Zahra had been pretty easy once inside. And probably that was the reason Abdul Zahra had chosen those places, to a certain extent; they were accessible for him to put down that floor tile with the symbol. Still, Abdul Zahra had to find a way to pass the short-dishdashes guarding those places. Unfortunately, no one would ever know how the old man did it.

"Are there any other landmarks?" Edward asked.

"I think it's the seven mosques," Abdullah answered. "An area with seven historical mosques all built at the time of the prophet."

"Okay," Edward said, turning the computer off. "Let's hit the road."

-51-

"We got the M.E. report, Sir," Lieutenant Sami announced.

Adnan gestured for the young officer to close the door. "Tell me."

"First the M.E. thought it was a heart attack, because of the colors of the tissues of the heart."

"Then…"

"He found some wax residue in his stomach."

Adnan frowned. "What wax residue?"

"It's a material used for enteric coating."

"Right." Adnan nodded, then leaned forward. "Have you seen the Saudi borders with Yemen?"

The young man took half a step back, his thick eyebrows met atop his nose. "No... but—"

"It's a shit hole," Adnan said, looking for his cigar pack. "It's a place where you live in shitty houses, see shitty people, and eat..." he gestured for Sami to guess.

"Shitty food, sir,"

"No, just plain shit."

Sami nodded. "But, sir, what has this to do with the—"

"That is where I will fucking send you if you keep smart talking with me, okay?" Adnan said in a low voice. "I don't send you on an errand to the M.E. office and you come back talking *Law and Order*."

"Sorry, sir."

"So what was this mumbo jumbo you said just now?"

"This coating is a material used to coat medicine pills."

"And?"

Sami swallowed. "Well, the medical examiner then got suspicious and started looking for any evidence of poison that might cause a heart attack."

Adnan smiled. "And he found some."

"Potassium Chloride," Sami said, then his face went pale. "It's just the poison name, Sir, a very difficult-to-notice poison, unless you are looking for it."

Okay, so Abdul Zahra was killed by a poison. Then why the cuts? If someone wanted to kill him with a poison that would look like a heart attack, why make all the cuts and alert people that it was a murder?

"This is not all, Sir," Sami said. "Potassium Chloride normally causes death in seconds, three minutes max, very painful way to die... but with this enteric coating the ME said it was possible that it took the victim from twenty-four to forty-eight hours for the poison to get into his body."

Adnan rubbed his chin. It did not make any sense. "If someone wanted to kill him, why give him time to call for help?"

"Well, there was the possibility of suicide—"

Adnan rolled his eyes. "How many years have you been in the force, Lieutenant?"

"Five, Sir."

"I have been in for thirty, okay? And the only suicide I saw was an old man who escaped the mental-illness hospital in Madeena."

Sami nodded slowly. "This is what the M.E. finally concluded as well."

Adnan frowned. "How?"

"Because, normally this Potassium Chloride has to be injected in solution, twenty CCs, but apparently our killer wanted to give the victim some time before he died. They used this special coating that kept the chloride inside his body then, after the PH changes to—"

"Yemen borders, just remember, Yemen borders."

Sami swallowed more. "Well, after some *conditions* are met, it releases the poison in intense quantities, but this will only take effect after—"

"A day or so, I got it. What is the big deal?"

"The thing, Sir, the M.E. said this entire thing is not something one can buy at a pharmacy, it is not even something the man thought actually exists. The only possible people who might have it are—"

"Some foreign intelligence agencies?"

Sami nodded.

Adnan let out a long sigh. He thought about the code of success, of pleasing the right people, of his retirement, of the complexity of the situation.

"Issue an APB for this American lady and her friend. I want them arrested at all costs." He sighed. "To hell with Fahad's orders to follow them. Get them here. Now!"

-52-

<Madeena City – Saudi Arabia>
<Time left until Zero hour is 7hrs:40min>
<Number of infected websites: 1,167,235>

The area around the seven mosques was another disappointment. Scattered shops here and there, nothing but sand surrounding the seven small houses that were supposed to be the mosques. No one in the street except for a group of workers in blue jumpsuits standing behind a road block. A narrow path went right into the middle of a white mosque a little distance from the others. The only one that had green grass and lush bushes around it as if a spotlight of green and life shone on the lonely white house. The sign said construction ahead. Abdullah was about to make a U-turn when Edward stopped him.

"Wait a minute, I want to go and talk to the workers."

He stepped out. Only Safiya joined him. Even though they didn't exchange words about their previous encounter, Edward felt that he didn't want to, couldn't, leave Safiya alone. Probably she felt the same.

Safiya wore her black-ninja dress. Edward wanted to ask her if there was a rule about when to put on the head cover and when to take it off.

Later. One mystery at a time.

"Hi." Edward flashed a friendly smile to the two men in blue jumpsuits.

They just stared at him.

He looked at the sky as if searching for clouds. "Good day today, yeah."

Mr. Social.

The two workers exchanged baffled glances.

"Say, what project are you working on?"

"Project?" the guy with a thick black mustache said.

"Yeah, what project are you guys working on?"

Thick Mustache shook his head. "*Mafee Maaloom.*"

"What?"

Safiya said, "He is saying he doesn't understand. I don't think they even talk Arabic."

Abdullah came in and talked to the workers in a language Edward did not recognize at first. Thick Mustache nodded and pointed at the white mosque near the construction, replying to Abdullah's question. They talked for another minute then Abdullah thanked the guys and turned to Edward and Safiya.

"That was Urdu, right?" Edward said.

"Yes," Abdullah said. "I asked them what the construction is for and—"

"And they told you they are here with Al-Gharee company," Edward said. "They are installing an ATM machine for the Ahli bank inside Fatima's mosque." Edward pointed at the mosque with the green area around it. Now he could see a group of workers with sledgehammers tearing down the mosque's main walls. Jesus.

Abdullah frowned. "You speak Urdu?"

"Apparently I can understand it."

They walked to the end of the small road and saw the drive-through ATM machine. Edward couldn't grasp the wisdom behind it. A road that went right into a historical mosque just to put a drive-through ATM machine? If New York City did this to a mosque in downtown Manhattan, wouldn't Muslims protest for days and nights against this "crime?"

Maybe Islam had special teachings when it came to Ahli bank ATMs.

Edward tried the ATM machine. A colorful message greeted him saying that Ahli Bank was the world's local bank.

Wasn't that HSBC? Maybe there were two world's local banks. Anyway, he goofed around with the ATM, trying to see if there was some hidden secret message in the ATM or a time portal of some kind. Nada. Probably only the faithful could see it.

They walked back to the car. Vane was on the phone. Kim rested her head on the back seat of the Bentley.

"We need to pick up Majida," Kimberly said. "We left her with a friend of hers, and she wants to come with us. She said she can help."

"Let's get her then," Safiya said. "Abdullah can bring the Hummer and we can all fit in there."

"Perhaps you want to think about it," Vane said. "I don't trust Fayazi's people."

They discussed it some more, and finally decided to go fetch Majida and drop her at her family's. After all, she had just been saved from kidnapping.

Another pick-up truck with the Gharee logo passed them. Six men, all in blue jump suits and yellow helmets, sat on the truck bed.

"Of course!" Edward slammed his forehead. Why couldn't he see it before?

Safiya asked what it was. He didn't answer. Edward needed to check one last thing. He dialed Abbie.

"Have you got the information on Abdul Zahra's business yet?"

"Yep, and I am hacking into the White House database now."

"Very funny, Abbie."

"Of course, you realize that what you asked is nearly impossible," Abbie said, chewing on bubble gum. "Not everything is as computerized in Saudi as in the States."

"Abbie..." If he didn't stop her she could go on forever. "What do you have?"

"Everything." She laughed.

"That's my girl. Can you see Al-Gharee on the list?"

"One minute..." Then she said, "Yep, it's here. It's not registered with his name as an owner, but the registration—"

"Abbie, what are the other projects they've done in the last five years? All his companies."

"I will email you the list."

"You are the best, Abbie."

"Do you want me to send you my promotion papers to sign as well, boss?"

"The line is breaking up!" Edward yelled, making the sound of static. "Abbie, I can't hear you."

"Never mind, you are the hottest boss I've ever worked for."

"I know." He smiled.

"There is no static now. Good, twenty percent is fine."

"Okay, just send me the list."

She yelled and kissed the receiver then hung up.

The truth was, she really deserved it. Sometimes, Abbie's work on the computer saved the cost of an entire team. Hiring her onto their small staff was a blessing. And the truth was, he and Kimberly were very surprised that Abbie accepted the low salary they offered, which was the best their small agency could afford at that time.

"Al-Gharee company belongs to Abdul Zahra?" Safiya said, her ardent eyes wide.

Edward straightened his back and adjusted his collar. "History detective on the case."

"Right."

When Edward saw the blue jumpsuit, he remembered what Safiya said about Zain dressed in one of them. It all added up, how else could Abdul Zahra have access to those places? Abdul Zahra was doing construction work for the government under a different name.

Edward explained his conclusion to Vane and Kimberly. No one cheered or applauded. They managed to hide their admiration well.

Safiya gave him her small Sony laptop. By the time he powered it on and checked email, Abbie's was already in his inbox. He opened the list. The company worked on about twenty construction projects. The prophet's house, the Uhud battle site, and the Baqee' cemetery were all on this list. He was right.

Kimberly asked, "How are we going to search through all of this?"

"We don't have to. We need to look at the historical ones only. Something to do with Fatima's time."

"Can I take a look?" Abdullah asked.

Edward handed him the laptop.

Abdullah had to pull over to read through the list. "The only one I recognize is this one," Abdullah said. "Number fifteen, the Two-Qibla mosque."

-53-

<Madeena City – Saudi Arabia>
<Time left until Zero hour is 6hrs:45min>
<Number of infected websites: 1,298,986>

Vane and Kimberly took a taxi and went to pick up Majida. Abdullah drove Edward and Safiya to the Two-Qibla mosque. The facade was surprisingly new. White marble covered considerable parts of it. A small water fountain replaced the now-familiar sight of long-bearded short-dishdashes in the big yard in front of the mosque.

No one gave Edward a second look. Safiya told him she had to go to the women's section if she wanted to get inside, so only Abdullah accompanied him. Abdullah gave Edward the Yamaka-like white hat. Edward wore it and took off his shoes and entered.

He didn't know what he had expected inside a mosque. Part of him felt unease, maybe because of the sign outside that said only Muslims were allowed. Another part wanted to take Safiya and go somewhere they could talk with no interruptions. But mostly, Edward felt, in a strange way, peaceful. He'd been here before; the place was familiar in a way he couldn't explain. The white board that showed the timing of prayers. The white halogen lighting. The green carpet marked with white lines for each prayer row. The feel of the soft carpet on his bare feet. The cold air coming from the central cooling. The murmuring sound of people praying. The wooden Islamic artwork. The Arabic calligraphy on the wall telling different verses of Quran. Even the verses were familiar.

The room started spinning. His hand reached reflexively to a black man wearing a similar white hat as his. The man held him with a friendly smile. The look in the man's eyes — that don't-worry-brother-you-are-home look — he had seen before. He lost his balance. Another man reached for Edward, they carried him. Abdullah's voice sounded distant. They took him to a corner. Abdullah and four other men stood watching.

"I'm fine," Edward said, still able to hear his heart thudding inside his chest. He had been here before. And not only once. He was here on a daily basis for a long time. He remembered the acts of Muslim prayers. Reading Quran while standing, then bowing and praising God, then kneeling, head to the ground, and praising God. He remembered how many times this had to be repeated for each different prayer.

A skinny man wearing a white dishdash brought him water in a plastic cup. Edward sipped and thanked him. "*Shukran Akhee*."

This was not happening, not to him. Something must be wrong. Maybe he had forgotten a lot of things about his past, but his beliefs were intact. His stand on religion, *all* religion, was clear. He wasn't part of any of it.

It took him another five minutes to gain full consciousness. The men around him were gone by then, only Abdullah remained.

"It's the long trip, Mr. Fleming," Abdullah said, "you need some rest."

Edward nodded with half a smile. His gaze wandered around the white walls, looking for something familiar. Then he noticed something. A wooden part had replaced the normal wall.

"What is that?" He pointed at the wooden window.

Abdullah shook his head. The skinny man who brought him the water was still nearby and caught Edward's hand pointing at the wall. "It's the other *Qibla*," Skinny said with an Indian accent, flashing a shiny smile.

Qibla was the direction where Muslims had to face during prayer, the direction of Mecca.

"What do you mean?" Edward asked.

"This mosque, it had two *Qibla*," Skinny answered as if it was obvious. "The great prophet was praying to Masjid Al Aksa in Qudos, Jerusalem, when he was in Mecca. He used to pray in a way where he face both Al-Kaaba and Al-Aksa. But when he migrated to Madeena, this was not possible anymore so he kept praying to Al-Aksa mosque, which created another problem."

"What problem?" Edward asked, his head swirling with too much information and memories. The 'System Overload' still flashed.

"Al-Aksa, Jerusalem, was a holy place for Christians and Jews, so some people in Madeena started to say that Mohammed's religion was just another version of Christianity and Judaism. The allegations went on until one day during the prayer, Allah ordered the prophet to pray to Mecca, so he shifted to this direction." The man pointed at a big recess in the wall, which fit a prayer place for a man. "This is the second *Qibla*, facing Mecca."

A man stood in the recess, praying. Six men stood praying in the row behind him. A group prayer, the man in the recess leading it.

Skinny added, "The other *Qibla* was closed two years ago, the government decided it was confusing to leave two *Qiblas* in one mosque."

"But this is history," Abdullah said. "It's the way this mosque was for hundreds of years."

Everyone was a historian today.

"I don't know, brother, we got the orders from the ministry of religious affairs and the next thing we know, a construction company came here to—"

That was it! Edward jumped to the wooden wall where the first *Qibla* was. Noticing the metal hinges, he pried the wooden window to open it. It gave way.

"Hey, stop it!" Skinny yelled.

Edward ignored him and pulled more. The window opened, revealing a small recess in the wall covered by a plate with the now-familiar rectangular symbol. No numbers on this one. The end of the treasure-hunt.

"What is going *on* today?" Skinny grabbed his shoulder. "First this crazy worker who came without an appointment and then you... leave this wooden wall alone!"

The words reached Edward as if from a distance. He focused on the metal plate, now ripped from the wall. Edward put his hand behind the plate, a smaller recess was in the wall. That was it! The Musehaf of Fatima *had* to be here.

Other hands pulled Edward away. But the make-shift closet in the wall was clearly visible. And, it was totally empty.

-54-

<Madeena City – Saudi Arabia>
<Time left until Zero hour is 6hrs:00min>
<Number of infected websites: 1,355,132>

The mood was not what one would call cheerful in Safiya's guest cottage. One of many across the country. The young princess sipped her tea, a distant look clouded her ravishing face. Edward sat in silence staring at Majida who held a cup of tea without even getting it near her mouth. The only sound was Kimberly talking to Abbie, telling her she was fine for the tenth time. Majida excused herself and went to another room.

Vane had left. But Edward knew he wasn't far. Safiya told Edward of a third room if he wanted to rest.

Some cottage.

They had failed. Zain had beaten them to the location of the Musehaf. The Indian guy working at the used-to-be-two-*qibla* mosque had confirmed that Zain took what looked like a book wrapped in a plastic bag of some kind.

Kimberly and Majida had gone through a lot in their search for this Musehaf. The same could be said of Safiya. She still had her houses and her fancy cars and probably even her big salary, but things would not be the same for her anymore. She would be more isolated within her family. The mean glares would be even meaner, the whispering around her would be louder. However, the princess didn't seem to care about any of that. For the past half an hour, all Safiya talked about was the few hours they spent together when they first met in September, 2001. Unfortunately, back then, Edward hadn't told her what he was doing or why he wanted to get into Saudi in such a way.

"After you left," Safiya whispered, holding his hand, "I waited for you to come. For days, I kept going to that place where we were supposed to meet…"

"Jeddah museum," Edward said, suddenly remembering. "I was supposed to meet you there after two days…"

She forced a smile, her green eyes peering into his soul. "I am sure you had your reasons."

Darkness engulfed him. He was running out of breath, people chasing him, a sound in his head kept telling him he was late, and people he cared about would pay for that. "I can't remember,"

"It's okay." She squeezed his hand. "You are here and that's what matters."

Safiya turned to face Kimberly, as if just realizing she was there, her hand tucking a wisp of black hair to the back of her head. "So… Kim, how are things back at the office?"

"Our office assistant is mad." Kimberly chuckled, then pointed at Edward. "Abbie is mad at *you*."

"Me? Why?"

"She said you should have called her to tell her I was okay. She insisted that it wasn't about her worrying about me, but because of her doing all the work tracing the people who kidnapped me for nothing."

Edward laughed. "Yeah, right. As if she managed to find them."

Kimberly gave him a reproachful look. She was right. He should have called Abbie, she deserved that. He had no doubt that she spent the day trying to find any lead on the group who kidnapped her colleague. Tracking the FTP site was a dead end, but she must have been scrambling another way. Abbie wouldn't give up so easily, and when it came to computers, she was the best.

An image from his long day flashed in his mind. He hadn't paid attention to it before because he was too busy with what was in front of him. But now... how could he not connect the dots?

Edward took the phone and dialed Abbie. The phone companies would be happy today with all the international calls.

"Abbie, listen, what have you found on the guys with the FTP site."

"Why, you want to send them a Christmas card?" she snapped. "You got Kim."

"Abbie, please, it's important."

"I gave them the document in PDF format."

"Good idea." He wasn't sure what difference that would make.

"So I inserted a small macro in the PDF; very simple and innocent-looking code."

"Ah huh, innocent looking, good, then?" How could a code be innocent looking?

"They took the bait!" Abbie said. "I got their IP address."

It sounded good. They took the bait, whatever it was, and Abbie got their IP address, which must be something the bad guys needed so badly.

"Great," he said.

"They didn't suspect that. Their firewall did not stop the code either because, like most firewalls, it was designed to keep things out, not to prevent my code from *going* out. We have them now."

"And they will not be able to hurt anyone because their IP address is with us, right? I mean they cannot go anywhere, they are crippled now."

"*Ed*," Abbie said. This couldn't be good. Abbie called him Ed only when she wanted to be nasty. "Don't be a dumb-ass. The IP address is just a way to find their approximate location. It's the Internet address."

"So how would that help us?" he asked, watching Kimberly smiling. Could they hear the conversation?

"I'm checking it right now. But so far it looks like your target is in the same city as you, most likely a nearby town. I'll send you the approximate address. Don't get your hopes up, it could be just a VPN tunnel."

Again with the VPN tunnel. He wanted to ask her what it was but it sounded like something better left alone.

Edward thanked Abbie and promised to call her once they had an update. His now-charged iPhone beeped, announcing new email. The email was a link to a Google Map location. Abbie wouldn't just give him the town's name. Once he touched the link, his phone opened the Google Maps window. The screen took some time to load. It showed him a desert — no surprise there — and lots of names. Then a red pin dropped at a small town with the name Rabatha.

He almost heard the click in his mind.

I.M.Hussaini

PART SIX

According to Wikileaks, Hillary Clinton wrote: "Saudi Arabia remains a critical financial support base to al-Qaeda, the Taliban, Lashka-e-Taiba (which carried out the Mumbai attacks in 2008), and other terrorist groups." She added: "Donors in Saudi Arabia remain the most significant sources of funding to Sunni terrorist groups world-wide."

-55-

<Madeena City – Saudi Arabia>
<Time left until Zero hour is 5hrs:30min>
<Number of infected websites: 1,431,332>

"Tell me again," Kimberly said in a low voice as if afraid to disturb Edward's search through the papers he printed from Abbie's email. "How do you plan on finding the men who kidnapped me?"

Abdullah drove the Range Rover as fast as it would go. Safiya assured them that it was one of her cousins', so whatever special agency was looking for her would not suspect them of being in this car.

Maybe it wasn't too late to ask Safiya how to join the royal family.

"Not those who kidnapped you," Edward flipped another page containing the list of Abdul Zahra's projects. He found the one he was looking for, which confirmed his hunch. He gave the address to Abdullah.

"It should be very close," Abdullah said.

The tinted windows revealed nothing much on the street. Few vehicles roamed. Calling them cars would be a stretch. Pick-up trucks from World War II. Shops looked dark and empty, more like blacksmiths' workshops from a western movie.

"This town is deserted," Kimberly said, looking through the side window from the backseat next to Safiya.

She had no idea. Edward used the time on the road to do a quick search on Abu Thar, the prophet's companion who was expelled to Rabatha during the time of the third Muslim ruler. Abu Thar was subjected to the ruler's wrath for his position on the new economic system. After Mohammed's death, a new system was invented to distribute the fortunes of the growing Islamic state. Instead of the equal-share-for-everyone system Mohammed established, the new system gave money based on loyalty to the Islamic state. Certain groups were receiving large salaries from the state while others got squat. The society was divided into two groups of the very rich and the very poor. Abu Thar used to walk in the markets and criticize the new economy, the trade transactions, and basically anything that he considered a deviation from Mohammed's teachings, telling people that what they did to Fatima was the start of the deviation. The ruler punished him by sending him to Rabatha to die alone there. His last words were that he did not regret anything he did for Fatima and her family —words that inspired many people afterwards, throughout history.

Including their friend, Zain.

The car stopped in front of a small structure. "This is it," Abdullah said. "Abu Thar'a tomb is here beyond the fence."

The two-story building in front of the abandoned cemetery was old but recently painted white. A small restaurant on the ground floor carried a sign in Arabic that read: "Food Restaurant." In case someone might mistake it for a weapons or medicine restaurant.

Edward stepped out of the car. He pressed on the two buttons on his watch. Vane would hear everything now. Edward knew his friend wasn't far, ready to back him up when needed.

Eight white plastic tables sat inside the dining area, all empty. Three cars were parked in front. No waiters in the food restaurant, just one cashier and another tall guy behind the counter. No warm greetings, no thank-you-for-choosing-our-restaurant or how-can-I-help-you clichés. Better.

"*Ayan Saheb Al-Mattaam*?" (Where is the owner of the restaurant?) Edward said to the cashier. The man just shrugged.

Edward repeated the question, pointing at the cars outside the restaurant. "I don't think they are yours."

The cashier exchanged a look with the tall guy.

Tall Guy shook his head, speaking in broken English. "Out, you go out."

Edward put both hands on the counter and spoke in clear Arabic. "Where is Zain?"

"I don't know Zain," Tall guy said, his unsteady voice confirmed Edward's suspicions.

"I know Gharee company owns this place."

Cashier picked up the phone and whispered something. Hurried footsteps came from a small spiral metal stairway at the back. Two men came in, both carrying baseball bats.

Not good.

The four guys surrounded Edward, all glaring.

"Out," Tall guy repeated, holding a kitchen knife.

Edward made a tusk-tusk sound. "No one taught you to say *please*."

Tall pointed with his knife at the door. "O..u..t."

"Yeah, I got that the first time," Edward said. "But I like the service here."

The four men stepped forward. Edward considered his options. These weren't trained fighters, he could take one of them, maybe two. But one unarmed man against four with baseball bats, well, Jackie Chan would be proud of him if he tried.

"You don't have to do this," Edward said, holding his ground. He shouldn't show fear. And he didn't have to, the door opened and Vane came in.

"You, pretty boy." Tall pointed at Vane who walked straight at him. Others laughed. Most people judge Vane by appearances. A deadly mistake. Tall guy chucked. "Go out before—"

Vane grabbed Tall's wrist and twisted upward. Tall let out a cry, dropping the knife. A man swung his bat. Vane ducked, still holding Tall's wrist. Once the strike passed him, Vane held the bat with his free arm and kicked the man's kneecap. Another cry of pain. Vane pulled Tall by his wrist then pushed him against the second baseball man, now charging at him. The two lost balance. With the same unearthly speed, Vane struck Tall on the throat and was about to punch the second baseball guy when both Edward and Cashier shouted, "Stop!"

Cashier added, "Please, stop."

"*Weena Zain?*" Edward asked the scared man.

"Upstairs," Cashier pointed at the spiral stairs.

Vane gestured to Edward to go up. "I'll make sure our friends here don't have any funny ideas about warning anyone."

Edward took the stairs, careful not to make a sound.

The second floor was nothing like what he expected. One open space the size of a basketball arena was filled with desks and computers and cables. Of the dozen young men, some operated the computers, two stood next to a big black rack filled with devices with small green, red and orange lights, and lots of cables. A very large guy who looked like Jabba The Hut, or someone who just swallowed Jabba the Hut, wore a red bandana and camouflage pants. The fat man carried a cable and examined the computers as if doubtful which computer he should plug into. Edward couldn't blame him. Four were immersed in a heated discussion over a small table in the middle of the room. He recognized two of them.

"Hi," Edward said, waving his hand, "can I check my email?"

No one moved. They all gazed at a young man in a blue jumpsuit. The young man laughed and shook his head, looking at an elderly man next to him. "See, Doctor Fayazi, I told you Edward would figure it out eventually."

-56-

<Madeena City – Saudi Arabia>
<Time left until Zero hour is 5hrs:00min>
<Number of infected websites: 1,502,392>

They all sat at the small table in Zain's hideout. Zain told Edward that it was better to let everyone inside. Vane had disappeared once he knew he wasn't needed. Edward introduced Kimberly and Majida, who sat next to each other at one side. Edward and Safiya on the other.

Abdullah didn't come in. As long as Safiya was safe, he was okay. It somehow reminded Edward of Vane. Vane would never admit it, but he liked acting as a guardian angel for his friends, probably even needed that.

A young man, the same one who gave Zain the talisman at the patrol station, came with a plate full of tea cups.

"You look fine, Doctor," Safiya said, "for someone who was kidnapped."

Fayazi held the top of his cane with both hands and nodded, biting on his lower lip.

Zain said, "I forced him to come with me. I couldn't allow for the secret my grandfather and father died for to be lost because of —"

"Some bored, untrustworthy princess," Safiya said, her hands on her hips.

"I did not suspect anybody, Safiya," Zain said. "It was just clear that the police were looking for one of you. I had a higher cause to pursue, my father's last will... would've..." Zain blinked looking at Edward with admiration. "I still don't understand how you found this place."

Everyone looked at Edward. He wiggled his eyebrows. "It was a matter of connecting the dots. It wasn't hard to conclude that as long as Kim's real kidnappers were not asking for the files from our library, the only reasonable choice would be that the caller was the same one behind this Internet virus, especially given the demands which indicated someone with good Internet knowledge."

"It could be anyone. Why did you suspect me?"

"For one, there was the way you fixed Safiya's laptop. You were good at computers and I saw that firsthand. Second, whoever put that virus on the Internet had to know something about Fatima's Musehaf. Not enough to be published, but enough to make a threat. Which is exactly what you, Zain, knew. You had only guesses as to what it might be but not the real picture, which was another reason for you to ask for the document. Then I remembered what you said when Safiya told us about the police suspecting Kimberly, do you remember what you said back then?"

Safiya snapped her fingers. "Yeah, right, he said Kimberly couldn't be attacked by Abdul Zahra because the man was sitting."

"Aha!" Edward pointed at Zain. "How did you know that unless you entered the house."

Zain winced and nodded.

Edward went on, "My guess is you somehow got Kim's cell phone and tried to take advantage of the situation."

"It wasn't like that," Zain said, rubbing his face a second too long. "I told you before, my entire life I was wondering, maybe resenting my father for not letting me say he was my father. He always gave me that cryptic talk about protecting me. Until last year, he started telling me about history, *our* history as Muslims, how the truth was manipulated, how Islam was controlled by politics and grudges once the prophet died. He told me stories about people across history who fought this alteration, tried to correct the path. Names from different ages, like Saeed Bin Jubair, like Maytham Al Tammar, like Abu Thar. He told me how all of them were following the lead of the first revolutionary leader in Islam. The one who taught all Muslims that they can object and protest without the sword, without bloodshed."

"Fatima," Kimberly said, her gaze fixed on one of the computer screens nearby.

"God's peace be upon her." Zain nodded. "My father told me about how that could be proved. How the truth could be shown to people at the right time."

"So he told you about the Musehaf," Edward said.

"Bits and pieces only. I guess I was pushing too hard to know. Until the day came when I read Dr. Fayazi's letter to him. Talking about his findings and how he was sure that Musehaf Fatima was not just a myth and his conclusion that my grandfather had it."

Zain turned to Fayazi. The old man gestured for him to go ahead while he pulled a chair and sat at the table.

"I guess my father freaked out, he did not want anyone to know about the book. I guess he also suspected I had something to do with letting Fayazi know, somehow. He was always skeptical about my work on the Internet."

"The virus," Edward said.

Zain shook his head. "It was already there, we just exploited it. Anyway, my father thought I was behind it as well and he did not speak with me for days after that. I tried to explain but he wasn't your best-listening type. Anyway, I didn't see him for three days, and then one night he called me, asked me to come and meet him in his place in Fadak. Only a few people knew about it, which made it the perfect place for him to meditate. I went there and he was not in his house. So I came the next day, and he was not there either. He called his secretary that afternoon and told her that he had been arrested and released but he needed some time away so she should cancel all his appointments for the week. So I stayed in Fadak, watching his house from a distance."

Safiya asked, "Why from a distance?"

"'Cause he once told me that if he ever get arrested I shouldn't contact him."

"He knew he was being watched," Edward said.

One of the devices made a loud beeping. Two of Zain's friends hurried to attend to it.

"I stayed there until I saw Kimberly and Majida arrive. I was about to go in after them, I thought that maybe he wasn't being watched. Maybe he needed me… I was about to go inside when I saw the black GMC."

Kimberly became rigid.

Edward said, "So it was you who saw Kimberly forced into the black GMC and not some scared villagers?"

Safiya's cell chirped. She opened it and frowned at the little screen.

"Edward, I told you what I know," Zain said in a low voice. "It wasn't going to make any difference who saw this."

"Hell, if it is! If I knew it was the government who took Kim, I would've gone to my embassy. I would have raised hell—"

"It wouldn't have worked," Safiya shook her head, her beautiful face pale. She tossed her cell to him. "They weren't the government. Someone else is running the show, powerful, resourceful, and supported."

Edward brought Safiya's cell closer. The text message on the screen made his heart plummet:

"They have you on their list, Princess, careful."

Edward's hand was shaking when he gave Safiya her cell back. "Go," he mouthed. *Please.*

She wiped her eye with the heel of her hand. "Good luck trying to get rid of me." She chuckled, but there was no joy in it. He was about to respond when she closed her eyes and whispered, stressing every word as if trying to convince herself, "I am not leaving you." Her soft hand reached his below the table, it was warm and sweaty.

"What happened next..." Zain's voice came as from a distance. "I am not very proud of it. After they left with Kim and Majida, I thought it was safe to go in the house now, so I did, and I saw my father ... well... you know how.."

They all nodded.

Zain added, "I didn't have the stomach to turn him and see the cuts but I took the ring." He lifted his right hand to show them the big red ring. "It's a family legacy, my father and my uncle got theirs from their father, I thought my father would've wanted me to get his..." Zain's voice choked. Fayazi patted his shoulder. The young man went on, "Then I heard a cell phone ringing in the old house and it was Kim's."

Yellow lines of text came rapidly on a nearby black computer screen. A young man with a well-trimmed beard hurried to the computer next to them and started typing something. Another young man joined him, checking the cables at the back.

"So you thought it a good idea to make demands?" Rage built up again. All this time, Zain knew what happened and he made use of the situation to get information.

"I read her blackberry messages and emails, and figured out what she was doing."

Edward grunted. "You have no idea what I went through—"

"You didn't see your father soaked in blood!" Zain fired back. "I had no idea if Kimberly was completely innocent. All that I knew... all what I cared about was that Musehaf. I had no doubt that my father got killed because of it. And I had to know what it was. I was only convinced that you and Kim were innocent when I saw you, and since then I tried my best to help you. At the old farm, I recognized you because you were calling Kim, and saved you from that man."

The tingling feeling of being watched. His spider senses did work after all.

"You said you did not unleash this virus," Kimberly said. "Who did then?"

Zain shrugged. "I don't know. Two weeks ago, around fifty pro-Fatima websites were hacked by some group. It wasn't the first incident; just this time the message was strange. They normally put pornographic materials with lots of insults, mostly targeting Shia, but this time they put a message that Musehaf Fatima will reveal the lies of Shia. It was what my father noticed and it came in the same time as Fayazi's letter. I think he concluded they were somehow connected and that was when he started to be cautious, even with me."

"Did you know about that, Doctor?" Edward asked, remembering what Vane told him about the old professor. Could it be true?

Fayazi shook his head. "I barely know how to send an email, even with that I always ask my students to help."

"Anyway," Zain said, "I was more than angry, because for the first time in my life I knew for sure that Musehaf Fatima was more than just an accusation of having another Quran. What my father had told me, and what I read in Fayazi's letter, left no doubt that it was the other way around. So I made up my mind."

"You turned the virus against them," Edward said.

Zain smiled. "That would be similar to saying that I used the invention of the wheel to build the car."

Edward frowned. "What?"

"The point is," Zain said, "their virus was a very rudimentary attempt. We took it to the next level."

Edward glanced at the racks of computers. From fifty websites to a virus that infected all computers and servers around the world. It must have been something.

"Come with me," Zain stood up, "let me show you our zombies controller."

<Rabatha town – Saudi Arabia>
<Time left until Zero hour is 4hrs:40min>
<Number of infected websites: 1,859,442>

"This is our data center," Zain said, standing in the middle of the room, his hands spread wide. "We started as a small group of bloggers, Tweeters and Facebook users with one objective in mind, that was to increase public awareness of the other side of our history."

Zain turned left and right, then yelled, calling for the large man who looked like Jabba the Hut, "Muhanad."

As Muhanad walked toward them, Edward could feel the vibration in the floor. Probably everyone in Saudi Arabia did.

"Muhanad is the heart of the technical team," Zain said, trying to put an arm over Muhanad's shoulder that was the size of a football field.

"Hi." Muhanad waved a hand that could double as a couch. To Edward, he looked like the entire technical team, not just the heart.

"Maybe you haven't notice that," Zain said, "but unfortunately what was published on the Internet of the Islamic history is just one point of view, one account that deliberately hid and even manipulated the truth."

"Especially on Wikipedia," Muhanad added. Despite his large physique — he was the same height as Edward and at least three hundred pounds more — and the red bandana, Muhanad had a baby face and a coy smile that helped people around him feel at ease. That he would not have them for dinner, for example.

"So we tried to do two things," Zain explained. "From one point, we have contacted universities and known researchers to help us with academic content and references."

"And from the other end," Muhanad said, "we built a team of social networkers to actively participate in publishing the other point of view. We built some websites, we contacted the editors at Wikipedia to allow us to add the second point of view... but..." Muhanad sighed, shaking his big head.

"They refused?" Kimberly asked.

"We got the first response two weeks ago," Muhanad said. "They said, your version is different from the one all Muslims knew and that will confuse people. Freedom of speech, my ass."

"Come on." Zain nudged Muhanad's belly. "We will try again."

"Use crayons," Edward said. "People like that."

"Come, let me show you how we control the zombies." Zain pointed at a group of three young men sitting at a table facing six or seven computer monitors.

"Zombies?" Safiya said. "Is that how you hacked into those sites?"

"It is far simpler than that, as a matter of fact." Zain walked to a desktop, held the keyboard with one hand while typing with the other. "Forget about what you see in the movies about hackers breaking into servers, accessing their data. Things like that take weeks of preparations and you can only do it for one server or one category of servers at a time. What we did here is a classic hacked-while-browsing case."

Zain's hand danced on the keyboard. A window came on the screen with something like a dashboard. "This computer is clean, no viruses, no malicious code, the same way your home computer is when you first get it out of the box. See, the virus scanner is showing no viruses found." He pointed at the screen with his chin. "Now I will browse Facebook, the Internet's most visited website. Look at the screen here."

The Firefox Internet browser showed a distorted version of Facebook. A lot of question marks took the place of the logos and animation.

"Is this the virus?" Safiya asked.

"No," Zain said, "it's actually the setting we *should* apply to our browsers. Like, set Firefox not to allow any script to run on the screen. It is the absolute safest way to browse the Internet. The problem is, as you can see, you won't be able to get much out of your browsing. Websites are designed now to run different kinds of scripts on your machine, most of them are safe, and if you don't allow them you will end up with an ugly web page like this."

Kimberly shook her head. "I don't understand, how did you get the virus into other computers?"

"First, it's not a virus, it's a malicious code." Zain rolled his eyes. "Second, it's not us who plant the virus, it's the people who compromise their own security." He then typed some more. Without using the mouse, he opened the setting window in the Firefox browser and changed some settings under the security tab. "Now, with these settings, the browser will ask me for my permission for every single script Facebook wants to run on my computer. See this."

A small window popped up. It told them that a long-named script wanted to run, and warned that it was an external one. Zain pressed on the Yes button in the box. The message disappeared. Another window popped up, asking for another script that wanted to run. Zain did the same. The process repeated six times. Each time, one of the missing logos and pictures on the screen came to life, showing the familiar content.

"Have you noticed the names of the scripts?" Zain asked.

No one answered.

"They were long," Edward said.

"Aside from long."

"Suspicious." Edward rubbed his chin, squinting at the screen.

Mr. Bill Gates.

Zain frowned. "Actually they are. If you notice the name, on the last one for example, it was referring to a server that is not Facebook. What happened is that Facebook ran some advertisements for other companies, those ads are just scripts pointing at other external servers. We uploaded ads to Facebook and they pointed to our server in Poland. Once the script is executed in your machine, you are linked with the server in Poland, not to Facebook. Our server in Poland will direct you to a computer we are controlling, a Zombie."

Safiya asked, "But what if I did not press on the ad in the Facebook page?"

"It doesn't matter. As long as your browser allows for the ad to be displayed, it means the script is already running. You have seen it yourself just now, how Firefox warned me. Of course, we had applied a dozen add-ons to Firefox to warn us against those scripts and at the end we took the risk and pressed on the *Yes* button."

Zain then brought up the virus-scanner window again. The scanner showed three codes found to be dangerous.

"I don't understand," Edward said. "Why does Facebook allow this?"

"They don't," Zain replied, "as a matter of fact, they have a very strict policy about what kind of script the ad is running. What we do is we gave them the script that is pointing at our server in Poland, they checked it out, it's safe, but once it is online, we change the script in Poland to point to our Zombie machine that contains a harmful code that will be executed on your machine. By the time the folks at Facebook delete the ad, we would have infected several computers around the web which happened to visit the page showing our ad."

Kimberly asked, "What will happen to those computers?"

"They became new zombies." Zain smiled.

"So what?" Safiya chuckled. "They eat brains?"

"They will start looking for their master, their controller. Which is one of the machines here." Zain gestured to the computers around them. He sure loved this room. "The Zombie will ask the master controller for the code it will run, the controller will give it to it, and we will be practically using this zombie to run more scripts that can hunt for more computers and make more zombies."

"So..." Safiya said, looking with disgust at her purse. "My laptop was a zombie? And... you had access to all my files."

Several young men in the room laughed.

"No, no," Zain said, "it's not like that. Zombies could only run a specific script, normally it's either a mail or web zombie. A mail zombie will send a spam email to all people in your address book, telling your friends to check some website. The website will be hosted in the web zombie, which could be Edward's machine at his office that is working fine and normally but at the same time running a small script waiting for Safiya's friends to click the link on the email she sent and join the zombie club."

Edward thought about what Abbie told him about someone hiring a large number of zombies during the last week. That must have been Zain and his group.

Edward's iPhone vibrated. A text message from Vane said: "A local guy went inside the diner. Suspicious. Be careful." Edward's fist tightened, but relaxed immediately. What harm could one local man do?

"We unleashed a large wave of attacks," Zain went on, "putting some ads here and there in some websites with our scripts. We also hacked some Salafisim websites, who were giving the false accusations about the Musehaf of Fatima, and put the script inside it. Then we instructed the zombies we had at the beginning, some of them were ones that we rented from the U.S.—"

"So," Edward scratched his head, "when Safiya and I browsed the CNN news website yesterday, it wasn't the site that was actually hacked, it was Safiya's laptop."

"*Exactly*," Zain said. "The script was in her machine, and whenever she opened a web page, it was instructed to bring up our message about Musehaf Fatima, but not all the times. Normally we were replacing some ads within the page so the people who were using the zombie machine would think it's the website that was infected, not their machine."

Edward could not grasp the idea. The Internet and computers were too complicated for him. "Impressive," he said to Zain.

Kimberly's blond eyebrows joined together. "They have infected thousands of computers around the world, and the only comment you managed to come up with is *impressive*?"

"Three million actually," Zain said. "But to be honest, we are using less than five percent of the processor of each zombie. So we are not really damaging those devices."

"I still don't understand one thing," Edward said, "you started your attack and put the message on the Internet a week ago. How come you were sure that you would get the Musehaf?"

"My father promised to show it to me..." Zain sighed. "I guess I rushed things." He then turned to Fayazi. "I just couldn't control myself after I read your letter to my father."

Kimberly said, "The doctor has a way of convincing people."

Fayazi smiled; it was forced and sad.

"Well, well," a voice from behind them said.

Electric shock went through Edward's body. Everyone turned. Despite the short white dishdash and the long black beard of the man who stood on the staircase, Edward immediately recognized the weathered face and the scarred cheek of Buzz-Cut.

"Why am I not surprised I wasn't invited to this party?"

"You." Edward grunted, his fists tightened, ready to launch at the man who attacked him in Fadak.

"Take it easy, big boy," the man said, his tattooed hand reached to his waist where the tip of a black gun handle was visible through the dishdash pocket. "Don't make me use it."

Safiya let out a muffled cry. Kimberly and Majida cringed and held each other's hand.

"What do you want?" Zain said, trying to sound unfazed by the sight of the gun.

"The book," the man said, pointing with his chin to the table.

Some of the gathering young men sneered. Others yelled threats in Arabic and English. But they all kept their distance from the man dressed like the religion police.

"I'm on your side, you morons," Buzz-Cut bared his teeth in an inhuman grin. "I want to publish this book for the world to see. This man, however," Buzz-cut pointed at Fayazi, "he works for the Saudis. I saw his name in their files, and they know he is here."

-58-

"Liar!" Zain yelled, hurrying to the windows with the view of the street. "No, one is there."

Muhanad ran around shouting orders for his team. "Backup everything! Upload all files!"

"You are working for them, aren't you, Doctor," Buzz-cut said, stepping toward the old man. "I saw your name in their files. They had orders to help you."

"What about *your* orders, Archer?" Fayazi said, his gaze locked with Archer's. "How much did Kareem pay you?"

Archer stopped in the middle of the room.

Fayazi leaned back in his chair. "What did he promise you in order to recruit you?"

"How?" Archer asked.

Fayazi smiled, eyes still sad. "Because I was the one who recruited Kareem in the first place and convinced him to find the Musehaf."

"You!" Archer said, pointing at Fayazi. "That means... Shit."

"Guys." Edward rubbed the back of his head. "I don't mean to be rude and interrupt this family reunion, but when you feel like it, could you tell us what's going on?"

"It was all my mistake from day one," Fayazi held up his hand in a mock surrender. "I already told Zain what happened and what I have done. So I guess you deserve to know that too. *Especially* you, Archer, you were a great help."

Fayazi turned to Zain. "Zain, since you already know what I am about to say, would you mind bringing what we found today for Edward to see."

Zain left. Fayazi sat back at the table. They all did except for Archer, who stood with folded arms, leaning against the wall.

"My family sent me to study religion in Saudi," Fayazi said. "Few people know this about me. I started as one of those Salafists, I grew a long beard and wore a short dishdash."

Doctor Fayazi in one of those ankle-length tablecloths. Edward had difficulty with the image. Then, once inside your head, such images were not easy to get out.

"To save you the boring details, I met Abdul Zahra Senior while he was working on the prophet's old house in Mecca. We had a chat, then another, and another until the man changed my mind. I wouldn't say that was an immediate effect. But he planted an idea in my mind. He made me start questioning history. Start looking at things from a different perspective. Anyway, unfortunately, Abdul Zahra was arrested. I spent another six months in Saudi, then decided that I could not listen to that crap anymore and went back home. I studied the only thing I wanted to really study, history. I was good at it. I cannot say I made money, or I got a better home. Actually, if anything, my entire life was damaged because of my research and my books. Arab governments put my name on their black lists; others put a reward on finding any dirt on me. I had a lot of death threats…" Fayazi took a long breath and let it out slowly. "I do not regret what I have done for Fatima."

Nobody spoke for some time. When it started getting awkward, Fayazi continued, "Then I started gathering bits and pieces about the Musehaf. I might sound naive, but trust me when I tell you that I felt God helping me on each step in this quest. When I was told about you, Edward, and your work on documents, I knew you would be the one."

"Told?" Edward asked.

"It doesn't matter." Fayazi fiddled with the papers in front of him. "What matters is that you were the right one for this."

"Uh huh, the one." Edward nodded. "Okay, the blue pill, please."

"What?" Fayazi squinted at him.

"I've seen the movie. First you give me that you-are-the-one pitch, next you tell me that we all live in a matrix."

Fayazi frowned, not appreciating the humor.

"For the record," Edward said, "I don't bend spoons with my mind power. And don't tell me the spoon is not there. I tried it, it didn't work."

Fayazi sighed and continued, "I surmised that Abdul Zahra would prefer an independent person like you to give him an expert opinion on what he had."

As if on cue, Zain came carrying a box and placed it carefully on the table.

"So I arranged for your visa, hoping that I could get you interested enough to visit Abdul Zahra and talk to him. But this wasn't my only concern. You see, I was never sure that Abdul Zahra had the Musehaf. So, I did something."

"You wrote to him," Safiya said.

"Yes, that and something else." Fayazi turned to face Archer. "I went to Abdul Zahra's brother, Kareem. Kareem is a multi-billionaire who lives in the UK."

"Kareem Al Makki," Edward murmured. The name meant something. He had heard it before. But where? The familiar unease of the *déjà vu* started again. Maybe he was living in a matrix after all. He needed to take bending spoons more seriously; maybe start with plastic ones first.

With the meticulous care of disarming a bomb, Zain took out a book wrapped in a transparent plastic bag and put it on the table.

"Kareem was still hurt from what happened to his father. He is the younger brother and the death of his father destroyed his life. So when I talked to him about the Musehaf, I was actually offering him a closure of some kind."

"Revenge." Archer sneered.

"Maybe. My reputation helped me to convince Kareem to start searching for the Musehaf. My objective was to make sure the Saudis did not get it when they arrested Abdul Zahra Senior, and that it was still either hidden by the father or Abdul Zahra Junior had found it."

Archer bit his lip and nodded. "Kareem hired me to trace down the people who arrested his father to see if they had confiscated that book of Fatima."

Fayazi put his hand over the book as if patting his favorite pet. "Kareem kept me informed about your progress. And when you confirmed that the Saudis didn't have the book, I knew Abdul Zahra Junior must've found it."

Zain signaled to two of his friends. They went to the window and checked the street, then reported it was clear.

"But why did you attack me?" Edward asked Archer.

Archer's teeth clenched, the muscles in his jaw popped out. "I saw communications to bring you and Kimberly to Saudi. The Saudis were expecting you."

"You were trying to *protect* us?" Kimberly asked.

Archer grimaced. "I didn't want to see more innocent people get hurt, I asked an old friend to stop Edward while he was still in the States—"

"Agent Summers..." Edward whispered, mostly to himself.

Archer nodded.

"I don't like it," Zain said, his gaze fixed on his men next to the windows. "It looks like someone knew about Doctor Fayazi's plan."

Safiya held Edward's hand and squeezed. "They were expecting you, Edward,"

She was right. They had to act fast. Edward checked his watch. It was almost 8, the sky still bright with the twilight light. According to the watch's GPS, Vane was very close. "So what will happen with the Internet message? What are you going to put on it? Have you got the Musehaf?"

"Sort of, I have to warn you that this might not be what you expected," Fayazi said, pointing at the old book. "However, I think we still have a case. We discussed it, Zain and I, and we decided to go for it. We are going to need Edward's expertise here, but you can do it anytime, once Zain finishes taking us through what he prepared for his zero-hour."

Zain pointed at a big plasma display on the wall with a laser pointer.

"You mean, I can *keep* this book?" Edward asked.

"For now, yes," Fayazi said. "Until you finish your verification and certify this as a genuine document. This is what you do, right?"

He nodded.

Edward ran his hand over the old leather cover. The papers were thick and brownish. The aroma of an old book. The distinctive smell of wood and dust and chemicals emerged through the bag.

Zain pressed on the pointer and the big LCD came to life. "Ladies and gentlemen, behold of the most dangerous secrets buried in history. You are watching what millions of people will see four hours from now."

-59-

Everyone, including Zain's team, gathered around the big LCD screen. Zain sat at one table with a keyboard connected to the computer that ran the screen. Fayazi stood right underneath the TV.

A video started, showing Fayazi sitting at the very same table they did now. The camera angle was such that nothing else of the room or the windows was visible.

"This is just one part of the video we are preparing," Zain said to Edward and Kimberly. "After you two take a look at the documents we have, we can add an interview with you to testify that what we are showing in the video is the real thing."

They wanted some credibility. After all Zain did today, Edward wasn't sure he wanted to help him. But, and Edward surprised himself by thinking this way, it wasn't about Zain, or even about him and Kimberly. Something bigger was going on here.

"Don't rush into any decisions, Edward. We have four hours for this to be broadcast," Fayazi said, his sunken gray eyes animated with... hope? "Take your time. Now, Zain, would you start the video please. I cannot wait to see how I look on TV."

The video started. Fayazi, sitting at the table holding the same book Edward now had, greeted the audience-to-be and introduced himself as a Jordanian historian, taking his time to talk about his Ph.D. and his books.

"Today, we came into a big discovery," Fayazi in the video said. "Part of this discovery is one of the first books that was written in Islam, a book that was written by a trustworthy companion of the prophet Mohammed, Sulaim. We have found an old manuscript for the Book of Sulaim, one believed to be the oldest, if not the original copy."

The camera shot a close-up of the ancient book. Fayazi carefully opened it and flipped through the brown pages. Edward did the same with the book on the table in front of him. The pages were made of an old brownish paper but not animal skin, which placed it somewhere between the seventh to the twelfth century. The wooden material of which the paper was made was thick and not chemically processed. More likely created in the early period of the Islamic state. Lab tests, lots of them, needed to be conducted to confirm this. Maybe even destructive chemical ones that would destroy part of some pages.

"Unfortunately, despite the great importance of Sulaim's testimony in his book," the camera zoomed out to show Fayazi. "Most Muslims still question the credibility of the book and its author, saying that it lacks any evidence. A point that I will address in detail after I take you on a quick tour through the book."

The camera zoomed in again to the book. Fayazi opened to the first page. "Sulaim started his testimony on the first day after the prophet's death. He told us how he and other men who were close to the prophet felt perplexed when they saw the people in Madeena decide to choose their own ruler as a successor to the prophet, ignoring the vow Mohammed secured from all of them to adhere to Ali Bin Abi Taleb as the successor chosen by God. Sulaim told us how he — along with several others — was dragged to the place where the first ruler sat and forced under the threat of death to announce allegiance to the king. Then Sulaim told us how other faithful companions went to Fatima's house and stayed there, refusing to give up and insisting on the right of Ali as God's chosen successor to Mohammed."

Fayazi flipped through pages. The camera zoomed in again on another chapter. Edward squinted hard to read the old Arabic script.

"The next chapter," Fayazi said in the video, "is one of the saddest stories in Islam's history. Sulaim told us how a group of men went to Fatima's house, carrying swords and torches, ordering those hiding in Fatima's house to come out and submit to the new ruler. The opposition, including Ali, Abbas the prophet's uncle, and several famous and devoted companions of Mohammed, tried to reason with the group, reminding them of Mohammed's last will. They refused to listen. Fatima's house was set on fire. They broke in and took everyone by force. Fatima, who was pregnant at that time, was beaten. And as a result of that beating, had an immediate miscarriage."

One of the men operating the computers covered his face, his shoulders heaving. Another wiped his eyes with the back of his hand while sniffling. The video zoomed in on the book again. Fayazi flipped to another chapter.

"Sulaim says after Ali was forced by the sword to shake hands with the ruler selected by that group, the ruler confiscated the land Mohammed gave to Fatima. A land that was not taken by the Muslim army in battle, which made it, as per the Quran teaching, for the prophet's use only, not to be shared by others. They justified taking Fatima's land as an important resource to finance the battles the ruler wanted to start against other cities that refused to join under his rule. Fatima went to the big mosque where everyone gathered, and there she gave her famous speech. The main subject was her land and her right. But she used this as an excuse to question the entire process of selecting the prophet's successor against predefined and clear orders from the prophet himself."

After that, Fayazi described the criticality of the situation during those days. Islam was in grave danger. On one hand, there was the prophet's death and the deviation from the course he had planned for Muslims to follow. On the other, people started rebelling against the new government, threatening the newly established Islamic state with dissolution. Fatima was keen on preserving Islam and at the same time correcting its path. Fayazi considered her Islam's first peaceful protestor, the woman who actually set a precedent for the right to peaceful protest when a ruler committed injustice.

Fayazi also talked about the big army Mohammed had prepared, prior to his death, to engage the Roman Empire's army, which was threatening the Islamic borders. The army was called Usama, in reference to the young leader Mohammed had picked despite a lot of criticism from other Muslims. Usama's army became another threat as they stayed close to Madeena and did not march as planned once the soldiers heard Mohammed was about to die.

"This was the basic tour through Sulaim's book," Fayazi said in the video. "Now it's time to go through the reasons why this book and its content should be considered. The first reason is that other writings from all Muslim sects referred to this book and to Sulaim on many occasions. Sulaim himself was a trustworthy person and no one questioned that."

The video showed Fayazi taking another collection of manuscripts and putting them in the camera. These were not made of paper but rather from animal skins — a material used widely in the first fifty years of Islam, during the Seventh Century.

"The second reason," Fayazi said, "is that we found another collection of documents, documents that Sulaim's book and other references in Islamic history have always referred to. Those documents provided indisputable accounts of the events taking place at that time, and the ramifications of what happened."

The video ended. Fayazi turned to Edward with an ear-to-ear smile. "What do you think?"

"Those documents you mentioned," Edward said, "it's Musehaf Fatima, isn't it?"

Zain brought another box that contained the animal-skin manuscripts and put it on the table.

Fayazi put his hand on Edward's shoulder and said in a low voice, "It is the Musehaf of Fatima, and when you read it you will understand why this can be more dangerous than several nuclear bombs."

-60-

<Rabatha town – Saudi Arabia>
<Time left until Zero hour is 4hrs:10min>
<Number of infected websites: 2,000,105>

"This is the first one," Fayazi said, taking out a manuscript and unfolding it carefully in front of Edward.

Now, he saw it up close. It wasn't animal skin, rather a large photograph of a manuscript written on a rag. Probably Zain had taken photographs of the original manuscripts. Old documents had to be preserved in a special environment, preferably air vacuumed.

"It is called Al-Saheefa," Doctor Fayazi said. "It is the most questionable document in Islamic history and the worst ever."

Edward's pulse quickened while he read the old writing.

"What does it say?" Kim asked, her pupils dilated.

Edward read slowly: "This is what we, who gathered here and signed this document, agreed on and took vows to do. That we will not permit under any circumstances and as long as any of us are alive, any of Bani Hashim to succeed Mohammed and rule the Arabs." Edward lifted his head. "What is Bani Hashim?"

Fayazi said, "It's the name of the prophet's family."

The rest of the document was about the place where it was written and that they decided to keep it in Kaaba. "In Kaaba?" Edward asked. "Why in Kaaba?"

"Read the names."

There were six, all men. "Holy shit. This… those…"

Safiya came over to read the names. "This is just—" Safiya shook her head, her face reddening. "It's blasphemy! You are trying to tell me those men were part of this."

"It's not me who is saying it," Fayazi said. "It is the document in front of you, Safiya. Don't you see, we finally have proof that—"

"Proof of bullshit!" Safiya snapped. "You are talking about the best people after the prophet, the men who supported Islam, who built the Islamic state."

"Unfortunately, they did that," Fayazi said. "You can imagine what kind of state was built on conspiracy, and not just any conspiracy, read the date— it is just after Mohammed made them promise to succeed him with Ali."

"They made their choice," Safiya said, her voice shaking. "It's a democracy."

"Hell of a democracy." Fayazi chuckled. "You will see what kind of democracy it was."

Kimberly said, "I don't understand."

"Me neither," Edward replied.

"It's simple." Fayazi turned to them. "The document here is a vow made by these six after Mohammed had told Muslims that God ordered him to assign Ali as his successor in guiding people to the teaching of Islam. They disobeyed a clear order from the prophet. Not only that, look at the way they described Mohammed— ruler of Arabs. This was how they used to see him, not as a prophet, not as the messenger of God. Also, look at the tone of hatred against the prophet's family. They did not say we will not let Ali succeed Mohammed. They have a problem with *anyone* from Mohammed's family."

Fayazi placed another photograph in front of them.

Edward read: "In the name of God, the most merciful, the most compassionate, this is what Mohammed Bin Abdullah asked to be written on his behalf for all Muslims on the day of Thursday in the month of Safar in the thirteenth year after his migration to Madeena…"

That was all. Edward looked down for any sign of deletion or invisible ink. Nothing. "What is this?" he asked.

"The tribulation of Thursday," Fayazi said. "Mohammed was sick, on his death bed, and he was concerned that some people were conspiring and undermining Islam. He wanted to put in writing what he already took their vows on. The three things he was most concerned about. He wanted his people to do three things: Send Usama's army to fight the Roman's attack, to be fair with women, and to adhere to Ali Bin Abi Taleb."

Kimberly asked, "Be fair with women?"

Fayazi rubbed his chin. "I am not sure of the translation. The language at that time was a bit more sophisticated than today's, but in principle he wanted Muslims to treat women well. Mohammed used to tell his companions, the best man is the one who treats his wife best."

"There is nothing *here*, Doctor," Edward protested. "The document is only those two lines."

"That's why we call it the tribulation," Zain said. "They never allowed him to finish it."

"They?" Edward asked.

"The same six men in the *Saheefa*, the first document we just read," Fayazi said. "One of them said, Mohammed was babbling because of the sickness and we don't need his will, we are fine with the Quran. People around the prophet were divided into two groups. Some said they had to honor the prophet's request and let him write his will, others refused. Mohammed dismissed them. Three days later, he died. We only know the content of the will because Mohammed kept repeating it over and over. I guess he wanted it to be in writing and everyone around him to sign it as additional confirmation."

"They had a point," Safiya said, her voice low and without confidence. "Why would they need a will from the prophet if everything was in Quran."

Fayazi's face turned crimson. "Haven't they read in Quran to listen to and obey the prophet?"

"Usama's army, Ali, and the women," Kimberly repeated, more to herself. "Why the women?"

Fayazi put the third photograph in front of Edward. This one was actually two. The first was a letter from the first ruler to

Usama. Apparently, the ruler was supposed to join the army as a soldier, based on Mohammed's orders. The man excused himself from joining the army because he became the king now and asked Usama to allow him to keep some men to help run the country. The second was Usam's answer, basically denying the ruler's request and reminding him that the prophet himself had mentioned the ruler and his friends' names specifically, and repeated many times that they should join the army under Usama's command.

Kimberly asked, "Why was sending Usama to fight the Romans that critical to Mohammed?"

"It's not the fight," Edward said. "I guess Mohammed had another reason for emphasizing sending that army."

"Exactly." Fayazi gave Edward a thumb up. "Mohammed knew what was going on. He wanted to send away those who were conspiring against Ali. If you read Usama's reply carefully, you would understand how big the army was. Most of the men in Madeena were assigned to that army. Which tells us two things. First, those who were asked to be commanded by a young man like Usama who was only a seventeen year old could never be candidates to succeed the prophet and run the Islamic state. The other thing was—"

"There was no democracy," Edward said. "If most of the people were in the army, what kind of election could they have conducted."

Fayazi looked at Edward with his mouth open. For a moment he was afraid the old man would do something embarrassing like hug him. Fortunately, he just made a long nod that bordered on a bow. "Absolutely right, Edward. Besides, we are missing an important point. We are talking about the Seventh Century. If Mohammed had orders from God that he should have his people *elect* his successor, then he should have given them some guidelines for this election. We are not talking about the Twenty-First Century where everyone knows what majority rule is. There was no way in hell a prophet would establish a country then leave it without any direction on how or what they should do after him."

Edward said, "I still don't like the principle that Mohammed forced his successor on his people."

"This is what Mohammed specifically addressed in his speech in Ghadeer," Fayazi said, walking around the room. The man still used his cane to walk but was moving with the speed of a young man. "During his last pilgrimage, Mohammed first asked the eighty thousand people who joined him if they believed in God. They said yes. Then he asked them if they believed that he was the messenger of God. They answered with yes. So he took Ali's hand and held it up saying: 'He who believes in me as a messenger should believe in Ali as my successor.' A decision from God not from him. Do you understand?"

Everyone nodded. Safiya tightened her lips and shrugged.

Edward wasn't sure what to say. It still sounded more like a dictator leaving his relative to rule after him. Was this because of Edward's position on religion in general or because he didn't trust Islam?

"Anyhow, I really recommend you read Usama's letter more in your free time. You will discover amazing things. It's agreed upon by all Muslims."

"Okay, what's next?" Kimberly asked.

"This one is actually five years after the prophet's death." Fayazi said. "It is a letter from the second ruler to Muawya, making him a governor over Syria."

The name rang a bell. "Isn't this Muawya guy the same one whose mother ate Hamza's liver after Uhud?"

"The very same one," Zain said. He was still standing next to the windows, watching.

Fayazi put his gnarled finger on the middle of the letter. "Read this, Edward, this is the interesting part. Read it and keep in mind that this was the letter where the king assigned his governor. This letter should tell the governor his policy. Why he's mentioning this here shouldn't be hard to conclude."

Edward read out loud: "And they told me that Fatima was inside the house. I said, so what. And I ordered the men to bring fire and set it in the house. They tried to resist but I pushed the door, she was behind it, we grabbed Ali and dragged him to shake hands with the new ruler and announce his allegiance."

"This is where she miscarried her baby," Fayazi said. "The man pushed the door so hard it knocked her off her feet. One of the men also hit her several times with a whip he carried. Ali was cuffed and pulled to the house of the ruler, where they put a sword to his neck, to accept the ruler or be killed. This is how their democracy worked."

Safiya asked, "But why would someone want to leave such evidence incriminating himself?"

"*Incriminating?*" Fayazi scorned. "He was the king, for God's sake. And he was setting his policy, the same policy they agreed upon in the *Saheefa* six years before when Mohammed was still breathing."

"Okay," Edward said, "what do we have next?"

"The first official order the first ruler issued." Fayazi put another photograph on the table, this too was actually two photographs. The second was a picture of a torn rag, the writing barely readable.

"What is that?" Safiya asked.

"Make a guess?" Zain chuckled.

She shrugged. "Fighting those who started rebelling against Islam."

Fayazi shook his head. "Not even close."

"Something about the new government?" Edward ventured, "Probably assigning someone as a minister or something."

Fayazi shook his head more. The corners of his mouth curved up in a sad smile.

Kimberly smiled. "Why don't you tell us hot and cold?"

"It's an order to confiscate Fatima's land," Fayazi said. "Imagine that, the king, with all the responsibilities, with all the challenges from the outside and inside with all the power, the resources, everything and what was his first order? To deny the woman who just lost her caring father the only property she had. To starve the prophet's family. Ali and Fatima had nothing else. Ali was known for being poor, he always gave everything he earned to the poor."

Edward examined the second photo, then handed it over to Kimberly. "Why does this one look like it's torn apart?"

"Fatima brought two witnesses, as per Islamic rules. They testified that her father had given her the land." Fayazi shook his head, letting out a deep sigh. "The first ruler argued about that, but Fatima was ready with an answer to every argument until he gave in and wrote another letter to the man he sent to confiscate the land to leave it to Fatima."

"Why was it torn like that?" Kimberly asked.

Fayazi swallowed, his eyes moist. "Fatima took the letter and left. One of the six men of Saheefa saw her going out with the letter in her hand. He had an argument with the ruler, something like: Today she asked for the land, tomorrow the kingdom. So they set out after her, and this man intercepted Fatima on her way home." Fayazi stopped, wiping a tear.

Kimberly's freckled face went pale. She murmured, "Be fair with the women."

Two of Zain's friends started weeping.

Fayazi continued, "According to her elder son, who was with her that night, they stopped her, took the letter and tore it, and beat her to the point her body had the marks of their beatings until she died a few weeks later."

More men were weeping now. Edward could not understand what they were saying but they kept repeating Fatima's name. It was both awkward and emotional. For the first time in his life he saw men, not just one man, crying. The puffed eyes, the reddened faces, the heaving shoulders. Kimberly wiped her eyes and stifled a sob. Edward tried hard to understand, to feel what they felt. But his mind kept asking questions, doubts still nagging at him.

"This was the main reason why she asked Ali to hide her grave. She declared that she resented the men who were responsible for taking what was hers. She did not want them later on to come and stand on her tomb pretending that they had regretted what they had done. To this day, Muslims don't know where Fatima was buried, which is in itself proof that something went terribly wrong."

Kimberly ran her finger over the photograph of the torn letter. "They beat a woman who just lost her father, for God's sake. Of course something was terribly wrong."

"Some believe that those beating marks were one of the reasons Fatima did not want her husband, Ali, to wash her body after she died. She was afraid that he would see those marks."

"And?" Edward asked. Asking felt insensitive; even Safiya had tears all over her apple cheeks now.

"*And?*" Fayazi said. "The man who killed hundreds, the man who was never challenged in a battle, the man who protected Islam and brought victory in every battle he had, the Achilles of Muslims, how do you think he would react if he realized that his wife, the prophet's daughter, the trust Mohammed gave him, was beaten?"

"If he was such a warrior," Edward said, trying not to sound skeptical, "why did he allow them to get to him when he was in his house with Fatima? Why not just fight them?"

Fayazi nodded and pushed over the last photograph. "This is one of Ali's speeches after he was chosen a ruler."

"So he *was* chosen?" Edward asked.

"Yes," Fayazi said. "History tells us that after the rebels killed the third ruler due to the bad economy and favoring his family with higher positions, people found themselves with no good candidate to rule except for Emam Ali. They went to him and he reminded them of Mohammed's will and how they deviated from it. He told them it was too late and it would be very hard to correct the path now. The people insisted. They finally threatened him to accept the position or they would kill him. Emam Ali was the only, I repeat, the *only,* ruler who was chosen by a majority of Muslims, all the other rulers were chosen by the predecessor assigning them. The very same thing they denied Mohammed from doing. Can you see the irony?"

Edward read through the speech. The name was Shakshakya. He had no idea what the name meant and did not want to ask. In his speech, Ali talked about what happened to him after the prophet's death. He disapproved of what his predecessors did, but acquiesced because he feared if he fought them, others, people like Muawya and his family, would take this chance to destroy Islam. With the prophet recently dead, such fighting could have destroyed the newly established state forever. He described how he preferred to renounce his right and try to fix the system from within. Then he told how the first ruler assigned the second, then how the third was placed.

"Okay, I can see his point," Edward finally said. The moment he uttered the words, a realization started sinking in. He was too harsh on Ali and maybe even Fatima, probably because they were Mohammed's family, the family of the man in power. Now he started seeing things from another perspective, a woman alone against a new regime that conspired against her father. She and her husband were the peaceful opposition in a time that was not ready for anything peaceful. Maybe this was why Kimberly was so enthusiastic about Fatima.

Edward inhaled deeply and said, "Now I assume you want me to take a look at the real documents and verify them."

Fayazi glanced at Zain then back at Edward and Kimberly. "Actually this is all we have."

-61-

"What do you mean, this is all you have?" Edward smiled. There must be some terrible misunderstanding. "This is nothing."

"They are photographs of the documents," Fayazi said, "it is proof that they did exist."

Edward shook his head. Zain and his friends gathered around the table where Edward and Kimberly sat, their gazes fixed on Edward, their eyes wide in anticipation, waiting for the verdict.

"Please, Mister Edward," a heavily built young man with a rounded face almost begged. His hand clenched as if in prayer. "*Please* try your best... I... we... will be always in debt to you..."

Another young man said, "If it's about money, we can pay you as much—"

Zain signaled to them to stop. "Edward, do you see all those men," he said in a low voice. "There are twenty more programmers, around the world. They were all working with us for nothing. I know what you are going to say, that they are hackers and they liked doing that. But it is not true. Those people are professionals, they have decent jobs, but they are like many other who got sick and tired of all the lies, they want to make a difference. They want nothing but the truth. And they found this as a cause worth sacrificing for."

He stopped. His black eyes zeroed in on Edward's. If there were such a thing as the eye being the window to the soul, then Zain's soul was in pain. "I am not sure if I am saying this right. But me and my friends had finally found a cause worth fighting for. We want the truth to come out."

Edward sighed. "I will see what I can do."

"Thank you." Zain put a hand on his shoulder. Others came and shook hands with him.

Archer, still standing at the corner, beckoned for Edward to come. Edward did, his muscles tensed as if preparing for a fight.

"What they found is useless," Archer said in a low voice. "Right? I mean, I cannot... they cannot publish it."

Edward studied the weathered face of the man who almost killed him. His blue eyes glistened with something akin to sorrow. Why was this man so desperate to get this book published? He remembered what Vane told him about Archer losing his mind after his wife's death. Was that it?

"We have developed a special system," Edward said. "We call it HILDA, it stands for Historical Information Lie Detection it uses advance correlation algorithms to—"

"Whoa," Archer raised his hands. "Easy on me. I don't want to understand what your HIDA does, I just need —"

"It is HILDA." Edward grunted. Maybe it was the fake beard the man wore, maybe it was the fact that he reminded him of the CIA and the FBI, people whom Edward, for reasons he couldn't really fathom, hated. Or maybe it was just his ego nagging at him to challenge the man for another — and this time, a fairer —

fight. "What I'm saying is that we found a way to detect lies and forgery in historical documents by correlating handwriting to —"

Archer raised his hand again. "Bottom line, you can prove whether this book is genuine or not with your HONDA system."

"It's HILDA." Edward rolled his eyes, Archer walked away.

"I can help," Kimberly said, coming up. "Photography is my forte, I can give you a lot of information about those photos."

He was sure about that. Edward had seen Kimberly discover forgery and manipulation in numerous digital and printed photos. "They talk to me," she often said. Probably the same way papers and documents talked to him.

They sat at the table. Kimberly asked Zain to digitally scan the photographs with the best resolution possible and to provide her with a computer with the latest *Photoshop* version.

After ten minutes of *talking* to the photos, Kimberly said, "Those were taken by Abdul Zahra Senior." They were old and long since lost the colors' hue so probably that was how she drew her conclusion. "I need more time on the computer to confirm this, but the pattern generated by the flash of the camera and shutter speed is similar to those in the photos Fayazi showed me in his apartment in Jordan."

Zain tilted his head at Fayazi. "You have photos taken by my grandfather?"

Fayazi winced. "Yes... I told you we were friends." He coughed. "They are photos of the old cemetery of Baqee', the prophet's house and some other historical locations before the Saudi government demolished them."

Kimberly was still looking at other photographs of the documents. She held one with slightly different colors. "This one is recent."

"How recent?" Edward asked.

"It was taken by a Nikon or Canon SLR something after the D500 series. You see how the light is focused in one area here, while other areas are relatively dark?"

"Uh huh."

"Well, that's because cameras try to adjust the brightness so that the picture is eighteen-percent gray, so it kind of balances the light. If you have very bright areas, other areas will be dark. However, new cameras came out with this nice feature where you can choose to ignore light coming from the sides and only focus on the center. Other areas will be either too dark or too bright."

"And this is important because..." Edward motioned for her to go on.

"This feature was released ten years ago."

Ten years ago. Abdul Zahra Junior had the originals. The question was still valid whether those originals were genuine or just forgery. But that was what Edward was best at.

"I need to run a test for the script in the computer," he said, more to Fayazi and Zain. "Our software will compare the writing against the one in the database to search for possible matches. I will need some time to compare it with other fonts from that era. There isn't much I can do without access to the paper itself — the results will never be conclusive, Doctor."

Fayazi rubbed his chin. "We still have the book of Sulaim, this one is original."

Edward had actually thought about that. It might be a good chance for him to put HILDA's lie-detector features to the test. It would prove whether Sulaim was lying or not when he wrote his book.

"But how can you know if he was lying?" Fayazi asked when Edward explained what he intended.

"There must be parts of the book where we know for sure it is absolutely true. We will compare the handwriting pattern against other parts."

"And will you certify this?" Fayazi asked.

Edward looked at Kimberly, who nodded. "We will give you in writing whatever we find."

Cheering erupted from everywhere. They came and shook hands with Edward.

Safiya stood next to him. "Do your best, Edward." She bit her lip, then looked at him with her big green eyes. This time it wasn't the moon and the sea poems he thought of. A woman whom he cared about needed help. "I need to know if this is really true. It's not about me or you anymore. This thing is way too big."

He didn't say anything. He wished he could. In the movies the hero always ignored the signals the heroine gave him until the end where he almost lost her. This wasn't the case with him. He had received every signal Safiya sent and he couldn't ignore what he felt toward her.

He glanced at her eyes again. Something, his heart probably, jolted inside his chest. He opened his mouth, closed it. Later. This wasn't the time or place. As if she could hear his thoughts, she half-smiled, still warm enough to melt his heart, and walked away to sit with Majida. Safiya flipped her phone and dialed a number.

In his peripheral vision, Edward saw Archer talking to Fayazi. Why would the Saudi government help the doctor? And how did they get those royal visas?

Kimberly stood next to Zain and another young man, watching the photographs being scanned. Next to them two young men sat in front of a computer screen. Their backs covered the computer so he could only see them pointing at something on the screen and talking.

"Abdullah said there are two cars watching the place," Safiya said. "It could be nothing, but it's better to take what you need and leave."

Archer came over and asked Safiya to repeat what she just said. Zain, Fayazi and Majida joined in to listen. They discussed whether they should leave or not. Zain pointed out that after cleaning the computers, the place was entirely legitimate.

The two young men in front of the computer called for Zain. "Omer Shaheen is gone," one of them in thick glasses that could be mistaken for binoculars told Zain, pointing at the screen. "I was on chat with Ibrahim, our website admin. He said the DoS attack at our servers stopped. He think this is because of the news about Omer."

"What news?" Zain asked. "Oh, you mean Omer from New Muslims Group."

"Yep," Thick-glasses said. "Ibrahim said he was found dead in his apartment today. Ibrahim knows that because—"

Zain slammed his head with his hand. He spun around. "Majida, your fiancé's name is Omer Shaheen?"

Majida blinked. "W... Why? I mean... yes." Her dark eyes popped as if something suddenly registered. "What... What did...your friend... say —"

Zain stepped back and turned to face Edward and the rest of them, pointing at Majida. "Her fiancé was the one who was attacking our servers for the past two weeks."

Majida stood, her long face ghostly pale, eyes wide. "What did your friends just say? Omer... was... found dead?"

Edward frowned at Fayazi. Did anyone tell Majida that they found her fiancé dead in his apartment?

"I am sorry, Majida," Fayazi said. "I didn't want to —"

"No!" She stepped back. "It's a mistake."

Fayazi extended his hand as if to hug her. She pushed him away. "It's all because of *you*! You crazy old fool!"

The doctor stepped back. "Majida, I... I had nothing to do with that, I swear."

In tears, she glared at Fayazi. "That is your problem, it is always about you and your fucking research, you cannot see anything else. I tried to tell you how dangerous your research was. You just, you just refused to listen. Among all people, among all the subjects, you picked up the best people of our history and dug to find dirt on them."

It was Fayazi's turn to blink. He shook his head in disbelief.

"Did you tell your fiancé what Fayazi's research was?" Archer asked.

"Not only him." She laughed hysterically. "I couldn't let this man go on destroying our legacy."

"What have you *done*, Majida?" Fayazi clenched his cane, trembling.

"I hoped by telling them, they could stop you. Oh my God, Omer..." She wailed. Her eyes were red. "But they had other plans. They wanted to help you to get the Musehaf. And then —"

"Who are they?" Edward asked, but he knew already.

"They wouldn't kill Omer, he was only trying to help…" She start sobbing again. "I shouldn't have told him about the Musehaf, I should've stopped him. I knew he was doing something on the Internet with his group."

"Your fiancé was studying computers, right?" Edward asked. "He was the one who launched the original virus attack."

Someone from the back said, "It's not a virus, it's a code, the difference —"

"Shut up!" Zain chided the young man.

"It's all your fault!" Majida lunged at Fayazi. Zain and Archer stopped her. "You crazy, you killed him, it's all your fault."

"I trusted you, Majida." Fayazi's face twitched in disgust. "How could you *do* that to me?"

Majida wept, slamming her cheeks with her hands. From the bits and pieces she told them, Edward understood that Majida told the religion police in Saudi about Fayazi's research. They asked her to help the doctor and promised her that they would keep an eye on him and destroy this Musehaf once and for all. They even helped getting the visas. Majida had also told her fiancé about how she was helping the religion police to find the Musehaf of Fatima. Omer got excited and started attacking pro-Fatima websites, and putting the first threat letter that the Musehaf of Fatima would prove the lies of the Shia. The same attack that Zain and his group then improved and redirected against all other websites in Saudi, then the world, with the new message and the counter. Edward concluded that, in their attempt to trace the source of the virus, this special government branch found Omer, and probably killed him.

"I don't understand," Kimberly said. "She was with me all the time."

"They were about to kill *you*, not her," Archer said. "It also fits with what I found. They were helping Fayazi because they were actually aware of everything he did through Majida —"

Archer stopped, his eyes wide.

Oh, no! The religion police knew where they *were*. Majida must have told them or they had her tracked. And no matter how things might look legitimate, Majida would tell everything.

Edward yelled, "We need to get out of here!"

Too late. Tires screeched on the pavement outside. Car doors slammed. Safiya's phone rang. She flipped it open. Nodded. Closed it. "Abdullah is saying they are here. We must run away!"

"The book!" Zain and Fayazi shouted at the same time. "Emergency format!" Zain ordered his group. They all hurried to the computers.

Edward and Fayazi flew to the table and started packing the documents.

"Come with me," Safiya pleaded, holding his arm.

"I can't." God, he wanted to. Then he saw Kimberly. Frozen and shocked. "Take Kim with you, please."

Safiya grabbed Kimberly. They ran to the stairs.

"You two come with me," Zain told him and Fayazi. "You are the most important ones now."

He led them to a small room in the back. Window glass shattered. A banging explosion sounded behind them. The big room filled with smoke. The scene was surreal and infuriating at the same time. No warnings. No talking through the loud speakers. They ducked in the back room and closed the door. Two black computer racks the size of a refrigerator filled the space, similar to those outside. One was full of equipment with a big label that said: "UPS power."

Zain bent over the floor and took out a tile. "This floor is built...with a datacenter specification." He panted. "False floor extended... all the way... to the other room... crawl to the end and you will see an opening to the ground level for power extension... we have prepared it to be used as an escape ladder so you can use it to go out."

"I can't," Fayazi said. "I am too old for this."

Edward said, "I'll help you, Doctor."

They both helped Fayazi get under the false floor, then Edward joined him. Zain closed the tile.

"What about you, Zain?"

"Protect the book, I will buy you time." He closed the tile. Darkness engulfed them.

-62-

Men shouted. Computers crashed. Heavy footsteps thudded on the floor they were hiding underneath. Then he heard Zain's voice. A thud of someone falling to the ground followed by Zain's crying for help. Men yelling and cursing. The floor tiles shifted under the weight of heavy boots. Dust fell down with each blow. The crack of ribs mixed with the agonized cries of the young man.

Edward crawled back to the tile they used to get in. He couldn't hide here and let the young man take the beating.

"No," Fayazi whispered. "Don't waste Zain's sufferings. He did it to save you."

The sounds were muffled. Footsteps moved to the other room. Did Safiya and Kimberly make it? Would they dare to hurt Safiya? The text message she showed him an hour ago. Why did they have the princess on their list? He wasn't sure he wanted to know.

They lay in the darkness for another ten minutes. Sounds came only from the main room on the first floor.

"Should we go now to the ground floor?" Fayazi whispered.

"Let's wait until they leave." They wouldn't be able to leave the place anyhow, so why risk exposing their location?

"Edward..." Fayazi said finally. "Do you think Majida was right when she said it was my fault?"

Unsure how to answer this, Edward opted for the best political answer he could think of. "You did what you had to do."

"Son, please don't insult me with patronizing."

To hell with political answers. "Fine, yes, I think she was right. Your blind persistence made you risk your life and others'."

Fayazi sighed. "I do not regret it."

Edward wasn't going to argue with him.

"Can't you see it, Edward? All the pain and misery in the Middle East, Afghanistan, even Europe, and the States. God sent Mohammed with Islam as a mercy. Along the way, Islam was turned into a tool for people like Bin Laden to spread death."

"If you say so." Edward wanted to shrug, but when crouched on his belly, it was impossible.

"What is that supposed to mean?"

Edward took a deep breath. "Nothing."

"Say it, goddamn." Fayazi's voice, even though he whispered, was too loud given the situation.

"Doctor, Islam was bad news the day it started. Sorry to say that but whenever you heard or read about Islam, it was always blood and wars." Edward slammed the dusty cement floor. "And don't start that lame discussion about the hundreds of Muslim scientists and their discoveries. That was a by-product, Islam was, is, an ideology of dictatorship."

"What if it wasn't?" Fayazi said. He let it hang in the air.

Edward felt a pang of guilt. He never allowed himself to go off-tangent like this. He was always objective, professional and agnostic.

Fayazi went on, "What if everything we know about that period of time was wrong? If they beat his daughter 'til she miscarried and died a few weeks after him, don't you think they would alter his teachings as well?"

"And you are going to correct this?" Edward sneered.

"We can. We should."

"How? By publishing a manuscript of a book we cannot prove whether the author was telling the truth or not? And some photographs of documents?"

"You said you can use your HEADA system of yours to get results on Sulaim's book, didn't you."

Someone opened the room's door. Heavy footsteps sounded right above where Edward was lying. He held his breath. Were their voices too loud? The footsteps walked away.

He listened, but couldn't hear anything from this floor. Maybe they had left the building. Better to give it another five minutes to be on the safe side.

Edward inched in the general direction of the wall where Zain had told them the ladder would be.

"Can you crawl to the wall, Doctor?" Edward switched on his phone so Fayazi could see him.

"I can... try," Fayazi replied, panting already.

Covered only with cement, the floor was a bit rough and filled with pipes and cables. Not only must he keep his head down not to hit the meshed iron bars supporting the floor, but he also had to avoid the short vertical beams rising from the ground.

"I have one question for you, Doctor."

Fayazi's voice sounded weak and out of breath. "Sure."

"Mohammed was the ruler of the Islamic State, right? He has this legendary warrior with him, Ali, as his forever-loyal soldier, and he definitely had some other strong people loyal to him, not to mention whatever pull he had with God, right?"

"Your point?"

"Why didn't he take this group out? He should've known what they were doing and what would happen because of them, if he was a prophet. Why then didn't he kill them or something?"

Fayazi stopped crawling. His heavy breathing grew louder. His head ducked between his arms. "We don't know everything that happened in that era. Lots of cover-ups happened after Mohammed. But what we know is this: Mohammed's mission was not to create a strong Islamic empire."

"I thought he was a messenger."

Fayazi shook his head. "He was. But his objective, his message, was to create and build the right society that respected morals and human life. No messenger ever forced anything on the people he was sent to. God supported them with miracles and with loyal people but they never used this pull with God that you mentioned to force people to believe. Quran says: 'No forcing in faith.' God wants people to believe with their hearts and to seek their way to him on the path he has laid for humankind. This cannot be forced."

Edward shook his head. "I am not talking about forcing belief, I am talking about punishing conspirators."

"But back then, Mohammed couldn't go to people and tell them that some men had to be punished for some crime they did not commit yet. He wanted to build a civilized society in that desert, a society that respected law. Mohammed, for example, didn't force everyone in Madeena to acknowledge him as a ruler. Neither did Ali when he ruled. They allowed the peaceful opposition."

"I don't know, Doctor."

History was a complicated matter. And when it came to the history of religion, that was the worst nightmare a researcher might face. Hard enough to investigate events related to men and by adding the extra factors of angels and demons and epiphanies and miracles, the thin line between truth and lies blurred and one suddenly found himself wondering whether there was an actual UFO sighting or one for Big Foot, and who was the aliens' contractor when they built the pyramids.

They crawled some more until Edward reached the wall. He then inched along the wall until he reached the opening for the power cables. A small plastic lid covered the hole. He switched on his phone again and examined the opening. Big enough for him to get in. The ladder was there, as Zain described. He waited for Fayazi to get his breath again.

Maybe it was his cell phone screen's light, but Fayazi looked as pale as a zombie. Edward gave him some time to relax.

"I am not a historian, Doctor; my job is to objectively validate the integrity of documents. What facts those might lead to is not my business."

"You... still... need... to know... the history." Fayazi's voice came low and weary.

"History maybe, but when it comes to religion... I don't know."

Fayazi didn't say anything, so Edward added with a chuckle, "References about religion always give me the feeling that it was either written to please a king or to satisfy someone's fantasy about finding a god."

If not for the sound of the doctor's heavy breathing, Edward would have thought that something happened to the old man.

He prepared to slide inside the opening when Fayazi blurted. "Have you read the Quran, Edward?"

"A few sections, part of my work when looking into old documents."

"Mohammed's name was mentioned four times in the Quran," Fayazi said. "Jesus' name, however, was mentioned around twenty-five times."

"Uh huh."

"Ever wondered why that was?"

"Ummm... I never checked statistics before."

When Fayazi did not reply Edward said, "Okay, I'll go down first, then I'll help you climb down." Edward turned back and let his legs go in the hole first. They found the ladder steps and he started descending, his hand holding the iron bar on top of him for support.

A loud clang of metal sounded. The floor tile above him collapsed, crashing. Light sliced into the darkness through the opening.

"*Fee Wahed Faowk,*" (Someone is upstairs) a man shouted. Two heavy footsteps followed.

Edward was already in the ladder opening, Fayazi pulled back. "Come, Doctor, fast!"

"Go down," Fayazi urged. "They should find someone, otherwise they will keep searching." He sneered. "Maybe I am finally paying for my sins."

"What sins? Come!"

"How do you think I got those old photos from Abdul Zahra Senior?" The calmness in the old man's voice made Edward shiver. "Go, Son."

Fayazi closed the plastic lid on top of Edward's head.

<Rabatha town – Saudi Arabia>
<Time left until Zero hour is 3hrs:20min>
<Number of infected websites: Unknown>

Ten minutes had passed since Fayazi was taken by the two men who came searching for them. It felt like ten eons. In the darkness, he stood in the small shaft between the first and the ground floors, with space barely enough to stretch his legs. Apparently, the wide opening was designed to allow a man to get into the shaft and use the ladder to go downward and escape. Once he was at ground level, the shaft had become uncomfortably narrow, which shouldn't be a problem in itself if the access panel in the shaft could be opened as it was supposed to be. He tried the panel once more. It didn't budge. No one remained in the building, he was sure of that. He even heard the rumble of cars driving away. The perfect time to escape. If only this panel would open.

Why hadn't it? Zain had told him he could use it to get out of this shaft.

Edward leaned back, away from the panel as much as he could, then threw his shoulder at it. Nothing. Just a muffled thud and pain. No space for such a maneuver. The good news was he didn't have claustrophobia or fear of darkness. But what about air? There must be something coming from somewhere, probably through the lid covering the opening, which wasn't giving way either. Soon Edward found himself worrying about food and water and missing the next episode of *Scrubs* and the Oscar ceremonies.

He leaned back against the other end of the shaft and used his legs this time to push the panel open. It moved slightly, less than half an inch, but that was all. Something was blocking it from the outside.

Could it be... the sounds he heard when he was hiding above, the crashing noise, could they have torn down the restaurant? Could furniture, a refrigerator maybe, be blocking the access panel?

He tried some more. Each time he gained only more bruises. This panel was not going to go anywhere today. The watch! He could use it to send a message to Vane. But once Edward brought the watch up close, he faced another disappointment. No signal. The metal surrounding him must be blocking it. He took his iPhone and switched it on. No signal. Of course, now that he needed it, the damn cell signal wasn't there. If he were on vacation in the Alps trying to spend some quiet time, his phone would receive ten calls from work every hour. And they say technology makes your life easy.

What had Zain done with all the technology? He wasn't sure how it would end with the young man and his group. One thing was for sure — they made a difference. A young man who saw something wrong and tried to correct it. Participating in editing online references was a positive step. Actually, when he thought about it, Zain had done a lot more than his father or his grandfather.

They did nothing but hide the Musehaf and document the destruction of the old shrines. Who knew what would happen if those documents were revealed twenty years ago? Most extremist Islamic groups were based on the ideologies of inherited Islam. Ruler-controlled Islam, anti-Fatima Islam. He remembered what he had seen today. Khadeeja's tomb deserted, Mohammed's house in Mecca turned into public toilets, then an abandoned library. Hamza and other people killed in Uhud defending Mohammed were left in those unmarked tombs. And the Baqee' cemetery, where most of Mohammed's family and companions were buried, was no better than Uhud. Then the alteration of the historical places, destroying the one-thousand-year-old mosque of Fatima just to install an ATM machine, hiding the first Qibla in the two-Qibla mosque, and demolishing the Ghadeer site.

Edward had seen these as just random and careless acts. But the more he saw, the more he knew something was occurring beyond laziness and stupidity. Not all graves were unmarked, not all historical sites were changed. Not to sound paranoid, but a pattern existed here. He could feel it. He never liked using his hunch on matters like these, but this time his hunch was so strong he couldn't just let it go.

He thought about Fatima, the way her mother prepared her. The way Mohammed prepared his followers to respect her. The way Mohammed established the fact that Fatima was more than just his daughter, that God had plans for her, that God would be pleased if she were pleased. Mohammed's last will said to treat women well. Then once the man died, Fatima was the first to be targeted. Her land, her husband, her house, the child she carried. When a young lady died because of sadness, it spoke of many things. When he'd first met Zain and listened to this tragedy for the first time, he couldn't fathom the sadness. Now he did.

All day today, Fatima was no more than a research project. Now, trapped in the darkness with nowhere else to go, he saw the lonely woman. He imagined her, just coming from burying her father, to see people surrounding her house, demanding her husband step down. Probably she thought of all the sacrifices she and her husband made for the cause; probably she recognized the men who came to her house to drag Ali out and beat her in the process. She recognized them from the times they came to her father, asking for money or advice or to pray to God to cure them.

Edward imagined her when she received the news that her land was confiscated, then when she was beaten again after convincing the ruler to get her land back. He imagined her talking to the crowd in the big mosque. Was she afraid? Did she stammer, looking at the numbers gathered? Being at the receiving end of the glares the ruler and his men gave her, had she thought about the son she lost when she saw the man who had hit her?

Kimberly was wrong. Fatima didn't defy the ruler and the men around him only for Islam's sake. She fought for the fate of all the nations Islam would extend to, all the people who would convert to Islam or live in countries where Muslims lived. Only fifty years after Mohammed died, Islam extended to cover almost half of the known world. In another one hundred years, the Islamic Empire dominated the world. But was it the same Islam Mohammed came up with? Was the man sitting on the chair heading the Islamic empire treating his subjects the way God wanted him to? Was the religion with one billion followers today the same religion Mohammed brought fourteen centuries ago?

He was no historian. But he knew the answer. Fatima made sure it would be easy to find, right in front of the world. Fatima made sure her contempt would be recorded forever, that her grave would never be found, that she didn't leave room for those who took her husband's place and conspired against her father to wiggle their way out. Signs existed everywhere for those who wanted to trace them.

Edward could see the pattern now. Fatima. Anything related to her was subjected to this ruthless hatred. Her mother's tomb, the house where she grew up, her house, her grave, her sons'. The same hatred of her was still alive today. In the past, Arabs used to bury little girls alive, today… well, it wasn't much different. And not just the Musehaf of Fatima revealed this to him. Abdul Zahra's clues had led them from one place to another. Each place spoke volumes of Fatima and people like Fatima, who established the religion, then were betrayed by their people. The hatred against Fatima, Khadeeja, Hamza, Abu Thar was still there.

Then he finally understood. The little treasure-hunt game Abdul Zahra played with them today wasn't meant to lead them to the Musehaf. He wanted to show them the path Fatima had left behind her. The path that asked a simple question: If it took only two months for Arabs to send Fatima to her death with a broken heart and a broken body, what could they do in fourteen centuries?

Aside from the green dome in the big mosque in Madeena, a minority who fought for their own existence, and the documents in his hands, nothing much was left of Mohammed or his offspring or his real teachings.

Suffocated, Edward pushed hard on the panel. He couldn't spend one more moment here. He pushed harder with all his strength.

For the first time in a long time, maybe since he had awakened from his coma, Edward felt he had a purpose.

-64-

<Rabatha town – Saudi Arabia>
<Time left until Zero hour is 2hrs:40min>
<Number of infected websites: Unknown>

The access panel did not give way. Just as fear started creeping in, a noise of metal clanking came from above. Edward lifted his head. A white light blinded him.

"I must feel very lonely," the familiar and bored voice of Vane said, Edward could almost see the annoying smirk on Vane's face. "Among all the places in the world, I am in this godforsaken place to save your ass."

"All my girlfriends say I have a nice ass."

"Maybe," Vane's voice came from above, "but the place is still godforsaken. Where the hell are the two trillion dollars per year going?"."

"What two trillion?"

"Apparently, Saudi Arabia makes that every year from the sale of oil. Yet, I have crossed the country from Bahrain, on the east coast, to Madeena, which is west coast, and I was totally struck by how poor those people are." Vane let out a sigh. If Edward didn't know him better, he would've thought that Vane actually cared.

"Would you please help me get out of here first? Then we can call Ban Ki Moon to look into your complaints."

Five minutes later, they were standing in the room on the first floor. The screens were all smashed, tables upside-down. Papers and cables and computer accessories scattered on the floor. He searched for the computers. Nada, they took them.

Vane was dressed in the same baggy white pants and white cotton shirt but he replaced the Arabic head cover with a white hat.

"Is that a fedora?" Edward pointed.

Vane shrugged.

"Desert camouflage?" Edward arched an eyebrow.

"Think of it as an extra layer of sun screen." Vane pointed at the broken window behind them. Then he frowned. "Well, you never know in this place when the sun will come up again."

"How did you find me?" Had he not been afraid of Vane's reaction, Edward would have hugged his friend.

Vane yawned. "Would it hurt your feelings if I told you your two-days-with-no-shower smell helped a lot."

Probably Vane heard the noise he made while trying to open the access panel.

"What about Kim and the others?" Edward asked.

They took the spiral stairs to the restaurant downstairs, what was left of it anyway. His guess was right, a large steel refrigerator leaned on the access-panel door.

"I saw her and the sexy chick taken into two different cars. The sexy chick was not particularly happy about being dragged."

The sexy chick must be Safiya. "So?"

Vane made a yes-no gesture with his hand. "She had nice lips, but she is not my type."

"I didn't mean *Safiya*." Edward rolled his eyes. "Where did they *go*?"

"Kimberly is safe, I intercepted the car that took her and had a nice chat with her captives."

"I am sure you can be persuasive." Edward felt the smile force its way to his face. Kimberly *was* safe. Thank God.

"That I am." Vane said, checking his manicured nails.

"And Safiya?"

Something might have crossed Vane's face. Hard to tell with him. "I don't know. I lost your GPS signal and thought...

Anyway, I figured you must be sitting there enjoying some fancy meal alone."

Vane, worried? That was something one didn't hear every day.

"Apparently," Vane said, faking a disappointed sigh, "there is not much food left here, and I bet the service is bad so we better hit the road."

Like in a cliché from a bad movie, the moment they stepped outside, four police cars surrounded the restaurant and blocked the road.

Vane whispered, "See, everyone thought you were enjoying the food alone."

"Maybe we should warn them about the bad service," Edward whispered back, looking at the dozen men, all dressed in green, stepping out, guns pointed at them.

"Probably you better keep the tip for the interrogation," Vane said. "Maybe they will like you and put you in a better cell."

The last one to get out of the car was Officer Adnan, another cliché. He wore a white dishdash and red head cover

"What happened here?" Adnan asked in a low growl, pointing with his chin to the broken windows in the restaurant.

"They didn't like the soup," Edward said.

"And the service," Vane added. "The service is bad."

"That was my tip!" Edward winced at Vane. "Maybe they have cells with TVs."

"Knock it off, you two," Adnan growled more. He chewed on something, and looked Edward in the eyes. Was it remorse that Edward saw in the captain's eyes? "Where did they take them?"

"No idea," Edward said.

"And Her Highness?"

Edward shook his head. "Gone too."

Adnan cursed in Arabic. He then turned and ordered his solders to check the restaurant.

"We just came across new evidence in the case," Adnan said in a tone of someone admitting he wore women's underwear. Hmm, women's underwear for someone who was four-five, over two hundred pounds and wore a white tablecloth. Not a very good thing to imagine. "We know who killed Abdul Zahra and we know you are innocent. Unfortunately, it looks like we arrived late."

"Yeah, traffic and all. Can we go now?" Edward started walking, passing Adnan. Vane followed. No one stopped them.

"Leave the country... now," Adnan said. Edward turned back. Adnan was still looking at the restaurant. "It's not a threat. But you better take it seriously, Mr. Fleming."

Edward held onto his leather bag. The documents and the book were still there. He couldn't just leave. What about Safiya?

"I can't."

"You have no idea." Adnan shook his head. He walked closer to Edward and tried to look him in the eye. Not an easy task with Edward's six-three. Adnan had to tilt his head all the way to the back. "Those people you are dealing with can and will get to you."

Edward shrugged.

Adnan sighed and smiled. "You think you are secure because you live far across the sea, or because of being an American? Is that it? You think they cannot reach to you? Or your parents? Or your wife and kids?"

"What about my dog? Are they going to spare my dog? Not that I have one but, you know, I want to know if can buy one if feel like it."

Despite his tasteless jokes, a cold shiver crept up his spine.

"Leave now. While you still have a chance." Adnan looked at Vane, then turned away a tad too quickly. "Maybe you haven't pissed them off yet and they will let you live."

"Help me find her," Edward said.

Adnan shook his head once more, and went inside the building.

Vane led him to a nearby street where a shiny white Porsche was parked.

"A Porsche?" Edward whistled.

"A replacement," Vane said, opening the car doors with the remote. "Courtesy of our friendly arms dealer."

Once in the car, Edward's phone vibrated. Another unknown number. What was the point of caller ID if everyone blocked his number?

"Edward!"

"Safiya! Where are you?"

She didn't answer.

The blood chilled in his veins when a male voice said, "Edward Fleming, I knew the moment I saw you that you would be our guy."

"Who is this?" He had heard this voice before, the arrogance, the inflated ego.

"We have a situation, Edward."

"What situation? She is a princess, a member of —"

"True," the voice said. "And you can imagine the frenzy if she were kidnapped and then killed by an American."

Edward closed his eyes, his hand clenched into a fist, shaking, ready to launch at some invisible enemy. Not Safiya, he couldn't lose her again.

"I will give you one hour, Edward," the man said, with a slight Arabic accent, hard to notice but it was there. "I want you to bring me all the documents."

"Let her go," Edward growled. "I will do what you want, just let her *go*."

"Shut up and listen! You have one hour, you understand, one hour to give me that Quran of Fatima. After that, I swear God I will —"

"Where?" He couldn't hear more threats. "Where do you want me to come?"

Silence. It lasted for a second or two, then the man said in a less-confident voice, "I will call you later to give you the location."

He hung up.

"Shit." Edward slammed his forehead. Vane's face didn't reveal anything, but Edward knew he heard the conversation. He always did. "I... I think..."

"He wasn't sure you had the documents." Vane nodded.

"How stupid I was... I should've told him I just don't have them." Edward let himself sink into the front seat of the Porsche.

"They would've killed her." Vane shrugged. "They kidnapped a princess, they wouldn't let her go and tell." He was probably right.

"So what shall we do?"

Vane tapped on his chin. "There might be one thing we can do." He started the engine and drove.

-65-

Vane drove so slowly Edward started shifting in his seat. The Porsche engine rumbled as if begging Vane to step on the gas. "The speed limit is in kilometers per hour not meters per hour."

Vane kept looking out the side window at the nearby houses. One heard about Saudi and thought of oil, petrodollars and luxurious villas. So far, Edward saw nothing but old houses in glorified ghettos. The only expenditure the city did was the big billboards of the King that were in every street. Sometimes other posters for the prime minister and the crown prince joined them. All were smiling as if they had heard a joke. And maybe, given the billboards and the poor neighborhoods, the entire thing was just a tasteless practical joke.

Hmm, maybe he needed to pick a better travel agent next time.

Next time? Would he ever come back here? Despite the cat-and-mouse game he was playing, and despite the friendly attitude of short-dishdashes around the historical sites, and yes, despite the likelihood that he, Kimberly and Vane might not make it out of here alive, despite all of that, Edward wanted to know more about this place. It wasn't because of the 'ancient mysteries' Fayazi kept telling him about, or the hidden documents, or any historical-slash-academic-slash-national-security secrets. He wanted to come back because he felt that there was some unfinished business for him here. Something to do with him, the real him, the lost chapter in his life. He had been here before, in this very same country. And whatever he had done here or what brought him here, he needed to know.

Vane parked in front of a yellow house two blocks from the restaurant. Yellow was the only color Edward could decipher from the mix of dirt, dust, and peeled paint. Graffiti covered the wall, that too was covered with dirt and joined the peeling process. A blood-red shiny Harley Davidson was parked on the pavement in front of the house. Next to the old facade, it looked like something out of a time-travel movie.

"An obese guy escaped," Vane said. "He was outside, shining his motorcycle when the police came in. I saw him drive to this house."

"Was he wearing a red bandana?"

"Cute, isn't he?"

Muhanad, from Zain's group.

"Any suggestions?"

Vane cracked half a smile. "Just one." He killed the engine and stepped out. So did Edward.

"Let's face him," Vane said, opening the front gate. The front yard was in no better shape than the facade. One palm tree stood alone with nothing but sand around it, no grass or bushes, just the tall palm tree.

They were in the middle of the front yard when the kitchen door opened and Muhanad beckoned for them to hurry inside.

"Oh God," Muhanad said, closing the kitchen door. He hurried to the nearby window and peeked from behind the curtains, looking into the street. "Anyone followed you?"

Edward shook his head.

"Three hundred pounds on a Harley," Vane whispered, "and he worries *we* were spotted?"

Muhanad, still in his camouflage pants and red bandana, wiped his forehead with the back of his hand. He was sweating, heavily, enough to fill the Grand Canyon. "I was polishing my motorcycle... when I noticed them... you know... you got to keep it polished... nothing worse than this sun and the hot wind with all the sands it carries. Do you know how they remove the paint from cars?"

"I really—" Edward looked at Vane.

Muhanad held up his hand, peeked through the window, and turned back to them, whispering as if revealing the Kentucky Fried Chicken secret recipe, "They sand blast it, you see, sand removes the paint from a car's body."

"So you escaped once they came in." Edward made a circular motion with his hand for Muhanad to go on.

"Yes, I guess they mistaken me as a restaurant patron."

Or another restaurant.

"I don't know," Muhanad said, scratching his bald head. "Maybe they were so focused on the raid they didn't see me."

"Maybe it was the pants." Vane pointed at the camouflage pants that were stretched nearly to exploding. "Camouflage is hard to notice."

Muhanad squinted at Vane and shook his head. "Anyway, I came here to pack my stuff, I will be heading to Bahrain today." He pointed at a big sport bag on the kitchen table. Next to it were three empty dishes. "There is nothing I can do to help Zain and the guys." Muhanad winced, then smiled sheepishly. "So, I thought it's better to have some snack before hitting the road."

Vane nodded. "It's hard to drive a motorcycle while starving."

"Well, there are some gas stations on the road, but they only have those stupid Subways or McDonald outlets, no real food."

"What is this house?" Edward asked.

"This? It's where we are staying," Muhanad answered as if that was the most stupid question. "Where do you think we spent the night?"

Maybe an airplane hangar?

Muhanad went to the refrigerator and picked out a new loaf of bread and stuffed it in his bag. Another snack for the road.

Edward looked at his own bag, it was small and slim, good only for a thin laptop or to carry documents. Like what he was doing now. Ah! "Do you still have access to your... um... zombies?"

Muhanad shrugged. "I guess, yeah."

"Can you access them from here?"

"Yeah," Muhanad said, his head tilted to the side. How could he do that without a neck?

"I think I have an idea," Edward said, taking his phone and calling Abbie.

-66-

"It sounds very risky," Muhanad said, rubbing the part of his face other humans called a chin. "What if we lost the documents?"

"It's just some photographs. And you guys scanned them anyway," Edward said.

"Yeah, everything is on our server in Holland now."

"I thought Zain said your server was in Poland."

Muhanad shook his head. "That one is the zombie master, the backups are stored in Holland."

The friendly laws of Europe. Maybe it made sense. You take places like China, Saudi and North Korea and look how strict their laws about information-exchange were, even a Google search for some topics was blocked. Then take places like Holland and Sweden, mix them together, and you end up with something moderate and reasonably free. At least until you consider the population ratio. It wasn't a free world after all.

Edward Fleming, human-rights activist. Or Google sales agent.

"But what about the Book of Sulaim?" Muhanad asked. "The book is an original manuscript."

Edward considered that. Of all people, he should appreciate the value of an original masterpiece. Regardless of what Muslims thought about the author and the contents of the book, it was still a valuable item.

"I..." The words didn't come.

"To hell with the book," Vane said, bored to almost yawning. The choice between saving someone and protecting an old book provided Vane with a moral dilemma on par with picking the color of his tie. For Vane, debates about saving the history of mankind and all academic arguments about how this book might be useful were... well, just academic arguments.

"Your friend is right, Mr. Fleming," Muhanad said. Edward's jaw dropped to his chest. "When compared to human life, to hell with anything else. There is nothing more important than a human life, right?"

"I... guess not."

"Of course, this book is not Fatima's Musehaf," Mohanad said, wistfully releasing a sigh that made Edward think of Hurricane Katrina. "I mean, it looks like the Musehaf was never there. Maybe it's just a myth."

"It's real," Edward said. "Those photographs we saw are proof that the Musehaf does exist and Abdul Zahra had it."

Muhanad's rounded face lit up. "So you think one day we will find it?"

Edward was about to comment when his phone vibrated. He didn't have to look at the caller ID.

"There will be a car waiting in front of the Marriott hotel," the same voice said. "Give them the papers and we will send your friend for you, alive."

"I have a better idea," Edward said, looking at Vane. Vane nodded for him to go on. "Why don't you watch the papers shown on YouTube. I can also put in some nice commentary of my own."

"I don't care." The man tried to sneer, but he couldn't pull it off. His tone was too edgy. "No one will see it anyway."

"Oh, they will."

"What do you mean?" More of the edgy tone.

Edward chuckled. "Do you really think by destroying some computers you could stop an Internet virus that big??

"Umm... it's actually a malware code, Mr. Fleming," Muhanad corrected.

"I will kill her!"

"Do that and I will put a special thanks for you on YouTube. I will say that without you, we couldn't have found this information."

The man cursed in Arabic. Good thing he didn't ask Edward how he knew his name, or what name Edward was going to put down if any. Details, nice to see people dumb enough to ignore them.

"I doubt your boss will be happy about that," Edward added.

"Don't tell me you don't care, I saw the way she was looking at you. *Princess Safiya*." The voice hissed.

Edward could almost feel the heavy, sticky breath that made the hair on the back of his neck stand.

Vane signaled, assuring he was doing good.

"You are going to kill her anyway."

"I will let her go if you give me the papers. You have my word."

His word. Edward barely refrained from scowling. "If you want to do that, then why don't we arrange a trade-off."

"You mean I give you the girl and you give me the papers."

"Yep, just like in the movies."

Silence, then the man said, "Fine, will wait for you in front of the Marriott."

"No."

"What? Why?"

"Sorry, I don't do hotels on the first date."

An old line, but hey, it was a tough day.

"What the fuck—"

"Not the Marriott, let's meet in the Aziziah Panada hypermarket in the children's clothing section."

"What? What children clothing? Why there?"

"Be there in half an hour with Safiya or else we will broadcast the video. And make sure her face is not covered." Edward hung up.

It went well, better than he had expected.

"Half an hour," Vane sing-songed while checking the refrigerator. "I have to go now if I am going to accomplish this plan of yours. God, do you people have nothing other than this alcohol-free beer?"

"Um... there is milk at the back," Muhanad said, then winced. "Although it's been there in the fridge for a week."

"Please," Vane pleaded, his face stern, holding the green bottle of the alcohol-free beer in both hands like someone might hold the gun he intended to use to commit suicide. He lifted his head and pointed the bottle at Edward. "Next time you want to pick an adventure, take us to somewhere where they have wine or women, preferably both."

Vane put on the white fedora, and left.

Edward and Muhanad sat at the kitchen table. According to Muhanad, the Aziziah hypermarket was a twenty-minute drive, probably ten for Vane.

"Do you think they will bring her with them?" Muhanad asked. "I don't mean to worry you, but what if they were planning a trap?"

"It is a trap," Edward said. "But Vane can handle it."

"Yeah, but what if they have a man... no... two men, maybe three, watching every entrance and exit?" Muhanad said taking a bite from a sandwich he just prepared. "You know, they will have radio communication and someone might be also watching the security cameras."

After ten minutes, and a dozen worst-case scenarios Muhanad came up with, Edward's iPhone chirped.

"I am at the market," Vane said.

"Can you see her?"

A crashing sound startled him. The door swung open. Archer stepped in. His gun pointed at them.

"Game over boys," Archer said, his voice calm and matter-of-fact. He was still in his white dishdash.

"Hey!" Muhanad shouted.

Edward told him to calm down. "I thought we were on the same team, Archer?" Edward said, putting the iPhone on the table. "Why the gun?"

"We are." Archer nodded. "But I will take the documents now. We will publish them."

"I need them for one last mission," Edward said. "I have a plan."

Archer put one foot on a chair and rested his gun on his knee, pointing at Edward. "You just want to save your girl, don't try, I saw the way—"

"She was looking at me, I know." Edward rolled his eyes. Everyone was Jerry Springer today.

"I was about to say the way *you* looked at *her*." Archer shrugged. "It doesn't matter, I don't have time for dancing. Give me the documents."

Archer removed the safety pin. Edward felt the click as if in his own head. He looked at the small black hole of the gun's barrel and felt everything around him was melting and sucked into this small hole. He forced his gaze from the gun.

"You can't kill me."

"Why not?" Archer scoffed. "Because of this psychopath friend of yours who think he's a French Vampire?"

Edward waved his index finger, signaling wrong answer. "First, he doesn't like to be called a psychopath vampire, a psychopath hunter is okay."

Archer laughed.

"Second." Edward held up his hand. "Even a man like you should know better than to insult Vane on the phone."

Archer's face slackened. He let out a silent curse.

"Pick up the phone." Edward pointed with his chin at his phone.

Archer closed his eyes, cursing in silence. "Put it on loudspeaker." He grunted.

Edward did.

"Hello, Archer," Vane said.

"Mister Vaserely." Archer wasn't sweating, but he might as well have been. Vane and his family's reputation weren't to be ignored. "Shame I didn't meet you."

"I'll invite you to my next birthday."

Archer forced a laugh. "That would be so generous of you, I always wanted to visit the great Victor Vaserely in his house."

"Ah, but my uncle might not be your type."

"Why?" Archer said, training the gun at Muhanad, who wanted to sit.

"He taught me this nasty habit, a code of honor, he calls it," Vane said, his voice slow and hoarse. "Not to forgive anyone who pointed a gun at me... or my friends for that matter."

"Is that a threat?" Archer smiled, his eyebrow arched in amusement.

"It is indeed. I know who you are, Archer, I know about your reputation. And you also know about me." Vane sighed. "God, I hate clichés, but please understand that if you hurt my friend, I will find you and I will *not* kill you."

Archer nodded. Then switched off the phone. "Now, Edward, give me the fucking documents."

Edward smiled. "I don't think so."

PART SEVEN

At the time of writing this book, women in Saudi Arabia were not allowed to vote or drive a car. To go to the hospital or take any treatment a woman had to be accompanied by a male relative. The law treated her as an adult only when it came to punishments.

-67-

<Madeena city – Saudi Arabia>
<Time left until Zero hour is 1hrs:30min>
<Number of infected websites: Unknown>

Adnan hung up the phone. This was the third call he received during the last hour reporting a woman who looked like the missing Princess Safiya being kidnapped by a large American whose description fitted Edward's.

The scenario fit. Edward came here to search for some historical book, he lured the princess to help him, using her enthusiasm for history, and when things didn't go as he planned, he decided to get rid of her. Or maybe she discovered that he was up to something bad and tried to stop him.

In any case, the princess ends up dead and Edward was the prime suspect. Which would also be in line with his friend Kimberly killing Abdul Zahra.

It all fit.

The problem was that Adnan wasn't born yesterday. Even if he set aside what he knew now about Fahad's involvement in killing Abdul Zahra, and that the American had refused to leave the country because he was worried about Safiya, even if he forgot all of this, those reports were way too convenient.

Safiya wasn't even a public figure for people to recognize her and call the police.

So what did all this mean? Fahad wanted a patsy? Was he going to harm the princess? Of course he was. The question was, what should Adnan do about it. Nothing much really. Those witnesses had come forward with official reports. He had to act. Later, there would be an investigation and he needed to show that he took action by chasing this American.

But how? He let him walk away an hour ago and now he had no means of finding him.

His phone rang, Hamdan, from control division.

"Sir, there is something strange with the American's cell."

"Yes, you already told me." Adnan sighed, turning on the TV in his office. The national TV station, as usual, showed the King sitting in some conference. Which probably meant that the old man was in the hospital. "It's an untraceable number."

How could they do that? Never mind. Maybe it was better this way. At least he had an excuse to not arrest the poor son-of-a-bitch. A squad force was on standby to arrest Edward once he showed up.

"Well actually, Sir, I don't know how it happened, but my team just told me, it just happened —"

"Hamdan, what are you talking about?"

"Edward's cell is traceable now, Sir."

-68-

<Rabatha town – Saudi Arabia>
<Time left until Zero hour is 1hrs:00min>
<Number of infected websites: Unknown>

"You still think this is your best option, Edward?" Archer sneered, having just finished tying him to a chair.

They were back at the restaurant that Zain's group used as a headquarters for their cyber activities. Archer stood near the broken windows on the first floor, watching the road. One yellow light in the ceiling above Edward's chair provided the only illumination in the room. A smell of burned wires and another of sweat — probably his — blocked his nostrils.

"Don't you think this is a tad too cliché?" Edward asked, trying to shift in his seat. The rope wasn't very tight. "I mean, tying me to a chair? What's next? Put a gag in my mouth?"

Archer gave him the flat eye. "If you keep talking, I might."

"What if I need to go to the bathroom? You have to untie me and then tie me again, it's a waste of time."

Archer was still looking through the windows. "I won't tell anyone if you go in your seat."

"No thanks." Edward shook his head. "I just changed my underwear." Edward tried the ropes again. Vane would've found a way to untie himself. "Come on, Archer, I won't run away, scout's honor, I swear."

Archer shrugged. "You could've just given me the documents. You wanted to play it this way."

Edward sighed. No point arguing with him. He looked at his cell on the table in front of him. The same table that they were sitting at earlier in the day. Hard to believe it had been only twenty-four hours since he landed in Saudi. Fayazi, Safiya, Zain and his group — God only knew what happened to them. He thought of the Musehaf of Fatima, of all the people before him who tried to find it. He was so close to putting his hands on it. He felt the rush of the discovery. And the disappointment of ending up with just photographs of the book; the book that could change history and probably the present and the future as well.

The cell rang. He and Archer looked at each other, then at the phone.

"Would you please pick up my phone, Suzy," Edward said. "My hands are a little tied up here."

Archer picked up the phone and put it to Edward's ear.

"Hello, Edward."

It was the man who had Safiya. "Hello back."

"You are late for our... meeting. You break my heart."

"Err... I am sorry, I don't do that normally on the first date, leave people with broken hearts, I mean."

"I am upset, and your friend Safiya is upset too. She thinks you abandoned her."

Archer pushed the phone harder on Edward's ear, signaling for him to be brief.

"I know this will sound like an old line, but I have an urgent situation here."

"Old what?"

"Forget it." Edward rolled his eyes. "I can't come. Tell you what, why don't you go to the movies instead? Buy a popcorn too, it's on me."

"I have a better idea. Why not bring *you* the popcorn?"

He imagined hearing the sound of speeding car engines coming from the distance in the empty street. Maybe it wasn't his imagination.

Archer grunted something.

Edward said, "I am sorry, I need to hang—"

Archer hung up and tossed the phone onto the table.

"Hey, careful with that thing," Edward protested, "it's an iPhone, not a Nokia, you can break it by looking at it."

But Archer had disappeared into the shadows of what was left of the big room.

Just as a few hours ago, window crashed, what was left of it anyway. Smoke bombs. Heavy boots thudded on the steps. Only this time he couldn't move. Edward closed his eyes and wished he were a religious man. Praying wasn't a bad idea now.

Minutes later, he was face to face with the man he saw at the murder scene in Fadak with Adnan, Mr. Sunglasses, the arrogant one who talked to Safiya. Even before Sunglasses spoke, Edward knew that he was the one talking to him on the phone.

"I don't like people making appointments and not showing up," Sunglasses said.

"I was about to send you some flowers and a nice apology," Edward said, trying to hide his fear. The man slapped him, actually *slapped* him, and the pain wasn't just his pride, whatever that meant. His left cheek stung as if on fire.

The hand came again. Edward couldn't do anything but close his eyes. It landed on his face. Blood rushed to his cheeks.

"Must be really heartbroken." Edward smiled, spitting blood.

Another hit, then another. One landed on his left eye.

"Can't you see?" Edward shouted. "I *couldn't* come."

Sunglasses stopped. He grabbed Edward's hair and used it to lift his head so he could look at him.

"You make more of these wiseass cracks and I will make Sultan fuck you right here, right now." Sunglasses pointed at a tall black man wearing a camouflage suit behind him. The man smiled and waved to Edward.

"Thanks... but I don't kiss on my first—" The air got knocked out of his lungs. Sultan punched him in the stomach. Edward fought to keep the tears inside.

Sultan moved behind him, his hands, big and rough, on Edward's skull.

"Where are the documents, Edward?" Sunglasses asked.

"Mommy didn't teach you to say please?"

Sultan moved his fingers slowly behind Edward's ears then dug them inside and pushed. Edward saw stars. Paralyzed, he tried to scream. Nothing came out. After seconds that felt like ages, Sultan let go. He heard Sunglasses saying something, probably repeating his question.

"My... bag," Edward said, even though he could not hear his own voice. "My bag, everything is in my bag." He tried to move his hand and point to the table where his bag was, but his body was shutting down.

Sultan's fingers slid on his temple, then moved down to the his neck, gently massaging it. Edward tried to brace himself against the pain, tried to tell his body to anticipate. It didn't work. This time all of his body screamed as if the pain traveled from the neck to every single nerve. Strange, but the only thought he could focus on was Safiya. Was she still alive? Did Sultan do to her what he was doing to him? The thoughts kept echoing in his mind until darkness engulfed him again. He was about to pass out when Sultan let go.

"M... my... bag."

This time Sunglasses heard him. He walked to the table and took Edward's black leather bag and opened the zipper. The book and the documents where all there. Sunglasses smiled. Sultan made some noise that was supposed to be a chuckle.

But the smile soon evaporated from Sunglasses" rat-like face. "Who tied you up?"

Edward wanted to crack something about Sunglasses' fast observations but thought better of it. "I don't know." Not his most convincing lie. Even through his sunglasses, Edward saw the doubtful look on the man's face. It was all too convenient to find Edward tied up with the documents right next to him.

Sunglasses signaled to Sultan. Sultan took a sport bag from another man and searched for something. Through the haze, Edward saw needles and electrical cables, plus some other metallic things. Not good.

"Are those the original documents?" Sunglasses asked.

"No," Edward said, as Sultan approached with two long needles in his hand. "Leash your dog, I will tell you everything."

"Start now, and fast," Sunglasses said.

Sultan cut the rope from the chair, Edward tried to move but his body stiffened. What had they *done* to him?

"We only found copies, photographs of the actual book of Fatima," Edward said.

Sultan grabbed his hands and pulled them. He called for the other guy to keep Edward's hands up.

"We found also the book of Sulaim. A man who lived and wrote about the events following Mohammed's death."

Sunglasses nodded. The other man grabbed Edward's wrists and pulled them up. Sultan unbuttoned Edward's shirt, leaving his chest naked. Sunglasses motioned to Edward to continue. He told Sunglasses about all the documents, one by one, their significance, what it meant, repeating every single word Fayazi said.

"So as you can see, the book of Fatima, the Musehaf, proves that Islam took a dangerous detour right after Mohammed's death. Fatima was the first to expose that. Everything about her, not only this book, is proof pointing us to the same conclusion."

Sultan put the two needles under Edward's arm pit. They tickled. His body started giving away. Sultan hadn't done anything yet, but Edward had a good guess what his intention was. Sunglasses yawned, he was about to signal to Sultan to start.

Edward had to stall them. "I can help you find the book, the original one."

"How?"

"I have an idea," Edward said, trying to improvise. "But I need to ask you one thing before I tell you."

"What do you want?"

"This document is very valuable, not only for Muslims but anyone who is into history. If I give it to you, are you going to sell it?"

Sunglasses laughed, his head tilted back, his chest heaved. Sultan laughed too. "Sell it? Is that all what you can think of? I will destroy it immediately."

"But why? You could use the money."

"Idiot!" Sunglasses slammed the table. "Do you know what this book can do to the faith?"

"It's not against Mohammed, as a matter of fact, all the evidence we found suggested that whatever happened after Mohammed might not be what the man had planned. All the—"

"Shut up, you filth!" Sunglasses kicked Edward on the knee. It was love kiss compared to Sultan's touch. "Where can I find the book?"

"You will need access to a very high-profile place."

Sunglasses squinted. "Where?"

"We need to dig under the Haram in Mecca."

"Easy," Sunglasses smirked.

Edward shook his head. "You don't understand. We have to go deep, into the restricted area. I know no one is allowed there."

Sunglasses leaned in so that they were face to face. He took off his glasses. He had brown eyes, nothing special about them. No glassy look, no soulless eyes, just a lot of self-inflated ego, and a terrible garlic smell. "Do you have any fucking idea who I work with? Huh? I have support from the big guys, I can dig wherever I want."

Sunglasses ranted on. Edward focused on the other man, who was trying to contact his friends via the radio. Finally Sultan interrupted the I-am-the-big-guy speech of Sunglasses.

"Lieutenant Fahad, Safiya escaped," Sultan said.

Sunglasses, Fahad, blinked. "What do you mean?"

"Our men were taking her back from the mall when he didn't show up." Sultan pointed to Edward. "But they were attacked. Three of them died, and she escaped... We don't know what really happened."

Vane *happened*. The plan was simple. They would be watching for a six-three muscular man not the delicate five-eight Vane, not that they would see him anyway. Vane would watch them until they gave up on Edward entering their trap, then would follow and get Safiya back.

"And, Sir," the other man said, holding the radio. "Our men outside are not responding."

Fahad frowned. "Have you tried calling them?"

"No one is answering, Sir."

Fahad's face lost color. He grabbed Edward by the chin. "Who is there? Who tied you to the chair?"

He tried to speak but Fahad's fingers pressed so hard on his jaw all that came out was unintelligible. Fahad signaled to Sultan. Edward felt the cold needles back on his armpit. The needles dropped to the floor. Something sticky and warm covered his neck. Half of Sultan's head was missing. His big body fell to the ground like a puppet released by the puppeteer.

The other guy's head followed, a bullet in it.

"Shit! Who is there?" Fahad shouted, pulling out his gun, pointing it everywhere.

Archer materialized from the corner behind Fahad. His gun pointed at Fahad. A muffled shot hit Fahad in the knee. Fahad tried to fire back. A bullet hit his hand. A cry, then Fahad fell to the floor.

"Who... who are you?"

Archer lifted Fahad from the ground, held his hand backward, then punched hard on the back of the elbow. The cracking sound was followed by Fahad's cry for help. Archer twisted the broken arm in a way the joint was never meant to be moved. Fahad's screams were silenced by Archer's hand on his mouth.

"No one will hear you. You brought six men inside. All are dead."

Fahad shook his head, his face a ghostly white.

"Whom do you work for?" Archer asked.

More head shaking. Fahad made a noise.

Archer loosened his grip on the man's mouth.

"The rest of my men… they will come."

"Maybe," Archer said, twisting the broken arm further to the back. "I will stop only when you start speaking."

Edward's stomach rolled as the arm and shoulder dislocated.

"Stop!" Fahad howled in agony. "I will speak."

And he did. Fahad spit out everything. Names, places, dates. Archer's and Edward's jaws dropped in astonishment. Neither expected that much.

Heavy footsteps and men shouting came from the lower floor and through the radio.

Archer leapt into the small room, the one Edward and Fayazi hid in, taking all the documents with him and leaving Edward alone with Fahad and the two dead bodies.

Fahad reached for his gun on the floor. Edward kicked it away.

"You can't prove any of it." Fahad laughed. "And my men will get you. You are surrounded."

Edward shook his head, putting on his shirt. "Wrong, and wrong."

Edward finished buttoning his shirt and sat, watching the room flood with police personnel wearing green suits, guns drawn, faces dead serious, everyone shouting for him to freeze and to raise his hands and not to move in both Arabic and English.

"Freeze or raise my hands?" Edward said. "Would you please decide and let me know what you want me to do."

More shouting from the police. Edward rolled his eyes. He thought of reminding them not to speak at once, when Adnan stepped into the room. He signaled to his men to lower their guns.

"You think you are funny." Adnan wasn't laughing. As a matter of fact, if his skin weren't so dark, it would have turned red. His face looked like an over-grilled steak.

"Just a witty conservationist." Edward flashed his best smile despite the pain.

"You are under arrest, Mr. Fleming," Adnan said, then turned to Fahad. "You too, Fahad."

Fahad shouted something in Arabic, an insult from the sound of it. Adnan's face reddened more, if that were possible.

"You are not going to read my rights?" Edward asked.

"We are not in the U.S., you moron."

Edward shrugged and pointed at a black spherical object fixed to the celling. "I just want you to look professional on the camera."

Adnan looked at the ceiling. His eyes bulged. Fahad cursed in Arabic and English. Nice when the translation came for free.

"Gentlemen," Edward tapped on his wristwatch, "please put on your best smiles, we are going live in… three… two… one… action, umm... Or whatever. You are on air."

-69-

Bullets flew above Edward's head, shattering the poor camera into pieces.

"You happy now?" Edward looked at the too enthusiastic policemen. "Adnan, you should let your team fire more from time to time."

"Shut up."

Edward made a tsk-tsk sound. "Can someone please turn on the laptop?"

Adnan did it himself. Edward opened Internet Explorer. The home page was set to load Yahoo. At the top of the screen, where the ads were normally displayed was a black line with writing in English and Arabic that read:

"As promised, Musehaf Fatima revealing the truth."

In place of the counter, a poor-quality video started, with a caption underneath suggesting another website for the full-HD video.

"It's on every website now all over the world," Edward said. He didn't need to bother them with how the virus... umm... the *malware* code worked, mostly because he didn't understand it himself.

The video showed Fayazi talking, the same one Edward saw when he first entered this very room six hours ago. Fayazi talked

about Fatima and Islam, and why Mohammed kept emphasizing
Fatima's rule. Even through the poor-quality video, Edward
couldn't miss the glitter in Fayazi's eyes. The aliveness, the joy of
revealing the secret to the world, the secret the old man worked
his entire life to uncover. Fayazi talked about the book of Fatima,
how it was created, how it was kept safe throughout history, and
then he flipped through Sulaim's book and read from his
testimony.

Adnan and his team kept making intelligent remarks such as,
"This is bullshit." And, "Let him go to hell." And, "Fuck him."
Edward told them that the next part would be even better. The
video continued to where Fayazi showed the photographs of the
Musehaf of Fatima, the documents and letters that told the real
story of what happened to that exceptional woman. Muhanad did
a good job of merging the videos.

Then Fayazi mentioned that those photographs would be
analyzed by two internationally recognized American scientists,
who worked for the Library of the Congress. He didn't mention
the names, and didn't describe Edward as an extremely charming
fellow, but the internationally recognized scientist part was a nice
touch.

Adnan and some of his men looked at Edward. Edward
waved for the gathered fans. "He's talking about me."

No applause.

The final part of the video was the grand finale. It started
with Fahad slapping Edward when he was tied to the chair.
Edward watched himself being tortured and couldn't help but
admire his acting, maybe a career in Hollywood would be good
for his talent. Wherever Archer was now, he would surely be
watching the same video and would agree that Edward's plan was
better than just giving him the documents. This way they got real
proof of not only Fatima's Musehaf, but also the black
operations carried out by Fahad and a man named Othman
Aruri, who was connected all the way up. Once Archer was
convinced, he helped him stage the scene. Edward did not
particularly cherish the idea of being tied to a chair during all of
that, but that was Archer's condition as he didn't believe that

Vane was out there busy saving Safiya. Archer insisted on tying up Edward to eliminate any surprises, which, Edward had to admit, played well in the overall staging. Maybe he should offer Archer a job in Hollywood once he was there. A janitor or something.

"You *knew* we were coming," Fahad growled. "You let us track your cell. You set up all of this."

Edward nodded. "You are brighter than you look."

He didn't need to tell them that Muhanad placed the call to the police to make sure Adnan and his team arrived at the right time.

Despite his new celebrity status, Edward was taken to the police headquarters in Madeena. From there, things went better than expected. Adnan and his boss figured out that the best way for them to get out was to appear as those who saved the poor American from the crazy, out-of-control Fahad. A press conference to all news channels followed later the next morning, where Adnan talked about his heroic part in saving Safiya and Edward, and uncovering the killing Fahad did.

Edward spent the night in detention and was interviewed several times by different officials wearing dishdashes, suits, and military uniforms. Names and titles and faces and different sizes of beards blurred to the point that he didn't care anymore whom he was talking to.

Two medical teams had seen Edward on different occasions. One was supervised by an American doctor sent by the embassy who insisted that Edward was to be admitted to a hospital immediately. The Saudis didn't allow it, but he was given lots of pain killers that put him to sleep almost immediately at the interrogation table.

Dreams about the Musehaf and Fatima and Fayazi and Safiya and Saudi Arabia haunted him like an overdue mortgage. He woke up several times, moving from one quasi dream to another.

Safiya. It wasn't the green eyes, or the melodic laugh that he missed most, but the warmness of her hand when she held his. So trusting, so electrifying, and yet so... familiar. Corny? Maybe, but with all the pain killers he was given, even Sundra Rajan's music started to have a sentimental value.

Despite his exhaustion, he couldn't sleep. Part of it was the guilt that gnawed at him. Had he failed Safiya? Was he ever going to see her again? Edward wished he had a pillow to throw, it always helped. Whenever he couldn't shake an idea off, he threw the pillow, or punched it, depending on how silly and annoying the idea was. Now he had only his folded arms to rest his head on and throwing them might be unwise. Maybe he should try punching.

But it wasn't only Safiya whom he thought about. Fayazi, and Zain and his group, were probably in serious trouble. Even if his embassy managed to get him out, Fayazi would not survive three nights in a detention cell like this. Dark, hot and humid. with no pillows to throw.

He opened his eyes. He wasn't in a dark cell. The room was lit by one yellow light bulb on the ceiling. A small wooden table stood in the middle of the room, with four chairs around it. The interrogation room, he never left it. They left him alone, sleeping on the floor. Edward sat, his back to the wall. With no watch or phone, it was hard to tell how long he slept or what time it was. He had a headache, annoying but not something two aspirins couldn't heal. His arms and shoulders were stiff, so was the back of his neck. A constant pain shot from his side. His kidney was on fire.

Sitting against the wall, his chin resting on his knees, Edward fell asleep again, interrupted several times by his head dropping or his legs giving way.

The door opened. Two men in suits entered, followed by Vane. Edward shut his eyes and opened them, and Vane was still there. Good.

Vane stood over him, his curly head tilted. He smelled as if having bathed in cologne, Dior most likely. "Where is Mr. Temoothi?"

"Mister what?"

"With this beard and the awful smell, all you need is a basketball with a happy face on it."

Life with Vane was an everlasting game of Tom Hanks' movies. The thing was, Edward wasn't sure he really liked Hanks.

"It was a volleyball."

"Ah, good to see you still have your mental health." Vane smiled and helped him stand. He wore a black Armani suit and dark crimson shirt.

The two suits introduced themselves. Edward didn't catch the names but they were working with the American embassy. One, a bald man with blue eyes, spoke a lot about the American-Saudi relationship, about the Middle East and the stock market and oil prices and the negotiation between the Israelis and Palestinians. He did not mention the book or the Musehaf or Fatima or Mohammed. But the impression Edward got was that someone somewhere was not happy about the mess they created. This and probably that Bald Head lost a lot of money in the stock market.

Edward murmured something about doing what he had to do. Both suits nodded but were not particularly excited.

Vane smiled. "It's over, Ed. You are coming with us."

-70-

Bald Head and his colleague took them to the Hilton. According to Vane, the impact the video made, in addition to the pressure from the American embassy, made releasing Edward go faster. Similar efforts took place to release Fayazi by the Jordanian embassy, but those might take a few days. No one knew what would happen to Zain and his group or if they were still alive.

Bald Head and his friend escorted them to a room on the sixth floor and promised to return at night to drive them to the airport.

Kimberly opened the door. She cried and hugged him hard. His muscles ached but he held her until she let go.

Vane told him that he had booked a three-room deluxe suite. He gave Edward a new set of clothes, pointing out for the third time that Edward needed a bath desperately, making a deliberate move of covering his nose when Edward was close.

"I drove her home," Vane said, probably reading his mind. "Her driver, Abdullah, took her once we were there."

Edward rubbed his face, a tremor in his chest. Silly him. "Is she... okay?"

Vane took a long breath then let it out. "If I say yes, will you go take a shower?"

"Vane."

"Okay, Okay." Vane raised his hands in mock surrender. "She will call you once things are settled down. She said you would understand."

He did.

"Can I ask something, O'great one?" Vane said while opening the bathroom door for him. "Perhaps you can enlighten me."

"About?"

"Why, among all the women in the world, the mighty Edward Fleming chose a princess, and not only a princess, no, one from the most conservative royal family."

Kimberly giggled. Edward just shook his head. Discussing matters of the heart with Vane was like explaining Beethoven to a tree. "It's a long story, I will—"

"Later, now, *la douche*, please." Vane shoved him to the bathroom and closed the door.

After he took the shower they ordered room service. According to Kimberly, there was no official comment about Fatima's Musehaf and the documents found. The Internet was another story, however. Discussions, often heated and filled with accusations, took place on every social-networking site. Hundreds of Facebook pages and groups were created with combinations of the words Musehaf, Fatima, and Quran. People from different backgrounds tweeted about anything to do with Fatima. Most of the groups were founded by women, Saudi women in particular were the most active ones. Even in this early stage, Kimberly believed that soon other subjects would arise. Women's right to vote, to drive, and to seek education would be on top of the list.

"As for the business," Vane said, his fork in mid-air, trying to choose which piece of steak. "The guys from the Library of Congress called twice today."

"Our contract will be renewed?" Edward asked, trying to sound enthusiastic.

"Much better," Kimberly said, her brown eyes filled with joy and happiness.

He missed her. The way she squeezed her hands when she got excited, the energy that emanated to everyone around her. "The library is ready to sign a contract with us to start on a new project."

"Which new project?"

She looked at Vane. Vane made a half smile and said nothing. Kimberly's penciled eyebrows were perfect half-moons, the freckles on her cheeks more pronounced as she spoke. "We were asked to start a new project to go through all the Arabic and Islamic literature and references in the past fourteen centuries, to see if there is anything that could support Fayazi's theory." Kimberly paused, her white teeth bared in a wide smile.

This should be the part when he showed how thrilled he was. "But that will be a hard job."

Kimberly exchanged looks with Vane. Vane shrugged. She said, "Vane said he will negotiate a six-figure contract."

"Really? That's a lot of money." He frowned, not exactly the perfect Mr. Thrilled. "Why?"

"Because this might change everything, you thickhead," Kimberly snapped. "This will be like re-writing Islam and Arab history. Edward, we have proof that whatever we are seeing now in the name of Islam is nothing but a mutant creature spawned by centuries of rulers who had only one thing in common."

"Funny names?" Vane said, chewing on something.

"Hatred for Fatima." She nudged Vane on the shoulder. "And this doesn't apply only to history. If the early rulers were not legitimate, the same will go for the current rulers. This is just the beginning."

"Great." Edward nodded. "I mean, really great."

"I think he needs some sleep," Vane said, pouring Perrier into her glass. Alcohol was not allowed in Saudi Arabia, especially in a hotel facing the courtyard of the big mosque.

Edward walked to the window. He stared at the green dome of Mohammed's shrine, then at the wall where the Baqee cemetery began. White pigeons flew above the dome. A group of pilgrims walked from the mosque to Baqee. Men in green military suits waved for them to go back. They didn't. More people gathered, probably demanding access to the cemetery.

Would what they discovered today change the way Muslims think? Would it encourage Muslims to reconsider their history and what they thought of as undisputed truth? Would they change the way they treat women? Could it be the start of another ideology, one that promoted life instead of death? One that lived in peace with other ideologies and other religions? Could this revelation change the way the Arab governments treated their people?

Maybe. And maybe there would come a day when all masks fell and the truth shone for the world to see. He wasn't sure what truth that would be, or what masks would fall, but he couldn't ignore it any longer, that premonition, the twinge in the base of his subconscious, the thought that there was much more than they had unleashed. That they had just touched the tip of an iceberg of forgery and accumulated lies. That much more about Fatima and her book existed than those sample photographs showed. That this Musehaf, this book of Fatima, had more secrets to tell. And he, Edward Fleming, the only history detective who had the chance to get close, had failed to find that book.

Perhaps it was as Sheikh Essa had said before, the Musehaf was not supposed to be unleashed now. Perhaps Fatima had a different plan for her book, as she had planned for her tomb to be hidden.

The pigeons rested on the green dome. The white marble gleamed with the orange of the sky and the setting sun. On the small desk near the window was his watch, his iPhone, and his leather bag. Some papers lay on the desk. There he saw it. His heart skipped a beat. His hand inched to the paper as if afraid that any sudden move would cast the thought away. He pulled the scanned copy of the letter Ayatollah Seerazi had sent to his student. The one that ordered the student to take the Musehaf to Saudi to hide it in a place where the Mahdi, the chosen one, would find it. He read it word by word, the document that started it all. The letter that changed the life of Abdul Zahra's family and started the chain of events when Kimberly gave it to Fayazi.

He read it again.

To make it close to the downtrodden scion.

Where the hands of her enemies would not reach.

Where the chosen one would find it.

Edward's gaze slid to the bottom of the paper, the signature of Ayatollah. The calligraphy artwork was not perfect but the resemblance could not be mistaken. The writing formed a half circle with two long pillars next to it.

"I know," he said, still looking at the green dome and the sun and the orange sky.

Vane and Kimberly, followed as he sprinted out.

-71-

Sheikh Essa stood amidst a large group of pilgrims. Edward stood next to him. The old man stared at the green facade, his eyes moistened.

"You knew," Essa said, his gaze never leaving the dome.

Edward nodded.

"I knew you would." Essa half smiled.

"How long did *you* know about it?" Edward asked.

Essa shook his head. He wore a small white turban. "I had a feeling. A strong feeling, that I should protect this place. So I figured out that probably God wanted me to do that for a reason. Do you know what I mean?"

Edward did. Which surprised him. "A purpose."

"Yes." Then Essa turned at him, the smile more prominent. "Tell me, how did you find it?"

Edward showed him the letter. "Look at the signature." He pointed at the Arabic calligraphy that resembled the shape of the dome and the two minaret. "In the beginning, I thought it was just a funny way of writing his signature, then I noticed the resemblance between the dome and the two pillars of the prophet's mosque."

"Just that?"

"That was the final piece of the puzzle," Edward said. "I always wondered how Ayatollah Seerazi or his student could leave the decision of placing the most important book in Islam history to a merchant. Abdul Zahra Senior was a fine person, but he would never be the one to decide on such a matter."

"Makes sense."

"Not only that, there was the fact that Abdul Zahra, of all people, knew that those documents would be at risk if he hid the book in any other place. He saw firsthand how the Saudis treated historical places."

"So he decided to go for the most secure place." Essa nodded.

"The only place the Saudis did not demolish."

"The prophet's tomb." Essa sighed.

"The only place close to Fatima's tomb."

"Speculations," Essa said, "suggest that she was buried somewhere nearby, maybe in Baqee or next to her father."

"A place the chosen one will find," Edward said, reciting the words from the letter.

"And we know that this is one of the places the Mahdi will visit, in which he will present evidence that will reveal the hidden truth."

An old man arrived in front of them, barely walking. He stood facing the mosque and raised his hands to the sky.

"But that wasn't what tipped me off," Edward added. Essa waited for him to continue. "The story about the man who tried to demolish the dome and got struck with a thunderbolt. Forget for a moment that it was too Walt Disney, it just reminded me that Abdul Zahra had a project here once."

334

"And what's better than the old mosque of the prophet to hide his daughter's Musehaf?" Essa said.

"Yes, then I thought that Abdul Zahra must have used the opportunity of doing some work there to hide the Musehaf in that rectangular box on the dome. Then someone made up the story about the man who was struck by the thunderbolt just to hide the truth."

"Otherwise people would keep asking." Essa smiled.

Edward almost heard the click in his mind. "It was *you* who made up that story, wasn't it?"

"Come, let me show you something," Essa said.

He walked inside the big mosque and Edward followed. People, especially those with short dishdashes and long beards, glared at Sheikh Essa. Good, no one even noticed Edward.

"This is the new part of the mosque, built during the past two decades," Essa said.

They stood under one of the big new cupolas of the mosque. The prophet's tomb and the green dome were less than three hundred feet away. White marble columns with corners made of fine oak wood extended from the floor to the high-rise ceilings. Essa pointed at the Arabic calligraphy around the spherical ceiling above them. "You can read Arabic, right?"

Edward nodded and started reading the writing on the ceiling. They were names, each one circled with drawings of flowers and tree leaves. Edward counted around twenty names.

"I don't understand," he said finally.

"Maybe because you are not so familiar with the Islamic history," Essa said.

"No, no, I get it," Edward said. A whiff of cold air from the fan blew on his face. "I see the names of Ali, Fatima, their sons, Hasan and Hussain, then I think this man is the son of Hussain. But I don't see what's the big deal. There are names of other known Muslims under other domes. Even those who signed that document against Mohammed and Ali."

"True," Essa said, "but first, all the names on other ceilings belong to people who lived during the prophet's time. Only this one had names of people born one hundred years after the prophet's death."

Edward shrugged.

"This is not all," Essa said. "This is the only ceiling in the new mosque where Mohammed's name is written. Others don't have his name."

"Okay, so what are those names?"

"They are Fatima's offspring. Mohammed had prophesied their birth, their names and what they would do. Mohammed told Muslims that Fatima is like an everlasting river that will keep flowing for humanity, her sons will bring mercy and knowledge to all those who believed in them."

"All those names are Fatima's sons?"

"Her great-grandchildren." Essa nodded. "See, this is Hussain's son, this is his grandson."

Essa went on pointing out every single name for Edward. All the names started either with Mohammed or Ali, except for the last one.

"Al-Mahdi." Edward frowned. "I didn't know that Saudis believed in the prophecy of the chosen one."

"They don't believe in Fatima and her sons either." Essa smiled.

Edward was missing something here. He rubbed his face, then, "Wait a minute - Saudis didn't write those names here. Abdul Zahra did."

Essa nodded. "And guess what's on top of this particular dome?"

"Another rectangular box?"

Another nod.

"This was how you found out about the location of the Musehaf, right?" Edward asked. A group of Singaporean pilgrims came their way, slightly pushing them back. Edward recognized the distinguished triangular hats the men wore. That, and the fact that all of their name tags had Singapore written in bold font.

Another history-detective trick. But Edward didn't brag about it.

"Abdul Zahra did the work on this ceiling and the old green cupola of the prophet's tomb, not directly, of course, but through another company. I don't think he told anyone, but I asked him when I noticed the names and concluded that there was no way Salafism would accept putting the names of Fatima's sons on the mosque. He admitted that he was behind it. Then I noticed the rectangular box on top of the two domes and reached to the same conclusion as yours."

"That Abdul Zahra hid the Musehaf under the green cupola, in that rectangular box."

Essa lifted his head and examined the ceiling, admiring it as if for the first time. "A smart place and I am sure even for those who knew the location, it would be hard to get the Musehaf."

For a normal person maybe, but not for Vane. "My friend and I can take care of that."

Essa's face clouded. "Take care of what?"

"Getting the Musehaf."

Essa shook his head and gave him the look of a father hearing his son's first swear word. "You should know better by now, son."

"But that's what Fatima wanted, right? For the truth to come out."

More people started staring at them, at Essa in particular. Essa took Edward's hand and trudged outside the big mosque to the yard in front of Mohammed's mosque. The air felt hot and sticky.

The old man was still praying there. When he saw Essa, he approached. "*Endi Maradh Khabeeth*," (I have a serious illness.) the man said, holding Essa's hand.

"You have chosen to pray in one of God's favorite places, my brother," Essa said. "Go visit a doctor now."

The old man frowned then broke into a smile and nodded.

"God will heal those who have faith and find the natural causes," Essa said, the man nodded more. "You can pray to God to give you food all day, but unless you go and search for a job, nothing will happen."

The old man thanked Essa and left. When the man was gone, Essa said, "Do you know what was the hardest thing on Fatima during all her tragedy?"

Edward cocked his head. "That she was betrayed by the people whom her father helped, that she was beaten and her land was taken, and she lost her son due to the miscarriage."

Essa shook his head. "She watched her husband, the man who fought all the Arabs alone in Uhud, the man who saved Mohammed's life when twenty men of Quraish wanted to kill him in his house in Mecca. That man, this loving husband, had to watch her beaten and mistreated without being able to draw a sword or defend her. You need to understand how Ali loved and cherished Fatima, and how he treasured her and the fact that Mohammed chose him to marry her."

White beams of light from the surrounding minarets illuminated the green cupola. Next to it, the cemetery of Baqee' looked even darker and more deserted. "I guess I can imagine."

"And Fatima knew how much her husband loved her. She could see the pain in his eyes, she saw the shame that tore him, restless that he couldn't defend her."

"Why didn't he do anything?"

"Because she told him not to," Essa said, looking down at the floor.

Edward remembered what Fayazi told him: "She wanted Muslims to make that decision, to choose the right thing."

"Yes, Fatima was not after winning a battle against those who betrayed her father, otherwise there was nothing easier than asking Ali to protect her. They were nothing more than a dozen of men at the beginning, none of them was known as a man of the sword, none of them was really a match for a warrior like Ali. But that was not the only reason. There is a more important one."

"Oh?"

"She wanted Islam to survive, even if what survived was just a body with no soul. If Ali had fought the people back at that day, a war would have started, a civil war right after Mohammed's death. Islam wouldn't survive it. The Roman

Empire and the Persian Empire were too eager to attack Muslims and eliminate them. Once they heard the news that Muslims were fighting each other, they would seize the opportunity. Ali knew that and so did Fatima. So she made the sacrifice, she accepted all that happened to her, she pleaded Ali not to fight them back and reminded him of the oath he gave Mohammed before his death."

"What oath?" Edward said, watching two men with short dishdashes, who stood scanning the crowd. Something about them, the way they looked at people, made Edward uncomfortable.

"Mohammed told Ali that there would be a day when he had to endure a pain that no man could endure and that he had yet to save Islam as he did in the past. He made him promise him not to take out his sword unless Fatima told him to."

"So he watched her beaten until she lost her baby."

"And she watched him suffer." Essa sighed, his eyes moist. "She probably listened to him begging her to allow him to defend her, to defend the religion he fought for since he was seven years old when Mohammed became prophet."

Edward shook his head. "And if we publish the Musehaf?"

"You saw what was there, part of it anyway, such a thing would destroy Islam, there is a reason why it was hidden all this time. Despite all the injustice against those who followed Fatima, despite the killing and the sectarian cleansing across the history, the wise men who were entrusted with the Musehaf knew that if it was published to the public, it would destroy Islam."

"But that Mahdi guy will publish it. That's the prophecy, isn't it?"

Another three men in short dishdashes surrounded two white men and asked them to show their papers. Essa took Edward's hand and walked away.

"He will, but Fayazi told you how the prophecy said he would have long battles against other Muslims until he cleared out Islam of all the lies and deception entangled within it since Mohammed died."

A man who fought Muslims and made truce with other nations. The folks at the CIA would love him for sure.

"I am sorry, Sheik Essa," Edward finally said. "Maybe Fatima sacrificed to keep Islam alive as you said, but that was a long time ago, when Islam brought civilization to the world, when the Islamic state encouraged science and art, and helped humanity. But now, when Islam is a religion that sends airplanes to crash into buildings, when it teaches young men to become suicide bombers..." He paused, then finally said, "Do you think if Fatima were alive, she would not want the truth to come out?"

"Not now, Edward, the time is yet to come."

"When? What should we wait for? More innocent people to die because of the ideology of death? Doctor Fayazi said that if the truth about what happened to Fatima came out, it would open the door for Islam to be corrected and brought back on the track Mohammed wanted. Don't you think that will save innocent lives?"

Sheikh Essa put his hand on Edward's shoulder and spoke in a pleading voice. "We have *one shot*, Edward, one shot that we were waiting for since more than a thousand years, we cannot rush this. We have to do it with diamond-cutting accuracy. No room for error, no room for half-baked plans, as you call them."

"No can do." Edward gently removed Sheikh Essa's thin hand from his shoulder and walked away.

Vane. Vane would find a way to get into that box. His friend would find a way to sneak in the night. Edward wasn't about to let this slide. The truth had to come out. He owed Fayazi and Zain this. He owed all the innocent people who died because of Islamic terrorists. And he owed Fatima.

"This wasn't what you believed in when we first met!" Essa called after him.

Edward stopped. A tremor started in his chest. "What?"

"I might be an old man but I have a good memory, son."

The tremor increased. His knees buckled. He turned to face Essa, scrutinizing his peaceful and confident face, searching for any hint of deception. "What are you talking about?"

"The religion police are on alert." Essa pointed at the men in short white dishdash roaming the yard. "They were informed that one of the Tawheed group had come back."

"What are you talking about?"

"This group tried to conquer the Kaaba ten years ago."

"But what does this have to do with me?"

Essa squinted at him. "You really don't remember, don't you?"

The tremor in his chest turned into a suffocating pain.

"This group came to me, nine years ago, in an unprecedented move to gain support," Essa said. "Among them was a man who had a different agenda."

Edward closed his eyes. He fought to keep his balance. He fought to keep the flood gates closed. No use, the memories were coming back to him, faster than his mind could digest.

"They are looking for... *me*."

"They don't know what the man looks like. But I do," Essa said, his eyes filled with remorse. "We met before, Edward... nine years ago."

-72-

"So?" Vane asked when he got back to the hotel.

Kimberly held his hand, asking if he were okay. He shook his head. Edward just wanted to reach the couch and collapse. He barely made it. His legs gave away almost instantly.

"Have you found it?" Kimberly's voice came as if from a tunnel.

The TV was on BBC. A bombed car in Iraq killed forty people, more were wounded. Suicide attack, Al-Qaeda. The report showed images of men and women running, another of a young child covered in blood. A woman dressed in a white blazer talked from a hospital full of people covered in blood and children with missing limbs.

Vane said something, so did Kimberly. He heard nothing other than the sea-shell noise and that voice that kept screaming at him: "Traitor!"

He ran to the bathroom and spilled his guts. Images of the suicide attack kept flashing in his mind. When nothing was left in his stomach, Edward sat on the bathroom floor, his back to the wall, his elbows resting on his knees, and his head between his knees. He started to cry, deep bone-crushing weeping, full-body sobs. Something had finally given way and he sobbed without ceasing. Kimberly came into the bathroom. Vane stood behind her. She said nothing, just sat and embraced him, letting him cry on her shoulder.

He told them everything, all the details, his point and Essa's argument.

Vane said in a monotone, "So, they are watching the place for an intruder?"

"Essa knew I wouldn't listen to him, so he leaked the information that a member of Al-Tawhid group was back, it's one that the Saudi fear so much. Al-Tawheed wanted to take control over holy places. Kaaba and Mohammed's mosque are under heavy surveillance."

"And you were with *this* group?" Kimberly asked, her wide gaze wandering between him and Vane. Vane's face showed nothing, as always.

Edward opened his mouth then closed it. "All I remember is that I met them in Egypt."

Kimberly said, "We can always go back or send someone to get that Musehaf."

"I guess." He shrugged.

"But you don't think so," Vane said. "You think when you know more about yourself, you might change your mind?"

Vane could be scary when he was right.

"The truth *has* to come out," Kimberly said. "Fatima would have wanted this."

"Maybe," Vane said. He shrugged. "This thing was hidden for a thousand years. Why do you want to decide about it in one night?"

Kimberly shook her head, opened her mouth to protest but didn't speak.

"Our plane is due in three hours," Vane said, checking his watch. "We'd better get our things packed before the embassy sends us our escort."

An hour later they were putting their bags in the Ford Explorer the embassy sent. A police car was parked on the other side of the street. "Just in case, they will escort us to the airport," Baldy from the embassy said.

Before he got into the Ford, Edward turned to see the dome. It still gleamed under the lights, still magnificent and still an architectural wonder. But that peaceful feeling of time stopping wasn't there anymore. Guilt took its place. Rage.

Edward closed his eyes and let the hot air blow on his face. Cars whizzed on a nearby highway. Aside from the confusion and the moral dilemma, aside from the guilt, aside from being grateful that he saved his friend and his job and maybe brought to light part of a scandal that was going on for God knew how long. Aside from all of that, Edward had a feeling that his life had taken a detour and he wasn't sure where it would lead.

Epilogue

Archer watched Kareem's shaky hand signing the check. Funny when he thought about it. Within less than a month, he made ten times the money he made his entire life. And for the very first time, he really did something that made him feel better.

"Thank you," Kareem said, handing him the check.

"I don't want to sound like I'm trying to kiss your ass or anything, but I... I mean the job... I liked it." He wasn't good with pleasantries.

Kareem waved him off. "Me and you, Mr. Archer, have one thing in common. You know that, right?"

Archer thought the question was rhetorical so he just waited. When the old billionaire said nothing, Archer said, "We both want the truth to come out."

"Don't patronize me." Kareem scowled. "Me and you want to bring this pile of lies they call religion down, don't we, Mr. Archer."

Archer thought about it, then said, "I have my reasons."

"True. And I have mine."

"So what's our next step?"

"Let's wait for Fayazi to be released, then we can talk about that."

"He told me that he was the one who convinced you to start this, is that true?"

Kareem let out a long exhale. He took off his glasses and put them on his desk. "He gave me a very good reason to trust him."

"And what was that?"

Another long exhale. "He told me who the informant was who tipped the Saudi authorities about what my father was doing. As you know by now, my father was trying to save the historical landmarks and took photos of the old sites."

"And who was that informant?"

"Fayazi himself." Kareem sneered.

Archer blinked. "And you are going to let him live?"

Kareem smiled, it looked like a wince. "He didn't know they would react like that. It was a different time and he was a different man."

Archer didn't buy it.

Kareem went on, "I still need him."

Okay, that was more like it.

Kareem's intercom buzzed. His secretary said in a British accent, "Mr. Kareem, she is here."

Kareem leaned into the intercom and said, "Let her in." He looked at Archer and said, "I want you to meet someone."

The office door opened and a young lady with blue spiky hair and a black leather skirt that was both too short and too tight walked in. Archer scrutinized the woman's face, searching his memory banks for whether he had ever seen her. She wore dark blue lipstick, dark blue eye shadow, and dark blue nails.

Maybe from *Star Wars*.

"Hello, Mister K," she said, stretching each word.

Kareem signaled for her to sit.

"Archer, I want you to meet my best computer analyst, Abbie. Abbie, this is Mr. Archer, he is working on Edward's case."

Abbie waved at him.

"Wait a minute," Archer said, "it was *you* who suggested Edward and Kimberly to Fayazi."

Kareem tapped on his checkbook then said, "Once the old man told me about his research, I knew that Edward would be the best one to help out."

Archer frowned. "You *knew* Edward?"

"He has a very valuable thing that belonged to me, maybe even more important than Fatima's book." Kareem plucked his lips then turned to Abbie. "I want you to brief Mr. Archer on your last report about Edward Fleming."

She crossed her legs. Abbie wasn't chewing gum but she should have been. "Well, nothing much after they came back, but you were right, Mr. Kareem. He started remembering who he was."

"Tell Mr. Archer what the name he used when he visited Saudi eight years ago was. This would be Mr. Archer's next mission."

Abbie smiled. "His name was Jamal Al-Afghani."

The End.

ABOUT THE AUTHOR

I.M.Hussaini is an Iraqi novelist and human rights activist. He worked as a reporter in Iraq and the Middle East during the war that ended Sadam's regime by the US-led collation. I.M. Hussaini is the author of the controversial series of Edward Fleming that attempts to bring to light the stories behind the scene of the new Arab revolt and discuss tabooed details from the Islamic history of the region. The author's decision to write in English came after his most famous book *The Detour* was banned in Iraq and other Arab countries. For more details about the author and his work you can visit his website at www.imhussaini.com

If you have any question about the historical subject, please feel free to email the author at imhussaini@imhussaini.com